08/11 2009 // 26 6 (4)

WITHDRAWN
FROM COLLECTION

Woman from Shanghai

Woman from Shanghai

TALES OF SURVIVAL FROM A CHINESE LABOR CAMP

Xianhui Yang

*Translated from the Chinese
and with an introduction by*

Wen Huang

Pantheon Books, New York

Introduction and translation copyright © 2009 by Wen Huang

All rights reserved. Published in the United States by Pantheon Books,
a division of Random House, Inc., New York, and in Canada by Random
House of Canada Limited, Toronto. Originally published in China as
Farewell to Jiabiangou (Gao Bie Jiabiangou) by Shanghai Arts and
Literature Publishing House, Shanghai, in 2003.
Copyright © 2003 by Yang Xianhui.

A portion of this work originally appeared in the *Asia Literary Review*.

Pantheon Books and colophon are
registered trademarks of Random House, Inc.

Library of Congress Cataloging-in-Publication Data
Yang, Xianhui.
[Gao bie Jiabiangou. English. Selections]
Woman from Shanghai : tales of survival from a Chinese labor camp /
Xianhui Yang;
translated from the Chinese and with an introduction by Wen Huang.
p.   cm.
ISBN 978-0-307-37768-5
1. Jiabiangou (Concentration camp)—Fiction.
2. Concentration camp inmates—China—Gansu Sheng—Fiction.
I. Title. II. Title: Tales of survival from a Chinese labor camp.
PL2971.X53G3613 2009
895.1'352—dc22   2008049528

www.pantheonbooks.com
Printed in the United States of America
First American Edition
2   4   6   8   9   7   5   3   1

CONTENTS

INTRODUCTION:
Preserving Memories of a Forgotten Era

Jiabiangou was the name of a forced labor camp, a Chinese gulag tucked away in the desert region of China's northwestern province of Gansu.

More than fifty years ago, nearly three thousand intellectuals and former government officials in Gansu were taken from their homes and sent to Jiabiangou to undergo what the Communist Party called "reeducation through hard labor." They were known as Rightists because some had expressed dissenting views of Chairman Mao's socialist policies or offended Party officials. Others were labeled Rightists simply because they had grown up as members of the "exploiting class"—in other words, their parents or grandparents were landlords or capitalists.

The large-scale persecution in Gansu was part of Mao's nationwide anti-Rightist campaign against his critics, who he believed had gone too far to the right in an effort to sabotage China's socialist system. To expiate this offense, he decreed they should be subjected to the same discipline of hard labor undertaken by the peasantry. Mao's campaign eventually ruined the careers and devastated the lives of more than five hundred thousand of China's intellectual and political elite.*

* Graham Hutchings, "One Hundred Flowers Movement 1956–57," in *Modern China: A Companion to a Rising Power* (New York: Penguin Books, 2001).

Between 1957 and 1960, the exiled Rightists at Jiabiangou slaved away all day long under the supervision of prison guards, cultivating farmland, growing crops, and raising livestock in harsh desert conditions. At night, they studied Chairman Mao's writings and wrote "self-criticisms," or confessions of their past misdeeds. Since the land around Jiabiangou was covered by barren salt marshes and desert, crops could only grow in some small oases. There was no way for the camp, which had originally been built to hold forty to fifty convicted criminals, to support roughly three thousand new arrivals. Since the government refused to provide any food subsidies, the Jiabiangou Rightists struggled for food from the day they arrived.

In the fall of 1960, food supplies dwindled further and a massive number of Rightists began to die from starvation. People combed the areas of grassland for food, eating leaves, tree bark, worms, and rats, and even the flesh of their dead fellow inmates. Since most survivors were too emaciated to bury the dead, hundreds of bodies lay exposed on the sand dunes.

At last the tragedy at Jiabiangou came to the attention of senior Party officials in Beijing. In November 1960, the central government dispatched a task force to investigate the situation at the camp. Upon realizing that the Gansu provincial government had gone overboard in its purge, the senior leadership soon issued an amnesty. Based on interviews with former Jiabiangou officials, by the time the government trucks arrived to move the Rightists out of the death camp early in 1961, there were only five hundred survivors.

Over the years, the tragedy was never made public. The officials in Gansu engaged in a systematic cover-up, sealing any documents pertaining to the camps. In January 1961, after all the Rightists were shipped out, a doctor was assigned to stay behind and rewrite the medical records of every Jiabiangou victim. The doctor spent six months fabricating their files. In letters sent to victims' families, the government attributed the deaths to various types of fictitious illnesses. Nowhere was the word "starvation" ever mentioned.

In October 1961, the central government ordered Jiabiangou to be closed for good. The tragic details of the camp remained a mystery.

The Gansu-born writer Xianhui Yang first heard the name Jiabiangou in 1965, when he was working at a military-style collective farm in the Gobi Desert. Yang was a nineteen-year-old high school graduate, full of revolutionary spirit. He had given up a comfortable urban life and joined hundreds of other idealistic young people in their lofty mission of conquering nature and developing China's backward northwest. They planted trees, cultivated farmland, and built irrigation systems in the desert.

At the farm, Yang became acquainted with some former Rightists who had served out their sentences and been assigned to work as staff there. One day, during a casual conversation, someone mentioned offhandedly the tragic deaths at Jiabiangou. When Yang asked about it, the person refused to elaborate and immediately dropped the subject.

The conversation, although brief, piqued Yang's curiosity. The idea that that the Communist Party would commit such brutality against its own people shocked him. He wanted to find out more, but it was at the height of another one of Mao's political campaigns—the Cultural Revolution. An attempt to investigate Jiabiangou might easily be construed as an anti-government activity.

Yang remained on the collective farm for sixteen years, from 1965 to 1981, first as a laborer, then as a salesclerk at the farm's department store, an accountant, and finally as a teacher at the schools set up for children of the staff. In his spare time, he began writing stories about pioneering life in the far northwest. During those years, China underwent dramatic changes: Chairman Mao died in 1976, and his successor, Deng Xiaoping, ended Mao's radical Communist policies and set China on the road to political and economic reform. In the late 1970s, the Party began to acknowledge the excesses of the anti-Rightist campaign, reversed verdicts against the majority of Rightists, and ordered the release of most of the prisoners. Yet there was never any official government apology or explanation for their imprisonment, nor was any compensation paid out to the victims. The Party had no intention of taking responsibility for the tragedy.

Yang became a professional writer in 1988 and subsequently moved back to the port city of Tianjin, where he wrote numerous short stories and novellas about the young people who volunteered, like himself, to settle the rural areas of China's northwest during the Mao era. He published such works as *Little Country Bumpkin*, *The Aristocratic Lady*, and *Thunder on the Distant Sea*.

Yet he never forgot about Jiabiangou.

In 1997, on the fortieth anniversary of Mao's anti-Rightist campaign, he officially launched his project. Emboldened by the lessening of the political tensions that surrounded the issue, he journeyed back to the Gobi Desert. First, he contacted the provincial government there and requested access to the official archives. As he expected, his requests went unanswered and nobody would speak with him. He wasn't deterred, however, and decided instead to look for the living archives—the survivors.

To get a feel for what the Rightists had to go through, Yang first visited Jiabiangou. Apart from some broken walls, there was nothing left. Local peasants told him that piles of human bones had lain scattered around the area for many years. In

1987, after the peasants had repeatedly filed complaints, the government finally sent a crew to bury the bones of the Rightists who had died there.*

Yang then traversed Gansu Province, visiting big cities as well as small villages, trying to locate survivors. Over the course of five years, Yang interviewed nearly one hundred former Jiabiangou Rightists as well as many of their relatives. Though some people were reluctant to speak about the camp for fear of further persecution, he managed to gain the trust of many who opened their hearts and shared their stories. The stories were often so heart-wrenching that Yang had often to interrupt the interviews so that he could go outside to take a deep breath and wipe his tears before finishing the session.

Upon his return, Yang adapted his interviews into a series of short stories. In 2000, *Shanghai Literature,* an influential literary monthly, published his first story, "Woman from Shanghai." The story recounts the tale of a woman who travels all the way from the coastal city of Shanghai to visit her husband in Jiabiangou, only to learn that he has died of starvation. His former roommate devises all sorts of obstacles to prevent her from seeing the body, because the flesh has already been eaten by fellow detainees.

"Woman from Shanghai" shocked the nation. Spurred on by strong public interest, *Shanghai Literature* magazine published eleven more of Yang's stories in the same year. In 2002, Ancient Books Publishing House in Tianjin selected seven of Yang's Jiabiangou stories and published them along with several of his non-Jiabiangou-related works under the title *Stories of Jiabiangou.*

---

* Tao Shi, "Call for the quick establishment of a Jiabiangou Museum," www.boxun.com/hero/shitao/45_1.shtml, September 2002; Yuxiao Li, "Yang Xianhui reveals the truth about Jiabiangou," http://www.huanguagang.org/library/jiabiangou.htm, 2005.

In 2003, as Yang continued his interviews to expand his Jiabiangou series, the Shanghai Art and Literature Publishing House gathered all the stories into one volume, titled *Farewell to Jiabiangou.*

The collection's nineteen Jiabiangou stories document, in simple unadorned language and a straightforward narrative style, the Rightists' daily struggles inside the labor camp. In "The Potato Feast," a group of starving Rightists who are assigned to transport seed potatoes from the city warehouse to Jiabiangou snatch a huge sack of potatoes, boil them, and then wolf them down with disastrous consequences. "Jia Nong" depicts the life of female detainees who struggle to raise a child born in Jiabiangou. "Escape" describes a Rightist's harrowing quest to break out of the camp. These and other stories in this book reveal with brutal honesty the dehumanized existence of the inmates at Jiabiangou.

Over the past three decades, numerous memoirs have been published both in China and abroad about life inside Chinese forced-labor camps (Harry Wu's *Bitter Winds* and Zhang Xianliang's *Grass Soup* being two of the most prominent). But never before has there been such an ambitious collection of stories told from the perspectives of people from all walks of life, about this dark and hidden chapter of Chinese history. They are, in the words of Jie Yu, an independent Chinese critic, "the Chinese *Gulag Archipelago.*"*

According to Yu, the Chinese government has engaged in a systematic cover-up involving the sabotage and elimination of many historical materials over the past decades. In such a controlled political environment, how did this *Gulag Archipelago* manage to rise from the deep water in China?

* Jie Yu, "Defending Our Memories, Defending Our History," Commentary on Radio Free Asia, January 13, 2006.

Yang writes what is known as documentary literature, a genre created in the 1980s by Chinese writers who disguised the journalistic nature of their work by incorporating some fictional elements in an effort to carry out what Yu calls "the mission of defending and protecting memories within a narrow space."

Yu says this type of writing, which is a necessity under a repressive regime, occupies the border between fiction and nonfiction:

> It's nearly unimaginable in the West, where freedom of the press is a given tradition. Literature is literature and news is news. One doesn't blur the lines. It's not that Chinese writers don't know the difference between fiction and nonfiction writing. It's just that the difficult circumstances of contemporary life have presented them with no choice but to deliberately blur these lines as a strategy.

Yang's editors went one step further to evade the omnipresent eye of the Department of Propaganda. They published Yang's stories under the category of fiction, even though they were well aware of the journalistic nature of Yang's works. They knew that the stories were closely based on true events and taken from the author's interviews with survivors.

Yang's Jiabiangou stories were an instant hit—especially in Gansu Province, where the tragedy occurred. He has won numerous national accolades, including the 2003 Best Short Story Award, granted by the Chinese Academy of Short Story Writers. Following the book's success, many survivors, who had never spoken about Jiabiangou for decades, stepped forward to share their stories with Yang. One reader was only a child when his father was sent to Jiabiangou. For many years he had been able to glean no more information than the official account that his father had died of illness. When he finally got hold of Yang's stories, he knelt in front of his father's portrait and read them aloud, with tears in his eyes. Yang hopes that his book will reach more members of the younger generation.

I was first introduced to Yang by e-mail through friends at the Independent Chinese PEN Center in 2005. During the next three years, Yang and I worked extensively over the phone and by e-mail to adapt the book for a Western audience. In 2007, the project was awarded a PEN Translation Fund grant, which motivated us to bring the manuscript to fruition. Acting on feedback from several magazine editors, members of the PEN Translation Committee, and U.S.-based China experts, we added some background information to provide political context, and we restructured as well as abridged some narratives. The English version offered here consists of thirteen stories that originally appeared in *Farewell to Jiabiangou*.

In a recent talk about *Farewell to Jiabiangou*, Yang says:

Today, only a few people know about this part of the history. Many survivors have either passed away or remained silent. The perpetrators continue to cover up what happened. I've made the effort to open up this black box and share these stories with the public because I want people to know the pain of those who have suffered. I hope this tragedy will not be repeated. More important, I want to bring closure to those who now lie under the vast desert sand.

Wen Huang
Chicago, 2009

Woman from Shanghai

Arriving at Jiabiangou

Qi Yaoquan was born in Dunhuang County, Gansu Province. In the fall of 1949, when Communist troops overtook the nearby city of Jiuquan, Qi was in his final year at Hexi Middle School. Inspired by the Communist plans to build a new China, he quit school and volunteered to join the Communist army. The Military Control Committee did not recruit him. In those days, the newly established government needed educated cadres, so the committee sent him to study for three months at a cadre training school and then assigned him a job as youth coordinator at Linze County. In early 1952, Qi became the general secretary of the Shahe Township Communist Youth League. In the same year, he was admitted to the Communist Party. Qi was a tall, handsome young man. An avid reader, he loved literature and was well versed in Marxist theory. He received several more promotions over the next few years, until in 1957 he was named the secretary of the Jinta County Communist Youth League.

At the beginning of August 1957, Qi Yaoquan received a short letter from the Jinta County Communist Party Committee, asking him to return to the county immediately for a conference. The request came as a surprise to Qi, who had been visiting an agricultural cooperative in the middle of the Badan Jilin Desert with a three-man work team since early July. This was his second trip to the region. The government had launched the collectivization movement a year earlier, and the county

3

had dispatched a large number of soldiers to different villages before the summer harvest. Their job was to urge peasants to fulfill the government grain quotas. Since the grain quotas were high and burdensome to meet, the work teams felt pressured to stay longer in the villages. Qi's team wasn't scheduled to return until late September or early October, after the peasants had dried and ground the wheat.

Upon his return, Qi learned that the county was about to mobilize the masses to start a campaign that Chairman Mao called the rectification movement. Citizens were urged to criticize the Party and thereby help officials improve the quality of their work.

Qi followed current events closely. He knew that Chairman Mao's new campaign, summed up in the slogan "Let one hundred flowers bloom and one hundred schools of thought contend," had already kicked off in major cities like Beijing and Shanghai, but he had heard two divergent opinions about it. The official party newspaper, *People's Daily*, carried numerous articles advising people to air their opinions. Yet Qi also read an editorial asserting that some people had used the rectification campaign as a way to attack and sabotage the Party. The Party was fighting back against its critics with great vehemence.

In Jinta County the rectification campaign kickoff meeting took place in the newly completed Baoshui Auditorium. All local officials, schoolteachers, artists, and writers attended. Lu Weigong, the county Party secretary, delivered the opening mobilization speech. Then all the participants broke into groups so that they could speak their minds and offer criticisms of the Party.

The reaction to the campaign was one of silence and indifference. For two days, nobody in Qi's group spoke up.

On the third day, Lu joined Qi's group. He further emphasized the significance of the campaign and encouraged everyone to speak their mind freely. Lu even said that when a Communist Party member refused to stand up and criticize the Party, it meant the person lacked strong principles. Silence indicated lack of patriotism.

Qi considered himself a red-diaper baby and a true revolutionary by nature. It had never even occurred to him to criticize the Party. But on the other hand, Qi had always admired and respected Lu.

Lu came from Qingyang County, a bastion of Communism in the early days of the revolution. He had grown up in an illustrious family of scholars and had left home at an early age and joined the Communist movement. During the civil war between the Communists and Nationalists, he was appointed the Party secretary of Qingyang County. After the Communist takeover, he was appointed chief of staff at the Gansu governor's office. In September 1956, he came to Jinta County as part of his training. During his stay there, he shared the county Party secretary's position with Qin Gaoyang, another revolutionary veteran, who came from northern Shaanxi Province.

Qi admired Lu because Lu was well educated and capable, modest and reliable. He spoke and wrote eloquently. On arriving in Jinta County, he visited ordinary people and listened to their problems and complaints. Based on what he heard, he helped to overturn several unpopular laws, and thereby improved the public image of the county leaders, who had been widely considered arrogant and rude. As a result, Lu earned the support of the local peasants and officials.

Lu, in turn, appreciated Qi's talents and capabilities. At the beginning of the year, the county Party committee assigned Qi to draft a report on the progress of agricultural collectivization in the county. Lu stayed up all night and completed a thirty-two-page draft. The next morning, he shared the draft with members of the committee at an expanded leadership meeting. Lu showered Qi with praises and approved his report without any changes.

On another occasion, Lu attended a night class on Communist theories that Qi taught on a part-time basis to county government officials. Afterward, Lu was heard telling several officials how impressed he was: "He is not only a good writer, but also quite an expert on Marxism. In my opinion, no other county official can surpass Qi in the area of Communist theory."

Later on, Lu had proposed promoting Qi to the job of deputy county chief. An official secretly passed the word to Qi: the promotion request had been granted by the provincial Party committee. Lu would announce the decision after the county wrapped up the rectification campaign.

Qi's respect for Lu and the news about his promotion prompted him to take action. The second day after Lu visited his group, he stood up and said, "I want to offer some suggestions for our county Party secretary Qin. First, as one of the most senior leaders in Jinta County, Qin should watch his public behavior and keep his personal life clean and discreet. At the moment, there is a coming saying that's popular among ordinary folks here: 'When Secretary Qin comes down to town, all the chicks' are called upon. You send him a married woman, he also lusts after a young virgin.' People don't just make up these ditties for no reason."

Qi spoke in a serious tone. Even so, his remarks aroused some murmuring among his group. Some people couldn't hold their laughter and had to cover their mouths.

Qi continued: "Comrades, please take this seriously. I'm bringing this up because I don't think it's merely a matter of personal lifestyle. Secretary Qin is a Communist official. To the people in Jinta, he represents our Party. I understand that he joined the revolution at an early age. What was his motivation then? It was to overthrow the old regime. Now that the old regime is gone, we Communists are in power. As an official in this new government, he engages in affairs with women— sometimes even two at the same time. What's the difference between him and the scoundrels from the old regime? As a matter of fact, we seldom heard such scandals about the county chief in the Nationalist era.

"My second criticism is about the county's overzealous approach to implementing the mandatory state grain-purchasing policy. I visited Shuangcheng village in the first half of this year. Many of the peasants I met looked feeble and pale. When I asked if they were suffering from any disease, they attributed their bad health to hunger. Apparently, the government had gone overboard the previous year in forcing peasants to fulfill their quotas. Peasants ended up without any food for themselves. Since government subsidies didn't arrive on time, many families had to subsist on wild grass. I hope the county leadership can keep ordinary people's interests in mind and come up with a reasonable quota to alleviate the situation."

Once Qi started speaking, he found it difficult to stop. Before he was done, he had listed seven complaints against the county leadership. After the meeting, he wrote down his seven complaints with a paintbrush on poster boards and pasted them on the walls of the county government office complex. As he did so, he remembered one more: A county official in charge of welfare took money from a relief fund earmarked for the needy and gave it to Secretary Qin every month in the form of a subsidy. In return, Secretary Qin promoted the official. Qi wrote about his complaint on a poster under the headline, THE VICE CHAIR REDIRECTS MONEY FROM THE RELIEF FUND TO ADVANCE HIS CAREER. Qi also criticized the county's misguided efforts to plant trees in the desert.

Qi went even further. He wrote an open letter to the County

7

Party Committee and handed a copy to Lu Weigong. In the letter, he made ten proposals, including: improve the unified state grain-purchasing system to ensure that peasants have enough to live on; remove incompetent officials from the Legal Department; give greater attention to collective leadership and the repudiation of dictatorship.

With Qi taking the lead, others began to follow suit and write their complaints on posters. The campaign finally took off. It was only two weeks, however, before Qi and the other activists began to lose their enthusiasm. Little by little, they noticed that something unusual was happening. Following a complaint meeting, the county would assign an official to seal the meeting minutes. When a speaker wanted to check if his words were recorded accurately, he wouldn't be allowed any access to the minutes. Qi also saw several strangers in the office complex every day. They seemed to copy down the writing from every complaint poster.

People grew scared and stopped their criticisms. Some even tore down their own posters.

Qi heard that the strangers had been sent by Secretary Qin. One afternoon, Qi pulled down all the posters he had written and burned them. Even so, he felt uneasy. He could sense that something ominous was moving toward him. He showed up at Lu's office and said, "Secretary Lu, please give me back my open letter." Lu told him that he had already passed it on to Secretary Qin.

Startled by what he heard, Qi raised his voice: "Why on earth did you hand my letter to Secretary Qin?" Lu answered back: "Did I do anything wrong? Wasn't it supposed to be an open letter to the County Party Committee?" Realizing that he shouldn't lose his temper in front of Lu, Qi immediately corrected himself: "If you have already given it to him, that's fine.

I'm just a little worried lately. The situation doesn't seem right. I sense that something bad is going to happen." Qi was hoping to get some news out of Lu, but Lu remained calm and professional.

As Qi left Lu's office, his heart was beating fast—he was scared. He felt as if a cold wind had been blowing on his back. He couldn't understand why Lu, who used to be so warm and friendly toward him, acted differently that day.

Two days later, Qi went to Secretary Qin's office and asked if he could be transferred to Dunhuang County.

"My parents are getting old," he said. "They need me to take care of them."

Secretary Qin answered in an icy tone: "We're in the middle of a campaign and you are not permitted to go anywhere. If you want a transfer, we can discuss it when the campaign is over."

"Why can't I? Didn't you just grant a transfer for Wen Keshuan?"

"You and Wen Keshuan are different."

Qi was surprised. "How am I different from Wen Keshuan?"

"I think you know the answer," said Qin.

Qi realized that the situation was getting out of hand. So he answered boldly, "No, I don't know. Please explain to me why I am different from Wen Keshuan."

"If you want the answer, fine. I'll tell you now."

Qin moved closer to Qi and asked, "Qi Yaoquan—how old are you this year?"

"Twenty-four."

"You don't act like a twenty-four-year-old. At such a young age, you've already burned all your bridges."

Qi froze. Secretary Qin continued, "You have gone to such extremes to ruin other people's lives. The only thing you haven't done is to kill them with a knife. Don't you realize what you are doing?"

A week after that conversation, attacks against the Rightists started in Jinta.

Overnight, new complaint posters began appearing on the walls of the county government office complex. This time, the criticisms were directed at Qi. His previous remarks had been condemned as vicious attacks against the Party. The ten points he had proposed in his open letter were now called "ten poisonous arrows shot at the Party." Every few days, a new layer of posters was pasted over the old ones. Since Qi refused to own up to his anti-Party crimes, the county held "public debates," which were in fact public condemnation meetings. Qi stayed true to his convictions and denied all charges and accusations against him. One time, Qi was dragged to a meeting jointly organized by the County Party Committee and the People's Legislative Committee. Secretary Qin happened to be there. Officials stood up and lashed him with criticism. As usual, Qi fought back vehemently. "My criticism against Secretary Qin was meant to help him improve. In no way should it be construed as attacks against the Party."

He then listed his ten proposals and supported each single one with quotations from Chairman Mao and Karl Marx. He could recite the original quotes by the Communist leaders word for word. Seeing that they couldn't win any arguments against Qi, many officials simply asked him to shut up: "You might talk the Party talk, but deep in your heart, you oppose the Party." Some speakers became upset with Qi. As he was debating them, they would go up to him, pushing him, poking his ribs with their fingers, and calling him a Rightist and a counterrevolutionary.

The condemnation meetings dragged on for weeks in various forms: department meetings, countywide leadership conferences, and group discussions. The meetings lasted as long as twelve hours a day. Qi had to appear at each one of them. On many occasions, he had to attend meetings both during the day and at night. Different departments lined up to condemn him. The meetings lasted for four months. Qi felt wounded, both physically and psychologically. He was on the verge of a nervous breakdown and had no strength to argue back. In the end, he simply remained silent at every meeting. He thought: If they want to label me a Rightist, so be it. So what if I'm a Rightist? Chairman Mao has said that people with ideological problems should not be treated like criminals or class enemies. I don't think they will disobey Chairman Mao's words.

Though he consoled himself with these thoughts, he could see that since January 1958, things had started to turn grim. The criticisms against him had escalated. Two countywide public condemnation meetings were held against rightists.

One night, after returning home from the second public meeting, he said to his wife, "Things don't look too good. All the accusations in the past several days have aimed at portraying me as a 'Rightist' and a 'counterrevolutionary.' Without the encouragement of the senior leaders, ordinary folks wouldn't dare bring these charges. It looks like they are ready to take action against me. I need to be prepared."

"How do you prepare for something like this?" asked his wife, who worked for the Chengguan Township government. They had been married for three years and had a one-year-old boy.

"It's very likely that they will charge me as a Rightist. The charge now carries severe penalties. Not only would I lose my position in the county, I might be sent away. I think we should file for divorce so our child doesn't get implicated."

As might be expected, his wife didn't react well to this.

"How could you think of something like this? What could

they do to you? Maybe they'd send you to the countryside or to a reeducation camp. So what? If that's the case, I'll go with you."

Unfortunately, the premonition Qi had that night soon came true. Around noon the next day, he was ordered to appear at the county government auditorium. He initially thought he was going there to attend another public condemnation meeting. The auditorium was packed. The meeting began with announcements by Zhao Zhengfang, the deputy chief of the County Public Security Bureau.

Zhao walked up to the podium with a list of those who had recently been labeled Rightists, and started to read off names, ordering them to step up to the stage. As the Rightists came forward one by one, Zhao said sternly through the microphone, "You are under arrest." He then beckoned to two policemen standing on one side of the stage and told them to bind the Rightists with ropes.

Soon, Qi Yaoquan's name was called. He knew that Zhao would give him the same treatment. He walked up to the stage, but stopped about two or three feet away from the podium. When Zhao made the official announcement of his arrest, two policemen approached him with ropes. Qi stepped back and said, "Stop."

The policemen were startled and froze there. Qi said loudly, so everyone could hear: "Comrade Zhao, as the Chinese saying goes, 'The guillotine is sharp but it doesn't behead the innocent.' Before you arrest me, I want to ask you: what crimes have I committed?"

Zhao stammered as he answered, "You still claim to be innocent?"

"The Party urged us to voice our criticisms, so I did. Was that a violation of the law? If so, I would say that the County Party Committee has also violated the law, because every committee member was involved in the campaign. They are the ones who encouraged people like me to speak our minds. Should they be under arrest too?"

Zhao was speechless. The auditorium became silent. Then some activists in the audience stood up and shouted: "Tie him up. Just tie him up. He's too arrogant."

The policemen seemed to wake from their trance. They seized Qi's arms and tied them behind his back. Qi didn't resist. It was pointless to fight. If he did, seven or eight more policemen would jump on him. But as he was pushed off the stage, he did shout, "Is it a crime to criticize the Party leaders?"

After Qi was gone, Zhao continued with his announcements. In total, he ordered twenty-six Rightists arrested and locked up at a detention center.

The whole process—from being tied up to being trucked off to the detention center—took more than an hour. After the police untied the ropes, Qi's arms stiffened and his hands and arms became swollen. He could feel sharp pains radiating from his shoulder blades, but he didn't moan or scream.

A sympathetic inmate who saw Qi's swollen hands told him to soak them in the big chamber pot. Urine alleviates the swelling, the inmate said. Qi stuck both hands in. He held his breath to ward off the pungent smell.

In the evening, a cook showed up outside his cell and yelled, "Time to eat." Qi didn't get up. He didn't want to eat. He decided to stage a hunger strike.

After the cook left, a blacksmith came and shackled Qi's feet with a pair of chains.

The next morning, Qi refused to eat. He didn't eat for three consecutive days. On the fourth morning, he changed his mind. He was starving and his body was weakening. He thought to himself: I have been on a hunger strike for three days and nobody gives a damn. They'd probably be thrilled if I starved myself to death. The Public Security Bureau would simply write up a report saying that I refused to admit my crimes and chose to cut myself off from the Party by committing suicide. I can't die. If I die, I won't be able to clear my name and seek justice.

A guard came to get him after breakfast. He escorted him to an interrogation room. Wan Shengxiang, who headed the Interrogation Section, took up his case.

The interrogation, which focused on Qi's various counter-revolutionary remarks, went on for eight days. On the last day, Wan asked Qi if he had anything else to add.

"Now that you have completed your portion of the interrogation," said Qi, "I'd like to ask you some questions. My first one is: do you believe that the editorials in the *People's Daily* represent the voice of the Party Central Committee?"

"The *People's Daily* is the mouthpiece of the Communist Party and they do represent the opinions of the Party Central Committee," said Wan.

"I agree. The *People's Daily* stated clearly that the Party wouldn't take extreme measures against Rightists and those who spoke out against the government. Why did the Public Security Bureau arrest me? Don't you think what you have done contravenes Party policy?"

Wan didn't answer. Qi continued: "The *People's Daily* also said that we have to take into account an individual's personal and family history before we decide if that person is a Rightist or not. I joined the Communist revolution at the age of sixteen. I grew up in a family with five generations of poor peasants. I have a perfect record. Why do you still bring the Rightist charges against me?"

Wan didn't answer. He simply grunted angrily. Before Qi could ask another question, Wan grew impatient and told a policeman to take him away. Qi was brought back to the cell.

The next morning, two policemen showed up in his cell. They grabbed Qi's arms and handcuffed them behind his back. The previous week, when Qi's feet were shackled, he could at least sleep and eat. Now, with both hands bound behind him, he couldn't eat or use the toilet without help from his fellow inmates. They had to unbuckle his pants for him when he used the chamber pot, and they helped him eat and drink. Sleep became almost impossible. He couldn't lie down flat with his hands tied behind his back, and sleeping on his side was also uncomfortable. All he could do was sit against the wall, from dawn to dusk.

Four days later, his fellow inmates reported to the guard that Qi's physical condition had rapidly deteriorated. The guard passed on the message to the prison authorities. Several hours later, an official came by and ordered Qi's handcuffs removed.

It was deep winter. Temperatures dropped below zero. People in the area normally wore heavy felt-lined boots at this season. Qi began to suffer frostbite on his feet. A guard who used to attend Qi's classes happened to recognize him. Qi asked if he could deliver a message to his wife, asking for a pair of cotton-padded shoes, with low tops because his ankles were shackled with chains. The guard didn't dare to visit Qi's wife at home or at work. He was worried about being labeled an enemy sympathizer. Instead he waited outside the Chengguan Township government building. When she came out after work, the guard caught up with her and whispered, "Your husband needs a pair of cotton-padded shoes." The next day, Qi's wife came with the shoes he requested, but they didn't fit because his feet had become too swollen. His wife promised to bring another pair the next day. Qi said, "Don't come yourself. Send the nanny over. I don't want you to be implicated in the case." She ignored his words and showed up two days later with a pair of handmade shoes that fit him perfectly.

The county prosecutor's office finally initiated an official investigation into Qi's subversive activities, and he was put on trial. The first court session was open to the public. The court-room was not very large; its gallery could accommodate twenty to thirty people. The seats in the gallery were all taken by activists handpicked by Secretary Qin.

When Qi was brought into the room, the judge was nowhere to be seen. A stove made from a metal cylinder stood in the middle of the room, not too far from the defendant's table. Qi could feel the heat from the flames. He moved his chair so that he was sitting next to the stove. Someone shouted from the gallery, "Move back to your place." He ignored their shouting and refused to budge. Then the judge and six members of the trial panel walked in and sat on the bench. The judge ordered him to move his chair back to the defendant's table. He still wouldn't move. A policeman got up, pulled him up from the chair and shoved him over.

With this little turmoil settled, the judge cleared his throat and asked Qi what his name was. "How could you not know my name?" Qi blurted out.

Laughter could be heard in the gallery. Even the panelists, who knew Qi well, laughed. The judge banged his gavel on the table. This court scene stayed in Qi's memory for many years. He was shocked to see a Communist judge wielding a gavel. In those days, Qi had only seen gavels in movies about the corrupt courts in pre-Communist days or courts in Western countries. He thought the Communist court would be radically different.

The judge banged his gavel once more and inquired about Qi's occupation and his birthplace. Qi straightened himself and dutifully answered each question. Then the six panelists took turns questioning him on the charges. Qi admitted or denied each allegation truthfully. The questioning lasted nearly two hours. In the end, the judge said, "Are you trying to tell us that you're innocent?"

"Yes," said Qi, "I am innocent. What's wrong with speaking my mind about the leadership? Chairman Mao says, 'Blame not the speaker, but be warned by his words.' How could you ignore Chairman Mao's words?"

The judge was speechless. He paused for a few seconds before adjourning the court.

Qi never had another public trial.

One afternoon in April, the police brought Qi and five other alleged Rightists to the courtroom where his trial had taken place. The judge stood and read the verdicts for each one. Qi was up first.

"Qi Yaoquan, a counterrevolutionary, harbored reactionary ideas, engaged in anti-Party and antisocialist activities. He refused to cooperate with authorities and to confess his crimes. Based on the above, the court sentences Qi to six years in prison."

Qi didn't protest. No member of the public was present. The court felt empty. After all six verdicts were read, Qi was taken back to the detention center. An official of the court came to visit him and asked if he was planning to appeal.

"Why not?" he said. "I just need a pen and some paper."

That night, with one of his fellow inmates holding a kerosene lamp beside him, Qi hunched over his pillow and composed a three-page appeal:

On the day of my arrest, I was charged with being a Rightist. For some unknown reason, the charges against me have escalated. Today I've been sentenced to six years in jail for being a counterrevolutionary. How did the court reach this verdict? I haven't shouted antirevolutionary slogans, nor have I committed a felony. The charges against me are baseless . . .

The next morning, as Qi was having his breakfast, a truck pulled into the detention center. Qi and the five other convicted Rightists were ordered to drop their food and board the truck. Qi handed his letter of appeal to the court official. As the truck was about to leave, Qi saw his wife walk in, with their child on her back. He asked permission to get off the truck. His wife whispered to him that she had received a notice from her supervisor saying that she could no longer keep her job with the township government. She would be transferred to a school in Shuangcheng Township. The news brought tears to Qi's eyes. He patted her on the shoulder and apologized for getting her into trouble. His wife told him to wipe away his tears.

"Tough guys never cry," she said.

As she was talking, she took a small stack of cash from her pocket and handed it over to Qi.

"This is two hundred and eighty yuan ($40). That's all of our savings. Take it with you."

Qi counted out eighty yuan and gave the rest back to his wife. "You need that to raise our child," he said.

The truck took off and drove through Yumen Township. The driver stopped at a restaurant, where each passenger ate a bowl of stir-fried noodles. They continued their journey for another two hours on a bumpy desert road before the truck pulled into Number Three Yinma Farm.

The farm, which had been built recently, served as a labor camp. All the prisoners lived in tents. Each tent, fenced in by barbed wire, could accommodate twenty-four people. A row of mud houses stood in a line outside the barbed wire. They were used as camp offices.

When Qi arrived, he was told that the top priority at Number Three Yinma Farm was to build an irrigation canal around the field. The next morning, policemen escorted Qi and the other prisoners out of the gate, which was simply an opening in the barbed wire. They walked three kilometers to the project site. Qi didn't mind the challenge of physical labor because he was in good spirits. He believed that his six-year sentence had been made in error, and that his appeal would soon succeed.

On the second day, several inmates tried to bully him. They swore at him for no reason at all, shoved him and punched him, just to see how he would react. Qi fought back.

One morning, as Qi was shoveling mud, an inmate working next to him started to yell: "You bastard! How dare you shovel the dirt in my direction? You've gotten dust all over my clothes."

Qi was outraged. "You're the bastard. With wind as strong as this, how can you dig without stirring up dust?"

The inmate walked up to Qi and pointed his finger in Qi's face. Qi pushed his hand away. Since Qi was a head taller, the inmate simply mumbled something and walked away.

Night after night, Qi had nightmares about being sentenced to death by the judge in Jinta County. He was put on a truck and sent to the execution ground. A policeman raised his rifle and shot him in the head. He woke up soaked with sweat. He could hear his own heartbeat. At lunch break one day, he sat behind a small sand dune and puffed on a cigarette until he dozed off. The cigarette butt fell to his chest and burned his winter coat. Another inmate smelled the smoke, woke him up, and poured some cold water on his chest to put out the fire. The nightmares and the fire put him in a sour mood that day.

However, when they finished work that evening, a camp

official showed up and called a brief meeting. He praised Qi for his good work and positive attitude and announced that he had been chosen as a group leader. Qi was put in charge of twenty-three people.

He had barely sat down inside the tent to absorb the good news when someone outside called his name.

"Where does Qi Yaoquan live?"

Qi immediately walked out.

The person looked like a prison officer. He told Qi to pack his luggage.

Qi was puzzled. He went back inside, folded his clothes, and rolled up his bedding. He hoisted his baggage onto his back and followed the man into the camp office. There he saw Dong Youcai, an official from the Jinta County Intermediate Court. Qi's eyes brightened. He went up to Dong, grabbed his hands and shook them, saying, "I can't believe it's you!"

Without offering a seat to Qi, Dong said, "I've been looking all over for you in the past three days. I knew you were at the Yinma Farm, but I didn't know which one. To make a long story short, I've gotten the result of your appeal. Let me read it to you.

'After reviewing the evidence against Qi, the court has decided to overturn the previous verdict. It's true that Qi made such Rightist remarks as "Communists are not as good as the Nationalists." But based on the principles of combining leniency with reeducation, the court hereby grants Qi's immediate release.' "

Qi was amazed at the news of his release, but he was also upset. "I never said that the Communists are not as good as the Nationalists," he said. "Someone made it up."

Dong interrupted him. "There is no need to dispute that. Let bygones be bygones."

It was summertime. Even late in the day, it was still quite bright outside. Dong decided to leave that very night. The camp arranged for a car to take them to Yumen Township. They boarded a train there and arrived in Jinta County by noon the next day. Qi was eager to go home, but Dong took him to the Public Security Bureau and handed him over to an officer at the detention center.

Qi was confused. "Didn't you say the court found me innocent and decided to release me?"

"We have overturned the counterrevolutionary charges against you, but you still remain a Rightist. Stay here for now. There will be a decision soon."

A couple of days passed and nobody came. Qi ended up staying at the detention center for a whole month. Every day, he would plow and cut grass at a small farm managed by the Public Security Bureau. The weather was getting hotter by the day. Finally, one sweltering afternoon, the county government dispatched a messenger to see him. The messenger asked Qi to pack and then brought him to the county government office complex.

The deputy chairman of the County Rectification Campaign Committee came out to greet him and read an announcement: "Qi Yaoquan has been convicted as a Rightist. He will reform his thinking at the Jiabiangou Reeducation Through Hard Labor Camp. Upon completion of his reeducation, he shall be permitted to continue employment with the county government."

The messenger led Qi directly to the County Intercity Bus Terminal. He was ordered to board a big truck. On the truck he saw Wei Derong, the former head of the Jinta County Taxation Bureau, and surprisingly, Zhao Zhengfang, the deputy chief of the County Public Security Bureau. Throughout the trip, Qi remained silent. Several hours later, the truck rumbled into Jiuquan County. The driver stopped at a small roadside village and got out of the truck; he walked into the village to rent an oxcart from some local peasants, while the three passengers waited under a poplar tree. Qi asked Zhao why he was there.

"It's a long story," said Zhao, looking depressed.

Qi was curious. "Remember when you had me arrested at the public condemnation meeting? You seemed so arrogant and authoritative. One day, you ordered your people to shackle my feet. The next day, you had my arms tied behind my back. How did you end up sitting in the same truck with me?"

Zhao looked uneasy. He spoke awkwardly. "My good old Qi, please don't blame me for your arrest. Your case was handled solely by Secretary Qin. He personally issued the order to have you shackled. It was my decision to put the handcuffs on you. This is how it happened. A couple of days after your arrest Secretary Qin called me at home, inquiring if you had been 'well taken care of.' I said not yet. He told me to have a second pair of shackles made by a local blacksmith and put them on you. I hesitated, saying that double shackling a detainee was a violation of the law. Nobody had done it before. Secretary Qin simply interrupted me: 'Do as I order. What kind of law are we violating?'

"I had no choice but to obey his command. So the next day I called my fellow policemen together for a meeting to discuss how to implement Secretary Qin's order. In the end, we all opposed the idea of shackling your feet with double chains. The alternative solution we came up with was to replace the chains with a pair of handcuffs. Please don't blame me. I'm not responsible for your arrest. It was Secretary Qin's doing.

"Even the announcement I read at the auditorium that day was drafted by Qin's assistant. Do you know why you ended up at the detention center after the court had released you from the Yinma Camp? Secretary Qin issued a secret order to have you detained. Qin said to me, 'If we can't get him prosecuted by the court, let's request the most severe administrative penalty possible.' Secretary Qin instructed the County Rectification Campaign Committee to write up report after report about your anti-Party activities. In the end, the provincial government agreed to send you to a reeducation camp, but fell short of terminating your employment."

Qi didn't speak. He stared at the loose dirt under his feet for a long time before asking Zhao what crimes he had committed. Zhao sighed.

"I've been charged with organizing a regional anti-Communist faction. It's a long story. As you know, Secretary Qin is a womanizer. In the past several years, we've received more than twenty complaints against him from peasants claiming that he raped their daughters or wives. It was a thorny issue for me. I invited Secretary Qin into my office and said, in a roundabout way, 'Secretary Qin, we've received complaints from the local villages about officials engaging in indecent behavior. These officials have tarnished the reputation of our Party. At your next meeting, it's important that you urge our fellow officials to refrain from committing any sexual indiscretions.'

"He asked me what I was hinting at. I didn't answer him directly. I merely wanted to give him a subtle reminder. So I said, 'It doesn't matter who the target is. The most important thing is to ask every official to act discreetly in the future.' He lost his temper and said, 'All I did was to mess around with a couple of women, but people like you keep stepping on my toes and bugging me.' After that, he began to consider me a nuisance.

"Of course, that wasn't the only thing that got me into trouble with him. He persecuted me for another reason: He accused me of following Zhang, the county chief, too closely. He believed that I had secretly formed an alliance with Zhang to oppose him. As you know, Zhang didn't always see eye to eye with Qin. Last winter, the district government requested information about the Jinta County's projected grain output. At a county meeting, Secretary Qin insisted on putting it down as three hundred kilograms per *mu* (0.16 acres). County Chief Zhang opposed that projection. He said, 'Local peasants have told us that we overestimated the grain output the last two years. As a consequence, the provincial government set an excessively high collection quota. After peasants fulfilled their quotas, they barely had enough to support their families. I would recommend one hundred and eighty kilograms per *mu*.' The county chief asked for the views of the other committee members. He said, 'Since I didn't grow up here, my projection of grain output per *mu* might be inaccurate. Most of you are Jinta natives. You tell me exactly how much grain a peasant can produce per *mu*.' None of the officials at the meeting answered, even though we all knew that the three hundred kilogram figure was outrageous. In the past, the average grain output was about one hundred or so kilograms per *mu*. Secretary Qin had deliberately inflated the projection to boost his reputation in the province.

"Seeing that we were all silent, Secretary Qin called on me. I felt obligated to give my honest opinion. I told everyone that Zhang's projection was more realistic. Qin gave me a dirty look and asked the other members. They all agreed with me. Qin lost his temper and walked out.

"Not long after that meeting, Qin plotted against County Chief Zhang, calling him a Rightist. I remained in my position for two more months before Qin succeeded in getting rid of me. Wu Peizhou, head of the Propaganda Department, was also removed from his position. All of us were charged with form-ing a regional anti-Party clique."

Qi was shocked. "What happened to the county chief?"

"He was sent to Jiabiangou to receive reeducation two weeks ago," said Zhao.

Qi shook his head. County Chief Zhang was a veteran Com-munist official from Qingyang County. He was warmhearted and low-key. Whenever he visited a village, he always asked to stay in the commune's cow sheds, just so that he could chat with the farmers. Unlike Secretary Qin, he was faithful to his peasant wife, who had bound feet. He took pride in his humble roots. Qi held him in high esteem.

"Where is Party Secretary Lu?" Qi asked.

"He lost his job in January. At the Provincial Party Con-gress, senior leaders who came from northern Shaanxi Prov-ince charged four officials from Qingyang County with forming a counterrevolutionary faction within the provincial govern-ment. The four were then stripped of their positions. Since Lu was friendly with them, he was implicated in their case. Secre-tary Qin delivered a speech at one of the plenary sessions and openly condemned Lu for secretly supporting a large number of Rightists in Jinta County. He said all the Rightists consid-ered Lu their mentor. Qin specifically brought up your name, and said Party Secretary Lu had directed you to launch vicious attacks against the Party."

Qi wanted to ask more questions, but just then the driver returned from the village. He was followed by a local peasant steering an oxcart. The driver pointed at the oxcart and said, "Get on. Stack up your luggage."

The oxcart was fitted with big wheels as tall as Qi. The Rightists sat on the cart, bobbing up and down on the rutted road for about two kilometers. They crossed a river, and then saw a row of low sand dunes in the distance. As they moved closer, a big wooden sign came into sight. On the sign, a line of big black characters read: JIABIANGOU STATE FARM.

Qi Yaoquan's heart began to pound violently. What's going to happen to me? he wondered.

Qi Yaoquan survived the Jiabiangou State Farm, known internally as Jiabiangou Reeducation Through Hard Labor Camp, and subsequently endured years of hardship at various labor camps and farms in Gansu Province. In 1978, the Jinta County Communist Party Committee cleared his name and removed all charges against him.

Woman from Shanghai

I heard this story from a former Rightist named Li Wenhan. Li was born in the central province of Hubei. After graduating from high school in 1948, he joined the Communist army. In 1950, one year after the Communists had taken over China, he was sent to fight against the Americans in Korea, where shrapnel from an American bomb broke three ribs on both sides of his chest. Li returned to China for treatment. Upon recovery, he was assigned a job at the Public Security Ministry in Beijing.

Li had grown up in a rich family and his nonproletariat family background became a liability under the new government. He was demoted and transferred to the Reform and Reeducation Bureau in Jiuquan. There he became a clerk at the production division. In 1957, Li was labeled a Rightist for writing an article that criticized the inefficiency of his local party officials. He was fired from his government clerkship and sent to Jiabiangou. In January 1961, the government released all the surviving Rightists from Jiabiangou, allowing most of them to return to their work units. Because Li had been fired, he had nowhere to go. The local government eventually assigned him to work at the Shigong Collective Farm in Anxi County.

At Shigong, Li was responsible for tending a vegetable garden, for which he earned a monthly salary of twenty-four yuan ($3.50). He stayed there until 1969, when China started preparing for a war against the Soviet Union; then he was transferred to the Xiaowan

Collective Farm. Li became a member of Division 14, which was in charge of managing the farm's livestock. He and I shared a room near a goat pen for three years. Over that period, we got to know and trust each other. In the long winter nights, he entertained me with many Jiabiangou stories.

Li's stories stayed with me. In the mid-1970s, I became a high school teacher in Lanzhou, Gansu's capital, and lost touch with Li.

In this world, anything can happen. One day in 1996, I went to visit my former high school teacher. As I approached the entrance to the school, someone called my name. I turned around and noticed a familiar tall figure—bald and tan, with well-defined facial features. Li Wenhan hadn't changed much, except that the remaining hair at his temples had gone gray. He said he lived in an apartment building near the school. He invited me over, and we downed a bottle of liquor and chatted the whole day.

After the verdict against him was overturned in the late 1970s, he went to work at the Wudaping labor camp in Jiuquan. He was a manager of the production division for more than ten years. When he retired, he and his family moved back to Lanzhou. During our conversation, he abruptly asked me whether I remembered the story of the Shanghai woman.

She was the wife of a convicted Rightist.

Before National Day on October 1, 1960, all the Rightists at Jiabiangou were transported to Mingshui, in Gaotian County. The Gansu Provincial Reform and Reeducation Bureau planned to convert about thirty thousand hectares of wild grassland and desert into farmland.

The project was hastily launched. Winter was fast approaching. Leaders of other camps in the region were sneaky and didn't send their laborers as planned. In the end, only the Jiabiangou Rightists went—about fifteen hundred of us. We set up shacks inside two gullies at the foot of Qilian Mountain. We had no wood to build houses, so we simply lived in caves we dug out of the gullies. The smaller caves on the shallow side of a gully were only about one meter high. You had to crawl in through a small opening, and once inside, you could barely sit up straight. Our group was assigned a location in the middle of a gully, so we were able to dig a larger cave. Twenty-one of us moved in together. The ones I remember very well are Wen Daye, Dong Jianyi, and Chao Chongwen.

Wen Daye had been the deputy dean of the Provincial Nursing School and a professor at the Lanzhou Medical Academy. He died in Mingshui after eating food unfit for human consumption.

Dong Jianyi died around the same time.

I can still remember the circumstances leading to Wen Daye's death. It happened in early November. One day, Wen came to me and said, "Old Li, I don't think I can live through this week. I've eaten the gluey soup."

I was stunned by what he had told me. The gluey soup that Wen mentioned was a soup boiled from a weed that the locals called "yellow cogon grass." You've probably never heard of it. It grew all over the grassland in tall clusters. Its stalks were long and thick and yellow. Some local peasants told us that they used to eat the seeds to stave off hunger during times of famine. We took our bedsheets to the grassland and spread them on the ground. We cut off clusters of the yellow cogon grass, beat them on the bedsheets to remove the seeds, and rubbed the seeds between our hands to strip off the husks. Then we'd hold up the bedsheets and shake them slightly so that the husks would blow away in the breeze. The seeds were the size of poppy seeds—we had to be careful not to lose them.

After collecting the seeds, we fried them in a hot pan and stored them in small bags, which we sewed inside our undershirts. We had to hide them well, since camp officials constantly checked up on us and would confiscate the seeds if they found them.

Preparing the seeds for eating was an equally complicated process. We would take a small handful out of the bag and boil them in a pot. This would soon yield a clear, sticky broth—something like thin rice congee. The broth still wasn't edible at this stage. We had to stir it rapidly with chopsticks until it cooled off and became a lump of dough. The dough was diffi-cult to stretch—it was like pulling a piece of rubber—and it was hard to break down by chewing. We cut the dough into small pieces, put them in our mouths, and swallowed. The dough had no nutritional value, but it wasn't poisonous either. It simply filled our stomachs, and gave us a false sense of fullness. You've probably heard about famine victims in some parts of China swallowing a type of white clay. This was a similar prac-tice. The dough wasn't digestible, so it would stay in the stom-ach for several days. Unfortunately, it was also hard to get out of the system. We needed to eat lots of wild vegetables in order to push it out.

We learned that it was lethal for people to drink the sticky broth before it cooled and solidified. If the soup hardened in the stomach, it could glue together whatever else the person had ingested—vegetables, weeds, leaves—into a large, hard-ened lump, which could get lodged in the intestine. At least thirty-some Rightists at Jiabiangou and Mingshui died after drinking the soup, including some who swallowed just a small amount of it, thinking a little wouldn't be harmful.

Wen Daye's words scared me. I couldn't help scolding him. "Didn't you know that the soup was dangerous?"

"I was starving. I just couldn't wait for it to cool down. I took a few gulps."

"A few gulps!"

"Actually," he said timidly, "I swallowed half a bowl."

I said I didn't know how I could help him. He suggested that I find him some castor oil seeds.

It wasn't a bad idea. Castor oil seeds were laxatives. Maybe the castor oil would dissolve the lump, and it would come out. I ran over to the camp clinic. The doctor swore at me and kicked me out.

"So many of our people are dying of dysentery from eating wild grasses and vegetables," he said. "They're shitting out their intestines. Now you ask me for a laxative. Where do you expect me to get it?"

I walked back to the cave, dejected. I couldn't bear the thought of Wen dying on me.

"Do you want to live?" I asked him. "If so, I'll dig it out for you."

We started the "digging" practice back at Jiabiangou. The abnormally heavy workload depleted our bodies, and the daily food ration of less than half a kilogram of grain wasn't enough to subsist on. In order to survive, we filled our stomachs with wheat husks, leaves, and seeds—anything we could find. A lot of what we ate was difficult to digest, and excretion was painful and strenuous.

In my hometown, there's a popular insult: "Your hiccup smells like weeds." It means the person is acting like a weed-eating animal. At Jiabiangou, we were literally turned into weed-eating animals, our excrement like goat droppings. Often, in the latrine, we'd help each other out. One person would lie on his stomach with his butt in the air. Another would squat behind him, digging. For this we used a special tool—a long wooden spoon made from a red willow twig. If we didn't have one, we'd use a metal spoon.

When Wen told me he had drunk the soup, his condition had already reached a painful stage: his lower abdomen was bloated like a drum and he couldn't pass anything. He leaned on a wall, his pants around his ankles. I knelt behind him and began to operate. I poked for a long time without success. I tried to break the hard lump into pieces but failed. Wen was moaning with pain. My tool had caused serious bleeding, but the lump inside his intestines remained intact.

Wen's stomach grew bigger and bigger. Five days later, the bloating killed him. We wrapped up his body in his quilt and left him outside the cave. That afternoon, the camp authorities sent over a burial team. They loaded him onto a horse-drawn cart and carried him north to a burial site right outside the gully.

Among our cave mates, Dong Jianyi was the only one who refused to touch anything he deemed outside a normal diet. Dong had been a urologist. He grew up in Shanghai and gradu-ated from a medical school there. I knew of him when we were at Jiabiangou, but we'd never spoken to each other. In 1959, before National Day, the camp organized an outing for pris-oners to see an exhibition put on by the Jiuquan Reform and Reeducation Bureau to showcase the achievements of the reeducation through labor program. After it was over, we stopped at a restaurant. Dong and I sat at the same table.

We struck up a conversation. He told me that he was the chief physician at a hospital in Shanghai. In 1956, the Commu-nist Party encouraged young professionals from urban areas to settle in the isolated northwestern region. As an idealistic young doctor, Dong volunteered, and ended up in Lanzhou. He chaired the Urology Department at the Gansu Provincial Peo-ple's Hospital. His wife was also a doctor; she didn't follow him when he was sent to Lanzhou because she was pregnant at the time. Dong looked like he was in his midthirties.

Dong's scholarly manners left an indelible impression on me. I remember telling a fellow Rightist on the way back to the camp that I didn't think Dong would survive. During our meal, he had chewed his food slowly, and nothing seemed to satisfy him. That person noticed the same thing about Dong—he was too fussy about his food. Others would supplement their limited food rations by combing the fields for wild vegetables, seeds, or rats. But Dong considered these things unfit for him to eat. He only ate the small amount of food supplied by the mess hall.

I didn't see Dong for quite a long time after our conversation. I thought he had died. But one day he showed up in Mingshui and was assigned to my cave. He told me that he had been hospitalized at a clinic in Jiabiangou for cirrhosis.

At Mingshui, Dong continued to turn down improper food. Our food ration was reduced to a quarter of a kilogram per day. The so-called food was actually a flour bun mixed with vegetables and a bowl of corn gruel. Without protein or nutrients in their diet, many people started to die. The gravity of the situation appalled the camp leaders, who took some special measures to reduce the number of deaths: fieldwork was temporarily suspended. During work hours, we were permitted to go scout the grassland for weeds, rats, or worms. We could also sleep in to save energy. We captured every rat and lizard in the nearby region and stripped the leaves and bark off every tree. Dong wouldn't eat any of that. Every day, after having his share of vegetable bun and corn gruel, he'd spend the whole day lying in bed.

"This isn't the time to show off your refined taste," I told him. "Eat whatever you can get your hands on. Survival is what's most important."

He turned his back on me and said, "Do you think what you're eating is fit for human consumption?"

Later on, I found out that his wife was responsible for

keeping him alive. She came to visit him at Jiabiangou once every two to three months, and would bring him crackers, powdered milk, and glucose powder.

Still, a month after his transfer to Mingshui, his health deteriorated irreversibly. He looked like a skeleton. His sunken eyes resembled dark holes. Soon he was too emaciated to walk. When he needed water, he would slowly crawl to the table in the common area.

One evening in mid-November, I was squatting in front of a makeshift stove, right outside the cave, boiling some perennial roots that I had dug up in the field. Dong appeared at my side. I thought he wanted to try my roots, so I pulled some out with my chopsticks and handed them to him, but he turned away.

"No, thanks, Li," he said. "I just want to ask you a favor."

I asked him what it was.

"I believe you'll go back to Lanzhou alive," he said. "There's no doubt in my mind about it."

I was puzzled. "How do you know? Haven't you noticed that my face is so swollen I can hardly open my eyes? I can't even wear shoes because my feet are too swollen. I'm dying."

I was being honest. By November, almost everyone at Mingshui had succumbed to some starvation-related illness. When we went to bed, we had no idea whether we would wake the next morning. Someone would die every few days. Most people died quietly, in their sleep, without a single moan or any sign of struggle.

In later years, whenever I talked about Jiabiangou, someone would inevitably ask me why we didn't try to escape. Some people did escape. But most of us stayed. Even in the worst of times, we had high hopes for our leaders. We were under the illusion that someday the party would realize we had been wrongly convicted and our verdicts would be reversed. We considered reeducation through hard labor a test of our loyalty to the Communist Party. If we escaped, it would have meant betrayal of our Party's trust. We would have regretted it the rest of our lives.

When I told Dong that I didn't think I would survive the winter, he looked at me with a faintly mischievous smile.

"Li, I'm sure you'll live," he said. "You are a very resourceful person."

I was taken aback. "What do you mean by that?"

"I know that someone is secretly supplying you with food. On two occasions Leader Kong came to our cave and asked you to meet him outside. When you returned, you would get into your bed and cover your head with the quilt, but I heard you munching on food."

I didn't deny this, because he was right. He had figured out my secret. It started in 1959, when starvation first hit Jiabiangou. People wrote to their families and asked for crackers and parched flour. I tried to figure out an innovative way to survive. After careful consideration, I decided to ingratiate myself with Leader Kong, who was in charge of logistics at Jiabiangou. It was not a high-level position. The job required him to ride a horse-drawn cart to the market in Jiuquan and purchase goods for the camp. Sometimes he'd pick up our mail at the post office. Realizing that Kong could be useful, I began to cultivate a relationship with him. One day, I received a package from a friend containing a piece of blue corduroy. I put the package in Kong's hand.

"I don't know what to do with this," I told him. "Why don't you take it to your wife so that she can make a jacket out of it?"

Kong, whose wife still lived in a rural area of Gangu County, accepted my gift, but he seemed embarrassed. He became sympathetic to my situation.

"Was this parcel sent by your family?" he asked. "Why don't they send you food? What we need here is food."

I was glad he brought it up.

"Leader Kong," I said, "I'm still single. My parents are quite old. I didn't want them to know that I had made a political mistake and that I'm undergoing reeducation here. That's why I don't have anyone to send me food."

My remarks seemed to achieve the desired effect.

"It's hard when you don't get any support from your family," he said. "But it helps if you have some money to spare."

I got the hint.

"What's the point of having money here?" I asked deliberately. "There's nothing to buy."

He patted me on my shoulder. "Not here, perhaps. But we can always find a way to get food in Jiuquan. It's not that hard. I travel to Jiuquan once or twice a week. Tell me what you want. I can buy food and bring it back to you."

It was exactly what I wanted to hear. I thanked him profusely.

"I have to ask you one favor then," I said. "The day I arrived at Jiabiangou, I had to hand over one thousand yuan ($150) in cash and three hundred yuan in government bonds to the treasurer's office for safekeeping. I can't withdraw the money now. Can you figure out a way to get it out?"

He thought for a moment. "It shouldn't be difficult," he said. "I'll go withdraw it tomorrow."

Leader Kong kept his promise. The next day, right before dusk, he called me to his office and said that he had managed to withdraw the money.

"I told them that your parents are ill and that you need to send money to pay the hospital bills."

After I received the money, I immediately gave the three-hundred-yuan bond to Leader Kong.

"I need cash now," I said. "Why don't you keep the bond? When it matures, cash it and use it to provide for your family."

He was quite pleased. Officials of his status earned a monthly salary of forty to fifty yuan, so three hundred was a big sum. I pulled out a twenty-yuan note and asked him to buy me some food during his next trip to Jiuquan.

One evening, two days later, after I had gone to bed, Leader Kong called my name from outside the cave. I followed him to a spot on the other side of the courtyard wall. He handed me a package with two oven-baked cakes inside. He told me not to tell anyone about it, and then he disappeared in the darkness. From that point on, I asked Leader Kong to buy me cakes once a week. Our secret deal lasted a whole year. The cakes weren't too big—probably just a quarter of a kilogram each—but they saved my life. By the time I arrived in Mingshui, I was nearly out of money. My health had started to deteriorate, and I was growing increasingly nervous.

Seeing that I didn't say anything, Dong grabbed my hand and continued.

"I want to ask you a favor. I received a letter from my wife several days ago. She is coming to see me in a few days. With my current situation being what it is, I don't think I can wait that long."

His words surprised me. "How can you say that? As far as I can see, you're doing fine."

He shook his head. "Listen—let me finish. There have been moments in the last few days when my mind has gone completely blank. My consciousness disappears, everything disappears. This is not a good sign."

"Maybe you just dozed off."

"Trust me, I know the difference between falling asleep and falling into a coma. Listen to what I have to tell you. I wrote back to my wife and told her that I might be transferred soon. I told her to come see me as soon as possible. I also told her that if she couldn't find me at Mingshui, to look for you."

37

"Dong! What am I supposed to do?"

Dong gave me a bitter smile.

"Be patient, my friend. I wasn't planning to tell you about this. I figured I could tough it out the next few days and live to see her, but when I got up this morning, I had another round of dizzy spells. I didn't think I could wait any longer. I had to tell you now."

"You miss your wife too much and you are losing your mind."

He waved his hand at me dismissively. "Please, don't interrupt me. What I'm asking you is simple and I hope you can do it for me. If I die before my wife shows up, would you wrap up my body with my quilt and leave it inside the cave over there? When you see my wife, tell her what happened to me and ask her to ship my body back to Shanghai."

He looked at me with dark sunken eyes and waited for my answer. I didn't say anything. My heart tightened. Dong pleaded again.

"Li, please, I beg you. I don't want to be buried here. When I decided to move to the northwest, I did so against the strong objections of my wife, parents, and in-laws. I ignored them because I was eager to devote myself to the development of the region. I wish I had listened to my family. I regret so much . . ."

Dong died three days later.

Unlike several of my cave mates who had died in their sleep, Dong passed away during the day, while he was sitting on his quilt and talking to me. He said his wife was coming soon and that there was a chance that he didn't have to bother me with his burial. In the middle of a sentence, his head drooped and fell to his knee. That was it.

Honoring his final request, one of my cave mates and I wrapped up Dong's corpse in his quilt and hid it in a dark corner of the cave. We waited for his wife to come and collect his body.

That's when events took a strange turn. The morning after Dong's death, the camp's director, Liu, appeared with several officials. He yelled at everyone and ordered his subordinates to go through the cave and check for dead bodies. They found Dong and carted him off to a place outside the valley for disposal. Remembering my promise to Dong, I followed the cart and saw where he was being buried.

The next day, we found out why Director Liu had made his sudden appearance. It turned out that several unexpected guests had showed up at Mingshui. They visited a number of the caves and asked the Rightists questions about how they had come to the camp and how much food they were given to eat each day. After the guests left, word got out that the visitors were members of a work team headed by the deputy director of the Central Party Committee's Supervisory Department. The team was investigating the situation at Jiabiangou and Mingshui. Apparently the massive loss of life at Jiabiangou had attracted the notice of senior leaders.

The news about the investigation stirred up a lot of excitement. We hoped that the investigation would result in our being allowed to leave Mingshui and go home.

Several days passed. Nothing happened. The excitement died down. Actually the visit did help in one way, which I'll tell you about later.

Five days after Dong's death, his wife arrived in Mingshui.

Since my bed was near the mouth of the cave, I was the first one to hear her voice calling Dong's name.

"Who is it?" I asked.

"I'm looking for Dong Jianyi."

I got up in a hurry and whispered to my cave mates, "Dong's

wife is here." I called out to the woman: "Oh, you must be Dong's wife. Please come in."

It was as if the cave was hit by a tornado—everyone got up from bed and scurried around, putting on their pants, tidying up their beds. The woman walked in.

"I'm from Shanghai. My name is Gu Xiaoyun. I'm here to see Dong Jianyi. Does he live here?"

"Ye—yes. He does live here. But recently, he . . ."

To be honest, I wasn't prepared at all. Dong had been dead for a week. I had assumed that the camp had sent her a death notice and that she had canceled her trip. I was at a loss.

She must have noticed my anxiety. With a bewildered look, she asked, "He isn't here today?"

I nodded my head ambiguously. I looked at my cave mates, hoping to get some kind of sign from them, but they just looked at me silently. That made me even more nervous.

"Please," I said, "please sit down."

But she just stood there, glancing around the cave. She seemed to sense that something was wrong.

"Are you Li Wenhan? Dong told me in his letter that I could turn to you for help if he was not at Mingshui. I am so glad you're here."

I nodded my head again. She went on: "Dong told me that he might be transferred to another location soon. He asked me to find him as soon as possible. Has he left already?"

"He just . . . stepped out."

I had no idea what to do. I avoided making eye contact with her. I knelt on the ground and cleaned off my bed so she could sit there.

Dong's wife put down a big bulging flower-patterned bag, untied the green silk scarf that covered her head, and looked at me. She had the typical face of a southern woman, an elegant face, with a full forehead, slightly sunken eyes, and a pointed chin. Dong had told me that his wife was in her thirties, but she looked much younger, like a twenty-five-year-old. I couldn't bear to break the news to her. I grabbed a mug, rushed over to give it a quick wash, and attempted to offer her hot water, but the thermos bottle was empty.

"Please don't worry about it," she said. "Just sit down and talk to me. Where is Dong? When is he coming back?"

I ignored her question, and called out to my cave mates, "Does anyone have any hot water for big sister Gu?"

One person gave me his thermos bottle, and I poured the water into a mug and sat it on top of a leather suitcase near my bed.

"Comrade Gu, you don't mind if we follow the Chinese tradition and call you big sister Gu, do you?" I asked. "Dong told me that you're a couple of years older than I am. You can call me little Li."

"Little Li, do you know where Dong is?"

I made up my mind that I would tell her the truth— I couldn't hold off any longer.

"Big sister Gu, Dong is gone. He's been gone for about a week."

To hide my anxiety, I called out to my roommates. "Dong's been gone for eight days, right?"

Nobody answered me. They simply sat there, watching the woman. I could hear their breathing.

I was afraid that the woman would burst into a loud wail, but she just sat there motionless, staring at me. Could it be that she didn't hear me? Did she not understand what I meant by "gone"?

"Big sister Gu, you understood me, right? Dong passed away a week ago."

She started to cry. Her wailing came from deep inside her chest. A great sob shook her frame. She covered her face and hunched over her bag. Tears streamed down her hands. Her tears touched our hearts, which had been hardened during the past few months by the massive number of deaths in the camp. We had forgotten what it was like to be sad. Her crying softened our hearts.

That poor woman! When her husband was incarcerated at Jiabiangou, she had traveled thousands of miles every three months to see him. Do you know how hard it was to travel in those days from Shanghai to Jiabiangou and Mingshui? She had to transfer from train to bus three or four times. It took her at least six days. Why? It was the emotional bond between a husband and a wife. She looked forward to their reunion when he finished his sentence. Now all her hopes and anticipation were dashed. The woman from Shanghai had endured all sorts of hardship and crossed half of the country, only to find out that her husband had died.

The thought of it made me weep. I could tell that other Rightists in my cave were also quietly shedding tears.

I waited patiently until her grief, anger, and disappointment had poured out. Finally I said, "Big sister Gu, please stop crying and try to restrain your grief. You should take care of your own health because you need to make it back to Shanghai."

My words were useless. Her weeping once again turned into a wail.

"Big sister Gu, let me explain the situation to you. Dong entrusted me with a couple of things."

She straightened her body and her wailing stopped. She turned to me, her sobs like hiccups. I told her that Dong had died peacefully, and that we had dressed him in a new woolen jacket we had found in his suitcase. I also told her that we had buried him in the cemetery. What I didn't tell her was that Dong had asked to have his body shipped back to Shanghai.

She sat there for a long time, just crying. When she finally stopped, she opened up her flower-patterned bag and pulled out several packages. She spread them on my bed.

"Little Li, I bought these two shirts in Shanghai. They were for Dong. I won't have any use for them. Why don't you keep them as a gift?"

She started crying again. Between sobs, she held a sweater up in her hands.

"I knit it all by myself, stitch by stitch. I think I'm going to take it home with me."

Then she pointed at food she had taken from her handbag—cookies, dried minced pork, and cakes—and raised her voice: "Everyone, please help yourself to snacks."

Under normal circumstances, a mob would have gathered, expecting to get a piece of cracker or a cigarette. But that day everyone sat on their bed, behaving in a civilized way. One person, assuming a noble tone, went so far as to say, "We're fine. I don't particularly care for sweet food, anyway."

"Don't you need the food for your trip back to Shanghai?" one man asked her.

"I don't need much," she said. "A couple of cookies will last me. If I'm hungry, I can always buy food on the train. You don't have anywhere to buy food."

"You're right," said the man. "I'm going to help myself."

He walked over, picked up two cookies and stuffed them in his mouth. He chewed a couple of times and then started coughing, and tears trickled down his cheeks. Another Rightist laughed.

"Try not to kill yourself with a cookie."

The man managed to gobble it down, wiped his tears and quipped, "If I choke to death, my wife would sue big sister Gu."

Everybody laughed. A faint smile flashed across the woman's face, and one by one, people came over to the food.

Those who were too weak to walk crawled over, and reached their dirt-stained hands into the snack bags. The food disappeared fast and a few minutes later, only crumbs were left. I was deeply embarrassed at my cave mates' desperate and impolite behavior, and apologized to Dong's wife.

"Big sister Gu, we're too hungry to mind our manners."

"I don't blame them."

After the food was gone, everyone went back to their beds. The Shanghai woman spoke up again.

"Big brothers, you were all Dong's friends when he was alive, and I'm grateful to you for helping him out. But I have one more favor to ask you."

Everybody quieted down and looked at her. The woman continued, "Can any of you take me to his burial site? If possible, I'd like you to help me open up his grave so I can take one final look at him. Then I'd like to ship his body back to his hometown."

"Of course," someone responded immediately. "It shouldn't be difficult. The pit is shallow and I don't think it will take much effort to dig him up."

My heart jumped to my throat.

"Big sister Gu, I don't think it's a good idea," I said. "We can't touch Dong's grave."

"Why not?" she asked in surprise.

"Think about it," I said. "He was buried a week ago. The flesh may have started to decay, but the body is still relatively intact. How do you expect to dig it out and ship it back? Will the railway authorities allow you to do that? Transporting a body is no easy matter. It's not like shipping a dead dog."

"What am I going to do?"

"If you really want to move him," I said, "wait a couple of years. Then you can take all the remaining bones back with you."

44

The woman was silent for a few minutes.

"Are you sure there is no other way? If not, I will follow your advice and come back later. Perhaps on the third anniversary of his death."

I adopted a deliberate, serious tone. "Three years is not long enough. It takes a long time for a body to decay. On the other hand, what's the rush? As the Chinese saying goes, 'Burial brings peace to the deceased.' "

"Okay," she said, "I trust you. I'll come back in a few years. But can you take me to his grave today so I can take a look at him before I go?"

It was the last thing I wanted to hear. My mind raced as I tried to figure out how to respond.

"Big sister Gu, it's probably not a good idea to visit Dong's grave."

"Why?" She looked stunned.

I dodged her gaze and stammered.

"No particular reason. It's just—it's only a small mound of dirt. What's there to see?"

Her face turned grim and her voice hardened.

"Little Li, I've come thousands of miles to see him—"

"We probably won't be able to find his tomb," I said.

"How come?" she asked.

I didn't know how to answer her questions. She looked suspicious. She had seen through me. My stammer became more pronounced.

"Th–th–the graves are scattered all over the grassland. It's really hard to figure out where Dong was buried."

"Didn't you just tell me that you buried Dong yourself? It's only been a few days. How could you not remember where it is?"

Damn. I should have been more careful about what I said. Now I was entangled in a web of lies.

"Big sister Gu," I said, "when I said 'we,' I was actually referring to members of the burial team, not me or anybody living in this cave. When a person dies, we carry the body outside. The burial team comes in a horse-drawn cart and takes it to the burial site. We ourselves don't go. We are all starving here—we don't even have the strength to walk, let alone carry a dead body."

Upon hearing my explanation, she paused for a second and then said, "Little Li, I need to identify Dong's tomb. If I don't know where he is buried, how am I supposed to bring his bones back in the future? All you need to do is to take me to the cemetery. I will search the graves one by one."

"You won't be able to find it. All the tombs look the same."

"Don't they have tombstones?"

"Tombstones? What do you think this is? A cemetery for Communist martyrs?"

"No tombstones?" She was almost screaming. "How can they do this to us? If relatives of the dead come to pay tribute, where do they go? This is inhumane and cruel."

"That's out of my control," I said, shrugging. "Listen, what I just told you is not completely accurate. Members of the burial team tie a small label on the body, with the person's name and unit number written on it."

"What's the point? The corpse is buried six feet under. Relatives can't dig up every grave and look for the labels, can they?"

"I don't think that's their intention. Officials use the labels for the sole purpose of collecting statistics, so they can put the numbers on a chart and submit it to the government. Providing convenient corpse identification to the relatives of a Rightist is not their job."

She started crying again.

"Looks like I won't be able to see Dong."

Seeing that I wasn't exactly being helpful, Chao Chongwen stepped in.

"What do you mean we can't locate his grave? Why don't we take her to the Supervisory and Disciplinary Department? They're in charge of burials; they must have a record of where Dong is buried."

The other cave mates murmured in agreement: "Good idea. Take her to the Supervisory and Disciplinary Department."

The woman wiped her tears and waited for me to answer.

"Okay," I said. "I'll take you to the camp administrative office."

I led the woman down a circuitous path inside the gully. We walked for ten minutes before I pointed to another valley about a kilometer or so away.

"The administrative offices are over there," I said. I watched her until she reached the valley and then I walked back to the cave. I heard Chao Chongwen's loud cursing before I entered.

"Li is such a bastard," he said.

Chao came from the central province of Shanxi. When he joined the Communist Party underground movement in 1946, he was only seventeen years old. After the Communist victory, he became a manager of political education at the Gansu Provincial Transportation Company. Chao was hot-tempered. Anytime he didn't like the way something was going in the Party, he would air his views at the next meeting, cursing and swearing. He claimed that he was singled out and convicted as a Rightist because he was constantly criticizing the Party secretary.

"What's that about?" I asked him. "What'd I do to offend you?"

Chao grabbed me and unleashed a torrent of angry remarks.

"You're lucky that I didn't do anything besides swear at you. Bastard! How dare you talk like that? Dong's poor wife was crying and begging you to take her to his burial site, but you put on airs and wouldn't do it. What a jerk—it's only a few steps away! You claimed not to know where Dong had been buried, but on the day his corpse was taken away, didn't you follow the cart? I remember you telling the officials that you wanted to mark Dong's tomb because his wife was coming soon. Now that his wife is here, you say you don't know where he is. What's your motive?"

I held back until he finished.

"Why don't you shut your stinking trap," I said. "I didn't realize you had such a dirty mouth. To tell you the truth, when the woman was here, I was worried that your big mouth could get us into trouble."

"What were you afraid of? That I might reveal your true intentions? You were mad because she didn't give you the sweater she knitted."

This incensed me.

"You don't know shit," I said. "There was a good reason I didn't want to take her to the cemetery. Two days ago, when I went to dig pepper plant roots, I found Dong's body lying abandoned, stark naked on the grassland. Someone had dug up the body and stolen his new clothes, probably to trade them with the local villagers for food. Even his quilt and blanket were nowhere to be found. I remember I told you when he died that we shouldn't have dressed him up in new clothes and wrapped him up in such a nice quilt."

"Is that true?" Chao's eyes widened.

"Yes, and it gets worse. There were huge holes in Dong's buttocks and thigh area, where his flesh had been hacked off."

Chao couldn't believe it.

"Go see for yourself if you don't believe me," I said. "The flesh was also sliced from his calves."

"Who did this? What bastard perpetrated this heartless deed?" Chao turned to Wei Changhai. "Did you have anything to do with this?"

Wei Changhai had just been released from solitary confinement for cutting flesh from dead bodies. During his incarceration, camp guards had tied his arms behind his back. The rope had almost cut off his blood supply. When he heard Chao's accusation, Wei's face reddened, and he yelled back in response.

"Don't blame me, Old Chao—I'm innocent. I've stolen flesh before and I admitted it. In the past few days, my arms have been so swollen that I haven't even stepped out of the cave. How could I manage to do something like that?"

"Who could it be then?" said Chao. "*Aii,* the human beings here have turned into animals. Even a tiger won't eat his own cub. Men eating other men—how can we call ourselves human beings?"

Everyone was silent. I was still fuming.

"You asked about my ulterior motives. Right now, the corpse is just lying out there in the open, frozen stiff. I just don't think his wife will be able to take the sight of the body."

Chao looked at me, and was silent for a while.

"Oh well," he finally said. "I guess I shouldn't have sent her to the administrative office."

It was almost dusk. The sunset cast a shadow over the gullies. There was only a narrow strip of sunshine visible on the cliff across from our cave. We streamed out to the mess hall, gulped down our ladlefuls of vegetable broth, and went to bed early, so as to conserve energy. But before I fell asleep, I heard the rustling of the dry grass curtain again.

The Shanghai woman had returned. I fumbled for matches and lit the kerosene lamp. The weak light cast by the lantern flickered on her face. She looked pale.

"Little Li," she said, "I had to come back to ask you for your help." As she spoke, tears welled up in her eyes again. I told her to sit down and calm herself.

"What happened?" I asked. "Did you find anyone?"

She wiped the tears off her face and sat down on the edge of my bed. I squatted down opposite her. It was tiring to stand inside a cave. The ceiling was low and we had to bend our heads. She told me that she did meet someone at the Supervisory and Disciplinary Department. The official had flipped through the death registry and confirmed that Dong had been dead for seven days. But he had no record of Dong's burial location. The official then referred her to a person named Duan Yunrui, a member of the burial team. Duan said he was only responsible for registering the names of the deceased and noting the time of their death. He didn't go to the cemetery himself. Duan took her to look for the other members of the burial team. One had died after eating unsanitary food and another one was hospitalized at the camp clinic. The rest of the team was too weak to walk and couldn't leave their caves.

The newly formed burial team had no idea where Dong was buried. The Shanghai woman stayed inside the administrative office building for a long time, sobbing. She told the official that she wouldn't return to Shanghai until she could find her husband's body. The official was infuriated.

"If you don't want to leave, fine," he said. "I'll find a cave for you. You can live there as long as you want."

The woman continued to cry.

"Where do you work in Shanghai?" the official asked her. "I'm going to write to the Public Security Department in your company, asking them to send someone to take you back. You're one of those spoiled city women. Your husband committed counterrevolutionary crimes and was sent here for reeducation. Instead of severing your ties with him, you have the gall to come all the way here to make trouble. You're clearly siding with our enemies—this is an act of protest against our government and against the dictatorship of the proletariat. We are going to notify your company and urge them to educate and discipline you."

Upon hearing this, the woman got very quiet, and left the office. In a way, I was relieved to find out that she hadn't learned the truth about Dong's body.

"What can I do to help?" I said. Her request remained the same.

"Can you take me to the burial site tomorrow morning and help me look for Dong's tomb?"

"How are we going to find it? There are hundreds of tombs over there. Some have been leveled by wind."

"I don't care—even if it means that I have to dig up every single grave."

"That's impossible. For one, you're not strong enough. Besides, it's not appropriate for you to dig up other people's graves just for the sake of finding your husband."

"Do you have a better idea?" She was sobbing again.

"There is no easy way," I answered coldly. "If we can't find him, we just have to give up. You've traveled all the way here and you've done your duty as a wife. The important thing is that Dong can rest in peace, since he is already buried. You should consider that you're not the only one who has this problem. I suggest you just try to make do in our cave tonight, and then catch an early train back to Shanghai tomorrow morning."

She was still sobbing inconsolably, but I ignored her. I

cleaned off my bed and offered it to her. I figured, as Dong's friend, offering my bed to his wife was the least I could do. I grabbed a long coat, went over and squeezed into bed with another Rightist.

Several hours passed. I raised my head and saw that she was still sitting on my bed. Maybe she didn't want to touch my dirty quilt and sheets. It had been three years since I had washed them. They were covered with lice and were disgusting just to look at. I heard her crying.

I don't know whether she slept or not. When I woke up the next morning, she was still sitting there, except she had covered herself with my quilt. Even though it wasn't yet the dead of winter, the temperature at night had already dropped to minus eighteen degrees Celsius. We didn't have a heating stove. We hadn't even seen one for three years. We used a heavy curtain knitted from dried grass to cover the cave entrance and ward off the cold air.

That morning I went to our group leader, obtained an extra food coupon, and bought breakfast for her—two vegetable buns.

She took the buns from my hand and put them on the suitcase next to the bed.

"I'm not hungry," she said. As she spoke, she started crying again. "Little Li, could you take me to Dong's grave? I won't be able to eat unless I find him. Dong, in his letter, said that I could depend on you for anything. I'm sure you know where he is buried. You told me yesterday that you went to bury him, but then you denied it. Why don't you want to take me to see him?"

I didn't know what to say. If I didn't tell her the truth, she would be grief-stricken and keep crying, which was tearing my heart apart. But I was afraid that if I did tell her the truth, she would be devastated. The more I told her not to cry, the louder her crying became. Finally I couldn't take it anymore. I turned around and walked out of the cave. I figured, maybe if I ignored her completely, she would give up.

I hung out in a different cave for the whole day, thinking that she might have left. At sunset, I went back. She was still sitting there on the edge of my bed, sobbing. The vegetable buns were perched on top of the suitcase, dry and shriveled. Someone had put a cup of water in front of her. She hadn't taken a sip. I got her another guest supper from the mess hall— half a bowl of sludgy vegetable soup—and handed it to her. "I know it doesn't taste good, but you need to eat something." Again, she refused the food. More tears.

When night came, she was still sitting there. I watched her from a nearby bed, worried that she might do something stupid. The lights went out after midnight. I could no longer see her face. I dozed off amid the sounds of her intermittent sobbing.

The third morning after the woman arrived at Mingshui, I woke up and found the sun beaming through the gaps in the curtain and onto her body. She was still sitting there, motionless like a clay statue. Her eyes were swollen like walnuts.

My nerves were jangled. I called Chao out of the cave.

"What are we going to do about her?" I asked him. "She hasn't touched any food or water for two days. I hope she doesn't die here."

Chao waved his hands in the air dismissively. "We've been suffering from starvation for over two years and we're still alive. I don't think two days without food will kill her."

"But we can't just leave her crying like this. What if she . . ."

I didn't finish the sentence. Chao looked up at the sky and said, "What else can we do? Not much. Why don't you just take her to the cemetery? You can let her take a look, and have it over with."

"No, no, no. I can't. What if she dies of grief after seeing what happened to Dong's body?"

Chao lost his patience. "You worry too much. What the hell are we supposed to do?"

Seeing that he was becoming impatient, I proposed a new idea. "Why don't you try one more time to persuade her to return to Shanghai? She doesn't trust me anymore. Maybe she'll listen to you."

Chao agreed immediately. "I can't promise anything. I'll certainly try."

But that morning, after Chao and I had breakfast and returned to the cave, something else happened. We found that another of our cave mates was dead. He had been an accountant at the Provincial Commerce Department. Several days before, I had seen him inside the latrine. He was squatting over a toilet pit. After he was done, he couldn't summon enough strength to stand up. I helped him up, but he was too weak to tie his pants. A starving person feels cold all the time. He was wearing a pair of summer pants on top of a pair of cotton-padded pants on top of a pair of woolen long johns. That morning, as everyone was getting up for breakfast, someone noticed that he was still lying there, with his head covered by the quilt. He didn't respond to questions, so the neighbor left him there. When he came back, he saw that the accountant was asleep in the same position. He pulled the quilt off and found that the body was already stiff. The man must have died sometime around midnight.

It was only another death. By then, we were all used to it. One cave mate said nonchalantly that we should just take care of it after breakfast. When someone died, several volunteers who were still physically strong would pitch in to handle the corpse. Chao and I were among the "strong" helpers. We opened his suitcase, dug out a clean shirt and a pair of pants, and put them on him. We wrapped up his body in his quilt and then dragged it to a vacant spot outside the cave.

The task left many of us panting. We sat down in the sun to catch our breath. I saw the woman standing outside the cave entrance, staring at us. Her pale ashen face was stricken with horror. The sight of death must have scared her. She stopped weeping. I nudged Chao to go talk with her, and tell her to return to Shanghai immediately.

It didn't take long. Three or four minutes later, Chao came back from the cave.

"Li," he said, "it didn't work. The woman won't listen to me. She thinks we're conspiring against her and trying to stop her from seeing her husband. She's going to go find Dong herself."

As Chao and I were talking, the woman stepped out of the cave. Her right hand shielded her eyes from the soft winter sun, which looked to me like the face of a jaundiced patient. She glanced in our direction, turned around, and walked north.

"Hey," I shouted. "Where are you going?"

She ignored me and continued walking. I caught up with her and blocked her way.

The woman stopped and stared at me with a reproachful look. She walked around me and kept going. Seeing this, Chao yelled at me from behind, "Li, don't stop her. If she's that stubborn, let her go. She'll give up if she can't find it."

I hesitated for a second, and then said to the woman, "If you don't want to listen to my advice, go ahead, but don't go in that direction. Most of the dead are buried on the south side of the gullies, in the direction of the administration offices that you visited."

She looked back at me, turned around, and walked toward the south end.

As she was walking away, Chao whispered to me, "Is Dong's tomb in that direction?"

I shook my head: "No."

Chao's face distorted with anger.

"Why did you send her the wrong way? Are you trying to harm her?"

"What do you expect me to do?" I said. "I found Dong's body on the north side, not far from our gully. What if she sees his body and dies from grief?"

None of us expected the Shanghai woman to be gone very long. After all, the tombs were scattered all over without any marks or names. But by noon, she hadn't returned. By sunset, there was still no sign of her. We went to eat dinner. Darkness seeped into the gully. She was still nowhere to be seen. I lost my cool and worried that something might have happened to her.

"Let's go look for her," I said to Chao. "I hope she hasn't run into any wolves."

We saw hardly any wolves when we first arrived at Mingshui, but as time went by, they started coming in packs, even before it got dark. They were not at all afraid of humans. The corpses fattened those wolves. Their fur got shiny and healthy.

Chao and I walked south. As we passed the mess hall, we saw a small figure moving toward us.

"Is that you, big sister Gu?" I called out.

She froze.

"What's taken you so long? Aren't you worried about wolves? If anything happens to you, I'll have to take the blame."

She was silent.

We walked back to the cave together.

"Did you locate Dong's grave?" I asked. Again, silence.

I had brought the two vegetable buns in my pocket. I didn't leave them on top of the suitcase because I didn't want others to snatch them while we were gone. She didn't touch the food. She simply gulped down a cup of water and lay down on my bed. She looked exhausted.

At dawn on the fourth day, I got up as usual, and brought back a bowl of corn gruel from the mess hall.

"Please have some, and then go home. Stop wasting your time here."

"Li, would it be possible for me to get a shovel?"

"What do you need that for?"

"When I was there yesterday," she said in a soft, hoarse voice, "I noticed some bricks placed on top of the tombs, with people's names written on them. I dug up two of the graves with my hands. They were shallow—only a couple of feet deep. I'm going to use a shovel and try to dig them all up one by one. I promise I will restore the tombs to their original states after I'm done."

The stubbornness of the woman touched me. My eyes moistened.

"Okay, big sister, eat your breakfast. I will take you to see Dong, I promise. I won't lie to you anymore."

After we came out of the cave, she faltered, but then she got up and started wobbling along.

We headed north that day. We had hardly stepped out of the gully before we started seeing exposed bodies lying on the sand dunes. The cemetery was supposed to be in the basin area, farther north from the gullies. But members of the burial team loafed on the job, simply digging a shallow hole in the wide stretch of sand dunes and dumping their bodies there. Since the burial was hastily done, the corpses were left exposed. Tattered rags and human hair fluttered in the cold, sweeping wind.

I signaled to Chao, hoping he could take the woman away for a while. He nodded and took her arm. I dashed over to

Dong's body, and scooped sand over him, covering him as much as I could. I had barely covered both of his legs before I was sweating and out of breath. I realized I was too emaciated to bury him.

The woman walked toward me. I pretended I was digging around and called out to her.

"Come and see if this is Dong," I said. "I think it looks like him."

To tell the truth, I began to worry that she might not be able to recognize her husband. Dong had been a young, good-looking man, tall with smooth, pale skin. He had looked sharp in his gray Mao suit. There was no vestige of that left. His body lay naked on the ground like a debarked tree, dry and stark. His brownish skin was like parched kraft paper pasted onto his bones. He had been dead for only nine days, but his body looked like a mummy excavated from an ancient grave. Two pieces of flesh had been slashed off from his buttocks and the bloodstained bones underneath were exposed.

The woman bent down and examined the mummy closely. Then she fell to her knees, let out a loud scream, and spread herself over the body. After her initial outburst of energy, her body lay motionless. For a whole minute, she was silent. I was scared, worried that she might have choked on her tears and passed out. Chao and I stepped forward and tried to pull her up. Her body jerked violently. Strange gurgling sounds spurted out of her throat and gave way to a sharp keening.

She came to life again. She shook the mummy, raised her head, and screamed at the top of her lungs, "Dong Jianyi!"

Her piercing cry rang out several more times, echoing in the gullies.

Chao and I stood there, waiting patiently for her to stop. Half an hour passed. Chao and I got restless.

"Big sister Gu, it's time to go."

We bent down and tried to pull her away, but her hands wouldn't let go of the mummy. We had to force her hands apart and separate her from the body.

"Okay," I said, "that's enough. Let go of him. It's not sanitary to keep clinging to him like that. Go. Let me bury him."

"Don't touch him!" She suddenly howeled at me. "I'm taking him with me. I'm taking him to Shanghai."

"How?" I said sarcastically. "Are you going to carry him on the train?"

"I will cremate him and take the ashes with me," she replied.

It wasn't a bad idea, but it wasn't possible because there was no firewood around. Dried camel thorns and achnatherum plants were everywhere, but there was no way they could sustain a fire that would generate enough heat to cremate a body.

"Are there any villages nearby?" she asked.

"The Mingshui People's Commune is about four or five kilometers away," I answered. She asked if I could go with her and buy some firewood from the local peasants. She didn't care how much it cost.

Seeing how determined she was, I decided to drag my swollen feet and take her there, while Chao went back to the camp. We walked for about two hours before we saw a peasant. He sold us three bundles of firewood. The woman asked the peasant if he would accept money to help her cremate her dead husband. The peasant turned down what he called "a spooky and inauspicious job." But he sent us to two villagers who agreed to do it. They hired an oxcart, and we all got on. On the way to the cemetery, we stopped at a small village store to get a big can of kerosene.

The villagers arranged the firewood in a big pile, soaked it with kerosene, and then carefully placed Dong's body on top. They set the pile on fire. The flames shot high. Soon the pile collapsed, and Dong's body fell into the flames. Then something terrifying happened: his body sat up, fully erect. As the wood ran out, we poured the rest of the kerosene onto the fire. Plumes of black smoke rose into the clear winter sky. Soon, all that remained among the ashes was a pile of bones. The leg bones were long, like charred wooden sticks.

"Why don't you take some of the tiny bones and bring them home," I suggested. "You can bury the rest over here."

"No," said the woman. "I'm taking everything home."

She untied her headscarf, spread it on the ground, and tried to lump all the bones together. But the fabric of the scarf was so thin it was almost transparent.

"There's really no need to carry every piece home," I said. "Even in a crematorium, they only give you part of the ashes, enough to fill an urn. Also, when you get on the train, the conductor will find out and kick you off."

She wouldn't listen. "I'll wrap them up with a sweater."

The woman carried all the bones back to the cave, and took a sweater out of her bag and wrapped it around the scarf. But the sweater was too small and no matter how many times she tried to adjust it, some of Dong's bones still stuck out. I rummaged through my suitcase and found a green military blanket, a souvenir I got from the Korean War, left behind by an American soldier. I unfolded the blanket and showed her the MADE IN USA label. I told her that I had had the blanket for more than nine years and couldn't bear to use it or trade it for food. The blanket memorialized an important period in my life—a time of glory.

The woman accepted the blanket. Since it meant so much to me, she said that she would wash it after she got home and send it back to me.

"Don't worry about it," I said. "The way things are going here, I'll be six feet under by the time it arrives. Just keep it at your place. If I can get out of here alive and have the opportunity to visit Shanghai one day, I will get it from you then."

She took my words seriously.

"Let me give you my home address," she said, and jotted down her address in a notebook on my suitcase.

Early the next morning, I walked with her out of the gullies, and pointed south, in the direction of a small train station. I stood there for a long time, watching her as she walked away. She was small and her shoulders disappeared under the big package towering over her. It was late November. The cold desert wind was blowing. She was wearing her green head-scarf. The tail end of the scarf was swaying in the wind, like the tail of a little cat.

I thought about what I had jokingly told her the previous night. Someday, if heaven had mercy on me and removed this crushing political baggage from my shoulders and made me a free man again, I would visit Shanghai. It wasn't that I really wanted the blanket back. I wanted to see that woman again. She left a deep impression on me.

In December 1960, the Rightists at Jiabiangou were in a life-threatening situation, and to get warm, we burned all of our papers and notebooks, including the one in which I wrote the woman's address in Shanghai.

As you know, I was labeled a Rightist because of some articles I wrote. After the government reversed its verdict against me in the late 1970s, I became restless and picked up my writing again. I published several articles analyzing China's reform-through-labor system. Instead of getting myself into trouble, one article won an award from the Ministry of Justice. The award ceremony took place in Shanghai.

On the last day I was in town, I had an afternoon all to myself. I went shopping along Huaihai Road, one of the main thoroughfares in Shanghai. Colorful shops lined the street and the sidewalks teemed with shoppers. I was looking to buy clothes for my wife, but I didn't see anything I liked.

I came across a large sign embossed with the words ELIZA-BETH WESTERN SUIT—A NAME BRAND SINCE 1942. That foreign name, Elizabeth, sounded so familiar. I paused in the middle of the street, trying to figure out where I had heard it. Then I remembered—the woman from Shanghai told me that her parents had owned a store before the collectivization movement began. It was called Elizabeth. Her family lived in a small Western-style building behind the store.

A wave of excitement swept through me as I walked inside. The store wasn't big, and it was packed with customers. I nudged my way toward a male salesclerk, who seemed to be in his late thirties. I waited patiently until he was done with his customers and then approached him.

"Sir," I asked, "do you know if the former store owner's name was Gu?"

The salesclerk looked confused.

"What store owner? Our store is state-owned."

"I meant early on," I explained, "in the 1950s, right after the Communist victory. Was this store owned by a person called Gu?"

I could tell he was surprised.

"Why are you asking me this? How am I supposed to know?"

I asked if there were any old folks around who might know something about the store's history.

"You can go upstairs and ask our accountant," he said. "He might know."

Following the salesclerk's direction, I walked along a corridor and went up to the second floor. Inside a small cluttered room, I found a man who appeared to be in his sixties. When I explained to him the reason for my visit, he told me that the owner before the collectivization movement used to be Mr. Zhu, not Gu.

"Could there be another store with the same name?"

"No," said the man, with confidence. "There isn't any other store called Elizabeth. I have been in this business for many years. I know all the old brand-name suit stores in Shanghai."

"Is there a Western-style house at the back? The owner's daughter told me that her family lived in the house."

The old man shook his head.

"No, there never has been, as far as I remember, and I've been with this store for more than twenty years. But wait . . ."

He stopped shaking his head, and changed his tone.

"Are you talking about the store on Nanjing Road, the Victoria Western Suit store? The former owner's name was Gu. There is a Western-style building at the back."

"Are you sure? I think she told me it was Elizabeth, the name of an English queen."

"I'm sure that's the one you're thinking of. If you want to look for the Gu family, go to the Victoria store. Both Victoria and Elizabeth are the names of English queens. You must have confused them. Time messes up people's memories."

The old man gave me directions to the Victoria Western Suit store. I walked a couple of blocks on the crowded Huaihai Road and then stopped. I decided to give up my search for Dong's wife. What if she had moved away to another city? What if she had already left this world? Wouldn't that be too disappointing to bear?

The Train Conductor

In December 1990, Li Tianqing, the Education Department manager of Wangjiaping Farm, received a call from the Gansu Provincial Reform and Reeducation Bureau. It turned out that police in the central city of Wuhan had captured two robbers who were runaway prisoners from the Wangjiaping Farm, a prison and labor camp for criminals with jail sentences of fifteen years or less. Li was asked to bring the criminals back. Without any delay, he left for Wuhan with two young officers the very same day.

Li, who turned fifty-eight that year, had joined the Communist revolution in 1948. His colleagues couldn't figure out why he was always passed over for promotion. The current camp director was twenty years younger than him, but his position was at a much higher level. Li held the title of manager for many years.

That evening, the train was packed, the air filthy and suffocating. Given that it was a long journey, one colleague suggested they purchase one sleeper ticket so they could take turns resting. Li reluctantly acquiesced and went into the conductor's office to inquire about ticket availability. The conductor, a man in his fifties, looked familiar. As Li was racking his brain to figure out where they could have met, the conductor seemed to recognize him as well. "Are you Li Tianqing?" he asked. That's when Li figured out who he was. His name was Wei Changhai, a fellow Rightist at Jiabiangou.

Returning to his seat, Li revealed his past to the young officers and shared some unusual stories about Wei, the train conductor.

I was labeled a Rightist in October 1957 when I was working at Wangjiaping. At first, I had been a detective at the Provincial Public Security Bureau.

I came from a family of capitalists. After the campaign to eliminate the counterrevolutionaries began in 1954, the leadership no longer considered me a trusted political ally. I was demoted from detective and was asked to serve in the bureau's propaganda office as a coordinator. I felt I had sunk to a low point in life. So, when my friend Su Zhenqi, a director at Wangjiaping, asked me if I wanted to be transferred, I accepted his offer. He was illiterate and had a crude manner. He needed my help and wanted me to serve as secretary.

During the anti-Rightist campaign, my family history once again made me a target. Following my conviction, I was sent to Jiabiangou in March 1958. Eight months later, they moved me to Xindiandun labor camp, a Jiabiangou subsidiary.

It was at Xindiandun that I met that train conductor, Wei Changhai.

There were more than one thousand Rightists housed at Xindiandun. We were divided into seven teams, one of which engaged in what was called "sideline businesses." They raised pigs, herded goats, grew vegetables, and took care of the horses. This special team employed about a hundred Rightists. The rest of the teams, each of them with about a hundred members, did farming and construction work. I belonged to the construction team that was assigned some of the toughest and most difficult jobs. We built houses, cultivated farmland, dug canals, sifted sand, cut stone from the mountain quarries, and carried it all the way to the farm.

Wei Changhai and I belonged to different teams. I didn't know him at all. I met him quite by chance.

In the winter of 1959, the camp ordered us to move grass from the swamps on the east side of Jiuquan to Xindiandun, which was built on a barren stretch of saline-alkaline soil. The agricultural teams planted wheat in the first and second years, but the yield was almost nonexistent. To improve the soil, members of the sideline business team spent six months in the spring and summer digging grass for fertilizer in the swampland near the Big North River, which originated at Qilian Mountain and meandered past the northern edge of Jiuquan. When winter approached, it was up to the Rightists at Xindiandun to transport baskets piled with bales of grass to the farmland. We had to carry the grass bales about eight kilometers per trip. The camp stipulated that an individual had to make at least six trips every day. Anyone who exceeded the quotas would be singled out for praise, while those who fell short would have their dinners taken away. At the beginning, people picked the dried grass bales, which were relatively light. When these were gone, we were stuck with the heavier wet ones.

Soon, several of the Rightists started collapsing. Fu Zuogong was one of them. Have you heard his name before? He was the brother of Fu Zuoyi, a prominent military commander in the Nationalist army. Fu had arranged the surrender of Beijing to the Communists in 1949. Chairman Mao rewarded Fu for his contribution by giving him a series of senior positions in the new government. Everyone had heard stories about Fu Zuoyi, but no one knew anything about his brother, Zuogong. Unlike his brother, Zuogong stayed away from politics. He graduated from Jinling University with a degree in forestry and embarked on the path of science, which he believed was key to China's revival. Following the Communist takeover, Zuogong worked as an engineer at the Agricultural and Forestry Department in Gansu. In 1958, he was labeled a Rightist and sent to Jiabiangou. When I first saw Zuogong, he looked fairly distinguished in a pair of broad, dark-rimmed glasses. He wore a long leather coat with a mink fur collar and chain-smoked from a black tobacco pipe. He would wear the same outfit even while plowing in the field. One Rightist once asked, "Aren't you worried about ruining your expensive coat?"

"My own life is in danger here," he replied. "Who cares about clothes?"

When we began carrying the grass bales together, I saw that he was very much changed. His former self had all but disappeared. He had allowed his hair to grow so long that he looked like a lunatic. His face was thin and sallow, his body a mere skeleton. His leather coat was stained and tattered. One of the temples of his glasses was broken, and he had to tie his glasses to his ear with a piece of string.

Carrying grass bales was particularly difficult in the winter. We would normally leave our bunkhouse at five in the morning and finish at about five or six in the evening. This time frame applied only to the physically fit. Those Rightists who were weak and emaciated wouldn't be able to meet their quota until midnight. Temperatures could drop to thirty degrees below zero. The roaring wind lashed your body like ice water or cut your face like a knife. A normal person would barely survive a week walking in those conditions for twelve hours a day, not to mention carrying a heavy load of grass bales.

One afternoon not long after the Chinese New Year, I was wobbling back to Xindiandun with bales of grass on my back. I saw Zuogong sitting on the side of a road next to two other Rightists. I walked up to them and asked if anything was wrong. One of the men told me that Zuogong couldn't move anymore. At that moment, an official named Zhao Laifu approached us and yelled, "Who's that sitting there?"

The shorter and younger of the two men standing there mumbled it was Zuogong.

Zhao came over and shouted in a fury, "What's the matter with you?"

Zuogong sat motionless, his eyes closed. When Zhao yelled again, he moved his lips slightly in response. "I can't walk. I'm dying."

I had heard people say that Zuogong behaved quite arrogantly in front of camp officials. If he was tired, he would sit down for a break, regardless of where he was. No matter how harshly camp officials scolded him or how much they threatened him, he wouldn't heed their orders at all. The camp orchestrated multiple public denunciation meetings, but he never treated the public humiliation as anything serious. On that particular day, Zhao began to scold him loudly, "You capitalist! By refusing the opportunity to reform yourself, you have made it amply clear that you're still dreaming of your past luxurious life and bullying ordinary working people."

"I wasn't a capitalist," said Zuogong. "I was an engineer."

"You are a bourgeois Rightist! Get your butt off the ground."

Zuogong didn't move. Zhao became outraged. He signaled to the young man nearby and ordered, "Wei Changhai, grab him and pull him up for me."

The man whose name was Wei Changhai responded with a "yes, sir" and stepped forward. He seized Zuogong's arms and dragged him while cursing all the while: "Get up, don't lie there like a dead dog."

That was how I encountered Wei Changhai. After Zuogong got back on his feet, he still wouldn't move. Zhao unhooked a piece of string from the basket on Zuogong's back. The string, made from grass, was used to wrap the grass bales more tightly. Zhao knotted one end of the string to the basket and looped the other end around Zuogong's neck. Then he asked Wei to pull the string, forcing Zuogong to move along. Wei acted as instructed. The dry grass string, rough and thorny, burned Zuogong's neck. Zuogong finally caved in and stumbled along after Wei.

In the days that followed, I saw Wei hauling Zuogong by that string on two separate occasions. The two of them looked like a pair of camels tied together.

Since this story is about Wei Changhai, I won't digress too much more about Fu Zuogong, who was found dead in a pigsty in the winter of 1960. He had snuck into the pigsty in an attempt to steal food from the trough; then he passed out. A heavy snow fell that night and covered his body. Nobody knew where he had gone. There was a rumor that he had escaped. When spring came, the snow melted and his body was exposed.

Having witnessed how Wei tortured Zuogong, I began to despise and hate him with all my heart. At Jiabiangou, I had seen all types of Rightists. Some were eager to speak at staff meetings and denounce other Rightists with a true passion. Others would spy on fellow Rightists and report them to the authorities. I understood their motives. They wanted to win favor from the leadership so they could have their Rightist labels removed sooner. But I could never forgive people like Wei—he was ruthless and brutal to his own kind.

He did benefit from his collaboration with Zhao. Several days after the grass incident, Wei was transferred to the camp kitchen. He didn't have to go hungry again.

Two months before our move to Mingshui, Wei was caught stealing wheat buns from the kitchen and swapping them for cigarettes. Angry and disappointed, the camp leaders sent him back to the construction team. Ultimately, when different teams merged in Mingshui, Wei and I were assigned to the same team.

It was during this time that I gradually became acquainted with Wei. He was twenty-four, about three years younger than I was. He had graduated from a polytechnic school and worked at the Lanzhou Railway Bureau.

At Mingshui, we worked for about two weeks to reclaim the wasted grassland. Then the project came to an abrupt halt. With the reduction of our food rations, the inmates who had been the first to arrive began to die in large numbers. As the situation turned grim, the camp authorities had no alternative but to stop sending Rightists to the fields.

After that, Rightists would guzzle down their share of corn gruel and then curl up inside the frigid caves to kill time. Some of them would roam the grassland looking for wild vegetables or the seeds of herbs to appease their gnawing hunger. The healthier or stronger ones would search the fields for mice burrows, snatching their stored winter food. Some caught lizards and boiled them.

When the weather turned colder, Rightists gathered grass seeds or stripped the bark from trees, and then boiled it. They ate grass seeds, which often caused severe constipation.

By the time the severe cold of November came around, emaciated Rightists were dying at a rapid clip and the healthier ones began to weaken.

Wei and I belonged to the ranks of the relatively healthy. I despised Wei and always avoided him. Yet Wei was shrewd. He knew how to detect a mouse burrow. Out of desperation, I was forced to abandon my earlier prejudice against him and join him one day to search the field for mouse nests. Every time we hit a mouse nest, we could collect three to four kilograms of millet or grass seeds. Later on, when my body swelled up and I was too weak to go digging mouse burrows, I dropped out of our partnership. Instead, I simply poked around a little, collecting dry herbal seeds. Wei wasn't able to continue the searches by himself. He gave them up.

By mid-November, my health had deteriorated. I could no longer venture far afield. Everyone else in my cave suffered similar ailments. Some had died, others were struggling for their last breaths. To my surprise, Wei had not changed much. There was no sign of edema on his face or legs. He was thin, but his arms were strong and his face exuded a healthy radiance. I noticed that he spent lots of time outside, saying he was collecting grass seeds, but he seldom brought any back. Two other young men close to his age often came to visit him. They all looked healthy and strode around briskly like normal people. When the three of them were together, they behaved quite secretively.

One cave mate told me that Wei's two friends used to be ticket collectors at Lanzhou Railway Bureau. They were not Rightists per se. They had said critical things about the Party during the Hundred Flowers campaign. The Party didn't label them as Rightist, but called them "bad elements." They were sent along with the Rightists to receive reeducation at Jiabiangou.

One day, at the tail end of November, I hobbled north through the valley, hoping to find some pepper roots in the wetland area. I ventured out a little farther than usual. As I reached the end of a gully, I saw Wei and the two bad elements cooking something at the foot of a small ridge. Most Rightists would bring their hunted treasure back to the cave and cook it in a porcelain basin on top of a makeshift stove. Why did those three cook their food outside in the desert? "What do you have there?" I hollered at them. "Anything good?"

Before I could get close, Wei and his friends hurried away with a sooty basin in their arms. They seemed quite skittish.

Why were they afraid of seeing me? Upon returning to the cave that evening, I reported what I had seen to Si Jicai, a walking stick. At Jiabiangou, people gave those who supervised fellow Rightists the nickname "walking sticks." As our supervisor, Si was fair and honest. If anyone encountered abuse or unfair treatment, we could count on him to argue with camp officials and defend us. He was well loved by the Rightists. After hearing my story, Si promised to investigate.

The next day, Si visited me at the cave and told me that my hunch was correct.

He didn't reveal what he had found. Instead, he merely asked me to go take a look with him. I followed Si all the way to the end of the valley. We stood on a wide stretch of desert dotted with sand dunes and tombs. Rightists who had died of starvation in Mingshui lay buried there. The burials had been carried out perfunctorily. In many cases, the wind blew away the sand and the corpses were exposed to the air. Every now and then, you could see rags and strands of hair rustling in the cold wind. I was spooked and asked why he had taken me here.

Si didn't reply, but kept treading among the tombs. He stopped by one of the exposed corpses: "Go remove the quilt from the body." I knew the burial procedure fairly well. When a person died, his fellow Rightists would wrap up his body in his own quilt. They would cinch the sections around the neck, waist, and legs with linen ropes before carrying it out here for burial. The body that I was about to examine seemed to have been rearranged by someone. The linen ropes had been cut. I slowly lifted the quilt and noticed that the deceased's winter coat had been unbuttoned. I pulled open the coat and couldn't help but scream: there was a long gaping hole in the chest of the corpse.

"You see it? That couldn't have been the work of wild dogs, could it?" Si asked me.

My head went numb, like I had been hit by a wooden stick. I stammered in disbelief, "Do you mean to say . . . ?" I didn't dare to finish the sentence.

Si continued, "Take another peek inside the chest."

I didn't have the courage to do it. I stepped back.

"Don't be afraid," said Si.

He stepped closer, bent down and held the hole open with both hands. "Come on over. Look inside the chest."

I glanced in: it was an empty cavity.

Si straightened the winter coat over the chest wound, covered the body with the quilt, and fastened it with ropes. Then he gathered some sand with his hands and spread it over the body. He rubbed both hands in the sand, as if washing the germs off them.

"Those bastards!" said Si, as we walked away. "They don't have a shred of humanity. You know what they were boiling that day? Human organs. They were cooking human hearts, livers, and lungs! The dead didn't have much flesh left on their arms or thighs. Years of hunger and hard labor had reduced them to skin and bones. When the bastards couldn't find anything edible, they hit on the idea of opening up the chest to harvest their organs . . ."

I was tongue-tied, still struggling to get over my initial shock. When I reported to Si about Wei and his friends, I had no idea they could have done something so heinous.

Later on, Si took me to see another exposed body, which had been slashed open with a knife. I turned over a paper tag fastened around his neck. It was Wang Yiwu's body. Wang had been a doctor at the Tianzhu County Hospital and was convicted as a Rightist for his anti-Party remarks. At Jiabiangou, he didn't suffer much because leaders had assigned him to the camp clinic to see patients. However, Wang continued to run his big mouth, talking openly about the fact that the massive number of deaths at Jiabiangou was due to starvation and mal-nutrition. As a consequence, he was booted out of the clinic and sent to the field as a laborer. A few weeks after his demotion, he was struck by a severe form of flu, and died a few days later. Since he hadn't toiled in the field for long, his body hadn't wasted away like the other one. The flesh of his buttocks had been sliced off, leaving two holes in their place. The calves were also stripped clean of flesh, their white bones sticking out.

On our way back, I asked Si what our next step would be. He said there would have to be further investigation. He thought we didn't possess enough evidence to prove that Wei and his friends were the culprits. "We can't do anything if they don't confess."

"If they did admit to it, what could you do?" I asked.

Si walked silently for a minute and then uttered a long sigh. "To tell you the truth, I don't know. If you commit murder, you will pay with your life. If you are in debt, you pay back the money you owe. But they've butchered dead people. There is no law to regulate this."

I couldn't come up with a good answer either. I simply said, "We need to think of something to stop this barbarism."

Si thought for a moment: "When I get to the bottom of this case, I will report it to Director Zhao and let him handle it. What do you think?"

I liked the idea.

The next day, Si segregated Wei and his friends and interrogated them individually. Using threats and scare tactics, he extracted confessions from all of them. He then passed on a report to Director Zhao. The following afternoon, Zhao and two staff members from the mess hall burst into our cave. He looked around and yelled, "Wei Changhai, where are you?"

Wei was actually sitting right in front of Zhao. He didn't respond at first. After the interrogation the previous day, Wei knew he was in trouble. He hadn't stepped out at all but simply squatted on the ground, looking preoccupied; at that moment, his face turned ashen. Since other Rightists in the cave had no clue as to what had happened, several pointed their fingers at Wei: "There he is, right under your chin."

Zhao's eyes gradually adjusted to the dim light. He recognized Wei and started swearing at him. "You bastard, why do you sit here without answering me?"

Wei jumped up immediately, smacking his head on the ceiling. He shrieked in pain. With feigned innocence he asked, "Director Zhao, what do you want with me?"

Zhao ignored him, turned around, and told the mess hall staff, "Tie him up for me."

At the director's order, the two mess hall workers pounced on Wei, looped a rope around his neck, then pushed his hands behind his back and tied them up high. Meanwhile, one of the henchmen grabbed Wei's shoulder and poked his knee against Wei's back, snapping tight the noose. Wei let out a loud cry and then curled up on the floor. As a public security veteran, I knew the power of that rope technique, which was normally used to subdue the toughest criminals. It was enough to break down even robbers and hardened criminals, let alone Wei.

It was common for camp officials to bind Rightists with ropes and then punch or flog them. Under normal circumstances, nobody dared to resist the brutality. But on that day, Rightists felt Wei's life was in danger. Hearing his piercing slaughterhouse cry, some forgot their own fear. One person risked his life by asking loudly, "Director Zhao, has he done anything wrong? Why do you tie him up like this?"

Zhao ignored this outburst and shot an angry look at Wei. "You motherfucker. How dare you eat human flesh?"

The rest of the people in the cave were astounded. One asked in disbelief, "Human flesh? What do you mean by that?"

Zhao continued to yell at Wei, without noting the comments from the crowd. "You lawless motherfucker! How dare you dig up dead bodies and cook their organs?"

Silence fell. The Rightists looked at each other in astonishment. Then, they burst out in a medley of cursing: "This bastard! No wonder he looks so healthy," someone said.

Amid the buzz of voices, Zhao stepped forward, kicked Wei in the back, and unleashed another torrent of obscenity. "This bastard didn't just stop at one corpse, but kept going. You lawless bastard! How dare you?"

Wei curled up tighter, moaning and yelping with pain, "Director Zhao, forgive me, I won't ever do it again."

A few minutes later, at Zhao's orders, the henchmen tossed Wei out of the cave like a chicken. He landed on the muddy ground with a loud cry of agony.

That same day, Wei's two cohorts were also roughed up and taken away. Zhao locked them up in a makeshift jail next to his office.

The stories about Wei and his friends spread rapidly. People were stunned and outraged by what they had heard. In the afternoon, nobody went out to scout for food. People either sat inside the caves or gathered outside in the sun, airing their views and speculating on the news. Wei was accused of lawlessness and moral degradation and some even suggested capital punishment. Others said he was worse than a dog or a pig. They recommended that Wei be sentenced to long-term imprisonment and undergo harsh reeducation at the Yinma Farm. Gradually, as the anger subsided, a few dissenting opinions came out: "What crimes did Wei commit? Did he rob or murder anyone? Did he rebel against the Communist government? What laws did he break?" The discussions were long and complex.

In my cave, the majority agreed that he hadn't broken any laws. He had simply violated the moral code—but how would one clearly define moral standards in a reeducation camp like Jiabiangou? Zhang, a former history professor at Lanzhou Teachers University, cited many similar historical instances in times of famine. "It's not like we haven't heard of this before," he said.

I didn't participate in any of the discussions. I was the one who had discovered Wei's secret and reported him to the leadership. Yet when I saw how he was roughed up by the two mess hall workers, I started to feel guilty. His constant screaming in pain and his begging aroused my sympathy.

Time usually passed slowly at the camp. The days were long and hard, to the point of becoming unbearable. Yet, on that afternoon, as we debated Wei's case, time flew by. Soon the sun over the Gobi Desert was going down, casting thin strips of light on the hills across from the cave. One person looked up and interrupted the conversation to remind everyone that it was dinnertime. People went to pick up their bowls and chopsticks.

I wasn't feeling hungry at all. My heart ached from the guilt I felt earlier. Wei had been incarcerated for more than five hours. I was worried his life could be in danger. I knew that the ropes that bound Wei could block the circulation of blood in his arms. His shoulders could swell up and his head could puff out like a hog. If Zhao didn't untie the ropes soon, Wei could end up losing both of his arms. He might even lose his life. This kind of thing had happened before at Jiabiangou. A Rightist attempting to escape was caught by the guards, who tied him up and threw him in solitary confinement. Exhausted from the chase, the guards went straight to bed. The next morning, remembering the captured Rightist, they dashed to the isolation room to release him, but it was too late: he lay dead on the floor. The more I thought about Wei, the more worried I became. I shared my concern with my cave mates but my repeated pleas for help went unanswered. I turned to Zhang, the former history professor, and begged him to go with me. He rolled his eyes and didn't even bother to move.

I gave up asking for help. After two years of starvation and exhaustion, we had become indifferent to human suffering. In recent months, as people around us kept dropping like flies and bodies were being carried out one after another, each one of us feared that we could be the next to fall. Sympathy for others was not a top priority. None of us was in any position to care for other people.

But I couldn't stand idle. I was the one who had reported Wei. If he died, I would be a murderer. If I managed to survive, I would be haunted with guilt for the rest of my life. Wei had certainly done something terribly wrong, but he didn't deserve to die.

I skipped dinner and went directly to Si. Then the two of us visited Zhao at his office and begged for Wei's release.

When we stepped into the isolation cell, I saw that Wei's face was swollen. He was moaning with pain and he kept smacking his head against the ground. We unfastened the ropes that bound him. His arms, which had become discolored and thick as logs, were numb. He was so weak he could hardly walk. Si and I carried him back to the cave.

In the first week, he could barely hold his bowl with his hands. I spoon-fed him. He expressed his gratitude profusely, often in tears: "You are my savior. Someday, when I'm able, I will repay your kindness." After two weeks Wei recovered.

I never took him seriously about paying back my kindness. I had no idea how long I would live. Besides, I never lost sight of the fact that he was a shameless, immoral scoundrel. I never intended to be his friend.

On the afternoon of December 2, several days after his full recovery, he pulled me to a quiet spot outside the cave and whispered, "I want to share a secret plan with you. I'm planning to get out of here."

His words took me by surprise. I feigned indifference. "Why are you bringing this up with me?"

"Li," he said, "I'm leaving for real. If I don't, I'll starve to death."

I kept my tone of indifference and said, "You don't have to tell me this. It's none of my business. If you decide to escape, I promise I won't report you. You don't have to worry about that."

"No, that's not what I meant. I know you won't report me. I want you to go with me," he said resolutely.

I was stunned. To be honest, I had also considered the idea of escape since we arrived in Mingshui. I just couldn't make up my mind. I had joined the Communist revolution at an early age, with the idealistic notion that I was helping overthrow an old regime in order to establish a new society. I took part in the war against the Nationalist government and was wounded in the Korean War against the Americans. After being convicted as a Rightist, I still clung to the hope that I could reform myself through hard labor and that the Party would eventually forgive me and embrace me. If I had escaped, it would have meant I had jettisoned all my old ideals. I would have undermined my future in China. However, as the situation deteriorated day by day, I came to the realization that I could die of hunger if I stayed.

After Wei told me about his plan, I said, "You should go by

yourself. I promise I won't tell anyone. I have too much to lose to think about escaping. I'm a veteran revolutionary and I don't want to give up hope yet."

Wei shook his head. "Why are you being such a fool? You've been kicked out of the Party long ago. Nobody thinks that you are still a Communist revolutionary, except you. You're an enemy of the people. You are receiving reeducation at a labor camp. You act like a foolish wife who prays for her treacherous husband to return. It's not going to happen. Even if we don't die of starvation, there will be no end to our exile here. Let's go together. In this world, the good people don't always win. You probably will have been buried somewhere long before your release date arrives. If you die here, your life will be worthless. We only have one life to live—don't you think we should put it to good use?"

Wei's words pounded me like a heavy fist. In the past two and a half years, I had been tortured with these same questions. There were times when I had even considered ending my life altogether. "Li," Wei continued, "I want you to come with me because you're a nice guy. If it were someone else, I wouldn't care. I hope you don't pass up this opportunity."

"I'm afraid I won't be able to go far," I said. "My legs are weak. I just don't have the strength to make it."

He knew what I meant and raised his voice. "I know you can't walk far. That's why I want you to come with me. If you encounter problems, I'll help you. I'll carry you or even drag you, whatever's necessary. You and I will go to Lanzhou together."

He spoke with such sincerity that I was touched. I used to despise him for his lack of morals. I rescued him from the isolation cell for my own selfish reasons—I wanted to relieve my guilt. I could never have imagined that my unintended gesture of kindness would be met with such deep appreciation. I considered his offer for a few more seconds and then accepted. "Okay. I can go with you. But what will happen if they capture us?" I asked.

"If we get caught, I'll find another opportunity and run away again," said Wei.

We acted fast. At two o'clock the next morning, we crept out of our caves and left the gully in Mingshui. It was a full moon and the gully, bathed in the moonlight mist, was eerily quiet. Our hearts beat as fast as our footsteps. About four kilometers away from the south end of the gully, there was a small train station. On a clear day, we could look out from our cave entrance and see the train running across the Gobi Desert and pulling into the station. That morning, we didn't go in that direction. We knew the station was heavily patrolled. Instead, we headed toward the north, passed the sand dunes covered with tombs, and ran west into the desert. That was my idea. Seven years of experience as a detective taught me how to throw false scents to confuse my pursuers.

We passed the Gaotai station, which was ten kilometers west. If the authorities at Mingshui found that we were missing, they would enlist the railway workers at Gaotai to help catch us. Our target was Qingshui station, about thirty or forty kilometers down the road. The station sat on the border with Jiuquan. A large number of troops were stationed nearby. Normally, an escaped Rightist wouldn't dare board a train at Qingshui. Wei and I intended to take advantage of this blind spot.

We raced ahead for some four hours. I didn't even know where I found the strength to make my weak and swollen legs carry me from midnight to the crack of dawn. The sun rose in the east and we were still rushing through the barren desert. No trace of human habitation was in sight. Nor was there even a single tree. Only the endless yellow sand. Wei finally suggested we take a break. "I don't think anyone is following us now," he said. We slumped to the ground, tired and hungry.

We rested for half an hour, munching on some wild berries that we had tucked into our pockets. On the previous afternoon, after finalizing our plans, Wei and I had tried to obtain some food for our trip. I had about forty yuan ($5.80) with me and attempted to use Si's connections to get some extra buns from the mess hall, but to no avail. Eventually, with thirty yuan ($4.40), we bought a bag of wild berries from a Rightist driving a horse-drawn cart. The berries were part of the horse feed and they tasted sweet and sour, quite pleasant. We were lucky to have remembered to bring a water bottle.

Not long after we had started walking again, I fell to the ground. I struggled to get up and cautiously moved a couple of steps, but then my body plummeted again. My atrophied legs could no longer sustain the weight of my body. I was perspiring and my heart was beating fast. Wei came over to pull me up from the ground.

"I can't control my legs. When I pinch them here, I don't even feel anything," I said.

Wei told me to slow down and rest up a little longer. "Perhaps we've overextended ourselves."

Half an hour later, I carefully rose again with Wei's help. I walked a few step and didn't fall, but my heart still beat wildly. We ambled along and stopped every few minutes. I was constantly gasping for air.

We moved, paused, then moved again. At about one o'clock in the afternoon, with the sun was hanging in the sky above us, I finally collapsed. Wei tried to haul me along but I couldn't get up. He glared at me and said, "You're such a wimp. We've only gone about twenty-some kilometers. What are we going to do about the rest of the trip? Qingshui station is still far away."

I didn't answer. I had noticed his growing impatience and

even anger. Each time he reached over to steady me, he handled me roughly. He was probably starting to regret bringing me along.

When I didn't respond, his face turned grim and ugly. He shouted, "Tell me, what are we going to do? You think a car is going to pick you up or something? We can't just wait to die here, can we?"

What else could I say? I was a burden. I had overestimated my stamina. He was still angry and continued to insult me: "You're so useless. If you won't move, I'll have to leave you."

His insults incensed me. I fought back. "Go ahead. I never asked for your help in the first place."

I really meant it. I was prepared for the worst. All night long, we had followed a route parallel to the Lanzhou-Xinjiang rail line, out of fear that if we strayed, we might get lost. If he abandoned me, I would continue to use the rail line as my guide and get to whatever station came next, even if it meant that I had to crawl the rest of the way. I wouldn't care if anyone was lurking in the station to capture me.

Wei gave me another fierce look and grabbed my arm. "Now you're just having a temper tantrum. Get up. I'll carry you for a little while."

I stood up, refusing his help. I turned around and kept walking. My body felt warm. I guess the anger made me stronger.

The sun was descending in the west. I was truly exhausted. I fell again and started to feel dizzy. I was kneeling on the ground, trying to push myself upright with both hands on the ground, when a gray fog clouded my eyes. The dizzy spell lasted only a few seconds. Then the yellow sandy ground under my feet reappeared. I knew the dizziness was a dangerous sign—my body was teetering on the verge of total exhaustion.

As I calmed down and tried to start out again, my body

began to sway. Every step I took, I was seized with the fear of falling down. Then my body started shaking uncontrollably, as if I had been attacked by a wave of cold air. The cold seeped into my bones. I plunged to the ground again. Wei rushed over and asked how I was. I opened my mouth but no words came out. My body kept shaking. Scared, he held my hands and asked again and again, "What's the matter? Are you okay?"

I began to fear that he might leave me behind. After the spasms in my body subsided somewhat, I looked at him, begging for another rest. "I'm feeling cold," I said.

We took a longer break this time. I forced myself to swallow some more wild berries. Once the shaking stopped, I stood up and pressed ahead.

I saw in the distance an irrigation canal that was built up above the ground. Two camels stood idly along the bank. I asked Wei to go find out whether there were people living nearby.

He walked over, climbed up onto the canal and yelled back, "Yes, there are."

I staggered over and saw under the golden sun a few low-lying mud houses not too far away. The houses were surrounded by farmland. I turned to Wei and said, "Don't bother carrying me. Why don't you go ahead and catch a train at Qingshui station on your own? I'll go to the village and see if I can find a place to rest for a couple of days. I'll board the train after I recuperate."

He frowned as he listened to me and then asked angrily, "What are you talking about?"

"Listen to me. My current condition doesn't allow me to walk far. If you carry me on your back, I'm going to slow you down. Neither of us will get home. If I can rest up a bit, we can both make it," I explained.

He considered my words and then stared at the village in

the distance. He said, "I can't let you stay here. If the villagers were kindhearted enough to offer you a room, that'd be great. But what if someone wants to report you to the authorities?"

I could see his point. When I had worked at Xindiandun, I had heard about how local peasants had caught escaped Rightists and turned them in.

So I wobbled on and passed the village without stopping.

Several times, Wei carried me on his back and put me down when he needed to rest. Our pace slowed significantly and Wei really tired himself out. Finally, we struck upon a new plan. Rather than heading toward Qingshui station, we decided to run the risk of stopping at the next station that we saw on the way. Luck was on our side that night. At midnight, we reached Sanwan station and happened to encounter a large group of migrants from Sichuan Province. They were traveling to Urumchi, the provincial capital of Xinjiang Uyghur Autonomous Region, in search of jobs. However, their train only went as far as Hami. When they disembarked there, the local police detained them for not having the proper work papers. Ultimately they were put on a different train back to Sichuan. Since the migrants didn't have money for tickets, they were kicked off the train at Sanwan station. Wei and I mixed in with the group and didn't arouse any suspicion. The next morning, we boarded a passenger train for Lanzhou.

The train roared eastward. Since it was a few days before the Chinese New Year, every car was packed. To escape the police and the ticket collectors, we crawled under the seats, pretending to sleep. Nobody paid any attention to us.

In the morning, the train pulled into the Lanzhou station. We left the station and ordered food at a small restaurant nearby. During the meal, Wei said he was planning to go back to his native city of Tianshui: "I don't dare return to the Railway Bureau. My managers there could send me back to Jiabiangou.

I'm going to my hometown first and see if I can get some odd jobs. If I can't, I'll travel to Xinjiang as a migrant worker."

As for myself, I couldn't even go home. My family lived in Wuhan. If I showed up there as an escaped Rightist, I could implicate my parents and make their life even more miserable than it already was. Without any options, I returned to Wang-jiaping Farm.

That was in 1960. Then I had lost contact with Wei, and I never saw him again until tonight.

Manure Collectors

Chen Yuming graduated from the University of Lanzhou in 1949, right after the Communist Party took over the city. The new government assigned him a job at the Gansu Provincial Public Security Bureau, and in 1955, he was transferred to the Outdoor Geological Reconnaissance Agency. On December 2, 1957, he was called into a conference room. In front of his managers and coworkers, he was charged with being an extreme Rightist.

Chen knew why he had been singled out. The previous year, he had openly criticized the government. He pointed out that building labor camps in the remote desert regions was a waste of government resources. He also complained to some friends in private that some veteran guards were mistreating prisoners.

At age thirty-four, Chen was removed from his job and ordered to receive reeducation at Jiabiangou.

Chen Yuming and one of his coworkers were the first Rightists to arrive at Jiabiangou. The second group, consisting of seven Rightists from the Jiuquan Transportation Company, came in the next day. A few days later, another eight people joined them. After that, there was a temporary halt in new arrivals.

Since Chen had worked in the provincial penitentiary system, he knew the deputy camp director fairly well. One day, the deputy director announced in front of all seventeen Rightists, "I'm temporarily putting Chen Yuming in charge here. If you have problems, discuss them with him first. He'll report to me."

For the next two months, Chen organized the clean up of the makeshift mud houses, the rearing of pigs, and the collection of manure. After the Chinese New Year in 1958, additional Rightists arrived in droves. Chen was promoted to section leader within the agricultural team. Chen had become a true walking stick.

The deputy camp director, Liu Zhenyu, was a former army officer, tall with the dark skin of a peasant. Chen had heard legendary stories about him. Liu, who was from Zhidan County, in Shaanxi Province, had joined the Communist army in 1935. He used to lead a small guerrilla force along the borders of Shaanxi, Ningxia, and Gansu provinces. In April 1947, his troops were ambushed by the Nationalist government forces. A bullet hit Liu's head and he fell off his horse. His comrades thought he was dead and retreated without him. Liu was captured and locked up at the Hualin Mountain Prison for two years. After his release, he returned to his hometown, where he farmed and occasionally dabbled in small businesses. In 1951, during a business trip to the city of Yinchuan, he ran into a former soldier who had served under him. The soldier was terrified. "We thought you had died," he said. "We even held a memorial service for you."

Liu was eventually able to return to military life, but there was one problem: nobody knew what had happened to him behind bars. Liu said he had never betrayed the party during interrogation, but he couldn't explain why the enemy had released him after only two years. After all, on the eve of the Communist takeover, the Nationalist government had gathered all the Communists imprisoned in Hualin Mountain and had them executed. Ultimately, they decided to put him on the "untrustworthy" list. In the mid-1950s, while his former comrades were promoted to senior positions within the province, Liu was transferred to Jiabiangou, where he became the deputy camp director.

Bad luck followed Liu to Jiabiangou. When Rightists died of starvation in massive numbers, the Central Party Committee held an emergency meeting in Lanzhou to reverse the extreme policies implemented by the Gansu provincial government. Liu became a scapegoat. A top Party leader ordered him to be shot. He narrowly escaped death when a work team that investigated the case concluded that the conditions weren't solely Liu's fault.

Liu was known for his explosive temper, but he treated Chen with sympathy, especially after he learned that Chen's wife, like him a former official at the Provincial Public Security Bureau, had also been sent to Jiabiangou. Liu twice arranged for Chen to spend a night with his wife. Liu even invited Chen to his house several times for dinner. Liu had his wife serve homemade noodles.

As a walking stick, Chen was in charge of thirty-some Rightists. They planted crops and dug irrigation canals. It was backbreaking work, but Chen was devoted to his job.

One day in July 1959, Liu summoned Chen to his office and said, "The vegetables we grew this year don't look too good. They need fertilizer. The camp leadership has decided to send some folks to the city of Jiayuguan to collect manure off the street. I recommended you to lead the job. What do you think?"

It was a very thoughtful gesture by Liu. He had tried to divert Chen from the harsh working conditions he endured in the field, out of concern that Chen's health might deteriorate. Besides, all Rightists at Jiabiangou longed for off-site assignments. It was the only time they could escape the watchful eyes of the guards. So Chen accepted the offer on the spot.

"Tomorrow morning," said Liu, "you can leave first and look for a shelter before the rest of the group. The others will join you in a couple of days."

"But what if someone escapes? I can't afford the blame."

"It won't be a problem," said Liu. "The people I assigned to the job are very reliable. They won't escape, I can assure you."

Jiayuguan was a newly developed industrial city built in the Gobi Desert. In those days, the downtown area was still in its infancy. The intersection of two main streets formed the core of the city's commercial and cultural life. In the middle of the intersection was a circular island decorated with a few small trees. On the four street corners there stood a movie theater called the May Day Workers Cultural Club, a two-story department store, a municipal government office building, and a grocery.

In the outlying areas, Chen found the site of a defunct iron and steel manufacturing plant. Half-finished production facilities lay abandoned in the open. Before Chen left, Liu had instructed him to check the plant site for vacant houses. Chen walked around the area and found nothing. The buildings in the plant's residential complexes were fully occupied.

It was getting late and the sun was disappearing below the horizon. Chen shuffled his way back to the city center on a pebbled sand road. He desperately needed a place to spend the night. His eyes lit up when he approached a small hill that jutted out in the distance on the south side of the road. There was a large dark hole at the foot of the hill. Since it was the middle of the summer, spending the night inside that hole didn't seem like a bad idea. He could resume his search for shelter the next day.

As he neared the hill, he was pleasantly surprised by what he discovered. It wasn't a hole after all. It was a cave that measured about ten square meters, several bricks and a thick layer of wheat stalks lay scattered on the floor. One of the walls was blackened by smoke. Someone had lived there before. He figured migrant workers had dug the cave. There was some dried horse manure outside, and two wooden stakes had been planted in the sand on either side of the entrance. A broken willow fence, apparently used as a makeshift door, was tied to one of the stakes. Judging by the human excrement on the ground, the cave must have been vacant for some time. Some passersby had used the place as a toilet.

Chen bundled up some tall grass and made a broom of it. He carefully removed the dried human waste and swept the floor. Then he sat down on the wheat stalks, drank from his bottle, and hungrily ate two buns that he had brought from Jiabiangou. Then, using his winter coat as a pillow, he lay down and fell into a sound sleep.

The next morning, Chen cleaned the cave thoroughly. First, he gathered up the wheat stalks and put them in the sun, then piled the bricks in a corner and scraped the soot off the wall with some rough grass. Then he brought the wheat stalks inside and neatly spread them on the ground to make a big mattress, which he surrounded with the bricks. Finally, he cleared away the horse manure outside and created a small open space in front of the cave.

Satisfied with what he had accomplished, he left to meet his fellow Rightists at the bus stop downtown.

All the long-distance buses to Jiayuguan stopped at the intersection downtown. Chen waited patiently near a row of small flowerpots in front of the movie theater. At dusk, he spotted a familiar horse-drawn cart heading in his direction. Several shabbily dressed men sat on the cart beside pots, pans, and empty bamboo baskets. He went to greet them.

The passengers jumped off the cart and asked eagerly if he had found shelter for them.

He got on the cart and told everyone do the same. He instructed the driver to move east toward the hill. "Where are you taking us?" shouted one Rightist. "We aren't staying in the Gobi Desert, are we?"

Chen kept his silence until the driver pulled up in front of the hill. He jumped off and said, "Here we are!"

The Jiabiangou Rightists were accustomed to hardships and had lived in caves before. Despite their initial trepidation and their whining, they were pleased with the arrangement once they stepped inside. They unloaded the cooking utensils and the luggage. Since they were all exhausted, they didn't bother to cook that night. They just munched on some buns and went to sleep.

In the summertime, hot and sultry evenings were common in the Hexi Corridor region. But later that night, a dry cool breeze blew in through the willow fence. They all slept soundly.

Early the next morning, they prepared their first meal. Chen sent a Rightist to fetch a bucket of water at Unique Place, a Tianjin restaurant down the street. Then they dug a hole in the ground outside to use as a makeshift stove. They put a pot over the hole and burned some dry grass underneath to heat up the water. They boiled a pot of thick corn millet porridge. Since their monthly ration was only twelve kilograms per person, they needed to plan carefully. But, because it was the first meal they had cooked on their own, they decided to treat themselves with an extra-large serving.

After breakfast, the driver went back to Jiabiangou. Chen and other Rightists sat down to plan the day's task. They loaded up some bricks at a nearby construction site to build a small stove outside the cave. Chen found a wood board and he converted it into a kitchen counter. They also mended the broken willow fence and reinforced their beds with bricks.

As they were finishing up, a Rightist named Zhang Jiaji

said, "This is unbelievable. It's like renovating a bridal room. All we need now is the bride."

Everyone laughed. They had not felt this relaxed for a long time. Since it was still early, Chen suggested they take a stroll to familiarize themselves with the city. In those days, the only place worth checking out was the department store at the intersection. Once they had finished window-shopping, they had nothing else to do. But nobody wanted to leave, so they sat on the ground to watch pedestrians and bicyclists passing by. Soon darkness descended. The streets became deserted. Lights came on. They reluctantly got up and wandered back. They were all hungry. Since they had exceeded their daily ration during breakfast, they limited themselves to a pot of thin corn gruel with pumpkins.

Dinner heightened their spirits. They sat around a small flickering kerosene lamp and chatted deep into the night. They felt overwhelmed by the freedom that had suddenly befallen them—the freedom to move through the streets without being watched by guards, to go to bed anytime they wanted, to eat to their heart's delight at breakfast and make up for it with a light dinner. They could chat as late as they were able to stay awake. Their newfound freedom seemed surreal.

There were five of them altogether. Yu Qingfeng was the oldest, in his early fifties. When Yu first arrived in Jiabiangou, he was a stocky man with a round face, pale and soft. Now he was nothing but a shadow of his former self, his features haggard and his body shrunken. Yu had owned a leather store in Lanzhou. After the Communists came to power, he became an ardent supporter of the new government. When the army entered Tibet, he donated a contingent of camels to help transport military supplies. He later gave up his business, followed the army to Tibet, and stayed with the troops for two years before returning to Lanzhou. At the onset of the collectivization movement, the government appointed him general manager of the Gansu Provincial Fur Corporation. During the anti-Rightist campaign, his capitalist venture during the pre-Communist era became a liability.

The second man in line was Xu Jingxuan, the former deputy chief of Tongwei County. Xu was over forty and having come from the countryside, was uneducated and provincial. But gradually he rose through the Party ranks. After moving into the city, he was convicted of bigamy when he married a young urban girl without previously divorcing his country wife. On top of that, he was heard making anti-Party remarks.

The third man was Gao Keqin, the former logistics director at the Provincial Postal Communications Department. Gao, in his late thirties, was the nephew of the Party secretary of Gansu Province. The youngest one in the group was the tall, lanky thirty-two-year-old Zhang Jiaji, who graduated from the Wugong Agricultural Academy in Shaanxi Province. He held the job of production director at the Shandan Military Horse Farm.

During their late-night conversations, Chen came to learn the background of each individual member. He told himself, No wonder Director Liu sent these people over here. They all have connections.

At the crack of dawn, they started a fire and boiled a pot of vegetable soup. They filled their bowls to the brim, gulped down the broth, and then prepared to leave.

While the others were adjusting their baskets and shoulder poles, Yu dashed away to the main road. He came back with a piece of metal wire. He shut the willow fence over the entrance and locked it with the wire. "Are you worried that someone might break in?" Chen teased him.

Yu became defensive. "You never know. It's better to be prudent."

Zhang interrupted, "Old Yu is loaded with money and he's worried about thieves."

Yu laughed. "I'm more concerned about my leather suitcase, which I took with me to Tibet. It carries a lot of political significance."

Zhang sneered. "What do you mean by 'political significance'? You jump at every opportunity to brag about your glorious past, but that couldn't even save you from Jiabiangou."

Yu said, "You may be right. I still don't understand it. I supported the Communist Party with all my heart and I ended up here anyway."

Chen found it strange to hear them argue like that. At Jiabiangou, everyone kept silent and avoided political topics at all costs. Now people were telling their stories without any reluctance. Chen cautioned everyone to keep their mouths shut.

But Zhang ignored Chen's advice and continued, "Old Yu, don't feel too bad. Look at Xu Jingxuan. He joined the Communist revolution during the War of Resistance against Japan and even he wasn't spared."

"Don't involve me," said Xu. "I was guilty. But to tell the truth, I didn't commit any crimes against the Party."

Everyone burst out laughing.

"We heard that when you were the county chief," said Zhang, "people accused you of repeating rhymes such as 'Working people are masters of our new society today. They still have to toil in the field all day. The summer sun bakes their bodies dry. The winter cold freezes their assholes tight.' You remember that?"

Xu was noticeably flustered. "I shared that ditty with some local folks when I was visiting the countryside several years ago. It was meant as a joke."

"A joke?" said Zhang, pretending to take an offended tone. "That little ditty tarnished the image of our working people and completely negated the benefits of our socialist system. Your remarks were quite vicious, you know."

Xu simply said, "Whatever the accusations are, I'm not anti-Party."

The gravity of his tone evoked another round of laughter. With that, they lifted their baskets on top of their shoulder poles and left for work.

Chen headed east on the main street and passed the Tianjin restaurant and a row of half-completed houses. It was such a new city that Jiayuguan lacked public sanitary systems. There were no public toilets. Many pedestrians simply defecated in alleys or on the pebbled ground behind the newly constructed houses. Chen went around to those places, picked up the dried or half-dried human waste with a small shovel, and dumped them in his basket.

By about ten in the morning he had filled up two baskets, so he headed back to the cave.

When he went to empty his baskets, Chen noticed that the other four Rightists had also returned. They had only gathered a small pile. Unhappy to see this, he entered the cave. The four of them were lying side by side on the bed. He tried to suppress his displeasure and asked, "When did you all come back?"

When they didn't respond, Chen raised his voice and repeated the question.

"At about nine o'clock," Yu answered as he slowly sat up.

Chen's anger rose by the second. "Why did you come back so early? Didn't we agree we wouldn't break until noon?"

No one replied. Then Zhang jumped up from the bed and said, "Fuck. It was just too embarrassing."

Chen was taken aback. "Do you mean to say that collecting manure is too embarrassing?"

More silence followed. Chen thought to lecture them but something made him hesitate. He sat down next to them. "So, I didn't realize you all have such thin skin. Tell me, what were you embarrassed about?"

Zhang almost yelled in response. "I guess you and I feel differently about this. When I carried those baskets of manure through the street, I felt like everyone was staring at me. Whenever I saw people speaking with each other, I felt as if they were talking about how badly that manure collector stinks."

Zhang had become quite emotional.

Chen looked him in the eye and said, "Kid, based on what you just said, I think you need another three years of reeducation at Jiabiangou. You never felt embarrassed when cleaning the toilet and picking up cow dung at Jiabiangou, did you?"

"That was different. We are all Rightists there and everyone was equal, but here we are in a free world. All the people around us are all free citizens. I'm a criminal in this crowd. That's what embarrasses me. Think about it. We've been reduced to the status of a manure collectors. It's truly shameful. Death is a much better option. What's the point of living? Has that ever occurred to you?"

Chen patiently waited for Zhang to finish. He paused for several minutes before responding, "Of course, there have been times when I thought about death. But now I see it from a different perspective. I don't know anyone at Jiayuguan and nobody knows me. So I'm not afraid if people laugh at me. Since I don't know them, I don't care."

"That's really comforting," said Zhang sarcastically.

Chen was outraged. "If you find it humiliating, you don't have to do it. I'll send you back to Jiabiangou."

Hearing this, Zhang smiled ingratiatingly. "Boss, I'm not going back. I would rather collect human waste than return to Jiabiangou. Fuck, no."

"Then stop complaining about losing face and do your job."

Their lives as manure collectors were uneventful. They followed a set routine, going out to the city twice a day to gather manure. They also collected pieces of coal or wood for cooking, putting them in a separate bag attached to the basket. Whoever came back earliest would go fetch water, start a fire in the stove, and cook. In the evenings, they would chat outside until bedtime. One time, they went as a group to tour the old part of Jiayuguan at the far end of the Great Wall. Unfortunately, the citadel was closed that day. They simply walked around outside and then sat for two hours in a meadow by the foot of a hill. The grass felt like a big green carpet, clean and dust-free. They found a pool of spring water welling up from under the ground. The men undressed and bathed themselves in the water. They then washed their clothes.

Everything was perfect, except for the food. They didn't have enough to fill their stomachs. At times, the hunger became unbearable.

Hunger posed less of a threat to Gao, Yu, and Xu, who were well connected and came from well-to-do families. They were frequently sent crackers, canned fruit, and cooked dry flour to supplement their rations. Chen and Zhang were not so lucky. They carried their baskets and tottered around all day with growling stomachs. Their health started to deteriorate fast. In the first week after they started collecting manure, Chen and Zhang kept their eyes on the dumpsters at residential areas. They spent hours hunting for half-rotten turnips, vegetable leaves, or a piece of pork skin. After dinner each night, when the others munched on their extra food supplies, Chen and Zhang would wash the foods they found in the garbage, boil them, and eat them.

Yu once chastised Chen and Zhang's scavenging activities, "You guys have no sense of shame. How can you spend hours hunting for food inside dumpsters? Even beggars don't do that. This is a matter of dignity. You can't reduce yourself to the same level as a beggar, can you?"

The sharp-tongued Zhang wouldn't let Yu get away with such snooty remarks. "Fuck you! What's wrong with being a beggar? Beggars at least are free citizens, which is more than I can say about a prisoner like you."

That shut him up.

Zhang continued with his foraging, but he didn't just search for discarded food. He burrowed deep inside dumpsters, gathering metal scraps and electric cords, and storing them inside the cave. Yu found them dirty and messy and the two of them squabbled over the metal scraps. By the end of the month, the group ran out of food. While everyone sat around feeling dejected and helpless, Zhang bagged his collection of metal scraps and sold them at a recycling center. He bought several oven-baked cakes at a black market and shared them with his roommates. After that, Yu never complained again.

The authorities at Jiabiangou sent a truck to the city and collected the manure twice a month. The driver also dropped off their biweekly supply of food and vegetables. One day in August, the truck arrived with Yuan, a supervisor at the agricultural team.

All the Rightists addressed him as Supervisor Yuan. He was one of the most ruthless officials at the camp. Camp leaders constantly beat up Rightists, but usually they ordered the guards to do the dirty work. Yuan was the exception—he would tie up people and hit or kick them himself. Many inmates had suffered at his hands.

When Supervisor Yuan stepped out of the truck, the Rightists were shocked to see him. Chen immediately went over to greet him.

Supervisor Yuan ignored Chen and rushed away to the other side of the hill to relieve himself. Chen turned to Zhang and asked if he had any money on him.

Zhang looked baffled. "What do you need the money for?"

Chen said, "Go get a couple of oven-baked cakes and a pound of roasted pork. Make some sandwiches for Supervisor Yuan."

"Nope," said Zhang curtly. "I don't have any money."

Chen begged him for help. "Brother, please . . ."

Supervisor Yuan returned. He circled around the area and then stopped by a pile of manure in the sun. "Is this all the manure you have collected?"

Chen nodded his head vigorously. "Yes, Supervisor Yuan. It's so hot out here. Why don't we talk inside?"

Supervisor Yuan entered the cave and looked around. "Look how messy your beds are. This place is like a pigsty."

Supervisor Yuan parked himself on the edge of the bed and lorded over them. He inquired about their work and Chen provided a full report. In a little while, lunch was ready. Xu had cooked a pot of corn gruel. Chen filled up a bowl and carefully handed it over to Supervisor Yuan. Then he brought the pork sandwiches over and put them on a piece of paper next to Yuan, who sipped the corn gruel and took a big bite from the sandwich. "You guys eat pretty well here," he said.

Chen forced a smile. "We bought those sandwiches with money sent by Zhang's family."

After lunch, the Rightists shoveled the dried manure onto the back of the truck. When Yuan noticed that the dried manure had barely added up to a single truckload, he complained, "Boy, you really know how to play hooky."

Chen said, "Supervisor Yuan, we are trying our best here."

"Are you really? You need to do your job and keep an eye on

these people. If you can't fill up a truck next time, I will have to send another group to replace you."

They didn't go out that afternoon. Chen called a meeting to discuss how to increase results. "You have all heard Supervisor Yuan's warning. We need to make a decision here."

"What the fuck was he talking about?" said Zhang. "We all worked pretty hard."

Since Zhang peppered every single one of his remarks with profanity, Xu gave him the nickname "Fuck Zhang."

The other members of the group complained that it had become too difficult to collect manure in Jiayuguan. All the human waste at public latrines was monopolized by the nearby communes. There wasn't much to collect at isolated street corners. Zhang tried to be funny again. "What can we do? We can't exactly grab people on the street and force them to take a shit in our baskets, can we?"

Chen devised a plan: they would assign two people to work at the crowded railway stations outside the city. Everyone liked the idea. The next morning, Chen sent Xu to the town of Dacaotan and Gao to Heishanhu. They would cover the railway stations there while the rest continued their work in Jiayuguan.

Adjusting the locations yielded results. When Supervisor Yuan showed up again a month later, he was pleased to see that the truck was filled to the brim.

After that, Supervisor Yuan didn't visit again for several months. In late October the first winter snow fell on the city. As winter approached, life became harder. There was less and less manure to collect on the street. In order to fulfill their quota, the Rightists had to travel to the outlying areas. Besides collecting manure, they wandered around the city looking for coal to feed their makeshift stove. They also covered the willow fence with a piece of linen rag.

During daytime, when temperatures dropped to less than ten degrees below zero, their bones ached. Their empty stomachs didn't help either. The cold weather exacerbated their hunger. Chen and Zhang spent more time at landfills, rummaging around for vegetable leaves and food scraps. Yu relied on his family to supplement his daily rations. He didn't know what it was like to starve. Every time he saw Chen bring back the rotten vegetable leaves, he would say with disdain, "One of these days, you're going to get food poisoning."

Yu's words proved to be true. One day not long before the Chinese New Year, Chen spotted a dozen kohlrabi, a beetlike vegetable. Local residents stored them in cellars before the arrival of winter. The kohlrabi that Chen had brought home that day must have been left in cellars for too long. They were dry and withered. In the evening, Chen and Zhang carefully peeled off the leathery outer layers and boiled the rest. Since the kohlrabi was in relatively good condition, Yu couldn't help but stuffing a couple of pieces in his mouth. But he began to despise their sweet taste and he stopped eating them. Chen and Zhang, on the other hand, gobbled up the whole pot.

An hour or so later, their stomachs began to hurt. Soon the two of them were moaning and sweating profusely. They suspected that they had gotten food poisoning. Yu didn't agree, because he had had two chunks and his stomach felt fine. Yu concluded that his two roommates had eaten too much and their stomachs had burst. Or, to put it in medical terms, Yu said they were suffering from gastric perforation and they were doomed. Yu even thought they might die any minute. So Zhang dictated to Yu a letter addressed to his parents, telling them he was sorry that he wouldn't be able to fulfill his filial duties in the future.

Yu also helped Chen draft a letter to Chen's wife, apologizing for the fact that his case had adversely affected her: "You were declared a Rightist and sent to Jiabiangou because of me. Now that I'm dying, I'm haunted by guilt. I will repay your love when we meet in the next life. Please take care of our children. When you are released from Jiabiangou in the future, please go ahead and remarry if you meet a nice man."

The two finished their "final" letters and lay down in bed, waiting for death to claim them. Another hour passed. Death didn't descend, but their stomach pain didn't diminish either. It occurred to Yu that he might have misdiagnosed their conditions. If they had in fact suffered from stomach perforation, how could they still be alive? He grabbed two bricks from the corner and heated them up on the stove. Then he wrapped the hot bricks with rags and instructed Chen and Zhang to use the bricks to warm their stomachs.

Another hour later, their stomachs began to growl. Then they started farting. They dashed out to relieve themselves and just like that, the pain was gone.

Despite the "food poisoning" episode, they continued to search for vegetables inside dumpsters. Hunger had warped their brains. When they woke up each morning, all they could think about was food.

Beginning in January 1960, the food situation became even more grim. The camp further reduced their monthly rations. They had to look for alternative food sources to appease their gnawing hunger.

Once a week, Chen would deliver food and vegetables to Gao and Xu. He would follow a rail line and visit Gao at Dacaotan first. Gao would treat him to boiled napa cabbage that he had stolen from a vegetable warehouse near the railway station. After lunch with Gao, Chen would walk another fifteen kilometers to Heishanhu to see Xu, who had taken shelter inside an abandoned house.

One day after the Chinese New Year, Chen paid his routine

visit to Xu, who offered him a bowl of boiled peas as a gift. Xu said they were undigested peas that he had found inside piles of horse dung near the railway station. He had eaten them for a whole week and he never had any stomach problems. "There was only one bad thing about the peas," Xu whispered mischievously. "They smell awful,"

Chen wolfed down half a bowl before he even noticed the stink. He didn't experience any stomach upset problems either. At dawn the next morning, Xu took him to an area where many horse-drawn carts were parked. They collected a big pile of horse dung, took it back to Xu's place, rinsed the dung with water and sifted out two kilograms of undigested peas.

After returning to Jiayuguan, Chen poured the peas into a pot and washed them several times more. He boiled them thoroughly, mixed them with corn, and cooked a pot of thick corn gruel. In the evening, when Yu and Zhang came back, they smacked their lips and enjoyed the food tremendously. They hadn't eaten solid food for months.

"Where does the smell come from?" said Yu.

"The peas were in storage for too long," said Chen casually.

Later, when everyone finished their meal, Chen told them the truth. Yu was furious. Soon, he started to throw up; his eyes filled with tears and his face took on the color of an eggplant.

"You idiot. How could you feed us with peas you found in a pile of horse shit? Are you trying to kill us?"

Chen was quick to defend himself. "I had quite a few at Heishanhu and I feel fine . . ."

Chen kept the leftover peas to himself. He soaked them in water for two days, added some salt, and boiled them. Every night he would snack on them, and nothing had happened to him. Seeing that the peas didn't cause any stomach problems for Chen, Yu eventually followed suit and began to munch on them. He was too hungry to be fussy. In 1960, famine had hit many parts of China. The snacks from his family came less and less frequently.

January and February were the coldest months. They struggled to collect enough manure. Each time they ventured out, they could feel the cold wind seeping through their bones. It was impossible to work outdoors. A couple of days before the Jiabiangou truck arrived, they stole human waste from public toilets to make up their quota.

One day in mid-March, pressured by the imminent arrival of the truck, they went to steal again. Chen targeted an outdoor latrine in a residential complex on the southeast corner of the intersection. In those days, houses in China had no indoor plumbing and families in residential areas used public latrines. Inside, there would be a row of holes in the ground. The holes were connected to a pond of human waste behind the latrine. At Jiayuguan, the government had built fences around the pond. There was a gate in the fence that was usually locked. Only the members of the local communes could access the human fertilizer.

Chen noticed a chink in the fence, as if it had been hit by a truck. He snuck in, then jumped down into the frozen pit of feces. Since the weather was turning warm, some of the ice covering the pit had begun to melt. Chen took his small shovel and scooped up enough to fill his basket. That's when he heard the footsteps. Someone had walked into the latrine. Chen stopped, tossed his shovel onto the ground, and tried to jump out of the pit, firmly grasping the edge with both hands. His arms weakened, however, and he fell back into the pit. He summoned his strength and tried for a second time. Again, he failed. He suddenly realized how emaciated he had become.

He stood quietly inside the pit for a few more minutes, waiting for the person to leave and then, with another jump, got out.

Someone yelled loudly at him, "Hey, what are you doing there?" Chen turned around and saw a young man poking his head through the gap in the wall.

"I'm collecting manure," said Chen.

"If you are collecting manure, why the hell were you standing there so quietly and peeping inside the latrine?" the young man said.

Chen blushed. The young man must have thought he was a Peeping Tom. "Oh, I was just exhausted from the job. So I was taking a break."

" 'Taking a break'?" said the young man, his voice rising. "Motherfucker. Why the hell are you taking a break here? Fucking pervert."

He jumped over the wall and lifted his leg to kick Chen's head. Chen ducked his head and shouted at the top of his lungs, hoping to get the attention of someone nearby.

An old man and a young woman emerged from either side of the latrine and stepped over. "Look at that pervert there," said the young man, pointing at Chen. "I saw him crouching down there quietly, watching people in the latrine."

"I'm not a pervert," said Chen. "I'm a manure collector. My body has become so weak, after I filled up my basket, I couldn't climb out of the pit."

Chen turned toward the old man and pleaded for help. The old man was puzzled by the whole episode. He moved closer and asked, "Where are you from? You seem to have an out-of-town accent. How did you end up collecting manure in Jiayuguan?"

Worried that the situation might get out of control, Chen recounted his life story. When Chen finished, the old man told the young fellow, "Don't beat up this poor man. Help him out of the pit."

The young man sneered at Chen in disgust. "I'm not touching him."

He spat on the ground and stepped back through the hole in the wall. The young woman followed him out.

The old man carefully climbed over the fallen wall and reached out his hand. Before Chen left, the old man led him to the front door of his house and poured two bowls of corn flour into Chen's hat. "Take it and make yourself a couple of corn cakes."

Before he went to bed that night, Chen touched both of his legs and stared at them for a long time. They were swollen. He said to himself, I'm suffering from edema.

One day in early May, Chen entered the city's railway station. Every time he went there, he would pass a platform at the south end and cross the rail to search for manure on the other side. Workers were building new rail tracks there. There was no toilet and many relieved themselves behind the piles of lumber and sand.

On that day, a throng of passengers had exited the train and was advancing toward him. Chen stepped aside and put down his basket for a break. For some unknown reason, a passenger in a police uniform suddenly stopped right in front of him and stared at his green army coat that he had gotten while working for the Provincial Public Security Bureau. At first Chen avoided the stranger's gaze, but he soon realized that the passenger looked familiar—the man was a former colleague of his at the Public Security Bureau. Chen immediately turned away, pretending he didn't recognize him. But the man struck up a conversation first. "Are you Chen Yuming?"

Feeling a little awkward Chen said, "And you are . . . ?"

"I'm Ma Jianbin."

Chen nodded his head. "Now I remember. Why are you here?"

"I was transferred to Jiayuguan several years ago, right after you left for a job at the Outdoor Geological Reconnaissance Agency. How did you end up like this?"

Chen laughed awkwardly. "Like what? Well, it's hard to explain in a few words. To make a long story short, I was labeled a Rightist and ended up at Jiabiangou. The camp sent me out to collect manure in Jiayuguan. What about you?"

"I'm still at the Public Security Bureau," said Ma.

"Have you been promoted? You must be a big shot now."

"I'm now the deputy bureau chief. Can't call that a big shot!"

Throughout the conversation, Ma appeared to be in a state of shock. He almost seemed embarrassed when he mentioned his current work title. Chen knew that his former colleague didn't want to hurt his feelings, but Ma's modesty made Chen feel even more awkward. He picked up his shoulder pole and said, "Ma, the bus is already here. Don't miss it. I also need to get back to work anyway."

As Ma mumbled his goodbyes, he searched frantically inside a coat pocket. He pulled out a small stack of cash and handed it over. "I–I have spent most of my money on the trip," he said, stammering. "Only thirty or forty yuan left. Please take it. Come visit me when you have time. I'll get you some more."

Chen pulled his hand back as if it had been burned by fire. "Ma, why are you trying to give me money?"

He picked up his basket and was ready to bolt. Ma grabbed his shoulder and almost yelled, "Brother, if you leave like this, I'll consider it a snub."

Chen was determined not to accept any money. "I don't want people to pity me," he said.

Ma shook his head and sighed. "You are just as stubborn as you used to be. Okay, but you need to promise me one thing—you need to come visit me."

Chen was touched by Ma's sincerity. "I promise. I will definitely go see you."

As a matter of fact, Chen dreaded the thought of visiting Ma, who had joined the Public Security Bureau in 1952, when Chen happened to be working at the office of special cases. Ma had served as his assistant for two years. Now he was branded a Rightist and Ma had been appointed deputy chief of the Jiayuguan Public Security Bureau. What a sharp contrast! He felt ashamed.

Yet as time went by, he changed his mind. In June his team suffered a crisis—they were short of food for four days. They had nothing to spare. Even Yu began to look for rotten cabbages in dumpsters. After giving it some careful thought, Chen decided to visit Ma and ask for some food or money.

He placed the baskets on his shoulder pole and left the cave.

The municipal government building was situated near the intersection, on the west side of the street. The Public Security Bureau was in the same building. Chen left his baskets at the curb and told the guard at the entrance that he was looking for Ma Jianbin.

The guard took one look at his shabby outfit and asked, "What do you want from Deputy Chief Ma?" Chen explained that he was a friend of Ma's and he was meeting Ma for some personal business. The guard told him to come back later because Ma was out of the office.

Since it was only eight-thirty in the morning. Chen decided to go collect some manure. He walked west, checking out street corners of construction sites. Around ten, he turned around and went back to the government building. As he was passing by the front entrance of the local hospital, he bumped into a woman hurrying out. The woman stopped him and said, "Big brother, could you do me a favor?"

The woman's eyes were red and swollen from crying.

"What is it?" asked Chen.

"My baby just died. Can you help me find a place to bury him?"

It was then that Chen noticed a baby in her arms, wrapped tightly in a small quilt. Chen's eyes brightened. He thought, I'm going to get what I need from her. So, he nodded his head. "Sure thing. As long as you pay me, I can do it."

"Would you take thirty yuan?"

Chen couldn't believe what he was hearing. Thirty yuan just for burying a baby? It was too easy.

Since Chen didn't reply right away, the woman assumed he wanted more money. "What about fifty? That should be enough, right? Big brother, please help me. That's all the money I have."

"I will do it. It's really no problem," Chen said right away.

The woman handed over the child and the money. Chen tucked the money in his shirt pocket and then switched the position of the child in his arms. The child was remarkably light. It was like carrying a package of cotton. He couldn't help but feel sad. He asked, "How did the baby die?"

"Pneumonia. Don't worry, it's not contagious. The pneumonia was caused by a cold."

Chen shook his head. "No, I'm not worried about getting infected. I was just curious. He is so tiny. How old was he?"

The woman burst out crying. "Twenty days . . . only twenty days . . ."

Chen's heart ached. He gently patted the woman on the back and asked her to stop sobbing. "Okay," he said, "I'm going to go bury him now."

He bent over to pick up his shoulder pole and the baskets. As he was trying to arrange the baskets with his free hand, the woman screamed, "Hey, you're holding my baby upside down."

Chen felt an impulse to yell back at her and say, "Does it matter if I hold him upside down?" Instead, he kept it to himself.

The woman continued, "Leave the baskets here. You can come get them after you're done with the burial. Nobody will steal your pole."

"I'm not worried that anyone will steal it," said Chen. "If someone throws it away, I wouldn't be able to get it back."

The woman didn't respond. Chen bid her goodbye and wobbled forward with his manure-collecting gear and the baby. A few steps down the road, Chen heard footsteps. It was the woman. "Why are you following me?" he asked.

"I want to see where you bury my child. I want to make sure you do a good job with it."

"Big sister, please trust me. I have taken your money and I promise I will do a good job. If I didn't, I wouldn't be deserving of your kindness."

Chen staggered west. A few blocks down, he glanced back. The woman was still standing there by the side of the street. He found a burial site in the desert. He could feel the woman's grief. With his shovel, he dug a hole in the ground, and then carefully placed the baby inside it. Then something came over him, and he bent over, scooped up the baby, and held it in his arms. He opened the quilt and looked intently at the baby's face. Then he wrapped it up and put him back in the grave.

He filled in the hole with sand and made a small mound on top. He knew that it didn't make sense to set up a little tomb because the mother would probably never come to see it. But deep down, he felt strongly that this had been a life, a person, who deserved a tomb. Someday, when strangers passed by or if the urban sprawl extended to this area, people should know a child had been buried here.

Chen never visited Ma after all. He returned to the cave and handed the money to Zhang, asking him to go buy food at the black market. At lunchtime, he told his roommates about the baby: his round face was pale, as pale as white limestone.

Many years later, he could still remember the face of that baby.

At the end of August, the truck from Jiabiangou came to gather the manure with Supervisor Yuan in tow. Everyone was surprised to see him. They all wondered what had brought him there. Chen figured something was wrong. He followed Supervisor Yuan to the cave.

"I want to see if you have collected enough manure to fill up a truck," Supervisor Yuan said. "If you have, I want you to pack up and go back to Jiabiangou."

Chen's heart sank. His worst fear had come true. He turned around and glanced at Zhang and Yu, who were cooking by the entrance. They all stopped what they were doing and asked earnestly, "Why? Don't we need more manure?"

"No, we don't. There is no need to ask why." Yuan gave them a stern look.

Yu didn't say anything, just added some wood splinters to the fire. Zhang excused himself to go to the latrine. Before he left, he signaled Chen to follow him. Once they were outside, Zhang removed some cash from an inside shirt pocket. "Chen, please go use the money I've saved for a rainy day to treat Supervisor Yuan to a nice meal. We need to make him change his mind."

As usual, Chen ran out and bought several oven-baked cakes, a bottle of liquor, and several slices of pork. Seeing that the supervisor was pleased, Chen took advantage of the situation and asked, "Do you know why they're sending us back? Is it because we are not fulfilling our quotas?"

Supervisor Yuan said, "No, not at all. You are doing a great job here. Rightists in Jiabiangou will be transferred to Mingshui. The provincial government is planning to build the largest farm in the region . . ."

So that was the reason for the pullback.

Chen didn't say a word. Supervisor Yuan took a large swig from the liquor bottle. "You all want to stay here and continue to collect manure. Let me do you a favor. I'll pick up the two folks at Heishanhu and Dacaotan first. The three of you can stay for a few more days. When you've gathered another truckload, I'll come get you."

Yuan finished the liquor and took his leave. The truck rumbled away and soon disappeared in the distance. The three manure collectors stood by the entrance to the cave for a long time. It was Zhang who finally spoke. "Fuck!"

The Love Story of Li Xiangnian

When I traveled last year to Jingyuan County, in Gansu, I heard about a Jiabiangou Rightist named Li Xiangnian. Li, who was originally from Tianjin, graduated from college in the 1950s. Before he was labeled a Rightist in 1957, he worked at Lanzhou's Municipal Sports Committee. While receiving reeducation at Jiabiangou, he escaped and ended up serving an additional six years in prison. The government removed his Rightist label in 1978. He settled down in Jingyuan, working for that county's sports committee.

Li's story stirred my interest, especially since I'm from Tianjin myself. I immediately paid a visit to him. The door of his home was padlocked. His neighbor said he had moved his family to Lanzhou ten years earlier. He was running a small art gallery in the area around Hongshangen Stadium.

I went to Lanzhou, but I didn't find him at the address provided by the neighbor. During a recent trip to Lanzhou, however, I mentioned Li to a painter friend of mine named Guan Qixing. Guan said he had met Li at a calligraphy exhibition ten years before and had come to know him quite well. Guan volunteered to introduce me.

Li's apartment building stood on a side street near the Lanzhou Railway Bureau. He was quite tall, his pale face marked with the indelible imprints of time. Two prominent lines, which looked as if they had been chipped by a knife, ran deep along either side of his *nose. After we exchanged pleasantries, I revealed the purpose of my visit. Li was unexpectedly forthcoming.*

It's difficult to summarize my experience at Jiabiangou in a few words.

Relatively speaking, my situation at Jiabiangou was good. I was a graduate of Hebei Teachers University. I majored in sports and physical education. I had a nice physique and I was dexterous. When I was a child, my father frequently took me to the theater, and I soon learned how to perform and sing Beijing opera. In 1959, not long after I arrived at Jiabiangou, I was selected to join the performance troupe and rehearse for a show to celebrate the tenth anniversary of the founding of the People's Republic of China. So I only had to sweat in the field for a few days.

I was also a calligrapher and painter. My grandpa used to be a scholar during the Qing dynasty and was renowned for his penmanship. Both of my parents had graduated from the Department of Economics at Nankai University in Tianjin. My father wrote beautifully with his paintbrush. Growing up in this intellectual family, I picked up their skills and became a good calligrapher myself. Following performances at the National Day celebration, one official asked me to design the outdoor bulletin board.

Thanks to my abilities in directing, performing, writing, and drawing, I was assigned numerous odd jobs and was spared the tough physical tasks in the field. In the first year, my health didn't deteriorate like so many others' did because I was able to figure out ways to scrounge extra food. For instance, I would write up short articles commending the good works of the mess-hall staff. Getting recognition on the bulletin board was conducive to their early release. They'd always ladle out a bigger portion to me at mealtimes. I also praised the medical staff at the camp clinic. In return for my kindness, the doctors there would grant me days off when I claimed to be sick. This is how I'd avoid heavy physical labor.

When we first arrived at Jiabiangou, we were naïve enough to think that our reeducation through hard labor would last only a year or so. But a year and four months passed and there was no sign that we might be released. Life became unbearable. I started to miss my girlfriend terribly.

Her name was Yu Shumin and she was then a student at Beijing Teachers University. She grew up in Shijiazhuang, the capital city of Hebei Province. I had met her in the spring of 1955 when I interned at the Shijiazhuang No. 2 Municipal High School. As a twenty-three-year-old, I felt in the prime of my youth. I was extremely outgoing, and talented at basketball and soccer. The soccer team at my university played against the provincial team three times, and Shumin came to watch. I showed off quite a bit. As a result, I noticed I had become Shumin's romantic target before the end of my internship.

Yu was just a high school sophomore, only seventeen years old, but she was quite mature physically—tall and slender with a fully developed bust and a pretty face. More important, she was also mature in her thinking. She always looked at me passionately. You know what I mean: when a girl is in love with you, her gaze is different. A couple of days before the internship ended, I was assigned to write a thank-you letter on behalf of all the interns and copy the letter on a red poster. Shumin fluttered around me, offering help. She ran around and managed to find a paintbrush and a bottle of black ink. As I was writing, she watched with admiration. She kept saying, "Teacher Li, your calligraphy is so beautiful." I could tell she was pursuing me. Of course, I liked her too. Even though she was young, she was stunning, a rare beauty in her school.

The night before I left Shijiazhuang, she invited me to visit her at home. After the visit she suggested we take a walk in the park. "Why rush back to the dorm? You need to enjoy this city before you go back to Tianjin." Once we got inside the park, she asked, "Teacher Li, after you return to Tianjin, will you still remember me?"

"How could I forget you?" I said. "You'll end up forgetting about me first."

"No, I won't."

After I returned to the university, I began to prepare for graduation. It wasn't long before Shumin took some time off and visited me in Tianjin. She had an aunt living there, and she stayed with her. She came to see me at the university every day. Sometimes we'd go walk in the park. When we parted, I gave her a photo album and some of my calligraphy as gifts. She showed them to her dad. She said in a letter that her dad spoke highly of my calligraphy.

After graduation, I was given a job at the Municipal Sports Committee in Lanzhou. I soon gained a good reputation as a coach and referee. In those days, the Lan Garden had the city's only outdoor basketball court, with lights installed for night games. I coached children's basketball teams during the day, and at night I served as a referee for all the municipal- and provincial-level basketball games held there. I ran up and down the court and reacted quickly. I judged every play accurately and announced my result with finesse. When I walked down the street, the young people would recognize me and call out to "the Lan Garden Referee." The *Lanzhou Daily* hired me as a stringer. I wrote about basketball and soccer, and commented on the newly released rules for the 1956 Olympic Games in Helsinki. I also worked as a sportscaster for the Gansu Provincial People's Radio Station. At major basketball games, I always had a prominent seat behind a microphone.

Throughout this time, Shumin and I corresponded with each other by air mail, because that was the fastest service in those years. In 1956, for the Chinese New Year, I went home for the first time since graduation to visit my parents, who had left Tianjin and moved in with my sister in Beijing. My sister was assigned a job at the Ministry of Construction after graduating from the University of Tianjin. She married a senior engineer at the Beijing Architectural Institute.

On my way to Beijing, I stopped by Shijiazhuang to visit Shumin and her family. Her father pulled me aside.

"Shumin is still young," he said. "You should protect her. Don't let your love affair jeopardize her studies."

After my visit with her parents, I took Shumin home. She stayed at my sister's place for several days. My father liked her very much, and found her considerate, diligent, and sweet. She acted as if she had become a family member. She called my mother "mom," and my father "dad." She put broad smiles on my mother's face. She shared a room with my sister. They got along well. Shumin was quite good-natured. She loved to sing and also played the violin. My sister adored her.

I have to mention a small distraction around that time. In 1956, the National Basketball Championship Games were held in Wuhan. I was promoted to coach the Gansu Province's men and women's basketball teams. All the players were amateurs chosen from the various government agencies and state-owned enterprises. We trained for a month before the games began. The men's team won a bronze medal, the highest placement ever for Gansu Province. It was quite an honor. During this period, a member of the women's basketball team developed a crush on me. She flirted with me constantly. On our train ride back from the championship games, she was bringing me tea one minute and slicing apples for me the next. All the players were picking up on it.

Back in Lanzhou, she invited me out every weekend. On Sundays, we hung out in the park. She insisted on paying for everything. She was a graduate of the Shanghai-based Tongji University, and was two years older than I was. She worked as a technician at the Gansu Provincial Construction Industry Bureau, earning a good salary, higher than mine. Her family also lived in Beijing, and before New Year's, she had planned a trip home to see her parents. I bought some local specialties—dried honeydew melons and raisins—and asked her to bring them to my parents. She dropped off the gifts and met my whole family. My father immediately wrote me a letter. My family could tell that she was in love with me. They liked the fact that she had a college degree, a nice job, and a good salary. But they preferred Shumin. My father warned me not to be too fickle and hurt young Shumin's feelings. A couple of days later, I received a long letter from my sister.

"We sense that your relationship with Shumin won't last. As the Chinese saying goes, 'Water from far away can't quench your thirst.' Shumin is still in high school. She has yet to attend college. I don't think you can wait that long. What if she changes her mind? Both your brother-in-law and I believe that the Lanzhou girl is the more suitable and practical choice."

To be honest, I liked Shumin much better. I was a young guy, and I liked pretty girls. The Lanzhou girl was taller and had nicer skin, but her eyes were too small and she was a little on the plump side. Shumin definitely beat her in the looks department. And my sister wasn't completely off the mark. Shumin still had to attend college for four years—not four months. If she changed her mind after college, I'd be ruined.

In the end, I let Shumin know about my sister's concern. I meant to tell her that I would wait for her and that I hoped she wouldn't change her mind after college.

She wrote back right away: "I truly love you. Don't doubt me. If you don't believe my sincerity, I'll travel to Lanzhou during the winter holiday and live with you for a month to give you my heart. Even if my parents objected to our union, I wouldn't listen to them."

It didn't happen in Lanzhou—our meeting took place in Beijing. During the Chinese New Year in 1957, I picked up Shumin in Shijiazhuang and then took her by train to Beijing. In Beijing, instead of going home directly, we stayed overnight at a hotel in Guangwumen. I was out of luck. Her period came that week. We slept together but I didn't get to do what people from my generation used to call "tasting the forbidden fruit."

After I came back to Lanzhou, we began to address each other as husband and wife in our weekly letters. We may not have been married at the time, but emotionally we were closer than most married couples. We expressed our feelings and yearned for our future together.

In November 1957, because my father used to serve in the Nationalist government, I was officially declared a Rightist. As a result, I stopped writing to Shumin. If I continued dating her, I would ruin her future.

Initially, I was not on the list for Jiabiangou, since I wasn't considered an extreme Rightist. But I was forbidden from serving as a coach and a referee. My new job was to sweep the basketball court before a game, heat up the boiler, and bring thermos bottles to the players. It was hard to swallow my pride. In the old days, the players respectfully addressed me as "Coach Li." Now, when they bumped into me in the boiler room, they'd say things like, "Li Xiangnian, go heat up the water for us. We need to do our laundry. Why is the water so cold? How do you expect us to take a shower?"

I got so upset about the way I was treated that I simply quit and refused to go back. My boss followed me to the dorm and lectured me. During the day, I would hang out at a teahouse and watch performances there.

One day in June 1958, an official at the Sports Committee announced at an all-staff meeting that I had been officially expelled from work for harboring a nasty attitude toward my coworkers and the Communist leadership. I would be sent to Jiabiangou for reeducation. On that day, a policeman was present. They had planned to take me away immediately after the announcement. I protested their decision and reacted strongly in front of the staff.

"I refuse to go to Jiabiangou," I said. "The Party has explicit policies in place to handle Rightists. Anyone who has been removed from his job should be allowed to seek employment on his own. If you force me to receive reeducation at Jiabiangou, it would be in violation of Party policy. It would mean you oppose the Party and the Party Central Committee, and I would take my case to the provincial government."

The leadership at the Sports Committee had never encountered such a situation before. Even the policeman who had been summoned to escort me out had never seen anything like it. They were speechless. After a minute, the director regained his composure and said, "The meeting is adjourned. Let's give Li Xiangnian some time to think about his mistakes. We will handle this tomorrow."

There was no way I would wait until tomorrow. I figured the leaders would probably call their boss at the provincial government after the meeting, and an order would go out to take me to Jiabiangou by force. If I waited until tomorrow, it would be too late.

As soon as I left the meeting, I headed directly to the train station and bought a ticket. At dusk I snuck back to my dorm and packed up my quilt and clothes. A tricycle cab peddled me to the station, and I boarded a Beijing-bound train.

When I arrived at my sister's house, I said I was home for a short visit. I didn't dare tell her the truth, because my mother was a Communist activist. She served on the neighborhood committee. She was what people normally referred to as the "neighborhood grandma," who would spy on each individual family and report everything she saw to the local police. She had won many accolades for her hard work. My father, a timid and prudent person, idled at home after retirement. He had served in the Nationalist government before the Communist takeover and was in constant fear that disaster could befall him. In 1957 I wrote him a letter explaining that the anti-Rightist campaign had reached a fever pitch and that I had been singled out for criticism. "It doesn't matter if they criticize you," he replied. "As long as they haven't officially charged you with being Rightist, you will be okay."

Back in Beijing, I was in a sour mood. Since I had nothing to do, I would go with my father to meet other traditional Beijing opera fans and listen to or sing arias to kill time.

A month after I came home, the Lanzhou Municipal Sports Committee delivered a letter to the Communist Party branch at my brother-in-law's work unit. Like my father, my brother-in-law was a timid, cautious man. He had grown up in a successful capitalist family, attended the prestigious Furen University, and had studied in Russia. The official took my brother-in-law aside.

"You are a politically progressive person. How could you let your family harbor a lazy and idling Rightist in your own home?"

When my brother-in-law insisted that he was completely in the dark about my political status, the official urged him to send me away so I could receive reeducation. When he got home that night, my brother-in-law broke the news to the family. My father was so upset that he skipped dinner. My mother and sister looked at me in disbelief. At bedtime that night, they persuaded me to return to Lanzhou. My mother even offered to buy me a train ticket. I didn't give them a definite answer. I knew that if I didn't leave, I would cause trouble for my family. But I didn't want to go back to Lanzhou.

I stayed at my sister's home for a few more days. My mother and sister stopped pressuring me, but the neighborhood police came looking for me. It was around noon and I was taking a nap. I heard my mother's voice.

"Xiangnian, get up. The police want to talk with you."

I woke up and almost screamed with fear, as if I had seen a ghost. The policeman asked why I had tried to escape. He said the practice of reeducation through physical labor was sanctioned by law. Once the convictions were approved, the order would go out for my removal by force.

"You need to go back and reform your thinking," he told me.

As soon as the police left, my mother started nagging. "You need to go back. You can't disobey government orders."

The next day, she gave me some money and accompanied me to the Guanzhuang Long-Distance Bus Station. In the waiting room, I pleaded with my mother.

"Ma, I really don't want to go. People always go hungry at the labor camps. They eat corn gruel all day. A reeducation camp is worse than a prison."

My mother didn't believe me.

"Our Communist Party follows humane principles, and it will help you to change your thinking. Surely you can't really believe that they would starve you."

I told her that many Rightists in Lanzhou had been sent to Jiabiangou in 1957. When relatives went for visits, they heard stories of starvation. But my mother was not persuaded.

"What choice do you have?" she said. "Whatever you do,

you can't deviate from the Party. If you do a good job reeducating yourself at the camp, the Party will take care of you."

The bus was approaching. I recited a line from a Chinese poem: "Once a heroic man goes, he never returns." Hearing that, my mother dropped to her knees, grabbed one of my legs and sobbed, "Son, don't say that. You need to trust the Party."

I did return home, but it took me twenty years. By then, my mother had died. For many years, our farewell scene at the bus station was etched in my memory. I was her only son, and she kicked me out of her house, sending me away to a labor camp to endure a subhuman existence.

But on that particular day, I didn't listen to my mother. I got off the bus at Tianjin. Many of my relatives still lived there, but I didn't contact any of them. I figured that if my own mother and sister didn't want to keep me, there was no way my relatives would. I briefly stayed with an old classmate, whose name was Zhang Jintao. He taught at a high school there. With the help of his cousin, I got a temporary job at the Xinhua Paper Manufacturing Company, which paid me 1.8 yuan (30¢) a day.

Two months later, I was in trouble again. I ran into my uncle walking on the street. He asked how I had ended up in Tianjin. I lied to him, saying that I had just been transferred back and was staying with a friend temporarily. He invited me to move in with him. I politely declined. When my uncle got home, he wrote a letter to my father in which he told him about our encounter and complained about my refusal to stay at his house. My sister read the letter and reported my whereabouts to the Party secretary in her work unit. The Party secretary in turn notified the police in Tianjin. A few days later, several officers came to my factory and ordered me to go back with them to the police station. I followed them and was immediately locked up at a detention center. Within a week, my employer sent a rifle coach to escort me back to Lanzhou. Upon arrival there, I was led to the administration complex. I went into the bathroom, where I jumped through the window and escaped. As I was running down a mountain path on Yuquan Mountain, the coach started shooting and several bullets hit the ground near me. I was so scared that my legs gave out, and the police swooped in on me. The next day, they put me on a truck to Jiabiangou.

After I had stopped writing to Shumin, I thought that I could end our relationship. I was wrong. In the cold, sleepless nights at Jiabiangou, my longing for her became ever stronger, as I thought for hours about her charming face and her supple body. I began to miss her to the point where I couldn't control myself. I wanted to escape and see her regardless of the risk. If I could only see her, I wouldn't mind if they sentenced me to death. I wanted to tell her the truth about my incarceration. I wanted to find out whether she was still in love with me. If she said yes, I would return to the camp and serve out my sentence. If she said no, I would go wander the streets.

Two weeks before 1959 gave way to 1960, the camp authorities picked several Rightists with performing talents to prepare for a celebration party, just as they had done a year earlier. Following months of hunger and physical exertion, we had all become emaciated. Nobody had the energy to create new performances for the party. We simply rehashed what we had done the previous year. Many of us accepted the acting assignment only because it got us an extra midnight snack and allowed us to avoid doing hard labor in the fields.

One night, a week before the Chinese New Year, I escaped. Around midnight, after rehearsal, everyone returned to their bunkhouse. I lay down on my bed without taking off my clothes and pretended to sleep. After an hour, I rose quietly, stuffed a suitcase inside my quilt, and put an old cotton-padded hat on my pillow. I covered half of the hat with my quilt. If the guard came in to check on everyone, he wouldn't be able to tell I had left unless he pulled down the quilt.

I put on a hat and a heavy blue coat, and carefully bundled up a metal water bottle and a couple of dried buns. I hid them inside my jacket. Then I put on another long blue winter coat, as if I were just going to the outhouse. I walked into the outhouse, climbed over a short courtyard wall, and then landed outside the compound.

I passed an old steel mill on the northwest corner of the camp, turned south from there and came to the Clear River. Since it was in the depths of winter, the river was covered with a thick layer of ice. I treaded carefully and crossed the river, ending up on the road to Jiuquan.

I had to be careful on the road. Once I got a few miles from Jiabiangou, I turned away from the road and waded through a wide stretch of grassland covered by knee-high shrubs. I tried to stay as close to the road as possible so I wouldn't get lost, but at the same time I had to run as quickly as I could. When the camp authorities realized the next morning that I had escaped, their officials would come after me on horseback.

At around ten in the morning, I finally reached Jiuquan and entered the downtown section. I checked myself into a small hotel with an identity card that I had stolen from a Rightist who used to work at the Lanzhou Petroleum Refinery Factory. I figured the guards from Jiabiangou must have found out about my escape by then. But I doubted they'd suspect I had the guts to check into a hotel.

I shut my door and stayed inside for the rest of the day. The next morning, I ventured out and found the Qiuquan train station. I hid behind a boulder opposite the platform.

At about nine in the morning, a train from Hami pulled into the station. I crawled under the train, and on the other side I merged into a throng of boarding passengers. It was right before the New Year and the train was packed solid. I sat on the floor in the middle of a car and dozed off with my head down. Nobody checked tickets. About twenty hours later, I arrived in Lanzhou. I got off and didn't leave the train station. I was terrified that the police were waiting for me at the entrance. I strolled down the platform and climbed into a train sitting idle on an auxiliary line. In the afternoon, I got out and managed to board a Beijing-bound train. Again, since the train was so crowded, nobody checked tickets. I really lucked out. I crawled under a seat and slept on the floor for forty hours, until the train passed Shijiazhuang.

Everything in Shijiazhuang seemed familiar from my internship and my visits with Shumin. I left the train station and immediately took a bus. I got off on a street near Shumin's home and found a hotel. I cleaned myself at a public bathhouse nearby and got a haircut. I also bought two live chickens at a market. Since I looked ill, I waited until the evening and headed toward Shumin's home, the two chickens a gift for her parents.

As I approached her family's courtyard house, it so happened that I bumped right into Shumin and her sister, who were about to go for a bike ride. She almost screamed with surprise.

"Is that you, Xiangnian?"

She was shocked, but her voice was filled with warmth. I began to feel embarrassed and acted awkwardly. I hadn't written her a single letter since the end of 1957. Many of her letters to me remained unanswered. I'm sure she thought my feelings had changed toward her. I really didn't know what to say. My heart began to tighten and my body turned cold. I stuttered and mumbled a simple greeting.

"Where are you going?" I asked her.

"We are going to visit a teacher," said her sister.

I pretended to be indifferent. "That's fine, go ahead. I'm just here to visit your parents."

"We don't have to leave now," said Shumin. "Let's go inside."

It had been three years since I last visited her parents' house. I didn't know what to expect. I was afraid her family would give me the cold shoulder. So I followed Shumin sheepishly to her parents' living room. To my surprise, they treated me warmly. Her father, who was a doctor, spoke in a measured tone and looked unusually calm, while the rest of the family were excited and demonstrative. Shumin's mother asked whether I had eaten and urged her elder daughter to go prepare some food for me.

"You look terrible," she told me. "Your face is dark and thin. Didn't you have enough food in Lanzhou?"

Of course I looked terrible. Years of sweating outside under the hot sun, in the dry northwest air, would do that to anyone. As Shumin went to the kitchen to prepare tea, her brother stayed at to my side, asking questions.

The warm atmosphere didn't last. Then as if on cue, everyone stopped talking at the same time. An awkward silence fell in the room, and I began to feel uneasy. I knew exactly what was going through their minds after the initial surprise had dissipated: why did this person suddenly pop up again?

My heart ached. For this family, I was no longer the person they had known three years before. I glanced at Shumin's teenage brother, who used to follow me around and call me "brother-in-law." I taught him how to play soccer and slept in his room during my visits. Now he moved away and was standing quietly by the door, examining me. Shumin was not her usual self either. She poured the tea and then retreated to a corner, sitting on a wooden bench without saying anything.

She would stare at me, but whenever I looked over to her, she'd lower her eyes and play with a button on her shirt.

Her chest was nicely developed and she was wearing a Beijing University badge. My heart sank further. While I had become an imprisoned criminal, she was a student at a prestigious university. I was no longer a match for her. I didn't belong in her family. I needed to leave. I stood up.

"Uncle and Aunt, it was great seeing you all," I said. "But I have to go now."

I bid farewell; Shumin didn't stop me. Only her mother asked whether I had a place to stay. When I said I was staying at a hotel, she didn't inquire further.

But as Shumin walked me out to the entrance, she said, "Come again tomorrow morning, at eight."

I didn't answer. I thought, Was there really any need for me to come back?

"Go back in," I said. Then I turned around and walked away.

I heard footsteps behind me. It was Shumin's little brother.

"Brother-in-law," he said, "if you want, you can still stay in my room."

I had to make up a lie.

"I can't stay with you tonight. My friend is waiting for me at the hotel. I have to see him to the train station tomorrow morning. I'll come back tomorrow morning."

After I returned to my hotel room, I tossed and turned all night long. When I woke, I felt like I was in a trance. I couldn't help myself, and I headed toward Shumin's house.

It had been hard to leave her. I wanted to tell her the truth, and to ask her one more time if she was willing to be in a relationship with a common prisoner. That's why I had come to visit her, after all. I had to bare my heart and tell her how much I loved her. Even if she decided that she didn't want to be my wife, I would get to see her one last time, look at her beautiful face, her slim body, and her smile. I wanted to listen one more time to her sweet and passionate voice.

As I passed the market, I saw her mother and her sister at a vegetable stand. It looked like her mother was planning to treat me to a nice meal. It occurred to me that she really didn't need to buy the groceries herself. Shumin's twenty-two-year-old sister could have handled the shopping by herself. I realized they were using the early morning shopping trip as an excuse to give Shumin and me some privacy.

As I got to her house, I lost all my courage, and began to hesitate. After all, I was a Rightist and a prisoner at large. I had no future. What did I have to offer her? Shumin was a university student, a future middle-school or university teacher. If she loved me and promised to wait, I would only ruin her career, and her life.

I stood outside the entrance for a few minutes, praying silently for her future happiness. I hoped she would find a wonderful husband. Then I turned around and left.

I got on a train and arrived in Beijing on the same afternoon.

I had escaped Jiabiangou with the sole intention of seeing my girlfriend. Now everything had changed—my future and my love had gone down the drain. What was I going to do? There was no need to return to Jiabiangou and serve out my sentence. I no longer had any obligation to the person I loved. I had just turned twenty-eight. Even though my health had suffered at Jiabiangou, I was still energetic and full of vitality. I believed I could live on the street. As long as I could stay free, I could put up with any hardship and survive.

Like many escaped prisoners, I thought first of going home, to seek protection and assistance from my parents. I was exhausted and desperately needed a clean bed and a nice home-cooked meal. After I left the Beijing train station, I decided I'd visit my family one more time before embarking on my life as a street person.

I waited until after dusk and then took the last bus to Guanzhuang, which was located in Tong County, about ten kilometers from Beijing. My sister and brother-in-law had moved into a residential complex for government officials. I got as far as the door to my sister's apartment, but I didn't have the guts to knock. Based on my prior experience, I was afraid that she and her husband wouldn't let me stay once they heard I had escaped from Jiabiangou. If they called the police on me, and I got sent back again, my sentence would be even worse than before.

I lingered in the neighborhood all night without knocking on the door. At dawn, I got on the first bus downtown. Any trace of familial love died in me that night.

I got off the bus downtown and tried to figure out what to do next. When I left Jiabiangou, I took seventy yuan ($10) with me, and now I was out of money. Without a Beijing residential permit or any connections, it was impossible for me to get a temporary job. I wandered the streets for four days. In the evenings, I would go to the train station and find a seat inside the waiting room. Since it was a peak time for traveling, the waiting room was packed with passengers. My presence there didn't arouse any suspicions from the police. As my money dwindled to three yuan, I got increasingly nervous. If I didn't find something fast, I would go hungry. I toyed with all sorts of ideas. I thought of joining those beggars at the train station, but I just couldn't get myself to do it. It was too humiliating. In the end, I decided to steal.

I used the rest of my money to buy a flashlight and a pair of pliers. I hid the pliers under my belt. That night, I broke into the Beijing Municipal Teachers Training Academy. I had scoped out the location during the day. The students had left for the winter holidays. The campus was empty and the guard's office near the entrance was locked.

I walked in around midnight. For some reason, the gate had been left wide open and no one was around. After entering the campus, I walked west, looking for a potential target. I had already prepared myself for possible questioning if I ran into anyone. I was going to pretend to be from out of town and say that I came in to look for a friend. Since I was wearing a nice blue winter coat on top of a neat Mao jacket, I didn't look at all like a burglar.

I finally stopped in front of a row of houses. There was a sign on the door of one house—OFFICE OF MEAL TICKET SALES. In those days, school cafeterias didn't accept cash. Students and teachers had to purchase special meal tickets. There was a padlock on the door. I pulled out my pliers and clamped down on the lock with all my strength. It snapped open. I entered and latched the door from the inside. There were four tables and a desk in the room. I hunched over the desk. There was a small lock on the drawers, and I pried it open easily. Inside the first drawer, I found over one hundred yuan ($14) in cash and thirty-five kilograms' worth of government-issued grain coupons. The second one contained a stack of stationery with a letterhead. I tore off five pages and put them in my coat pocket. They could be useful later. If you wanted to stay in a hotel in Beijing, you needed to present a letter of approval written on official letterhead.

With the money and the grain coupons, I treated myself to a nice restaurant meal. I bought a bag of cakes from a grocery store so I could snack whenever I felt like it. That put me in a good mood. I was tempted to write out a fake recommendation letter on the letterhead and check into a hotel, but I didn't dare, and continued to sleep inside the train station at night. During the day, I began showering at a public bathhouse, and napping for a few hours on a comfortable couch there.

I lived like this for about a month, until I ran out of money and had to commit another burglary. I found an opportunity in an office building next to the zoo. I didn't know the name of the place. All I could tell was that the building was part of a military office. I broke in at night and snatched a thick stack of grain coupons, and a hundred yuan. I also took some coupons for cooking oil, which I mailed to my sister.

I planned to leave Beijing after this. After all, I had been on the street for more than a month now, and I was afraid that the local police would notice me. I was especially nervous about carrying the big stack of grain coupons I had stolen. They could probably be traded for four hundred kilograms of food.

Before my departure, I wanted to clean out my bag and count what money and grain coupons I had. I went to a public toilet in the train station, and had begun to count, when I heard a noise. I raised my head and saw that an old man in the adjacent stall was peeping over at me. I immediately put the coupons back into my bag, pulled up my pants, and walked out. I checked myself into a public bathhouse to shower and nap. After I woke up, I went back to the train station and bought a train ticket. As I turned away from the ticket window, two plainclothes policemen stood in my way.

"Comrade," they said, "we are with the Public Security Bureau. You are suspected of a crime. Please come with us to the station."

Policemen in Beijing were really polite and courteous. They even said, "If our investigation shows that you're inno-cent, we'll give you an official apology for our mistakes."

The old man in the toilet stall had called the police on me.

They had followed me to the public bathhouse. There were no lockers there, like we have today. Customers simply left their personal belongings on a bed. The police checked my bag and found the stack of grain coupons and the pages of letterhead. They wanted to wait and see what I was going to do next, so when I bought my train ticket, they nabbed me.

I was locked in a detention center, and the next day, a military officer met me in an interrogation room. I learned that the office building that I had broken into belonged to the civilian administrative section of the Defense Ministry.

Three days later, the Public Security Bureau in Lanzhou sent two officers to Beijing. I was tried before the Lanzhou Municipal People's Intermediate Court and sentenced to six years in jail. I didn't go back to Jiabiangou, but was sent to a prison near Baliyao. In 1961, they transferred me to a suburban reeducation camp for criminals in Dunhuang County.

Despite the fact that I ended up in jail for six years, I never regretted my actions. If I hadn't run away from Jiabiangou, I would have died of starvation. Many of Jiabiangou's three thousand inmates received help from their families. Even so, most of them were dead by the end of 1960. Throughout my incarceration there, my family never wrote me a single letter, let alone sent food or money. How could I have survived? I got lucky.

By 1966, I had served out my jail sentence, but I was not allowed to return home. The local government gave me a job at the Shigong Collective Farm. Over the next four years, I was transferred to four different farms in the region. All in all, I had worked at various reeducation camps and collective farms for eighteen years.

How did I make it out alive? The first six years behind bars were miserable. We worked under the watchful eyes of gun-toting public security officers. They treated us like animals. In the early morning, we were herded out into the fields. In the evening, the iron gate clanged shut behind us. Everything else took place inside a crowded cell—eating, shitting, and sleeping.

I held out hope for a government amnesty, or at least a reduction in my sentence. Neither came, and I lost all hope. I knew I would never be able to see Shumin again, but I wondered whom she had married, and whether she was happy.

After I served out my time and became an employee of the camp, I lived on a salary of twenty-four yuan ($3). I squeezed every penny. For example, I would buy a wash towel, cut it in half, and use only half at a time. I saved money and then spent my savings on tobacco. I was a chain-smoker because I was depressed. Tobacco became the most precious commodity and the number one necessity in life. At lunchtime, we were normally given two steamed buns at the mess hall. I would eat one and exchange the other for a pinch of tobacco. When I ran out of tobacco, I would roll up dried sunflower leaves, wild roadside plant leaves, and even sawdust.

I also learned how to cheat. I told all sort of lies to avoid work: I would go tell the unit leader that the group manager needed me to water crops. Then I would go to the group manager, saying that unit leader had assigned me to help a local village copy Chairman Mao's latest teachings onto a billboard. Since the unit leader and group manager seldom communicated, they never found out about my lies. I would sneak into a village to pick up an odd job, such as painting caskets for extra cash. At all staff meetings, I always volunteered to stand up and speak about how much I supported the Party. In this way, I could have a day off in the dorm, with the excuse that I needed to prepare my speech. When the Cultural Revolution started in

1966, everyone wanted a portrait of Chairman Mao to hang on the walls of their offices or living rooms. I painted many portraits for the camp. Then factories and villages nearby heard about my painting skills and they would hire me to do theirs. When I was out on those painting assignments, people treated me nicely, offering me food and occasionally tobacco. My painting and calligraphical skills saved me.

In those days, the government forbade inmates to return home after reeducation was over. I craved my freedom, so I wrote to my sister. I told her how much I missed home and complained about the miserable quality of life at the farm. Guess what—my sister passed my letter on to the farm's Party secretary, as a way of demonstrating that she had drawn a clear line from her Rightist brother. As a result, I was beaten up by the guards and sent to isolation for two days.

By 1972, I was determined to get out of there. My only option was to find a wife in the rural area nearby and settle in her village. It was a pathetic fantasy. When I was working at the Heqing Camp, there were about fifty single guys, all of whom were college graduates from the 1950s and political exiles like me. We got into terrible fights of jealousy over a disabled woman who lived in a nearby village. All the normal or pretty women were married off to local peasants with good family backgrounds. The women with physical disabilities were snatched up by camp employees.

I began to look seriously for a wife when I was transferred to Beiwan Camp. Locals fixed me up with four different women. The first one was a widow, whose husband had been head of the Tianyuan Commune Tractor Station. When she paid a visit to the camp, one official said to her, "You are a Communist Party member. How could you marry someone who was a convicted Rightist?"

She broke up with me. Next a village elder took pity on me,

and fixed me up with a local woman. On our first date, I found out that she was a hunchback, and only half my height. She needed a stool to stand on when she cooked.

The third woman was a young widow who lived close to my work unit. A friend introduced us, and we went on a date. She said she was willing to marry me. At the age of twenty-eight, she already had five children, and desperately needed a husband to help raise her kids. I closed my eyes and accepted her proposal. I was willing to put up with anything for freedom. I visited her parents, who took a laissez-faire attitude, and said that the decision was totally up to her. Even the camp authorities had put in a good word for me. For a while, it looked like our union would work. But several days before our wedding, something came up. Her brother made his living as a painter, painting doors, furniture, and caskets. I had been doing a lot of similar painting jobs, and had greater skill in it. Her brother was afraid that if I moved into the village, I would take his business. So he strongly opposed our marriage and made a big scene at their family's house. Not long after that, we broke up.

I ended up marrying the fourth woman I had met. Her name is Wei Wanhua. At that time, she had just turned thirty, and had three children—two daughters and a son. Her husband had been killed in a landslide. I was an old bachelor with political baggage and she was a widow with kids. It was a good match. Our wedding took place inside Beiwan Camp, in a bunkhouse I shared with two coworkers. They moved out to make room for us. My supervisor even granted me a week off for my honeymoon. After the marriage, I immediately submitted a report requesting permission to leave and take care of my family. In 1976 I was registered as a peasant at Pingpu People's Commune and became a free citizen.

On the occasion of my wedding, I didn't have any money to buy a gift for the bride. So I wrote to my sister, asking if she could send me some money and a piece of corduroy so the bride could make a jacket out of it. My sister bought the corduroy and gave me fifty yuan. She wrote me a note saying, "We are happy to know that you are getting married. The countryside will be good for you and we hope you have a bright future there. I have sent you some cash. This will be the only gift you will get from me."

She enclosed a second note from my mother: "We can tell that you have changed and reformed. Keep up with the good work."

In the Pingpu People's Commune, I was treated as a second-class citizen. Our commune was poor and the grain yield was pitiful. The village chief didn't even allow me to work in the field, since he didn't want one more person to share the limited food supply. This actually worked to my advantage. I took out a small loan from the commune and purchased brushes and several cans of paint. I traveled from village to village, painting furniture and caskets. The villagers loved my work and offered me food as payment. The bartering enabled me to support my whole family.

At the end of 1978, when Deng Xiaoping took over the Communist leadership, the government reversed its verdict against me. I was assigned a job at the Jingyuan County Sports Committee.

When I heard the good news, the first thing I did was to write a letter to Yu Shumin. Then I went to Beijing to visit my family. My mother had died six months before. When my father broke the news to me, I shed a couple of tears, but I really didn't miss her that much. I had severed my blood ties with her a long time ago. After listening to my stories from the past twenty years, my father burst into tears.

Then I confronted my sister.

"Why did you turn your back on me? What crime did I

commit? How could you be so cruel and devoid of any human feelings?"

She told me she was a believer in the power of thought reform. She believed that the labor camp was a humane place and that I wasn't being mistreated.

I stayed at home for a month. One day, my father asked me about Shumin. His questions triggered my feelings of loss. I was desperate to know what had happened to her and whether she had received my letter.

I returned to Jingyuan County and started my new job at the sports committee. One day, I saw a letter on my desk. It was from Shumin.

Her parents had passed on my letter to her during the New Year's family reunion. After reading my letter, she started crying.

I had written my letter in question-and-answer format, recounting my life over the past two decades as well as my love for her during that period:

QUESTION: I stopped writing to you in the spring of 1958. Do you know why?

ANSWER: Once I was branded a Rightist, I knew that I would no longer be a good match for you. I made the painful choice to let you go. I wanted you to find someone who could make you happy.

QUESTION: Why did I show up unexpectedly at your house in the winter of 1960?

ANSWER: I missed you so much that I escaped from the labor camp to see you.

QUESTION: Why didn't I keep my promise and see you the next morning?

ANSWER: I came to your house but I changed my mind as I stood in front of your door. If I had walked in, I would have lied about my situation because I didn't dare tell the truth. If I continued to conceal my political situation, I would have ruined your future by pulling you into a bigger lie.

At the end of the letter, I wrote, "Dear Shumin, I paid a large price for escaping the labor camp to see you. I was arrested and thrown in jail for six years, after which I was transferred multiple times between labor camps. It wasn't until today that the government overturned its verdict against me."

In her letter back to me, Shumin wrote, "You shouldn't have hidden the truth from me. Even if your status as a Rightist prevented us from forming a family, I would have at least helped you by sending money. I didn't know about your suffering and I didn't realize that you've been in love with me for the past two decades. I thought you dumped me for that female basketball player you met on the train. I will repay you for all your past sufferings."

She kept her promise. One month later, during winter break, Shumin, who was then a professor at Tianjin Teachers University, sent me a telegram asking me to meet her at the Baiyin train station on Wednesday evening. I showed up at the station and saw her.

It had been nineteen years since we parted in Shijiazhuang. She was forty now, but she didn't look her age at all. She was as charming and pretty as ever. She had gained some weight and had lost her figure, but there was an elegance and maturity about her that still made my heart beat fast. For nineteen years, I had moved around the barren desert of the wild northwest and had never seen such a beautiful woman. To tell the truth, I felt embarrassed. I hardly resembled my former self. Even though I was considered a midlevel county official, I wore a faded blue Mao jacket and a black peasant coat, and I was quite pale.

She spoke first.

"Don't look at me like that. Let's find a hotel nearby."

Actually, I had already booked a room at a guesthouse near the train station. After we got to our room, I gradually overcame my initial uneasiness. We shared our past and cried together. It went on like that for half a day. Then she wiped her tears and said, in a hoarse voice, "Let's stop crying. That's not why I came here."

We went to a grocery store where she purchased loaves of bread and several dozen bottles of beverages. I was puzzled.

"Why do you want to horde so much food?" I asked. "Are you suffering from starvation phobia, like we prisoners do?"

She simply laughed and piled the food in my arms. After we hauled the groceries back to the hotel, she shut the door, put on the DO NOT DISTURB sign, and said, "We aren't leaving this room for three days!"

And that's what happened. We stayed in bed for three days and three nights, like a pair of young lovers. We made love, cuddled, and sweet-talked each other, resolving an affair that had been unconsummated for nearly twenty years. In those three days we forgot our regret and our sadness. Everything disappeared, the earth, the heavens, the universe—all that existed were two pounding hearts.

Three days later, we traveled to Lanzhou together. We checked in as husband and wife at a hotel there and continued to enjoy the bliss of our togetherness. Ten days later, she returned to Tianjin.

That was our first meeting. The following summer—the summer of 1980—she invited me to come to Tianjin for a monthlong visit. I had many relatives there, but she didn't want me to stay with them. She booked a hotel room for me near her university and visited me every day. Her husband, who was a senior city official, was home for the first ten days, but then he went on a business trip to Yunnan Province. Since her son was on summer break, he joined his father on the trip. When they left, Shumin invited me to her home. For two short weeks, we lived like husband and wife. She showered me with a love and tenderness beyond what a wife could give.

"Shumin," I told her often, "if I were to die tomorrow, I'd be happy. The happiness you've given me is greater than all the suffering I have endured."

After her husband and son returned from their trip, I had a chance to get a glimpse of her husband. She took him to eat at a restaurant near my hotel, and arranged for me to eat at a table nearby. During the meal, I saw that Shumin's husband treated her nicely. He kept putting food on her plate. I thought to myself, What a nice couple. I shouldn't see her anymore. Our affair should come to an end.

In the following years, she twice visited me in Lanzhou, telling her family she had to attend an academic conference there.

This year, Shumin will be sixty-two. She has retired. I'm almost seventy and my hair has turned completely gray. I miss her every day.

I Hate the Moon

In the fall of 2003 I found Xi Zongxiang, a Jiabiangou survivor, who lived on the top floor of an old apartment building on Lanzhou's Dongchengxiang Street. He had very short gray hair, and his face looked healthy and robust. He told me he was sixty-seven, but he didn't look his age at all. He had the build of a professional athlete.

When I told him I wanted to interview him about his life at Jiabiangou, he appeared shocked and somewhat nervous. As he led me into his living room, he scratched the back of his head, like an awkward teenager. "How did you know about my connection with Jiabiangou?" he asked me. "How did you find me?"

I pulled a letter out of my bag. He grabbed it and sat down on an old couch. As he skimmed the first couple of lines, a smile began to appear on his face. "Ah, my buddy Yu Zhaoyuan sent you."

I had interviewed Yu Zhaoyuan when I was in Jinta County three years earlier. Yu explained that he and Xi were close friends at Jiabiangou. He asked me to look up Xi if I traveled to Lanzhou. "Yu told me you are a very open and candid person," I said. "He said you wouldn't dodge my questions."

You want to know how I ended up at Jiabiangou? Well, we have to go back to my school years. In 1951, I was a freshman at the senior high school attached to the Lanzhou Teachers University. It was the best school in the entire Gansu Province. It still is, and it has the highest college admission rate. That was why I chose to go there—I wanted to get into a prestigious university.

Then something happened in October 1951 that changed my life forever.

In those days, the facilities at my high school were not particularly impressive, despite its excellent reputation. The desks were old, dented, and scratched up. I often covered mine with a piece of newspaper. One morning, I tore a page from a newspaper and replaced the old one on my desk. I saw a big portrait of Chairman Mao in the paper. Mao's portraits were everywhere in those days, so we usually just took them for granted and never bothered to take a closer look. But on that particular day, I had the chance to examine Chairman Mao's portrait up close. I suddenly realized how elegant and feminine his face appeared. It wasn't at all imposing. I didn't know why I felt that way. I guess I compared Mao's face with that of Stalin. During the 1950s, portraits of world-famous Communist leaders hung side by side in most classrooms: Karl Marx, Friedrich Engels, Vladimir Lenin, Joseph Stalin, and Mao. Stalin, with his thick moustache, wore his marshal's uniform. He looked tough with that moustache. So I picked up a pen and carefully added a shaggy moustache to Mao's face. I wanted him to look like Stalin.

I was proud of my artistic creation. With that added hair on his lip, Mao looked masculine and majestic. In my next period, I had basketball practice. Since I was tall and athletic, I played on the school team. In the middle of a game, a friend came over and pulled me off the court. He said my teacher wanted to see me in his office right away.

I didn't think too much of it at first, because it was quite common for my head teacher to summon me to his office. I chaired the students' sports committee and he constantly brainstormed with me on how to encourage the whole class to engage more actively in athletics. But when I entered his office, my teacher looked quite grim. He said one of my classmates had showed him the doctored picture of Chairman Mao's face. I admitted that it was my doing and explained my reasoning. Before I could finish, he shouted, "It's a serious political issue. You're insulting our great leader Chairman Mao!"

I didn't agree with him, and I defended myself by citing a similar incident that had happened the previous summer.

"Do you remember when an administrator dumped a stack of old alumni pictures into a trash can?" I asked. "Some students pulled those pictures out, brought them back to the classroom, and drew moustaches on the women's faces and pigtails on the men's heads. You saw what my classmates had done and didn't say those drawings had insulted the alumni."

My teacher was taken aback. "There are some serious problems with the way you see things, kid. I guess you haven't figured it out yet, but you're in deep political trouble. I want you to go home tonight and give it some serious thought. Write a self-criticism and turn it in tomorrow morning."

To tell you the truth, I wasn't that politically sensitive. Most of my classmates were just like me. It was only two years after the 1949 Communist revolution. Communist ideas hadn't taken root in my mind. Joining the Communist Youth League or the Communist Party or pledging to devote your life to Communism hadn't yet become popular. Only a few of my classmates had expressed interest, and they were constantly being teased by their peers for harboring political ambitions. There was a popular belief among the students that mastering math, physics, and chemistry would entitle you to a good job anywhere in the world. We were pragmatic and naïve at the same time.

That night I stayed up late and wrote a carefully worded self-criticism. In those days, "Long live Chairman Mao" had already become a daily slogan in our country. Worried that my teacher might escalate the incident into a more serious political issue and accuse me of being anti–Chairman Mao and anti–Communist Party, I wrote, "It was disrespectful to draw a moustache on Chairman Mao's picture. What I did was an insult against Chairman Mao."

The next day, the teacher called the whole class together to hear my self-criticism. The school's headmaster was also invited to the meeting. After I finished my speech, several political activists in my class stood up one by one and denounced my action. They even shouted slogans like "Down with Xi Zongxiang's reactionary act."

Fortunately, they didn't say "Down with Xi Zongxiang," because the political climate was still relatively mild then— nothing compared to the tension in 1957. The policies hadn't become radical yet. They didn't categorize me as a class enemy.

I wrote up four or five additional self-critiques and apologized at several group criticism meetings. Then the whole incident was laid to rest. But I still felt a deep sense of shame, and it just seemed too awkward for me to continue with my studies at the school. During the winter holiday, I submitted my resignation and dropped out.

My family lived near Shuimo Valley, not far from the A-Gan Township coal mine. We had lived there for two generations. My grandfather started a pottery business when he was young. In the summertime, he would mix the clay and mold it into different types of small vessels. He would buy some cheap coal from the coal mine and fire the pottery in a small kiln. When winter came, he would sell them to local peasants or street vendors—thirty cents for a single vessel, and seventy cents for a set of three. My father and his brother inherited the business. During busy times, our whole family pitched in. But I really didn't care too much about the pottery business. After attending school for ten years, who would want to spend his time playing with clay?

I stayed home for six months, helping with the family business. Then I left and got a job with a construction company. It was a managerial position. I had to roam around several construction sites, handling all sorts of trivial business all day long, without any breaks. I wasn't too thrilled about it, but there was no other opportunity available, and it was better than staying at home.

In January 1954, China launched a top-down political campaign to ferret out what the Party called "counterrevolutionary elements." The construction company organized a winter political study program. All employees were asked to examine their activities before the Communist revolution. Since I was only a kid in prerevolutionary days, I didn't feel that the campaign had anything to do with me. At meetings, I simply sat there, saying nothing. But the Party secretary singled me out without mentioning my name. "Someone at our company made some serious political mistakes in the past," he said, "but refuses to confess."

I knew he was talking about me. I was mad as hell. All I did was draw a moustache on Chairman Mao's portrait. They just wouldn't let it go. The next day, I skipped the meeting. Then I asked for a leave of absence, with the excuse that I needed extra time to prepare for my national college entrance examination.

The college exam was a total lie. I didn't even finish high school. How could I expect to pass the college entrance exam? So I went home again. At the end of 1955, the government began to implement a nationwide collectivization program. My family's pottery shop merged with six other small pottery businesses in the area and formed a government-run firm, called the Shuimo Valley Pottery Cooperative. Initially, the company couldn't find any educated staff to do bookkeeping, because all the craftsmen were illiterate. An official showed up at my house and asked if I was willing to become the company accountant. I had just gotten married then, and needed a job badly. When my family owned the business, my parents supported me. But when we lost our businesses in the collectivization movement, my father became a regular employee and earned a meager salary. Life became really hard. It didn't take much to convince me to accept the job. The salary was quite good—sixty yuan ($8.80) a month.

Two months after I started at the pottery cooperative, the government transferred me to a newly formed vocational school run by the Municipal Light Industry Bureau. Since qualified teachers were hard to come by, I was assigned to teach full-time there. We held our classes in the evenings. In the daytime, I would travel with several top municipal government officials and help them with speeches or other publicity materials. It was quite a demanding job, but they reduced my salary by half. I expressed my dissatisfaction to my boss. He said, "You are now a government official, not a pottery worker. Your political status has improved. What does it matter if you earn less?" I didn't buy his argument. With my small salary, I couldn't even support my family.

Before the revolution, a teacher earned two or three times more than a policeman. Under Communism, a teacher's salary was less than half of that of a policeman. I requested a transfer back to the pottery cooperative; my request was rejected.

Two years later, the Hundred Flowers campaign started. Again, I chose to remain silent. Drawing the moustache on Chairman Mao's portrait had already ruined my chances of attending college. I just didn't have the guts to criticize the Party anymore. Around that time, our school was jointly run by the Qilihe District government and the Municipal Light Industry Bureau. The two agencies constantly held joint public meetings. One afternoon, as people slowly filed into the meeting room, the director of the Municipal Light Industry Bureau got irritated; he told everyone to sit down and be quiet so he could start the meeting. Most of the attendees ignored him and kept chatting. I was sitting in a corner with a fellow teacher, puffing on a cigarette.

For some reason, the director began to pick on me. He said over the microphone, "Xi Zongxiang, could you shut up?" I was incensed and shouted back, "Did you see me talking? Why, of all the people here, are you randomly accusing me?"

I could tell he was mad. The next morning, he dug out the moustache incident in my file and orchestrated public meetings and wrote up big posters to condemn me; some of my coworkers dredged up my earlier complaints regarding my reduced salary. My complaints, they claimed, indicated that I felt nostalgic about the old regime under the Nationalists.

The director accused me of harboring deep hatred against Chairman Mao and the Party. I refused to give in and continued to argue with him and other activists. It only exacerbated the situation.

On April 10, 1957, the campaign committee officially declared that I was a Rightist and would be sent to a labor camp for reeducation.

After the announcement, an official at my school gathered me and three other Rightists in his office to study the reeducation guidelines. Based on the government document, reeducation was considered a severe form of administrative disciplinary action. The official made an effort to reassure us.

"If you change your thinking through hard labor, you'll be able to come back in a couple of months," he said. "You can get your jobs back. If you refuse to go, however, you'll be expelled from your work unit. You will have to find new employment on your own."

I immediately raised my hand. "Why don't you expel me from the school? I'm not going to a labor camp. I will find a way to support myself."

The reeducation guidelines were blatant lies. When I got home, my mother said that an administrator from my school had visited my family that morning. The man asked for my family's residential registration booklet, saying that he needed to update my information. Since my mother couldn't read, she had no idea what was going on. She handed the family registration booklet to the school administrator, who returned it around noon. When my mother showed me the registration booklet, I found out that the Public Security Bureau had canceled my city residential permit. Under the cancellation stamp, he had written: "Transferred to Jiabiangou Reeducation Through Hard Labor Camp."

Without a city residential permit, I wasn't even allowed to stay at my own home, not to mention find a job. The local Public Security Bureau frequently patrolled the neighborhood. If a family had out-of-town guests who intended to stay for more than three days, they had to apply for a temporary permit. Otherwise, the police would come every day to harass them, or take them to a detention center if they refused to obey orders.

On April 20, the campaign committee labeled three more teachers Rightists. Two policemen came and escorted us all the way to Jiabiangou.

That was how I ended up there. When I first arrived, I had a lot of time to think about life. I felt unlucky. Most of the Rightists at Jiabiangou were scholars or senior government officials. As a high school dropout, I wasn't even considered well educated. Nor was I an independent thinker. I had never engaged in any anti-Communist activities before or after the revolution. It was ludicrous that they had locked me up there. The more I thought about it, the more depressed I became.

After attending nightly study sessions and doing lots of inward examination and reflection, I realized that I was to blame. For example, I had never applied for membership in the Communist Youth League. I had made no effort to involve myself in political activities. That was due to my ingrained bourgeois thinking, which had stifled my political awakening to Communist ideas. Besides, I grew up in a nonproletariat family. My parents and grandparents were small-business owners.

After identifying the root causes of my mistakes, I was determined to reform. I wanted to purify my thinking through physical labor. I drafted a lengthy report on my new political awareness and pledged to start a new chapter in life.

Initially, I was assigned to the task of digging an irrigation canal. Our daily quota was to dig ten cubic meters of dirt. I exceeded my quota every day. Then I was transferred to the agricultural team.

We had all sorts of competitions. We competed with each other in the field to see who could plow the most amount of land. The winner would have a tiny red paper Communist flag attached to his name on a chart. One day, I got up at midnight and worked twenty-four hours nonstop. At the end, I couldn't even see straight. I plowed three and a half *mu* (2,334 square meters) and won the top prize. Do you know why I worked so hard? I wanted to be released early.

Since I had won so many prizes, people speculated that the authorities might remove my Rightist label and commute my sentence around National Day, on October 1, 1959.

I waited impatiently. Finally National Day arrived. At the celebration ceremony, only three Rightists—I mean three out of over three thousand—had their verdicts reversed. I wasn't one of them. But even those three guys couldn't go home. They were ordered to stay on as employees.

The three reformed Rightists were paid twenty-four yuan ($3.50) a month and were given slightly better treatment.

In the past year, we had put up with hunger and exhaustion and worked our butts off. My health had already shown signs of deterioration. The hope of getting a reduced sentence had kept me going. Now the so-called reeducation turned out to be life imprisonment. The terrible news hit me hard. I collapsed. In November I couldn't even get out of bed. I didn't even have the strength to walk over to the mess hall for food.

By the spring of 1960, during the sowing season, I was a bag of bones. Our food ration was further reduced, but we had to plant wheat from morning until evening. Many Rightists became too emaciated to work. In the daytime, they simply sat outside in the sun. Every week, two or three people would die.

My friend Yu Zhaoyuan helped me. Yu used to be a human resources director for the Xigu district government in Lanzhou. He was a very smart and resourceful guy. Since he grew up in the countryside, the supervisor frequently asked him to take the lead on various farming tasks, so Yu maintained very good relations with our supervisor and unit leader. He was a very compassionate man. Seeing that my health was deteriorating fast, he went to the unit leader and asked him to put me on the irrigation team, which was responsible for watering the crops. Initially, I declined the offer. At Jiabiangou, water was as expensive as gold. I was worried that if the irrigation canal had leaks and water was wasted, I would be held accountable. Yu allayed my concern by saying: "You don't know how lucky it is to work at the irrigation team. All you need to do is to let the water flow through a small gap into the field and then fill the gap after the job is done. The rest of the time you can just sit in the field and rest. Occasionally, you can dig up carrots or some potatoes from the field and steal wheat or corn to stave off hunger."

Upon his advice, I agreed to the transfer. Yu was right: it was a cushy job. At the same time, I had learned to be more resourceful and skillful at stealing. In the fall of 1959, I stole more than ten kilograms of corn from the field and buried it in the sand dunes. The corn sustained me throughout the winter.

One evening, the director ordered us to work an extra shift to plow the field and plant wheat, because there was a full moon shedding light over the field. We took a break around midnight. I sat on the ground and looked at the bright moon. For some reason, my heart became filled with anger.

"I hate the moon," I said to Yu.

He looked surprised. He was chewing on a handful of pesticide-soaked wheat seeds that he had stolen earlier. After he swallowed the seeds, he asked me, "What did the moon do to make you so mad?"

"Each time we have a full moon, we're ordered to work an extra shift. That damned moon is squeezing every drop of blood from us."

Yu laughed. "If you can figure out how to cover up the moon and stop it from rising, we can all go to bed early."

"I wish I could be the legendary Hou Yi," I said, "so I could shoot down the moon with a powerful bow and a set of arrows."

Yu laughed harder. "You're useless. All you do is whine. Why don't you get yourself a job in the kitchen or in the barbershop? Then you won't have to work the night shift."

I shook my head. "I'm unlucky because I don't know how to suck up to the leadership like you do."

We chatted about all sorts of things that night. Yu told me about a woman who had recently come to visit her husband at Jiabiangou. The woman said criminals at the labor camp on the outskirts of Jiuquan were treated much better than we were. They were given twenty kilograms of grain every month and had regular eight-hour workdays. Since all the detainees at the camp were criminals, they had to be monitored by security guards when they worked outside. The authorities at the camp wanted the criminals to work extra hours in the evening, but the guards objected, so the criminals never worked at night. On rainy days, the guards were reluctant to let the criminals outside because it was more difficult to monitor them in bad weather. As a result, the criminals ended up resting in their bunkhouses. Only a few of them had died of starvation and exhaustion.

Yu shared the story as a piece of gossip, but it got me thinking: if I stayed much longer at Jiabiangou, I would die. There was no doubt about that. Why couldn't I figure out a way to be transferred to the camp in Jiuquan? I remembered a Jiabiangou Rightist who had wounded a guard while attempting to escape during National Day. He was publicly denounced and sentenced to two years in jail. They sent him to the Qiuquan labor camp as punishment.

Over the next few days, I became obsessed with the transfer. The Jiaquan camp might have a bad reputation because only common criminals were locked up there, but it was better than waiting to die at Jiabiangou. Our monthly food ration had been reduced to twelve kilograms of corn and wheat. We also had to work fourteen hours a day. There wasn't a glimmer of hope. A regular criminal could probably be released after he served out his sentence. A Rightist could never go home, even if his verdict was reversed.

The more I thought about it, the more determined I became. I decided to commit an offense that would be just severe enough to get me a one- or two-year jail term.

How could I achieve that goal? Could I beat up a unit leader or a supervisor? Nope. Zhang Yusheng, a former state's attorney in Gansu, once had an argument with the unit leader. He hit the man over the head with a shovel and ran away. The police seized him at the Jiuquan train station. He was sent back to the camp, where he was executed.

What if I broke into the warehouse and stole some grain? That wouldn't be considered a criminal offense. The authorities would probably send me to a "specially monitored" group. Belonging to that group might be even worse. It was solitary confinement. I'd be tied up with heavy rope for days.

I racked my brain, trying to figure out what crime to commit. Then an opportunity landed squarely in my lap.

One evening in early May, I was watering the vegetable garden in front of the camp administration building. A pig broke away from the pen and ran into the garden. The pig burrowed around in the dirt, dug out a turnip with his snout, and munched on it. The first thing that flashed through my mind was—kill the pig. That could make my wish come true. In the previous fall, a guy named Li Zhi had killed a stray rabbit in that very same vegetable field. He was starving, and he roasted and ate the animal. Someone reported him to the camp authorities. The guards tied him up with ropes and paraded him around. The director gave him a demerit. According to the camp regulations, if a Rightist accumulated three demerits, he would be arrested and sent to a camp for criminals. I thought to myself, Killing a rabbit got Li one warning. A pig is three times bigger and much more valuable than a rabbit. Killing the pig could probably get me three demerits. I'd be eligible to be transferred to the criminal camp.

I got excited; my heart beat fast. I approached the pig quietly, a shovel in hand. When I got close, the pig raised its head, stared at me for a moment, and then went back to burrow for more turnips. I raised the shovel and whacked the pig on the back. The blow was so fast and powerful that the pig collapsed on the ground. But it didn't die. The pig started squealing, its front legs pawing at the air. The squealing was loud. It scared the hell out of me. I summoned up my strength and hit it again, two and three times more, until the squealing stopped. The pig lay motionless, surrounded by turnip leaves.

I seemed to be possessed by some demonic spirit. I raised the shovel again and smacked the pig repeatedly until I broke into a sweat. Then I sat down and took a break. Yu and another fellow Rightist, Cao Huaide, hurried to my side. They had heard the pig's squeals. When Cao, a former professor, saw the dead pig, his face turned ashen and his voice quivered.

"You are going to be in big trouble."

I was calm. "Don't be afraid. I killed the pig. I take full responsibility. Get a knife. Let's roast it and have a feast."

Cao was shaking and ranting, "I don't want to touch the meat. You're so reckless. If the authorities get wind of this, all three of us will be in big trouble."

Cao went on and on. But Yu wasn't scared at all. He patted me on the shoulder and said, "Good job. This pig will last us a whole week. Let's drag it to some place behind the sand dunes and skin it. Remember, it's our little secret. None of us should report it to the camp authorities. Otherwise, we'll all be tied up and sent to the 'specially monitored' group."

I was disappointed. I killed the pig so that I could become a criminal, but Yu thought I had killed it because I was desperately hungry. I couldn't share my secret with him, so I ended up sharing the pig with Yu and Cao. We lit a small fire, roasted a big chunk of meat, and split it. We wrapped up the leftovers and hid them in the sand. The next four days, we snuck out every night and roasted a piece of pork. On the fourth day, the leftovers were all rotten. Yu cried over the reeking pork. I cried about the failure of my plan.

After the pig was gone, we resumed our daily struggles with

hunger. More and more people died, and the idea of a transfer came to haunt me again. I had to commit another offense.

I soon had a second chance. One evening, as I was watering a field of wheat, I saw several goats in the field. We raised about two thousand goats at Jiabiangou. They were divided into eight groups, each tended by a Rightist. That evening, I noticed only seven groups pass by. One was still out grazing somewhere. So I held my shovel and waited by the side of the road. I waited and waited. The last flock finally appeared. I dashed forward and hit the head of a goat with my shovel. The goat plumped onto the ground. It died without even making a sound. As it so happened, I knew this goat's herder. He was the former principal of an elementary school attached to Lanzhou University. He was an old, bookish man. He and I had arrived at Jiabiangou around the same time and had been put in the same study group.

The poor old guy was stunned by my sudden violent action, and started screaming, "Are you crazy? Don't you want to live?"

"No," I said, "I'm not crazy. I'm hungry and desperate."

"Even if you're hungry, you can't do this in broad daylight. They're going to kill you."

He was a timid but kindhearted man. He was scared and unable to control his emotions. He began to weep.

"What am I going to do? How am I going to explain this to my boss?"

I grabbed his hand. "Go run back to your unit leader. Tell him to come hunt me down. Tell him I killed a goat. Blame it all on me!"

The old man shuddered with fear. He wiped his tears and slowly led the goats away. I dragged the dead goat to the same place behind the sand dunes, started a small fire, and had a nice meal. After I filled my stomach, I lay down and waited for the guards to show up and arrest me. After a while, I fell into a deep sleep. I woke up at midnight. Nobody had come. I was disappointed, and reluctantly returned to my bunkhouse.

Nothing happened the next day or the day after. Later on, I learned that the former school principal told his unit leader that a goat had strayed and gotten lost. The unit leader sent him and three other Rightists to search the grassland all day.

For a whole week, I snuck behind the sand dunes and gorged on the goat meat. Sometimes, I would go eat the meat during the day. Even so, nobody found out about it. It made me complacent. I had wanted to get arrested, but no matter how badly I behaved, nothing happened to me. Instead I just fattened up on pork and goat meat. As the saying goes, "Heaven favors the bold." It's so true.

I soon gave up my hopes of becoming a criminal. I was prepared to stay at Jiabiangou for a long time. I decided to supplement my food ration by occasional theft. I was hoping to survive another year. By then, with heaven's blessings, the worst would probably be over. Maybe everyone would be allowed to go home. After all, being a Rightist carried less of a stigma than being a criminal.

A few days later, I got called to Director Liang's office. It was right after supper. Director Liang's quarters consisted of two rooms: an office and a bedroom. As I walked in, Liang was holding a unit leader meeting. When he saw me, he adjourned the meeting, but told everyone to stay around for a bit. He wanted them to witness a small ceremony.

Before I had a chance to figure out what Liang was talking about, a uniformed policeman walked out of his bedroom. He pulled a piece of paper from his breast pocket, and read, "Lanzhou Municipal Public Security Bureau Arrest Warrant. Following investigation and review of the evidence, we charge

Xi Zongxiang with the crime of conducting counterrevolutionary activities . . ."

My mind went blank. I didn't even hear what came next. I
kept thinking, All I did was kill a pig and a goat. How am I a
counterrevolutionary? Is it possible they've brought up my
moustache drawing again? I asked what I had done.

A second policeman stepped out of the bedroom and told
me to shut up.

"Lie down," he said. "For your own safety, we are going to
handcuff you. You have to sleep here tonight. You're forbidden
to leave the room."

The next morning, the policemen dragged me to Jiuquan
station and put me on the first train back to Lanzhou. After
my arrival, they locked me up at the Changjia Lane Detention
Center.

When the interrogation started, I discovered that my arrest
had nothing to do with the killings of the pig and the goat. I was
suspected of forming a counterrevolutionary organization with
two friends, Ma Xin and Yao Jiada.

To understand this ridiculous case, I have to take you back
to my pre-Jiabiangou days. Ma and Yao were my former colleagues at the vocational school. Unlike me, both of them were
high school graduates, but they were denied entrance to college because they both had parents who were big business
owners before the Communist revolution. As buddies, we used
to hang out together and shared similar political views. In
1957, all three of us got in trouble. I was sent to Jiabiangou. Yao
was also labeled a Rightist, but he was lucky. He only got a
demotion. Since Ma was cooperative with the authorities, he
didn't get a Rightist label, but he was sent away for three
months to transform his political thinking through physical
labor at a nearby collective farm.

A week before I was sent to Jiabiangou, Yao and Ma came to visit me every day. Since I was going to a faraway place and we didn't know when we would be reunited, we decided to have a picture taken. Ma, who was a talented calligrapher, wrote a poetic line on the photo: "Let our friendship remain evergreen like the forest." A neighbor saw that the three of us constantly gathered at my house. He reported it to the authorities, saying that we were planning to cross the border and escape to a foreign country. When the school sent an official to talk with me, I lost my patience and exploded. I swore at the neighbor and accused him of framing me and my friends.

The official tipped off the Public Security Bureau. The police put us on a blacklist and monitored our mail. They even put Yao and Ma under surveillance.

Of course, we were totally in the dark about all this. After I settled down at Jiabiangou, Yao, Ma, and I constantly wrote letters to one another, swapping tales about our lives. We sometimes complained about the people around us. One time Yao told me he had resigned from the vocational school and become a waiter at a restaurant. He said that he'd rather wait on tables than teach, because many of his former colleagues had mistreated him. He also mentioned that he had befriended a chef, who was smart and friendly. In my response, I wrote to Yao about my friend Yu Zhaoyuan. I said how capable Yu was and how he had managed to avoid starving at the camp.

When the Public Security Bureau read those letters, they reached the conclusion that we were truly a counterrevolutionary organization and that both Yao and I were trying to recruit innocent people to join us.

In April 1960, I was sentenced to five years in jail. Yao and Ma got four and eight years respectively.

Eleven months after I went to jail, the court revisited our case. The judge reversed the earlier verdict, on the grounds that the police lacked sufficient evidence. All three of us were set free.

The day of my release, a local official came to my house and ordered me to attend a study session at the local public security branch. I had to check in every week to report about my activities. In the words of the local official, I needed to "put myself under the supervision of the proletarian dictatorial organization."

For a long time, I couldn't get a job. Then the street committee organized a transportation cooperative. I borrowed money from relatives and purchased a tricycle with a flatbed on the back. I began to make a living by transporting goods. In 1966, when the Cultural Revolution started, my Jiabiangou record resurfaced. I was sent to my ancestral home in Baishi Commune, Gaolan County. I became a peasant.

During my exile, my wife moved in with my parents. My father took over the tricycle job and helped raise my kids. He continued with the tricycle job until he was in his midseventies. In 1979, I was allowed to come back home. I was given a job at the Shuimo Valley Elementary School. I wasn't qualified to teach, so I was put in charge of logistics.

Things are much better now. The fact that you and I can sit down together and speak candidly about what happened is a sign of true progress.

The Thief

Yu Zhaoyuan arrived at Jiabiangou in the spring of 1958. Before his conviction, Yu headed the Xigu district government's Human Resources Department in Lanzhou. He was at Jiabiangou for three years. Following his release in 1961, he was sent back to his native Jinta County, where he was ordered to do farmwork under supervision. His Rightist label was officially overturned in 1979. Once, during a casual conversation, a neighbor asked Yu how he managed to survive Jiabiangou when thousands had died of starvation there. He replied, "I was a shrewd and notorious thief." I interviewed Yu at his apartment in Jinta County.

In his second year at Jiabiangou, Yu began to suffer from edema. His legs became swollen; his face puffed up like a pumpkin. At that point, Yu had never stolen a single item of food. This had a lot to do with his upbringing. He was born in a rural area of Jinta County, but his father, an herbal doctor, had received some formal education. He taught Yu how to read at an early age. He indoctrinated his son with stories about Confucius. In one of the stories, the sage refused a bowl of water on a hot summer day, because the water had been drawn from a spring called Robber's Spring. A righteous person would rather die of thirst than drink water from an unclean source, Yu's father explained.

Confucius's teachings on nobility remained etched in Yu's

mind. When he arrived at Jiabiangou, he found the idea of stealing shameful. When he suffered exhaustion, and his stomach grumbled, he would chew on leaves and weed seeds to appease the hunger.

In the spring of 1960, Yu began to steal food after two of his roommates died within three days, right before his eyes.

The first to die was a former schoolteacher from Yongdeng County, named Ba Duoxue. Ba had graduated from Beijing University. Many who lived with him would describe him as an honest, timid person, who would "worry about getting injured by a falling leaf." One time, a fellow Rightists secretly took a cucumber from the vegetable field and offered to share it with him. Ba was so scared that he pushed the cucumber away, saying, "Are you trying to get me into trouble?"

When spring came, Ba was so hungry he couldn't get out of bed. He asked the people around him for a cigarette. Yu went out and managed to get a small pinch of tobacco leaves from a Rightist he knew. He rolled up the leaves, lit the cigarette, and gently put it between Ba's lips. Ba haltingly raised one arm and held the cigarette with his dry, twiglike fingers. He took a couple of drags and then closed his eyes forever.

The second person Yu knew was Shen Dawen, a botanist and former professor at the Gansu Agricultural Academy; Shen had studied in the United States. He and Yu had shared a bunkhouse for more than two years. In the first months after their arrival, the camp authorities organized farming classes for Rightists, and invited Shen to teach. Shen took to his bed several days before Ba. He had lost the ability to walk, but he insisted on getting food from the mess hall himself, without bothering the others. He'd crawl on his knees all the way there and back. He padded his knees with a pair of shoes, tied to each other with the laces, to alleviate the excruciating pain he felt from scraping them against the ground.

Two days after Ba's death, Yu was awakened by Shen in the middle of the night. "I'm craving corn cake," said Shen.

"It's almost midnight," said Yu. "Where could I possibly find you cake?"

"Please," begged Shen. "Get me some cake. It's all I want."

A Rightist sitting nearby nudged Yu on the elbow. "I think he's about to die," he said.

A numbing pain spread around Yu's scalp. He put on his coat and went directly to the official in charge of the mess hall, to ask if he could get a baked corn cake for Shen.

"Shen wants a cake?" said the official. "What if Wang or Li wants one too? Where am I supposed to get all these cakes?"

Out of desperation, Yu knocked on the door of Liang Jing-xiao, a camp division director. Yu had impressed Liang with his farming abilities when he had arrived in the camp, and Liang trusted him with many of the most challenging farming operations. Yu woke Liang and told him what had happened to Shen. On this night, Liang honored his special connection with Yu.

"Go tell the mess hall manager to give you two corn cakes," he said. "Tell him Liang said so."

With the two baked corn cakes in his hand, Yu rushed back to Shen, thinking that he could prolong Shen's life for at least a couple of days.

The next morning, when Yu got up, he noticed that Shen lay in his bed motionless. He called Shen's name and there was no answer. He touched Shen's head and it was icy cold.

The deaths of Ba Duoxue and Shen Dawen shocked Yu. His belief in the principles of moral virtue weakened. Shen was a botanist and knew how to survive on seeds and plants without poisoning himself. Even so, he still succumbed to starvation. How, wondered Yu, will I be able to survive Jiabiangou?

After several days of contemplation on this subject, he

reached a decision. While taking a break in the field one day, he walked over to his close friend Yang Naikang, who used to head the Propaganda Department of the Xigu District government in Lanzhou. They had known each other for a long time.

"Old Yang," said Yu, "we are too hungry to walk. We need to figure out how we're going to survive."

Yang didn't say anything.

"We've got to come up with something," said Yu. "You think we should just wait to die?"

"What can we do? You were always the smart one, Yu. You tell me what we should do."

Yu paused for a few minutes before speaking again.

"I have one idea, but I'm not sure how to pull it off. I'm too scared."

"What is it?" asked Yang, looking Yu in the eye. "Spit it out and then we can decide whether we have the guts or not."

"Okay. Let me share with you my idea of how we can conduct business transactions without putting down any capital."

Yang's eyes widened. "You mean robbing and kidnapping?"

"What? No! I was thinking about stealing grain from the warehouse. Will you join me?"

Yang was silent for a few minutes.

"Damn it," he said at last. "Worst-case scenario, we die. We're going to die of hunger anyway."

Three days later, around midnight, Yu and Yang met in front of the camp's grain warehouse. Yu carried a bamboo pole. He had sharpened one end of the pole at a forty-five-degree angle. Their footsteps woke up a large black dog sleeping near the warehouse entrance. The dog barked and began to jump at them. Yu knew the dog fairly well, because he frequently transported seed grain from the warehouse to the field. He growled back at it in a deep voice, and then quietly called the dog's name. It worked. The dog stopped barking, circled around Yu's legs, sniffed his feet, wagged its tail, and walked away.

Yu and Yang stayed put in a corner for a few minutes to ensure that the coast was clear. They were standing in front of the largest warehouse in Jiabiangou. A mill house and a small office were attached to one end. A guard, whose only job was to guard the warehouse and the mill house, lived in the office.

As expected, the office door opened, and the guard stepped out. Yu could see his dark shadow move around the warehouse. He passed a mud wall on the east side and continued to patrol on the west. He swore in his low voice, "You little bastard. What are you barking about?"

Then he went inside, and everything was quiet again.

The warehouse was divided into two rooms. Yu knew that bags of seed wheat were piled against a wall on the north side of the small room, almost as high as the ventilation window. Yu and Yang crept up closer to the warehouse, and crouched under the window. Yu spread a bedsheet on the ground. He squatted down and leaned against the wall. Yang climbed on top of Yu's shoulders, and Yu tried to stand up. He failed twice.

"My legs are too weak," he said.

They traded positions. Yu climbed on Yang's shoulders and found himself at eye level with the ventilation window, about three meters above the ground. He tried to hold on to the window frame with one hand, using the other one to pry open the window. He managed to open it up a small crack. He took the bamboo pole from Yang and wedged it into the crack. The gap grew larger. Yu slowly squeezed the pole inside. He couldn't see anything inside the warehouse, but probed around with the bamboo pole. His heart beat so powerfully that he could hardly breathe. He paused for a few seconds, took a deep breath, and then probed some more. The tiny noise caused by the friction between the bamboo pole and the window frame sounded like a thunderstorm. Yu stopped every couple of minutes, pricking his ears to make sure nobody had heard him.

Finally, he felt the bamboo pole hit the linen sacks. He tightened his grip and poked the sharp end, with all his might, into a sack. It seemed to work. Slowly, little by little, he pulled the pole out through the window. He reached a finger inside the sharp end. He felt several wheat seeds.

He tilted the pole downward and emptied the seeds onto the bedsheet on the ground.

"I got it," he whispered gleefully to Yang. Yang was equally excited. He straightened his back. "Good. Keep on poking!"

Yu summoned up his strength and poked his bamboo pole inside again and again.

After a while, both of Yang's legs started trembling. "I can't hold you any longer. Come down quickly."

Yu retrieved the pole and shut the ventilation window. As Yang was repositioning himself, his legs gave out on him and he collapsed to the ground. Yu was thrown off, and his head struck a piece of concrete. He screamed with pain. The dog at the other side of the warehouse started barking again. Yu and Yang had no time to agonize over their injuries. They rolled up the bedsheet, picked up the bamboo pole, and bolted. A few steps later, the dog caught up and jumped at them. Yang was bending down to pick up a rock, when Yu stopped him.

"Please don't! Don't hit the dog. We'll never get out of here if you do."

Yu moved closer to the dog, and whispered tenderly, "Blackie, don't bark. Come over here."

The dog stopped barking. It came up to Yu and circled around him. Yu patted its head. The dog circled around one more time and left.

"Let's run," said Yu.

But it was too late. They had barely run twenty steps when

they heard the guard chasing after them. The guard called out to the dog, "Get them, Blackie! Go!"

Yu and Yang reached a vegetable field on the north side of the warehouse. There were two big trees in the middle of the field. They raced over and hid behind the trees.

"Thieves!" shouted the guard. "There are thieves robbing the warehouse!"

"There's no way we can escape," said Yu. "That bastard is in much better shape than us. We need to come up with a plan."

Yang was so nervous that his voice changed. "What do you think we should do?"

Yu turned toward the shadow in the distance, lifted his voice, and howled, "You son of a bitch. I'm going to kill you if you follow me any further."

The guard stopped. He couldn't see how many people were hiding behind the trees. He simply yelled again, "Help! There are thieves robbing the warehouse."

Yu used an even more sinister tone. "Bastard. If you scream again, I'm going to blow your head off."

The guard wouldn't back down. "Don't talk tough, mother-fucker. Step out, if you have the balls to face me."

"You bastard, I'm trying to throw you a bone—don't waste it. I'm asking you to return to your office. If you don't, I'll kill you tonight."

The guard grew silent. The dog kept barking. Yu knew that the Rightists living nearby wouldn't get out of bed even if they heard the commotion. Only the camp officials would get up. And they had guns. He had to end the confrontation. Seeing that the guard didn't move, he grabbed Yang's coat and the two of them walked out from behind the tree. He shouted at the guard, "Hey, buddy, let us pass. I'm sure our paths will cross someday." Then they headed toward the sand dunes on the northeast side of the camp. They looked back a couple of times.

The shadow was still standing there, and the dog kept barking. They quickened their pace.

They couldn't believe how easily they had gotten away. They had stolen almost one kilogram of wheat. Instead of returning to their bunkhouse, they ran directly to an area of grassland on the east side of the camp, where they had hidden a bowl during the day. They collected some dry weeds, set up a campfire, and cooked the seed wheat. As they munched on the delicious wheat, they decided to do it again in a few days.

The next evening, after they came back from the field, Director Liang suddenly showed up with several walking sticks, who conducted a thorough search of their bunkhouses, pulling off all the sheets and bedding, and opening up suitcases. Even though they didn't find anything, Yu and Yang realized the leadership must have suspected that members of the agricultural team had committed the theft. When Yu visited the mill house the following day, he saw that Blackie had been replaced by a light-colored dog with brown spots. As Yu passed by, it barked at him fiercely.

They didn't go back to the warehouse, but emboldened by their initial success, they decided, during the Chinese New Year's celebration, to attack the camp kitchen. With Yang's assistance, Yu climbed on top of the kitchen roof. Through a skylight, he slipped in a bamboo pole with a hook and stole some dough. They escaped to the grassland and baked a cake.

In the weeks after New Year's, Rightists started to mix seeds. Yu started to steal with more regularity. Every day, he'd fill his shoes with wheat seeds, or wrap the grain in a small packet and hide it inside his straw hat. He even changed the handle of his shovel into one made of hollow bamboo. He'd stuff grain into the handle before leaving work and then carry it back to the bunkhouse. Before long, an official discovered his trick. He went to Yu's bunkhouse and pulled a suitcase half-filled with seed wheat from under his bed. Yu was denied one dinner as punishment. He was dragged outside and a public denunciation meeting was held against him.

During planting season, Yu and several other Rightists stole wheat seeds and ate them raw in the field. They couldn't do this during work hours, but only during breaks, after the guard and the supervisors had left. The members of the planting team would lie down on the ground, reach their hands into the linen seed sacks, and stuff the seeds into their mouths. The process was a bit like a whale eating plankton. First they would move their tongues to produce saliva, so they could wash the fungicide off the seeds. They spat out the poisonous saliva between their teeth, chewed the seeds, and swallowed them. At dinnertime, when they were given a bowl of corn gruel, nobody could tell whether it was salty, bland, or sour, because the insecticide had destroyed their taste buds.

One day, after eating too much fungicide, Yu got a terrible stomachache. He rolled around on the ground and his shirt was soaked with sweat. He was sure he was dying. Two hours later, the pain disappeared. His stomach let out a loud growling noise, and then he got hit with a terrible diarrhea that lasted for several days. He could hardly walk. A week later, he was back to stealing seeds to feed his hunger.

In the spring, they were sowing seeds nonstop—first wheat, then flaxseed, corn, and sorghum. They stole whatever they sowed.

In June, the wheat began to flower. Yu and other Rightists pulled off the wheat heads and sucked out their starchy juice. By the end of June, the wheat heads were still green, but kernels had been formed inside. They would rub the wheat heads between their hands to remove the chaff, so that they could get at the kernels. They chewed the kernels raw.

Everyone stole wheat from the fields, but no one more than

Yu. He didn't just steal it; he hoarded it. He would dig a hole in the field, bury the stolen grain, and mark the soil so he could retrieve it later. He stole food on every possible occasion, no matter how high the risk. His efforts paid off handsomely—his edema disappeared. He rolled up the bottom of his pants and pressed his shin with a finger. It was no longer swollen. Hundreds of people were dying, and many were too hungry to do so much as walk, but his health had improved.

There was one thing that Yu didn't anticipate. In October 1960, the camp authorities ordered all the imprisoned Rightists at Jiabiangou to be relocated to Mingshui. Only the weak and the sick would be left behind. The next day, Luo, an agricultural team supervisor, showed up with his two assistants. They picked one hundred and fifty young and relatively strong Rightists to join the first group. Yu was among them. He felt his heart ache. The grain he had hidden would be wasted—the rats would have a grand time with it. Many years later, when he talked about his relocation, Yu still burned from the loss of his grain.

When the train pulled into the Mingshui River station at ten the following morning, Supervisor Luo told them to continue walking east. The group carried their luggage and walked until dark. They finally arrived at a stretch of barren land near the Gobi Desert. At Mingshui, their job was to dig a canal so it could link up with the Black River, and divert water to irrigate farmland. They'd leave for work after breakfast every morning, and not return until dark.

A week later, work was halted temporarily. A cook, while carrying a wooden steamer over to a huge wok filled with boiling water, fell in. The skin on his body instantly turned crispy. He was pulled out, but when someone touched his arm, the skin peeled right off. Supervisor Luo hurriedly ordered several people to carry the cook to a nearby hospital. The doctors had neither the expertise nor the equipment to treat him. They put him on a truck and shipped him to the county hospital. He died on the way. After the accident, nobody showed up at work for two days.

After a few days, work resumed and then stopped again. The camp authorities reduced the daily food ration from half a kilogram to a quarter of a kilogram. Worrying that the reduced food ration could lead to mass death, Supervisor Luo walked from one bunkhouse to the next, telling Rightists to take a break for a couple of days and wait for further notice from the senior leadership.

They waited, but they heard nothing. The weather was turning colder. Supervisor Luo didn't push the Rightists to show up at work. They simply gobbled up their two meals of corn gruel and slept in order to conserve energy.

It was in this period that Yu got busy. He remembered seeing a large stretch of green in the far northeast that looked like it might have been crops—perhaps either corn or sorghum. One night, he folded up a towel and thrust it into his breast pocket. He told Duan, the group leader who slept by the entrance to his mud house, that he needed to go get food.

Duan didn't stop him. He even offered Yu his flannel hat.

Yu left the bunkhouse and followed a path that headed northeast. The wind painfully scraped his face. He pulled down the flaps of the flannel hat to cover his face. It was a moonless night, so dark that he could hardly recognize any signs. He felt his way forward. A few minutes later, he tripped over a ridge. He bent over and realized that he was standing next to an irrigation canal. He walked along the canal for a long time before he found a cornfield. Peasants had already harvested it, so all that was left were cornstalks. He patted one stalk after another. No matter how thoroughly a field was harvested, you were always sure to find a few ears of corn that were missed. Not that night—he didn't spot a single one.

Just as Yu was feeling that his trip might have been for naught, he saw a yellowish oval spot in the distance, shining like a lamp in the darkness. When he moved closer, he found himself in front of a mud house. The light shone through a thin veil of white window paper. Yu crept up to the window and heard people talking inside. He spat on his index finger and carefully poked a small hole in the window paper. He saw two people sitting in the middle of the room. From their heavy black uniforms, Yu could tell they were staff members at the Xinhua reeducation camp. If the two of them were up at this late hour, they must have been called to guard something important. The courtyard was dark and Yu could see a ray of faint light through a slit in the front door. He looked around and saw a dark pile. He stepped closer and touched it. Good heavens! They were ears of corn. He knelt in front of the pile and hurried to fill his towel with the corn.

By this point, Yu had become a professional thief. He rolled up the flaps of his hat and acted quickly, but calmly. He tried to maximize the space in his towel by putting two rows of corn horizontally and then vertically inserting several more. While he was doing this, the door squeaked open. A kerosene lamp cast a beam of light on the pile. Yu was startled, and threw himself on the ground.

A tall shadow emerged. The person untied his pants and began to pee on the ground. After he finished, he turned around and looked in Yu's direction. He simply stood there without buckling his pants. Yu's heart tightened: Had this person heard anything? Had he smelled or felt anything unusual? Yu lay there motionless.

He couldn't understand why the man wouldn't go back to

the room. Instead, the person bent over and looked in Yu's direction a few more times, tilting his head to the left and then to the right. Damn, Yu thought: the man must have adjusted to the darkness and seen him. He wondered whether he should make a run for it. He didn't want to abandon the bag, but carrying it would hinder him.

Then something unexpected happened. The tall man suddenly turned around and ran back to the house. The door slammed shut. He heard the man speak, in a nervous voice, from inside the house.

"There's a wolf."

Another voice responded: "Are you sure? Did you see it clearly?"

"Yes!" screamed the man, "I could see clearly. His ears stood erect and he was chewing on the corn."

"Quick, get a shovel," said the other voice. "Let's go take a look."

Yu realized that the two wolf ears were the flaps on his flannel hat. He jumped up, grabbed his bag, and ran out of the yard. The door burst open, and then he heard loud swearing: "It's not a wolf—it's a thief!"

Yu heard their heavy footsteps behind him. He ran for a few hundred meters, crossing several ridges in the cornfield and jumping over an irrigation canal. He stumbled and fell, and saw that the two guards were still after him. He got up and ran over the crest of a small sand hill. He lost his balance and his body rolled down a steep slope like a piece of loose rock. When he hit the bottom, his hips hurt and he couldn't stand. He simply sat there, waiting for his two pursuers to reach him. Since the hill was steep, Yu could see them standing there on the top. They cursed loudly and then walked away.

Yu continued sitting there without moving for another half hour. He worried that the guards would take a different route to get to him, but other than the howling evening wind, he heard nothing unusual. Yu finally uttered a sigh of relief. He got up, but when he tried to walk, an excruciating pain emanated from his hips. He clenched his teeth and slowly climbed up the hill. He was deeply happy for his good luck.

As he wobbled into the desert, his excitement quickly evaporated. He realized he was lost. Should he go east or west? He looked up at the sky and located the three bright stars that, as he had learned as a child growing up in the countryside, normally pointed south. He found his orientation and headed west.

Not long after this, he heard the wolves. Their howling was moving closer and becoming clearer. There were two of them. He knew how to outsmart one wolf, but if two attacked at the same time, he wouldn't be able to fight them off.

His first priority was to get away from the wolves. He decided to take a different direction, and go south. As a child, his father used to tell him that a wolf could smell the scent of his prey half a kilometer away. He could sense that the wolves were coming from the west. He wanted to walk at least a kilometer south to dodge his predators.

His steps quickened and his heart pounded. His nerves were so jangled that he forgot about his hip pain. He broke into a sprint. The sound of the wolves grew louder, and he was soon exhausted. His body became warm and he gasped for air. His lungs hurt from the large quantity of cold air he had taken in—it felt as if someone had sprayed hot-pepper powder in his mouth. His throat was dry and painful. His legs weakened. Sweat streamed down his back. In a few minutes, he'd drop from exhaustion. Why don't I stop and take a break? he thought. I'll leave my fate to the hands of the Heavenly God.

As despair and hopelessness took over, Yu slowed down. He noticed that the howling started to become distant. The wolves had turned east. The northwest wind had blown his scent away from the wolves. He dropped to his knees in exhaustion.

He sat on the ground until his heartbeat returned to normal. He couldn't sit long because his sweat-soaked shirt soon turned icy cold. He got up, turned around, and walked west, where he believed his farm was located. After a few steps, Yu found several small mounds of dirt. He almost screamed for joy. He was standing next to the dry canal, which had led him to the shed with the pile of corn. In a way, he was grateful to the wolves. If he hadn't gone south to run away from the wolves, he would have walked in the wrong direction.

Yu traced his steps back for a quarter of a kilometer before finally reaching his bunkhouse. Leader Duan was awake when he walked in.

"What took you so long?"

"I was lost in the desert for half of the night," said Yu.

Yu took six ears of corn from his bag and handed them over to Leader Duan, who immediately hid them inside his quilt. Yu felt his way to his bed and pulled his suitcase from under his bed. He emptied his bag, and the rest of the corn, into it. Altogether he had stolen forty-two ears of corn, so he had thirty-six left. Before he locked the suitcase, he put aside four more on his bed. He covered his head with a quilt and quietly chewed on the corn. Each time he took a bite, he felt the milky juice—sweet and delicious—ooze from his teeth.

The next morning, Yu gobbled up a bowl of gruel from the mess hall and was ready to go back to bed for a nice sound sleep. Both his hips hurt badly from the fall the previous night. But Supervisor Luo blew his whistle and ordered everyone to follow him to the mountain and look for food. He explained that the peasants living in the local villages had told him about a type of edible yellow herb. "I want you to go dig yellow herbs today," he said.

Before Supervisor Luo finished his talk, Yu flew into his bunkhouse, opened his suitcase, and stuffed four ears of corn in his coat pocket. Then he joined the others. Walking quickly despite his injuries, he was a kilometer ahead of everybody by the time the other Rightists crossed the rail line and entered the mountain area. He intended to find a secret place to set up a fire and roast the corn. He collected some dry twigs on the way and then took a small side road, away from the main path. He soon found a clearing in the woods, started a small fire, and placed the corn on top. The outer leaves were burned. He stripped the leaves and munched on one ear after another. The cooked corn tasted delicious. Within minutes, all four ears of corn were eaten. The stripped cobs lay scattered on the ground. Yu dug a small hole near the fire and buried the cobs. Then he peed on the spot. He had to be careful. Supervisor Luo was a strict leader.

When Yu joined his fellow Rightists, someone asked if he had found any yellow herbs.

"No fucking luck," he said.

Two days later, Yu went back to the little mud shed, hoping to scout the surrounding areas and see if there was anything else worth stealing. The door was padlocked. He peeped through the window and it was vacant—no ears of corn, no guards. But the trip wasn't a total waste. On his way back, he stumbled upon a small patch of peanut plants. He chewed one and found that the juice tasted sweet. He figured the peanuts had probably been planted by the guards in the shed. They weren't ripe yet. When he left he carried several bunches of the peanut plants with him. He boiled the leaves to supplement his diet.

He made several more trips to the area in the next few days, but he didn't see anything worth stealing. He stopped bingeing on corn, limiting himself to one ear of corn per day. If his hunger became unbearable, he would return to the peanut field and bring back some more peanut leaves.

By mid-November, the cold season came to the foot of the Qilian Mountain. More Rightists died. The living ones waited quietly for their last moment to come. Only a small minority, unwilling to accept their fate, took the extraordinary risk of escape.

Yu didn't even toy with the idea of escape because he didn't want to go home. When he was a teenager, his parents had pawned a small piece of land—the only source of livelihood for his whole family—to support his education. They expected that he would bring glory to his family. If he showed up at home, as an escaped rightist, his father would die of a heart attack. He had no intention of going to Lanzhou either, because he didn't have anyplace to hide or stay. He decided to stay put and find a way to survive.

While the others slept all day in the cave, Yu forced himself to patrol the areas near the camp. He found a plot of turnips sandwiched between two gullies. The turnips had been harvested. There was a big pile of turnip leaves in front of a small shed, near the edge of the field. The local peasants must have donated the leaves to the mess hall—Yu remembered seeing some turnip leaves floating in his corn gruel. A former prisoner named Zhou lived in the shed. He had served out his sentence and was transferred to Jiabiangou. as an employee. During the day, Zhou always sat outside, but in the evening, he would watch from his window and walk around the shed with a wooden stick in his hand every ten minutes. After visiting the location several times, Yu decided to act at night. He hid behind a wall near the turnip leaves. After Zhou made his circuit and went inside the shed, Yu crawled to the pile and filled a bag with leaves. He and three of his roommates boiled the leaves and feasted on them for several days.

He went back again. While he was bagging the leaves, Zhou pounced on him from behind, and smacked at his legs with his wooden stick.

"You bastard! I've been waiting for you."

Yu limped his way back to the cave. He never made another attempt to steal the turnip leaves. He knew it was a lucky break for a former prisoner like Zhou to get a cushy job like that at the camp. He didn't want to wreck his career.

After his legs healed from the smacking, Yu shifted his target to a field of corn millet at the far south end of the camp. It was already late November and nobody had harvested the crops. He was puzzled. Was it because all the peasants had been drafted to build irrigation projects, or was it because local villagers didn't consider the millet an important crop? Yu didn't know, but he spotted only a couple of women watching over the crops. They lived inside a shed and patrolled the field every now and then. Yu again collaborated with his friend Yang Naikang. They crawled up to an open space near the field one night. Yu howled like a wolf, and the women ran into their shed. Then Yu and Yang jumped into the field and filled their bags with the ears of corn millet. They'd stop every couple of minutes to howl and kept bagging the millet.

Since the corn millet was considered good stuff, they didn't want to share it with the others. They found a spot near a sand dune and buried the grain. When they went back the next evening, their bags had disappeared. They suspected that someone else had stolen their corn millet. Some Rightists always hung out near the sand dunes, looking for hidden treasure. Yu and Yang went back to the corn millet field again. This time, they carried their stolen grain all the way to the cemetery on the far north side of the camp and buried it next to a grave. They went back night after night to boil the millet or chew it raw. The millet tasted sweet when eaten raw, but they often ended up coughing badly because the tiny millet grains got stuck in their throats.

The good days didn't last. By the end of November, a group of local peasants arrived and harvested the crops. The field was swept clean, as if it had been hit by a winter storm.

As Yu continued to wander around the area searching for food, he noticed something strange. At a corner of the gully, not far from their caves, there was a goat pen with seventy to eighty goats. Two Rightist shepherds lived in a cave next to the pen. They looked different from the others—they were healthy, with ruddy faces. Yu couldn't figure out how they remained so strong. He asked around, and one person, whose last name was Zhang, revealed their secret: every week or so, the two Rightists would come back with a dead goat on their shoulders, its intestines dangling from its bottom. The shepherds would tell the camp authorities that a jackal had bitten the goat's rear end and pulled the intestines out. Each time it happened, the two shepherds looked extremely upset, and some people actually believed their story. Camp officials simply asked the shepherds to hand over the dead goat, and never investigated the matter further. Zhang said it was evident that the two shepherds killed the goats, pulled the innards out, and ate them. Officials ate the meat.

Upon hearing the story, Yu wasn't jealous at all: in times of starvation, people did all sorts of things to survive. He asked where the officials put the skins. Zhang replied that they normally tossed the goatskins on the roof of Director Liang's office.

Yu went to look for Director Liang. Nobody was in his office. He quickly climbed on top of the flat roof and stole two pieces of goatskin. He ran all the way to the far end of the gully and started a small fire to burn the wool off the skin. It was a difficult job but Yu handled it with patience, spending almost a whole day removing the hair. Finally, the skin was as crisp as a piece of strawboard. Yu broke it into small pieces and had a feast. He took the leftovers back to his cave and shared them with his roommate. Yang Naikang chewed on the crispy goatskin, saying, "The Peking duck in Lanzhou's best restaurant isn't half as delicious as this."

There wasn't much left to steal at Mingshui, but Yu wasn't ready to sit still and wait for death. He climbed up a nearby mountain to look for weed seeds and herbs. On his way back one day, he saw several bones, bleached by the sun, scattered on the side of the path. He figured they were animal bones, not human bones, so he brought them back to the cave. His roommates didn't think they had any nutritional value. Yu agreed but figured there was no harm trying. He set up a fire and placed the bones on top. A small miracle occurred: the bleached bones turned brown and a layer of small bubbles emerged on their surface. Yu scraped the bubbles off with a piece of tile and licked the powder in his hand: it had a light salty flavor. Yu was encouraged by his discovery. He put all the bones on the fire and then scraped the bubblelike substance onto a sheet. After some time, he had a full handful. He ate it like wheat flour. His roommates followed his example and began searching for animal bones.

By mid-November, the death toll reached an alarming rate, with more than ten people dying a day. Liang Buyun, the Party secretary of Mingshui (no relation to Liang Jingxiao, the division director), became concerned. He reported the grave situation and appealed for more food, but the head of the district government was a die-hard revolutionary. "Death is inevitable in a socialist revolution," the man said. "Don't crap your pants."

Liang returned to the camp dejected. After careful consideration, he decided to set up a special patient ward to reduce the high death rate. Liang gathered all the emaciated and dying Rightists into seven clinics, converted from Rightist bunkhouses. He installed a stove in every cave and assigned two relatively healthy Rightists to take care of the patients.

In early December, the supervisor transferred Yu to one of these clinics. He was ordered to collect the bowls from patients during mealtimes, fill them up with food, and deliver them. He also handled the patients' bathroom needs, making sure they stayed in bed without wasting energy.

There was one other task for Yu and his fellow caretakers: they had to remove the dead bodies, wrap up their belongings, and leave them outside the clinic to be buried. Yu was a smart person. He discovered that most deaths occurred around midnight—patients fell asleep and never woke up. He began waking all his patients around midnight, ordering them to chat with one another. Some swore at him, but Yu was never upset. He'd smile and pull the patient out of bed, saying, "Sit up and talk, you bastard. You won't have me to blame if you die in your sleep."

His method actually worked. The ward he supervised had the lowest death rate.

Yu didn't steal any food during this time. He was too busy taking care of thirty to forty patients every day. After a couple of weeks, his health began to deteriorate. His face and legs became swollen.

It was then that an unexpected event occurred. In the second half of December, the central government came to their rescue. A bus drove into Mingshui; the most seriously ill patients were to be transferred to the Xinhua camp to recuperate. Yu was running back and forth, helping patients to board the bus, when Director Liang told him to get on so he could continue to look after his patients at the new location. Yu rushed back to his cave to collect his luggage, and came upon his friend Yang Naikang. Yu couldn't bear to leave Yang alone. He went back to Director Liang and said that Yang was dying. Liang agreed to let Yang go with him, so Yu and Yang squeezed into the bus together.

Fifty-one Rightists arrived at the Xinhua camp and lived in two separate big rooms. They slept on the floor, which had been cushioned with wheat stalks. Yu found himself out of a job there. Prostitutes, dance girls, and civil servants under the former government from Shanghai had been incarcerated there previously, and now had been assigned to look after the patients.

Yu was treated like a patient himself. Every day, he got one meal—a bowl of thick rice congee with minced pork. He still felt a gnawing hunger and continued to steal. He wandered around the camp every day. One day he walked into an office and saw two bags of rice standing against a wall. He sat outside the office, pretending to doze off in the sun. When an official left for an errand, he went in and filled all his coat pockets with rice. Then he returned to his usual spot, leaning against the wall and moaning. When the official came back, he noticed that the bag had been opened and someone had stolen rice. He dashed out of the room and asked Yu whether he had seen anyone come in.

Yu opened his eyes and said, "I did see someone. He wore a long yellow coat and he walked west."

The official ran after the "thief" in the direction Yu had pointed. After the official left, Yu walked leisurely back to his ward. He woke up Yang and together they went outside, found a quiet spot, and chewed on the raw rice.

Four days later, Yu and Yang were transported to the Jian-quanzi camp, which was about seven kilometers away from Mingshui. They were put in a big warehouselike barracks with many other emaciated Rightists from Mingshui. An official told them that they would be allowed to go back to Lanzhou after a brief period.

Jianquanzi camp was facing problems similar to those at Mingshui. Many criminals locked up there were dying of starvation. Soon the daily meal of thick congee with minced pork disappeared. The quarter-kilo food ration was reinstated. Death continued to spread.

One day, after squatting inside a latrine, Yu couldn't stand up. He tried to touch the ground with both hands, raise his butt, and then pull up his upper body, but his hands gave way and he collapsed on the latrine floor. He stayed there for a while until a fellow Rightist found him and helped him up. That incident scared him. No matter how weak he was, he had to look for food.

In an interview many years later, Yu said that if you don't give up your will to live, you'll find unexpected ways to survive. The evening after his fall in the bathroom, he walked around the camp, looking for things to eat. He saw several horse-drawn carts pull up in front of the warehouse. An official gathered several Rightists to unload sacks of beans from the cart. A couple of sacks had holes in them and the beans leaked to the ground. Yu squatted down, trying to pick them up. The official yelled at him to go away, but Yu didn't want to miss such a rare opportunity. He loitered until darkness descended. The bright moonlight cast a shadow on the ground. A horse happened to stand in the shadow. Yu moved stealthily toward the horse, crawled between its legs, and curled up under the cart. Since the official was busy directing the unloading, he didn't see Yu. Yu reached out his arm and carefully swept the beans toward him. He filled both his coat pockets with beans, and then crawled away. But as he stood up, he was suddenly overcome with dizziness and tumbled to the floor. The sound of his fall alerted the official, who ordered two Rightists to drag Yu all the way to Director Liang's bunkhouse.

He pointed at Yu's bulging pockets and said to Liang, "Look what your people have done!"

Liang simply waved his hand. "This guy has passed out. Don't be too harsh."

The official was surprised by Liang's response, and let Yu be.

On January 1, 1961, Rightists recuperating at Jianquanzi received a notice that they would be allowed to leave the camp in groups. The government had sent several doctors from a hospital in the Zhangye region. They would check up on all Rightists, granting permission for the healthy ones to leave first. During Yu's medical exam, the doctor pinched him on the thigh. Yu didn't take the pinch well, and he fell to the ground. The doctor wrote his diagnosis: "Not fit for train ride."

Several days later, another group was to be selected for departure. Before the medical exam, Director Liang called Yu to his office and said, "If you really want to go home, try to look healthy, and be tough."

With Liang's encouragement, Yu took off his Jiabiangou uniform and put on a new winter coat that he had brought from home and had stuffed in his pillowcase. He scrubbed his face and shaved with a razor that he borrowed from Liang. When the doctor pinched his thigh again, he clenched his teeth and stood still. The doctor said, "Put him on the train."

When his train reached Lanzhou, several trucks waiting at the station took the passengers to a guesthouse run by the Civil Affairs Administration. The moment he walked in, Yu started to scout for food. He saw some celery hanging on a wall outside the cafeteria, and immediately snatched a bunch. At night, he had minced pork congee for dinner. After supper, he and his roommate munched on the celery. On the second night, he was planning to go back and steal more celery when he found out that the vegetables had been moved. He saw a dumpster outside the cafeteria. He reached inside and pulled out clumps of burned rice, scraped from the bottom of a pot. He washed the dirt off and then boiled the rice again in his room. He and his roommate shared burned-rice soup.

Several days later, Yu noticed a pile of oven-baked cakes on top of the desk inside Officer Zhang's room. He recognized those cakes. Officer Zhang, who had escorted them from Jianquanzi camp to Lanzhou, bought the cakes in the café car on the train. Rather than giving each Rightist a whole cake, Zhang simply distributed a couple, asking the Rightists to cut them into several pieces and share. When they got to Lanzhou, Officer Zhang piled the leftover cakes on a desk close to a window. Yu walked outside, to the back of the room and noticed that the window was broken. He could stick his hands in, but there were always people in the room. Every day he would walk around near the room, waiting for opportunities. One morning, after Yu came out of the cafeteria, he saw Officer Zhang and several policemen walking into a conference room. He jumped at the opportunity. He ran to the back of Officer Zhang's room and poked his arm through the hole, but couldn't reach the cakes. As he was maneuvering, he accidentally pulled the curtain, which swept the pile of cakes onto the floor. As Yu was pulling his arm out, the door burst open. Officer Zhang's assistant, Little Li, walked in. Two policemen appeared from both sides and seized him.

Officer Zhang came up to him and pointed his gun at Yu's stomach. "Yu Zhaoyuan, you have become a stealing maniac. You stole food at the camp and you've continued to steal here at Lanzhou. If I find you stealing again, I'm going to blow your brains out!"

Yu felt humiliated and depressed. He unbuttoned his shirt,

bared his chest, and pointed one finger at himself, as if to say, Why don't you just kill me?

Officer Zhang shook his head and softened his tone. "Can't you just stop stealing?"

"Of course I can. If you give me a couple of those cakes, I promise I won't steal again."

"Those cakes aren't for me and you can't eat them either," said Officer Zhang. "If I allowed you all to eat those cakes on the train, you would have died. The doctors told us that your intestines are as thin as paper. If you overstuff yourself, you could cause them to rupture."

"You're wrong. My intestines have been toughened so that nothing can poke through—not the twigs and leaves I ate at Jiabiangou, nor the raw celery I eat here. Compared with the stuff I ate at the camp, the cakes would be easy to digest."

Yu recuperated at the guesthouse for a week. His wife was notified and came to pick him up. She carried a bag with some steamed wheat buns inside. Before they left, Officer Zhang instructed Yu's wife not to feed him too much at once. "If he overeats and dies, I won't be held responsible," he said.

Yu and his wife walked to the railway station to catch a suburban train to Xigu District. While waiting for their train, Yu begged his wife for a steamed bun. His wife couldn't give it to him. Yu burst out crying.

"I had nothing to eat during my three years at Jiabiangou. I almost lost my life. Now that I'm home, you still won't allow me to eat."

His wife was stunned. It took her a while to grasp the full meaning of his sadness. She broke the bun in two halves and offered him a piece. As she watched him devour the bun, she began to cry herself. "You never mentioned it in your letter. You always told me things were fine," she said.

Three months after Yu returned home, he had gained

strength in his legs, but he still suffered from unbearable hunger. He thought about food all day and night. He craved raw grain. No matter how much he ate, his stomach still felt empty. One day, while his wife was at work, he opened a wooden box where she had stored all the corn flour. He found a big teacup, filled it up with corn flour, and hid the cup behind the books on his bookcase. Before he went to bed every night, he would munch on a few spoonfuls of raw corn flour. Without his daily fix of raw food, he couldn't sleep well and his stomach would growl with hunger. Yu didn't overcome his raw-food eating habit until the winter of 1962, when his wife filed for divorce. At court, his wife accused him of stealing corn flour and insisting on eating it raw—this was one of the reasons she cited as the basis for divorce. She said her neighbors had learned about his habit. They thought she was abusing him by withholding food, and that her stinginess had forced him to steal food in his own house. His wife told the judge that she couldn't stand his stealing habit anymore. The judge granted her the divorce.

The Army Doctor

I first met Dr. Shang Chunrong in the winter of 1970, when I was employed at the Xiaowan Collective Farm. A mysterious rash appeared on my thigh and soon spread to the rest of the leg. I was hospitalized for three months, under Dr. Shang's care.

Dr. Shang was in his early thirties. He grew up in Tongwei County, Gansu Province, and joined the army in 1956, first serving as a medical assistant and then being promoted to doctor. In 1965, he left the army and worked at a civilian hospital. He was later transferred to the medical clinic affiliated with Xiaowan farm.

Most of the doctors at our clinic were graduates of medical universities or technical school. Two were farm employees who had been promoted to assist the medical staff. If possible, we always tried to avoid those two, but the truth was that the professional doctors weren't much better—they acted arrogantly and talked down to us all the time. Everyone's favorite doctor was Dr. Shang. He had no official medical training, but he had been in the field for many years and was experienced in treating common ailments. As a former soldier, he was outgoing, sociable, and warm. He was always hanging out and chatting with employees.

During my hospitalization, I had the opportunity to see Dr. Shang every day. In the evenings when he was on call, I would visit his office and listen to his stories.

In 1956, the military adopted a compulsory draft policy. Recruiters came to my county and I entered the first group of soldiers under the new system. I undertook a three-month military training period in Lanzhou, and then the army sent me to a military hospital at Qilihe District for three months to learn basic medical skills. After the training was completed, I was assigned to work as a medical assistant at a regiment that was stationed in Jiuquan. My job was to guard prisons and forced labor camps.

Three years into my job, the medical director of my regiment decided to transfer me to a clinic at the battalion level.

"You've been a medical assistant for a long time now," he said. "You should be able to improve your skills at the battalion clinic, so you can aim for promotion."

I understood what he meant. In my current position, I was only allowed to treat patients with minor illnesses, like colds or headaches. Patients with serious health problems would be handled by professionally trained doctors. The situation was handled differently at the battalion clinic, since they only had two or three doctors on staff. When it was really busy, medical assistants were called on to treat patients. It would be good training for me. Soon after my arrival, the clinic granted me the right to offer diagnoses and prescribe medicine. All of a sudden, I was a doctor. Everyone looked up to me.

Our battalion was headquartered inside a labor camp, about ten kilometers east of Jiuquan. The camp held two thousand prisoners who grew grain and vegetables. One mid-November day in the 1960s, the battalion commander came to the clinic and passed on a telephone message from Ji Zishen, who headed the clinic at the regiment. Director Ji came from northern Shaanxi Province and joined the Communist army in 1938. He was conferred the senior captain's title in 1949 and promoted to be a major soon after. He was a serious person and quite amiable around me. He liked my work and trusted me.

"Looks like you'll get a new assignment," said my commander, but he wouldn't tell me what it might be. So I was somewhat baffled as I rode a horse-drawn cart toward the regiment clinic in Jiuquan.

Director Ji greeted me.

"We have been instructed by the senior leadership to send a doctor to help save lives at Jiabiangou," he said. "Many Rightists have fallen sick and a large number of patients have died. You're a good fit for the assignment."

I was taken aback. "Director Ji, I'm only a medical assistant. Why don't you send a professional doctor?"

"You'll be perfect for this job," said Ji. "You're bold and not afraid to handle dead people. Don't worry about your lack of medical skills. Jiabiangou has plenty of doctors. Many Rightists there are former doctors or medical professors from the major hospitals and universities in the province. We want you to learn from those doctors and improve your skills."

After considering Director Ji's words, I decided that I agreed with his reasoning. Over the past three years, I had been picked for several special off-site medical assignments because many doctors felt nervous around prisoners. One time, a counterrevolutionary riot broke out at the Jiayuguan Commune when peasants protested against government grain quotas and clashed with the local police. Government troops were called in to suppress the riot. The two doctors who accompanied me became scared and collapsed. I ended up treating both the wounded soldiers and tending the doctors.

Before I left, Director Ji advised me to pack up some medicine, especially cardiac stimulant and glucose IV bags.

When I stepped out the door, Director Ji called me back in. "Come back. Don't leave too fast."

I saw him staring at a blank wall, smoking a cigarette.

"You can stay with one of the nearby army units," he said.

His advice was redundant. It was the only option available.

"Where else can I go?" I said jokingly. "It's not like there's a nice hotel there or anything."

He laughed. "If you encounter anything unusual there, please report it to me directly. Remember—even though you're staying with the army unit, don't report to the company commander. Always consult with me first."

"What type of unusual circumstances should I expect?"

He hesitated for a few seconds and appeared to brood. "It's hard to say. I just want to remind you that all the residents of Jiabiangou are Rightists, some of them big-name Rightists. The political situation is complex. Anything can happen. If you run into anything tough, don't make a rash decision without consulting with me first."

I nodded.

"You're on your own this time," he continued. "Be careful and stay out of trouble."

I found Director Ji's behavior somewhat strange. During my previous assignments, his instructions had always been short and precise, never so verbose.

The next morning, I carried the package on my back and left on foot for Jiabiangou. In those days, the army possessed few trucks or cars and it was difficult to get a ride. It was more common to walk. I arrived at the army barracks first and then visited the Jiabiangou administrative office building.

Do you know why a company of soldiers was stationed near Jiabiangou? In 1959, severe food shortages occurred in Gansu Province. The army's monthly ration was reduced to nineteen kilograms, not enough for young, energetic soldiers. To improve matters, the leaders of our regiment posted an army unit near Jiabiangou to cultivate farmland and grow crops. In the first year, officers at all levels, including medical staff, participated in farming and irrigation projects. At regular training classes, our political adviser warned us not to loiter around Jiabiangou camp.

"We don't want Rightists to get the impression that we are guarding the camp," he said. "That's not our job. If a riot breaks out, however, we will step in immediately to suppress it."

Our barracks was about several hundred meters away from the Jiabiangou camp. On the day of my arrival, I stopped by the office to introduce myself to members of the camp leadership, but nobody was around. So I went directly to the camp clinic.

Three people were sitting inside the room. Before I even had the chance to greet them, they all stood up at once. I guess they were surprised to see a person in military uniform. I wore a Red Cross lapel badge. I asked if the head of the clinic was available. They said that their supervisor had gone to the city to request more medical supplies.

Seeing that they were all just standing there, I gestured for them to sit down.

They sat down, but looked nervous.

"Don't be afraid," I said. "I've been sent by the military in Jiuquan to help treat patients and save lives. I don't get involved in anything other than medical cases."

I asked them for their own life stories. As it turned out, they were all Rightists. One person's name was Yang; he had been the chief physician at the Lanzhou Medical Academy's hospital. The second doctor was rather short. He had been a chief physician at the Lanzhou Municipal Workers Hospital. The third person was a woman who had headed the Nursing Department at the Gansu Provincial People's Hospital. They all looked up to me as their leader, and reported in detail the various cases they were handling. The clinic had to cope with an overwhelming number of cases. Many deaths were caused by low blood sugar, compounded by depression.

"Why is low blood sugar the leading cause of their deaths?" I asked.

They didn't respond. I didn't probe further. I knew they wouldn't dare tell the truth. They became Rightists and ended up in Jiabiangou because they had spoken truth to the Party.

"Why don't you take me to see the patients?" I asked.

Dr. Yang led the way. We walked into a big residential compound, with rows and rows of makeshift houses. I didn't understand why they stood vacant.

"Most people were transferred to Mingshui three months ago. Those who are dying or too sick to move were left behind. These are our patients."

"How many patients do we have?" I asked.

"About three hundred," Dr. Yang said.

We entered the first room. I was impressed by its sheer size, almost three times the size of a regular office. Beds made of clay were arranged around the left, right, and center of the room, in a shape like a horseshoe. Even with more than twenty patients, the room still felt empty. It was upsetting to see all those bedridden patients. In their pre-Rightist days, most of these patients had been respected officials or intellectuals. At Jiabiangou, they more closely resembled a group of beggars with tattered clothes. Several of them had tied linen ropes around their waists. I didn't see any stoves. They tried to keep warm by tightening the clothes around their bodies. Some of them lay in bed with their eyes closed. Others sat staring at the wall. One person had converted a cookie can into a stove and had torn pages from a book to feed a small fire he had lit in it. There were several additional books on a pile next to where he knelt. He was boiling something in a tin cup set on top of his stove. I asked him what he was cooking.

"Dry vegetable leaves," he said.

I examined each patient closely. Their expressions were horrifying and their suffering palpable. Their bodies were dried up like thin wooden sticks, their eyes sunk deep into the sockets, and their faces stuck like parched paper to their skulls. The edema patients were bloated. Their faces had ballooned until they were as round as the bottom of a basin. All of the patients were terrified of cold and covered themselves with many layers of shirts, sweaters, pullovers, and cotton-padded coats. I asked each patient where he had come from and what crimes he had committed. Their replies were short and simple. My military uniform probably instilled fear in them.

That changed when Dr. Yang explained that my only task was to offer medical treatment. Seven or eight patients jumped down from their beds and surrounded me. Several handed me letters, begging me to mail them.

I had no idea how to handle the letters, so I didn't accept them. Besides, Director Ji had warned me about this kind of thing. But the Rightists were persistent. They began to shove the letters into my coat pockets. One Rightist tugged at my coat and pleaded his innocence. Another begged me, saying, "The Central Party Committee doesn't know anything about our suffering. If you only sent my letter out, the Party would know about it and come to rescue us."

"Don't put your letters in my pocket," I said. "I'm not in charge of this. You should give your letters to the officers at the camp."

They ignored me and kept stuffing the letters into my pockets. One person whispered to me, "The officers here review our letters. They never deliver petition letters to senior leaders."

When I finally made my way out of the room, there were seven letters in my pocket.

The next day, I followed the Rightist doctors as they made the rounds. We checked up on patients and conducted a couple of resuscitations. I hardly had a quiet moment to myself. Each time I returned to the office and was about to take a break, a nurse would rush in with the news that someone had passed out or stopped breathing. The doctors and I would follow the nurse to the ward and give the patient a shot of cardiac stimulant or a glucose IV. The medicine worked miracles. Several minutes after the glucose IV dripped into the patient's veins, he would open his eyes. Once the patient woke up, he had no recollection of what had happened to him. He would simply look around at the people standing by his bed and couldn't figure out why the doctors were there.

On the third morning, another patient lost consciousness. Since the Rightist doctors were tending several other similar cases, I had that patient all to myself. I applied what I had learned from the Rightist doctors the day before, injecting him with cardiac stimulant first, followed by 50 cc of the glucose IV. I later added another 100 cc of glucose. None of this worked, however, and in the end, the nurse and I wrapped him up with his quilt, tied a rope around his body, and placed him near the entrance for the burial. When I returned to the office, I felt dejected: a human life had slipped away from my hands. How could I be so useless?

Dr. Yang walked in and, noticing the gloomy expression on my face, asked whether I was all right. I told him about my disappointing performance.

"You saved many patients with the glucose IV. How come I couldn't do it?" I asked him.

"Don't blame yourself," he said. "It was not your fault. We had brought him back to life twice already. His time had come. Nobody could have saved him."

"How could you know? I've never heard this explanation before."

"It's what we call experience. The first time a patient passes out, you can bring him back with 40 cc of glucose IV. The second time it happens to the same person, you need to double the amount of glucose or increase it to 200 cc. If the patient falls into a coma for a third time, nobody can rescue him, no matter how much glucose you inject into his bloodstream."

At lunchtime, I returned to the army barracks and telephoned Director Ji. "I ran into an issue here that I need your guidance on."

"What is it?" He sounded tense.

I explained to him about the letters that the Rightists had shoved into my pocket. I was wondering if I should return them or drop them off at the post office.

There was a pause on the other end. Then, Director Ji said haltingly, "Why don't you mail the letters out? Just don't give them to the postal coordinator at the barracks. If possible, try not to use the post office at Jiabiangou, either. Bring the letters when you visit Jiuquan and send them from the post office there."

In the next four days, I followed the Rightist doctors and learned how to handle many emergency cases. I felt my medical skills had dramatically improved and I was confident enough to treat patients all by myself. Since I spent most of my time in the wards, the patients got to know me better and the intimidation of my uniform soon dissipated. They started to pour out their life stories to me. One man, a former official at Shandan County, had gotten himself into trouble by openly challenging the county Party secretary's attempts to overstate the yield on crop production. Another man, an engineer at the Northwest Railway Design and Construction Institute, had been asked to build an interprovincial railroad. When his design failed to appeal to the taste of a senior official, he was charged with sabotaging China's socialist construction plan.

Whenever possible, I would stroll around the camp to familiarize myself with the surroundings. One day, as I stepped into the mill shop, I caught a young woman stealing flour. She was stuffing the raw flour into her mouth and the white powder covered her face. She looked like a white rat. She was frightened that I would report her. I struck up a conversation and found out she was, like me, from Tongwei County. I promised that I would keep quiet about her stealing.

"Don't worry," I said. "You are from my own county. I wouldn't betray you."

I met another woman who used to be a teacher at the Lanzhou Medical Academy. When she complained about her low salary, the leaders at her department labeled her a Rightist.

On the morning of my fifth day at Jiabiangou, I made the rounds alone. An old man stopped me and asked to have a word with me.

I had noticed him two days earlier. Each time I passed by, he was always lying in bed, covered with a heavy quilt. On top of the quilt was a winter coat with a fox-fur collar. He was emaciated and seemed not to have enough strength to sit up. When the old man talked with me that morning, he was sitting there, leaning against a quilt.

"Are you part of the Seventy-second Regiment? I want to inquire about someone you might know," he said cautiously.

"How do you know my regiment number? Who do you want to know?"

"Do you know a person called Ji Zisheng?"

His question came as a surprise.

"Yes. He is the director of our clinic. How did you know him?"

"Yes, I know him. I know him."

I probed further. "Tell me, how did you know him?"

"Your unit used to be stationed at Wuwei County, right?" he said. "While Ji was there, he married my daughter."

"Really? Is your family name Wu?"

"Yes. My name is Wu Chengxiang and my daughter's name is Wu Xiuying."

"So you're Director Ji's father-in-law," I said.

He nodded again, humbly.

I looked more closely at him. Sadness overcame me. His body had been reduced to a skeleton. His long gray beard extended to his chest. His shirt was covered with food stains. From the way he talked, I could tell he used to be a person of status. His long beard must have looked distinguished in his pre-Jiabiangou days.

"Do your daughter and her husband know you're here?"

He murmured incoherently in response.

"Do you ever write to your daughter?"

"No."

"Why not? Your son-in-law heads our clinic. If you wrote to him, he would certainly be able to help you."

The old man was silent.

"Do you want me to pass on a message to your son-in-law?" I asked him.

He seemed to contemplate my offer. After a few minutes, he replied, "If it's not too inconvenient, could you ask him to bring me some hot pepper sauce?"

"Don't you want some sugar?" I asked.

"Does my daughter have access to extra sugar?"

"Of course! Your son-in-law is a military officer, so he has special privileges."

"Oh, I didn't know. Why don't you have him bring some sugar for me, then? Would it be a problem if I ask for some cooked flour powder?"

"Of course you can—he's your son-in-law. You're starving over here. There is nothing wrong with asking your children for food. I will go get it for you."

He was grateful, and asked for my name. As we continued talking, I learned that he had been a merchant in the fur trade before the Communist takeover. In 1949, he served as the director of the Industrial Business Association. His daughter attended the Lanzhou Teachers University and was a high school teacher in Wuwei County. She met Director Ji at a joint event between the army and her school.

I asked whether it was true that his daughter and son-in-law had no idea about his incarceration at Jiabiangou.

"I think they know," he said hesitatingly. "I wrote a letter to my wife, asking her to tell my daughter about my situation. I was hoping that my daughter could send me some food. My wife did send the letter out but we never heard anything back."

"So your own daughter is turning her back on you."

"The letter must have gotten lost in the mail. Or maybe my wife never sent it, and she has simply lied to me."

"Why would your wife lie to you about the letter?"

"Perhaps she worried that my Rightist status would harm the careers of my daughter and son-in-law. I'm now considered a class enemy. It wouldn't benefit anyone politically to help me out. People would be accused of 'not drawing a clear line with the enemy' or 'harboring too much sympathy toward a Rightist.'"

"It doesn't matter whether your daughter is aware of your situation," I said. "I will take care of it for you. I will go talk with Director Ji. I don't care about drawing a clear line with our enemy. Do you think he would stand idle while his father-in-law is starving to death?"

At lunch, I meant to call Director Ji, but decided it would be too risky to telephone him during regular work hours about what had happened that morning. What if the switchboard operator overheard our conversation and spread the news to the others? I remembered those awkward moments when Director Ji first assigned me my tasks at his office. He must have known that his father-in-law was receiving reeducation at Jiabiangou, and that helping his father-in-law might spell political trouble for him. I needed to be prudent.

Before leaving work that day, I told the doctors that I was going to Jiuquan to pick up more medicine from the army pharmacy. They all liked the idea. The cardiac stimulant and glucose drips I had brought had long run out.

Early the next morning, I walked the thirty kilometers to Jiuquan, dropped off the letters written by the Rightists, and then headed toward the clinic. I ran into Director Ji at the clinic entrance. He was surprised to see me.

"Has anything happened?"

He was relieved to learn that I had come back to get more medical supplies. Director Ji took me to the pharmacy and granted approval to my request for medicine. Before he left, he asked me to stop by his office afterward.

I figured he must have lost his cool, and was eager to know if I had discovered his secret. He told me to close the door and sit down. Then he offered me a cigarette. Director Ji normally smoked the cheap Flying Horse brand, but now he removed from his desk drawer a pack of Peony brand, and handed me one. He even struck a match to light it up for me. I was embarrassed. I took the matches from his hand and insisted on lighting the cigarette myself.

As I inhaled greedily from the cigarette, he asked me how everything was going.

"Have you been able to improve your medical skills? Those Rightist doctors are very experienced, and you must have had a lot of opportunities to treat patients."

"It's true that we have lots of patients and cases. But their cases are all similar—low blood sugar. All I've done is inject cardiac stimulant and give glucose IV drips."

"Have you encountered any troublesome incidents?"

"Like what?"

"Have you met anyone special? Any friends from your hometown?"

"All sorts of people," I said. I mentioned the young woman I met at the mill shop, and Fu Zuogong, the brother of a well-known Chinese general named Fu Zuoyi.

Director Ji stopped smoking and looked at me distractedly. I felt it was time to spill the beans and tell him what he wanted to hear. I took another puff on the cigarette and said, "I hope you don't think I'm too inquisitive. There is something I need to share with you. I met a sixty-year-old man from Wuwei County. He claimed to know you."

"What did you tell him?" asked Director Ji.

"I didn't say much. I was concerned that he might get you in trouble. Our encounter took place yesterday. As instructed, I'm reporting this to you directly. That's the reason I'm here."

"You've done the right thing. Did the old man tell you how he knows me?"

"No," I lied.

"Have you told anyone else about this?"

"No." That was the truth.

Director Ji uttered a sigh of relief, and leaned back in his chair. He lit a cigarette and sat there, thinking. I waited quietly, trying to figure out what was going through his mind. I didn't want to share too much information about my meeting with Mr. Wu because I didn't know how Director Ji was going to react.

"Are you sure you haven't shared this with anyone else here?"

I shook my head emphatically.

"That's good. It'd be dangerous if more people knew about this. You know what I mean. I want to tell you the truth. When the senior leadership instructed us to send medical personnel to Jiabiangou, I specifically recommended you. Do you know why? It's because you're reliable. I trust you. The old man you met is my wife's father."

"Really?" I pretended to be surprised.

"Yes. Last year, my mother-in-law wrote to us, saying that her husband was at Jiabiangou. She begged us to help out. I was afraid of getting drawn into this political mess, so I didn't do anything. Please don't ever repeat this to anyone."

"Director, trust me. I know how important it is to you. I won't tell anyone."

Director Ji relaxed. "Did he tell you what he needs?"

"Nothing particular," I said, continuing my lie. "I didn't tell him I knew you. I guess that's why he didn't tell me what he needed."

"What do you think we can offer him? I can't let that old man starve to death."

It was my turn to utter a sigh of relief. I could finally do something for Mr. Wu, as I had promised.

"What about some salt and hot pepper sauce?" I said casually. "The mess hall offers two meals a day—a bowl of corn gruel at each meal. The camp leaders worry that salt can hinder water retention, so the cooks never put any salt in the gruel. It's hard to swallow the bland, soupy stuff. Your father-in-law would probably appreciate something that added flavor to his meals. You can also get him some cooked flour powder so he can mix it with water and drink it."

"Of course, of course," said Director Ji. "I can also probably prepare some meat for him."

"It would be better if you could mince the meat and stir-fry it so he can add some to each meal. The poor man suffers from malnutrition and is very thin."

Director Ji suggested a glucose drip and some new clothes.

"He doesn't need clothes. So many people have died and there are plenty of clothes left. He needs food. A pair of socks would help, though. When I saw him, I noticed that he didn't have any. His feet were covered with a piece of cloth."

Director Ji told me to stop by his home the next morning. When I arrived, he had already prepared the food: cooked flour powder, crackers, hot pepper sauce, and a cup of minced pork. I bundled it all together and packed it with my medicine.

"We appreciate your help," said Director Ji. "I was planning to order a car for you, but I changed my mind because I thought it might arouse suspicion."

"It only takes me four or five hours to walk back," I said. "It's no problem."

I noticed the absence of his wife. She was a teacher, and I had heard she was quite attractive. I asked him where she was.

"She left for work already," Director Ji said.

But I was certain that his wife was home. It was only seven-thirty, and still dark outside. It seemed inconceivable that she would have gone to work that early. When Director Ji went into the bedroom to get cash for his father-in-law, I heard a woman's voice. I assumed she must have decided not to introduce herself to me.

I reached Jiabiangou a little after one o'clock in the afternoon. Instead of unpacking at the barracks, I went directly to the Jiabiangou clinic. I poured a cup of hot water and munched on the oven-baked cakes I had brought from home. I was planning to rest up a bit and then go visit Director Ji's father-in-law. But before I could even finish the cake, a nurse rushed in and informed the doctors of an emergency. The doctors followed her out. I swallowed the rest of the cake and joined them with my newly replenished supply of medicine.

The patient who had needed help was Director Ji's father-in-law. When I got there, he was no longer breathing. We applied cardiac stimulant and glucose injection, but we couldn't rescue him.

I was outraged at the doctors.

"This patient was in good condition when I left yesterday. I can't believe that none of you bothered to take care of him."

The doctors and the nurse stood at attention. None said anything. They were too afraid to breathe.

After scolding them for a few minutes, I realized how futile it was to assign blame. No matter what we did, he was not coming back. My heart ached for the old man. I felt so guilty that I wasn't able to save him. I asked the nurse to bring a small cart. With the help of others, I placed his body on the cart and wheeled him to an area near the sand dunes. I dug a deep hole and buried him.

I returned to the clinic. Seeing that I had calmed down somewhat, Dr. Yang came over to me and explained what had happened. "On the day of your arrival, the old man had twice fallen into a coma. We were able to save him twice. Today was his third time."

I gave the cooked flour powder and the minced pork to the doctors. I looked up the young woman I had met at the mill shop and offered her the hot pepper sauce and the salt.

Two days later, I took another trip to Jiuquan and told Director Ji that his father-in-law had died. I had been thinking of how best to break the news to him. I apologized profusely for failing to save his relative. I asked for his forgiveness. I waited for his anger to flare up. I was certain I'd lose any chance for a promotion. Most likely, he would have me pack up and go home. But Director Ji seemed calm when he heard the news. He uttered another one of his long sighs.

"Okay," he said. "That's good."

Two weeks later, the provincial government sent a rescue team to Jiabiangou. All the Rightists were released. Among the patients I had treated, there were fewer than two hundred survivors. I said goodbye to the young woman from my hometown and the teacher at the Lanzhou Medical Academy before they were shipped home. The next day, I packed and returned to the barracks.

In the spring of 1960, I was promoted. In 1965, Director Ji was appointed deputy commander of the army's Logistics Department.

The Potato Feast

"The most memorable thing? You're asking me to tell you the most memorable thing I experienced at Jiabiangou?"

This interview took place in the early winter of 1999. I was sitting with Gao Jiyi inside his plant clinic, in a corner of the Jianlan Free Market in Lanzhou's Qilihe District. This flower market wasn't big. About forty or fifty shops formed a little courtyard. It was cold outside. Night temperatures dropped below zero. During the daytime, shop owners put the flowers and plants outside the stores to attract customers. The flowers turned the small courtyard into an oasis in the blighted yellow landscape of the northwest.

There were no flowers outside Gao's plant clinic. People who lacked experience in nurturing flowers and plants consulted with Gao on how to grow them, as well as how to treat plant diseases and prevent bug infestation. On a table near the window, there were all shapes of bottles and pots, each containing a different type of solution, liquid, or powder.

On this particular day, Gao, who is sixty-four years old, was sitting on an old wooden chair with his back to the table. He invited me to sit on a short chair next to the door. The store was about four square meters. Several bags of potting soil were piled in one corner. The dirt was for sale. He would package the dirt in small plastic bags and charge customers thirty cents per bag. Since the store was so small, he could only accommodate a single customer at a time.

This was my second visit. Two days before, a friend of mine who was also a Jiabiangou survivor brought me here to meet Gao. We chatted briefly about Jiabiangou. Before I left, I urged him to spend some time thinking about his life there. I told him that I would come back for an official interview with him a couple of days later.

I looked him in the eye, trying to open him up: "You were at Jiabiangou for three years. There must be something that is forever etched in your memory." Gao repeated my question and then remained silent for a long time. He raised his head, which was full of gray hair, as was his beard.

"There is truly one thing that I can't erase from my memory," he said at last. "I have never shared it with anyone, not even my wife and my children. But the past gnaws at my heart, tormenting me. I'm constantly awakened by nightmares."

Gao seemed to be holding back something. The first time I met him, he had struck me as being open, straightforward, and articulate. I straightened my back and waited patiently for him to talk. I didn't want to rush him. Based on my past experience in interviewing people like Gao, I knew that pushing too hard could lead to the opposite result—a person would either give a perfunctory answer or would withdraw completely. Most Jiabiangou survivors are easily scared. They'd probably mistake a falling leaf for a piece of rock that could hit them on the head.

After another long pause, Gao began his story.

It was 1960, in the beginning of April. One day, the camp director plucked eight healthy Rightists from each division to retrieve truckloads of seed potatoes from Jiuquan. Under normal circumstances, loading and transporting seed potatoes fell under the responsibilities of the agricultural team. But finding eight able-bodied laborers on the agricultural team was an impossible task. We were into our third year at Jiabiangou. Most Rightists were on the verge of physical and mental exhaustion. Some had died. The director had to cast a wider net for an assignment like that.

Several of the people were selected from the agricultural and construction teams; Jin Zhenzhu, a walking stick at the construction team, led our team. He was a couple of years older than I was, short and plump. As a team leader, he didn't have to slave away in the field, and he could enjoy a larger ration of food than we did. Those perks kept him in better physical condition. His face always looked rosy, a rare sight at Jiabiangou.

An ex-convict named Wei, who served out his time at Jiabiangou and stayed on as an employee, was also picked to supervise us.

I was selected too. I was transferred to the carpentry team not long after we arrived at Jiabiangou. Carpentry work wasn't as physically challenging as field labor. Even though my body weakened, I still had more energy than the others. I was only twenty-one years old at the time, in the prime of my youth. I was the youngest Rightist at Jiabiangou.

In the morning, we rose before dawn, gulped down a bowl of corn gruel, and departed. The morning desert air was chilly. We huddled in the back of the truck, our heads tucked inside our coats to ward off the wind. The truck rambled on for more than an hour before we reached Jiuquan. We entered a large empty courtyard, where we saw ahead of us a huge holding room.

A pile of seed potatoes took up half the room. The potatoes looked quite clean; they must have been transported from another province. We squatted down by the pile and hand-shoveled them into sacks. Each time a sack was filled, four of us would carry it outside. A fifth person would bend down under the sack and raise it up on his back while the other three lifted it onto the truck.

Before ten o'clock that morning, the truck was fully loaded and ready to go. Wei, the ex-convict-turned-supervisor, told us to open up one sack and take out eight kilograms of potatoes. He said each one of us would be awarded one kilo, which we could boil and eat before returning to Jiabiangou.

We all applauded the idea. During the past two years, we had never had a full meal. We were salivating at the thought of so many potatoes. I was even bold enough to ask Wei whether he could grant us a couple more kilos so that we could give our stomachs a real treat.

"You're as hungry as we are, aren't you?" I asked.

Wei shook his head.

"No," he said. "It's not that I don't want you to eat. The problem is that if you overstuff yourself, you won't be able to work in the afternoon."

We each ended up eating one kilo of boiled potatoes. It wasn't enough, but it was better than the food at Jiabiangou.

Loading the potatoes was a two-day job. We filled the truck twice a day and didn't need to accompany it back to Jiabiangou. We stayed in the courtyard and slept in an empty room. The next evening, we loaded the last truck and packed our luggage. As we were ready to take off, Wei suddenly stopped us.

"I'm going to reward you with a full meal tonight," he said. "Let's unload a sack, take the potatoes out, and boil them."

In a corner of the courtyard, there was a large clay stove, with a huge wok on top. We picked the heaviest sack—at least eighty kilograms—and filled the wok to the brim. We were truly desperate, and began to stuff the half-cooked potatoes into our mouths.

Remember the saying about hot potatoes? Well, those steaming potatoes were really hot. It was hard to put them in our mouths. We would break a potato in half, blow air onto it, and wolf it down.

When an opportunity for a full meal arose, those of us who lived with constant hunger literally gobbled up the potatoes without even chewing them. We ate, ate, and ate. My stomach bloated, but I didn't want to stop. Everyone knew this was a rare opportunity that wouldn't present itself again in the future.

We filled our stomachs right up to our throats. We couldn't even sit. One person threw up after he tried to bend his back. So we ate standing up. At one point, a Rightist stretched out his neck so he could shove more potatoes down his throat.

Eventually, the nine of us, including the driver, finished off every single potato in the wok.

As we crammed the potatoes into our stomachs, nobody ever thought about the health consequences that we might face. We suffered terribly on the journey back. In those days, the road leading to Jiabiangou was paved with sand and poorly maintained. The truck bounced in and out of ruts and potholes. Each jolt was accompanied by violent vomiting among the group, and piercing stomach pain. We blamed the driver for driving too fast. I pounded on the driver's window, begging him to slow down. He did. As the truck wobbled along, our vomiting gradually subsided, but the pain persisted. We simply lay flat on top of the potato sacks, faceup, with both hands holding on to the sacks to reduce the impact of the bumps.

The two-hour ride seemed endless, and the pain became so overwhelming that I wanted to die. Finally the truck pulled into Jiabiangou and stopped in front of the administrative building. The driver asked us to get off, but the only people who were able to were Jin and Wei. They had fared better because they hadn't eaten as much as we had, and they got to sit in the front seat next to the driver. The rest of us lay on top of the sacks, paralyzed, our bodies weakened from the pain. We were moaning and couldn't summon enough strength to lift our vomit-covered bodies off the sacks.

Director Yan at the construction team saw us and got wind of what had happened. He walked up to Wei, cursing and swearing.

"You bastard, your job was to supervise this group. How could you allow such uncontrolled gorging? Didn't you realize that they could kill themselves with overeating?"

Yan's concerns proved to be justified. That night, after we were carried off the truck and sent back to our bunkhouses, one Rightist from the agricultural team died after midnight. His stomach had burst.

My own stomach pain wouldn't let up. My moaning turned into loud screaming. "I'm going to die!" I shouted. I tossed around in bed. I sat up and then lay down. No matter what I did, I couldn't get relief.

It so happened that there was an emergency in the camp that night. At about midnight, a sluice gate in a small reservoir broke. The camp leadership ordered the carpentry team to rush over immediately for repairs. The reservoir, about eight kilometers west of Jiabiangou, was operated by the Xindiandun camp.

I was spared the task because of my stomach pain. Shi Si-liang, our team leader, assigned Niu Tiande, an elder Rightist, to stay behind to take care of me and watch out for thieves who would sometimes steal lumber from our backyard.

Niu was a university graduate in the pre-Communist era and had worked as an engineer in the northeastern city of Shenyang. In the 1950s, when the new government began to cultivate China's northwest, Niu came to Lanzhou, working for the Gansu Provincial Construction Bureau. By the time he was sent to Jiabiangou, he was already approaching sixty. Niu was bookish, clumsy, and weak. Labor-intensive assignments in the field were way out of his capability. Shi was his former colleague at the Provincial Construction Bureau. He was very sympathetic toward Niu's plight. To protect Niu, he convinced the authorities that Niu could do good carpentry work and had him transferred to our team.

Niu and I soon became good friends. I was the first Rightist to be assigned to the carpentry team, a founding member. In the summer of 1958, when large groups of Rightists arrived at Jiabiangou, the camp found itself short of farm tools. Leaders purchased shovels, plows, and other equipment, but there was no carpenter to assemble them. I volunteered myself for the task. Even though I had no carpentry skills, I had grown up in the countryside and had assembled simple farm tools before. They were not all that difficult. With permission from the camp leaders, I worked day and night, examining some old tools at the warehouse and learning to assemble the new ones. After I completed the project, the authorities simply kept me on the carpentry team. Later, several professional carpenters, who were sent to Jiabiangou because of their anti-Party remarks, joined the team. With their coaching and training, I became a bona fide carpenter myself.

On our team, I admired Niu's intellect. He was very friendly. As you know, I was young and restless. My shirts and pants wore out fast and I never bothered to mend them. Niu would patch up the holes for me. He was a little bit of a compulsive cleaner, and couldn't stand it when I wore dirty and smelly clothes. He would force me to change and then hand-wash my clothes.

That night Niu took good care of me. He put his own washbasin under my bed to catch my vomit. Niu had me lean on my quilt and he slowly and gently massaged my stomach, which hurt terribly. Gradually, the massage produced results. By early morning, after a night of intermittent vomiting and diarrhea, my stomach had emptied out. Niu caught all the disgusting stuff from my stomach with his basin, dumped it out on the ground outside the tent, and came back for more. All night long, he ran around, without a wink of sleep.

He put a small makeshift stove near my bed, gathered some firewood from the yard, and heated up the room. I fell into a deep sleep.

When I woke up the next afternoon, the stomach pain was gone. I had gained back some strength. I drank a bowl of cold water, put on my clothes, and walked out. The sun had already gone down. It looked like it might have been three or four o'clock. Members of the carpentry team lived in a courtyard bunkhouse next to the carpentry shop. The courtyard was eerily empty. Everyone was out on assignments somewhere.

I passed the carpentry workshop and was planning to look for some food at the mill shop. My stomach was growling with hunger. A few steps farther, I noticed something strange: a broken wooden rake in front of the carpentry workshop had been moved to the side of the building. It was an old-style horse-drawn rake, with a big rectangular wooden frame and long iron nails to loosen or level soil. The agricultural team left it there for us to repair. The rake was leaning against the wall. I assumed that someone had used it as a ladder and climbed it to go up to the rooftop. I wanted to find out who it was.

I stood on top of the "ladder" and looked around. A few meters away, I saw someone lying flat on his stomach, his rear end toward me. Even though I couldn't see his face, I knew it was Niu. It came as a surprise. Niu had reached an advanced age and his body was quite weak. Why did he climb all the way up here? What was he doing?

I found it quite strange. I climbed onto the roof quietly and crept up to him. I stood behind him and peered over his shoulder. There was piece of square blue cloth wrapper on the ground. I recognized it—he'd bundle up his shirts and pants with that piece of blue cloth with a white flower pattern and use it as a pillow. I noticed a thin layer of sticky, yellow brownish matter evenly spread on top of the cloth. It had apparently been in the sun for a while and was semidry. I recognized pieces of white and yellowish potato chunks. My heart tightened. Good Heavens! Niu had collected my vomit and excrement from the previous night, spread it on his cloth wrapper, and put it out to dry in the sun. He was carefully sorting out the undigested fingertip-size potato chunks and stuffing them into his mouth.

My heart tightened. I felt like I had been hit by an electric current, and my brain went blank. I didn't know how long I stood there, ten or twenty seconds maybe. Then I came to my senses. I stepped forward, pushed him to one side, and kicked at the blue cloth. Some of the sticky chunks and the cloth wrapper went flying in the air. I kicked and kicked. The stuff fell from the roof to the ground below.

Niu let out a loud piercing scream, and his face distorted with anger. Like a cornered animal, he jumped up and threw himself at me.

His scream scared me. I had never heard him scream before. I thought he was going to hit me and push me off the roof. I didn't realize a kind old man like Niu could rage and charge at me like a lion. Shocked as I was, I moved a couple of steps back and found myself standing on the edge of the roof, with no way to escape. I balled my fists and got ready to fight back. But when he moved closer, he simply grabbed both of my wrists, paused, and then began to shake my arms.

"Little Gao, I treated you like my very own little brother," he said. "I thought you were a good man. How could you be so brutal to me?"

He didn't hit me, or push me. He simply vented his anger through his words. "Why? Why are you so cruel?"

"How could you eat that stuff?" I said.

He yelled back, "Why not? What's wrong with eating it?"

I was struggling with myself. I meant to tell him how filthy he was. I wanted to say that the half-digested potatoes were for pigs, not for human beings. But I didn't want to hurt his feelings. So I simply repeated, "You can't eat that stuff. You can't eat it."

"Yes, I can!" he screamed back. "Yes, I can."

Waves of sadness swept over me. Here he was, a well-educated and respected engineer. How could he humiliate himself by eating another person's vomit and excrement? I had tried to protect his dignity. How could he think I was evil for trying to snatch his food away? As I was going over those thoughts in my mind, tears welled up in my eyes. I began to sob.

"Niu, let's not fight anymore. You are an intelligent man, college-educated. You should know what is edible and what isn't."

Niu was startled by my words. He slowly let go of my arms, and then he suddenly pulled me into his bosom and cried like a child. I could feel teardrops falling on my face. His emotional outburst was contagious. We huddled together on the rooftop and wept like two children.

This incident happened almost forty years ago, but I remember it like it was yesterday. I'll never forget Niu's wailing. When the carpenters returned that night, I didn't share the story with them. I didn't know whether I had done the right thing by intruding on him like that. Even today, I still wonder about the same question. Maybe I overreacted.

The incident on the rooftop actually brought us closer. As a veteran member of the carpentry team, I knew lots of people and could always get extra food. I began sharing my food with Niu. I stole flour from the mill shop and would share that with him too.

I had another special assignment. As you know, there were mess halls in Jiabiangou, one operated by the agricultural team and the other one by the construction team. Steamed wheat and corn bread were our staple foods. But the bamboo steamers in the mess halls constantly broke. Each time something went wrong with a steamer, I was the person they called for repairs. While fixing the steamer, I would scrape off the bread crumbs stuck on the steamer and put them in a bag so I could take them back to my bunkhouse. Sometimes I would steal a couple of corn cakes. The cook pretended not to see it. I always split whatever I had with Niu.

When summer harvest arrived, Niu was transferred back to the agricultural team. It wasn't a good year. After the harvest, our food ration was reduced. As food was scarce and hard to come by, I no longer had any extra to share with him. I myself was hungry all the time. So we fell out of touch for a long time.

At the end of October, I saw Niu again, after we moved to Mingshui. The carpentry team had been disbanded. I was the only one left. The other members had been reassigned to the agricultural team. At Mingshui, I lived by myself inside a small cave. I was ordered to bring with me some simple carpentry tools and take on small repair jobs.

As our food supplies dwindled further, some Rightists started to comb the oasis for edible weeds. I didn't think the weeds had any nutritional value. It wasn't worth the effort.

Occasionally, I would go out to the grassland and collect some dried cow dung to fuel a small stove inside my cave. I covered the cave entrance with an old blanket to ward off the cold wind. I lay in bed all day to kill time. Soon I began to suffer from edema, and my body became swollen. I felt cold even when I wore cotton-padded coats and pants.

One day, as I was dozing off, I heard a rustling noise outside the entrance to my cave. I thought it was a wolf—they converged at Mingshui once the corpses started piling up, and they even began to attack the living, knowing that we were too weak to fight back. One night, a wolf actually poked its head into my cave. I had to chase it away with an ax.

I grabbed an ax, but then I heard a soft voice.

"Little Gao, are you there? It's me."

I opened the curtain. It was Niu. He was crawling on the ground and gasping for air. I tried to pull him inside, but he refused. He just wanted to see me one more time. He didn't think he was going to last long.

He was living in a bigger cave, which had been converted into a makeshift patient ward, at the south end of the camp. He had come over to ask me a favor. Before he stopped panting, he took out of his coat pocket a shoe brush made from palm fiber and a hand-knit sewing kit.

"If you survive and return to Lanzhou," he said, "can you go visit my family and tell my wife what happened to me here? Take these two items. My wife and my daughter will recognize them. Before I left, my wife gave me this brush because I used to be finicky about shining my leather shoes. My daughter made this sewing kit so I could patch up my clothes when they got worn-out. When they see the brush and the sewing kit, they will believe what you tell them."

I accepted the brush and the sewing kit. I didn't say anything to comfort him. I simply promised that I would deliver it to his family if I was able to leave Mingshui alive. I could tell from the look of him that he wouldn't last for more than three days. I had already witnessed many deaths at Mingshui and was familiar with the symptoms of a dying person. First they suffered from edema. It would disappear for several days and then return. When that happened, it meant imminent death. Sometimes, patients' faces swelled up to the size of pumpkins. Their eyelids bulged like soft pears, while their eyes shrunk to slits. When they walked, they hobbled along, stopping for a few seconds between steps. Their lips were so swollen that they couldn't close their mouths. From a distance, you might think that they were perpetually smiling. Their hair stood upright. When they talked, they sounded like whimpering puppies. On that day, Niu's face, voice, and his gait matched this description of a dying person.

Five days after I saw Niu for the last time, I escaped Mingshui. I was still young and I didn't want to die like Niu. I was afraid that if I didn't do something fast, I'd become as sick as Niu and wouldn't have the strength to run away. One night in early November, I left, carrying a wooden stick as a weapon to protect myself against wolves. I didn't bring anything else besides a couple of my medical books and Niu's shoe brush and sewing kit. I used to be an herbal doctor and those books were valuable to me. At about nine or ten o'clock, I boarded a train at the Mingshui River Station.

The journey was filled with perils and hardships. I escaped to Lanzhou and met up with my sister and my mother. Before I left the city, I took out Niu's shoe brush and sewing kit and handed them to my mother. I jotted down the names of Niu's wife and daughter and their address, and told Niu's story to my mother.

With the help of my mother and sister, I secretly returned to the village where I had grown up, in a remote isolated region of Shaanxi Province. I spent a winter there. In the spring of 1961, I heard about the release of all the Rightists at Jiabiangou. Eager to find out how my former work unit would handle my case, I went back to Lanzhou. I stayed with my mother and my sister for several days. My mother told me she had met with Niu's wife and his daughter, and had broken the sad news to them. Niu's wife and daughter cried for a long time.

Escape

I went back to Gao Jiyi's floral clinic for the third time. Sitting on the same wooden stool near the door, I continued with our interview, asking him details about his escape from Jiabiangou. Before starting his story, he filled me in on how he ended up running a floral clinic.

Gao had been an herbal-medicine doctor at what is now the Lanzhou Municipal Traditional Chinese Medicine Hospital. In 1957, he was branded a Rightist. In 1978, after the Party reversed the verdict against him, the Lanzhou Public Health Bureau assigned him a job at the First People's Hospital, where the leaders urged him to continue his old job as a doctor. Gao declined. It had been more than twenty years since he had last practiced medicine. He felt that he was too rusty to be a competent doctor. He was worried he might jeopardize people's lives.

Instead, Gao volunteered to became a gardener. The hospital was bare, without even a lawn. One couldn't find a single pot of flowers. The municipal "greening" committee had criticized the hospital several times for its failure to create a green environment. Gao said he had tended orchids and grown flowers at his home village and managed to convince the hospital leaders that he could make the hospital a "green" model for others to emulate in three years. They hired him and gave him an administrator's salary and benefits.

Gao attended a gardening seminar in Beijing and used his car-

pentry skills to build a nursery, where he nurtured a variety of common as well as exotic plants and flowers. He gained quite a reputation in the region. Gardens sprang up within the hospital premises. Plants and flowers adorned patient wards and offices. Within a year the city awarded the hospital a big plaque for its greening efforts.

Gao worked for the hospital for over ten years and applied for retirement when he turned fifty-eight. He was then hired by a floral company. When the company switched ownership, Gao resigned in anger after getting bullied by the new owner, and opened up a small floral clinic that could earn him twenty to thirty yuan a day. He felt leisurely and carefree. He liked the fact that he didn't have to worry about food and clothing, or getting harassed by the police.

Gao was sitting on the same chair, his left hand resting on a counter covered with bottles and small flowerpots. He had the face of a Chinese peasant—tan and rough. He wasn't that old, only sixty-four. Gao looked serious and seldom laughed. When he did, the laughter lasted only a few seconds before it froze abruptly. His eyes were dark, focused, and stern. His voice was loud, but he spoke in a monotone. "My escape was filled with risks," he said.

I left Mingshui one night in early November 1960. That was five days after my friend Niu Tiande visited me in my cave. I don't know exactly what time it was. I didn't have a watch at that time. I used to wear an expensive Plum Flower watch, but one day, soon after I arrived at Jiabiangou, Chen Fenglin, my group leader, cornered me and forced me to take it off and hand it over to him. He said confiscating my watch would prevent me from running away. He promised to give it back after I served out my time there. Anyway, since it wasn't too long after dinner, I'd guess it was about eight o'clock. I picked up a wooden stick, put on a long winter coat, and snuck out of the cave, heading toward the train station in Mingshui.

I had obtained information from relatives visiting other Rightists that an eastbound passenger train stopped at the Mingshui River Station every night around nine o'clock. The camp was about three kilometers away from the train station, so it didn't take me long to get there. I waited for a while before the train pulled into the station.

There were guards patrolling the station. Camp officials on duty would go on patrol after eight-thirty in the evening. It was difficult to catch Rightists on the road—escapees could easily hide behind the sand dunes—but the guards knew that the only way out of Mingshui was the train station. The guards would seize runaway Rightists right before the train arrived. Those who were caught would be put under arrest, have their hands tied behind their backs, and then be shipped to Yinma camp, where serious criminals were incarcerated. If the camp leadership showed leniency and treated the escape as a lesser offense, the culprit would only be locked up in solitary confinement for several days and publicly denounced at staff meetings. Then he would be reassigned to a specially monitored team.

I lucked out that night. I didn't run into any guards on patrol. In those days, a passenger had to show an authorization letter from their work unit when purchasing a ticket. I didn't have the letter, nor did I have any money. I simply hid in a dark spot under a viaduct near the station, waiting for the train.

I did face other problems—I encountered two wolves. I saw them from a distance, but they never got too close to me. Maybe they were intimidated by the wooden stick I was carrying. Or perhaps they had just feasted on a dead body and weren't hungry anymore.

I waited in the dark until the train's blinding white lights flashed past the waiting room and the ticket office. There were only a few passengers waiting on the platform. Two railway workers in blue overalls waved their signals. After the train came to a full stop, the conductors descended the stairs and stood by the entrance to greet passengers and check tickets. The passenger cars were well lit. It was a good time to board the train, but I didn't move. Without a ticket, I was afraid that the conductors would catch me and prevent me from getting on. I was also afraid that my capturers might jump out from their hiding place and seize me. The conductors went back up and closed the doors. The railway workers waved the lanterns up and down. The train whistle pierced the air. As the train clanked away, I jumped out from the dark and ran after it. I grabbed the handle of a car door and climbed on. I assumed that the railway worker didn't see me; otherwise he would have sent a signal for the train to stop. The train kept moving and gradually picked up speed. Within seconds, we were out in the wilderness. I held on to the handle and pressed my body close to the door, which was locked. I could see people walking around inside. The conductor was nowhere to be seen, so I banged my fist on the door, hoping to catch the attention of a passenger.

The sound of my banging was lost in the deafening noise of clanking wheels and roaring wind. It was freezing. My hands were numb from the cold and I could hardly hold on to the handle. If I stayed outside any longer, I would plunge to my death under the wheels.

I banged harder and harder, and finally a passenger saw me. He tried to scream something. I couldn't hear a word. Then he left. A couple of minutes later, he came back with a conductor. He opened the door, grabbed the collar of my jacket, and dragged me into the car. After he had securely fastened the door behind me, he began to lecture me.

"How dare you! Are you trying to kill yourself?"

Once his tirade was over, he asked if I had a ticket. I said I had purchased one and then patted my various coat pockets, pretending to look for it. I was wearing a brand-new woolen jacket that I had dug out of my suitcase. I had shaved and trimmed my hair before I left. He didn't suspect that I was an escaped prisoner, and he was quite polite to me. He simply ordered me to move into the conductor's room. Then, without saying anything, he locked the door and left.

Realizing for the first time that I had finally left Jiabiangou, I started to relax. Fatigue from my escape caught up with me. I leaned my head against the chair and dozed off.

Someone hit my forehead. I opened my eyes and saw a policeman standing in front of me. I was too emaciated and exhausted to respond, so I shut my eyes and went back to sleep.

The policeman hit my head harder. I woke up fully and struggled to sit up, knowing that I was in trouble.

"Why'd you hit me so hard?" I mumbled, pretending to be nonchalant.

The policeman seemed stunned by my reaction, and feigned a smile. "Did you get hurt? I was just trying to wake you up. Can I see your ticket?"

I knew I couldn't lie to the policeman about the ticket. "I didn't have money to buy a ticket. I haven't eaten for two days. Do you have any food?"

The policeman stared at me as if I were crazy. "Who are you? What do you do?"

I told him I was an official at the Organization Department of the Party branch at Fufeng County, Shaanxi Province. "I came to Mingshui camp for an assignment, but was robbed. I lost my bag and everything. I haven't had any food for two days."

I could tell that he was rather dubious about my story.

"What's your name? What are the names of the Party secretary and the deputy secretary of Fufeng?"

I answered calmly. Apart from my name, which was fake, the rest was true. I had learned the names from an official who had stopped by Mingshui to visit a friend.

My answers, smooth and prompt, didn't quite dispel his suspicions. He probed further. "You should have sent a telegram to your supervisor to ask for help. Why did you climb aboard a train in the middle of the night?"

"My good comrade," I said, "my assignment involved an investigation at Mingshui. That's a forced labor camp. There's no food there and they're starving. How could I just sit around, waiting for help to arrive?"

My story seemed to convince him. His tone softened somewhat.

"Whatever happened to you," he said, "you're not allowed to ride the train without a ticket. You can go ahead and find a seat. We'll let you off near Zhangye station. It's a big place and you can ask the local Party committee to help resolve your difficulties."

I didn't argue with him. If I had refused to get off, it wouldn't fit with my status as "an official from Shaanxi." My true identity could be exposed. So I simply thanked him and picked an empty seat.

When the train reached Zhangye, the policeman gathered me and a dozen other passengers without tickets and ordered us to get off. I tried to walk around the train and find another way to sneak back on, but he saw me and stopped me. He handed me over to another policeman at the platform. I tried to repeat the same lies to this officer, hoping to get some sympathy. But he just ignored me and ordered me and the other offenders to move on.

I followed the crowd out of the station and found myself inside a dark courtyard packed with people—some standing, others squatting. They murmured nervously to one another. From their conversations, I could tell that many of them were migrant workers from the rural areas of Henan and Sichuan provinces. The light was on in one room off the courtyard, and when I looked in, I saw two policemen sitting behind desks. I realized that we were supposed to register, and that meant we'd be put in detention. I always heard stories about how local police rounded up migrant workers, detained them for a short time, and then shipped them to the collective farms along the Hexi Corridor, where physical laborers were in short supply. As the Chinese saying goes, I was in danger of going "from a tiger's den into a cave of wolves."

The line moved slowly. I noticed the policemen had left the courtyard to continue their patrol duties outside. I quietly moved out of the line and merged with the crowd at the back. The courtyard was fenced in by a low mud wall. I climbed over it and ran away.

I went back to the train station and spent the rest of the evening inside a waiting room. Occasionally a policeman would walk by. I sat there calmly and read my book, pretending I was waiting for the train. Since I was dressed nicely and didn't act like a migrant, the police didn't bother me.

In the morning, the sun rose and it became warmer outside. I left the waiting room. I was tired and my stomach was empty—I had to find something to eat. I wandered along a small street leading to Zhangye County. I saw several restaurants and a bakery, where oven-baked cakes were piled up neatly inside a glass counter. I didn't have any money or anything valuable to trade. The only treasures I had were two reference books: *A Pocket Edition of the Acupuncture Encyclopedia* and *A Comprehensive Guide to Chinese Herbal Medicine.* I had brought them to Jiabiangou and then to Mingshui. During the winter, when many Rightists burned their books to keep warm, I saved them and burned dried cow dung instead.

But now I had to trade the books for food. I walked up and down the street with the books in my hand, and anytime I saw someone who looked as if they might be literate, I would catch up with them and ask if they wanted to buy my books. Most ignored me and kept walking. Some would stop to check the covers before handing them back to me. The books were useless to them if they weren't doctors.

By afternoon, I was desperate. My legs were weak and I was hit by a dizzy spell. If I didn't eat soon, I would drop dead on the street. I thought to myself that I'd better go back to the waiting room. If I collapsed there, the railway workers might be able to intervene and offer me some food to save my life, or they would send me to a detention center, where free food might be provided.

As I headed back toward the station, I bumped into two men with long gray beards, sitting in the sun in front of a house. From their clothes and their manners, they looked like educated people. I decided to try my luck one more time.

"Grandpa," I said, "I have two books with me. Do you want to buy them?"

They both looked at me and one of them took the books out of my hands, flipped through the pages, and asked where I was from. I blurted out another lie.

"I come from northern Shaanxi Province and grew up in a family of herbal doctors. But lately my hometown has been hit by famine. I'm on my way to Xinjiang to pick up a construction job. But I ran out of money and have to sell these two books."

Upon hearing my story, one of them stood up and said, "Kid, put your books away. I'll buy two oven-baked cakes for you."

The two kindhearted men bought me two cakes at a state-run restaurant. They even asked the waiter to bring me a bowl of hot water before they left. I devoured the cakes and drank up the water. With the food and water in my stomach, I felt much stronger. I went back to the waiting room and started to figure out ways to board the train again.

Throughout the afternoon and early evening, three east-bound trains stopped at the station. All the boarding gates were closely guarded by conductors. It was impossible to get on without a ticket. Several migrants with large bags on their backs had been taken away by police after they tried to get on illegally. I didn't dare try it.

I didn't get on the next day either. But as I was lingering outside the waiting room, I found a used ticket stub on the ground.

Around midnight, a train pulled in. I waited until the train was about to leave, and then ran over to the boarding gate, shouting, "Don't close the door. Let me on."

I flashed the used ticket in front of the conductor while he was locking up and hurried into the train car. Luckily he didn't stop me.

I immediately ran into another car and sat on a seat near the entrance, checking to make sure that the conductor wasn't following me. Since the train was crowded, I crawled under the seat and stayed there until the train arrived in Lanzhou.

I didn't dare return to my former work unit. I figured the authorities at Jiabiangou would have issued a notice about my escape to all the local public security bureaus and street committees. I waited until ten o'clock that night before I visited my sister's house. My sister was a veteran Communist soldier. She joined the Communists while they were fighting against the Nationalists near my hometown. After the Communist victory in 1949, she became a doctor at an army hospital. Before I was convicted as a Rightist, my mother left our village and moved in with my sister and her husband.

My mother was thrilled to see me. She assumed that I had been released, but when I told her that I had run away from Jiabiangou, she didn't blame me. She was just happy that I was home. My sister, however, was scared.

"What are we going to do?" she kept asking me. "The Public Security Bureau in Lanzhou could be here to search for you any second now."

I understood her fear that my appearance would implicate her and her family. I promised that I would only stay overnight and would leave the next morning.

"I'm going back to our village," I said. "If the police don't arrest me, I will live as a farmer for the rest of my life."

My sister finally became resigned to the fact that it was my only way out. I then asked her one more favor.

"Could you buy me a train ticket? You're a military officer and can buy a ticket without an authorization letter."

My sister put on her uniform and left right away. After my sister had stepped out the door, my mother broke into tears and asked me not to blame my sister.

That night, my mother cooked me a big bowl of noodle soup with pickled vegetables. In the early morning, I bid them goodbye and went to the station. My sister tucked forty yuan ($5.80) in my pocket. She also gave me four cartons of expensive cigarettes, which were only available to military officers.

"These aren't for you. You have more obstacles to get over before you reach home. You might need them to trade for favors."

It was an easy train ride. After seven hours, I found myself in the central city of Xian. On the train, I befriended the person sitting next to me. I used his authorization letter and purchased another train ticket from Xian to the mining town of Tongchuan, where I needed to change to a bus. It turned out to be a big hassle to buy a bus ticket. There were only three buses going to my hometown every day. Each bus could accommodate only thirty-some passengers, but the bus terminal was packed with seven hundred people.

I sat in the waiting room, worrying myself to death. A uniformed man walked in. He looked like an employee of the bus company. Mr. Uniform stopped in front of a young fellow sitting not too far from me, and ordered him to show his ticket and identity card. The fellow handed over his ticket, explaining that he didn't have an identity card. Mr. Uniform examined the ticket and barked, "If you don't have an identity card, how did you get this? I'm confiscating the ticket."

The poor fellow begged and protested, but to no avail. Mr. Uniform even pushed him out of the waiting room. My heart beat very fast. I didn't realize there were such strict rules at the bus terminals. I wondered if I might be the next target, and would be sent to the police station as a criminal.

Mr. Uniform left without inspecting anyone else. After observing him closely, I found him quite suspicious. It occurred to me that he could be one of those scam artists or gang members who dressed up as a staff member of the bus company and bullied poor, ignorant country folks. Just then, an idea hit me. I stood up and followed Mr. Uniform.

He walked into a restaurant. I did too. He sat at a table. I sat at a table next to him. To avoid arousing his suspicion, I took out a cigarette and started to smoke. Now and then, I would glance at him and he'd glance back at me. Finally he spoke, asking me where I came from. I told him I was a doctor from Lanzhou. He paused and inquired if name-brand cigarettes were readily available to ordinary residents in Lanzhou.

I answered casually. "It's hard to get cigarettes. But I'm a doctor so it's fairly easy for me."

His tone changed. He begged me, "Could you give me a pack?"

I pulled one pack out of my bag and tossed it to him. As he tried to pay me money, I pushed his hand aside.

"Don't worry about it," I said. "I'm here on a visit. Since I don't know anybody there, could you help me get a ticket to Yan-an?"

Mr. Uniform hesitated for a couple of seconds. He looked around, reached his hand into his pocket, and handed me the "confiscated" ticket.

"I bought this one for a relative. Why don't you take it?"

I was overjoyed. I paid him the money and gave him four more cigarette packs as gifts.

I couldn't believe I had managed to obtain a ticket so easily. The next morning, I rode the bus to Yan-an, where I had to transfer to another bus that went to the city of Sui-de. I ran into a ticket scalper, haggled with him over price and paid three yuan for a ticket that carried me to Sui-de.

After I came out of the bus stop, I had about four yuan with me, and more than sixty kilometers to walk to my village. There was no bus going there. I spent one yuan at a cheap hotel and began my journey early the next morning, without breakfast.

Two or three kilometers outside Sui-de, I felt so tired and hungry that I couldn't walk any farther. I stopped a farmer driving a horse-drawn cart. His head was covered by a piece of white cloth and he was carrying a bag bulging with steamed buns. Once we started talking, I found out that he was traveling to Sui-de to pick up his son, a migrant worker who had fainted at the bus station.

"People are so heartless nowadays," said the old man.

"When they saw my son pass out from hunger, nobody offered him food or tried to save his life."

"Grandpa, I'm in no better position than your son. He's lucky, because he'll see you soon, and be fed. I have sixty kilometers to walk before I reach my home. I haven't had any food since last night."

The warmhearted old man removed the bag from his back and took out six corn millet buns for me. Then he hurried away in a different direction. I subsisted on those buns and walked for four days before I finally reached my village in Jia County.

I stayed with my uncle for a month to recuperate. Once I had recovered, I went home. I rested for a whole winter and as the weather turned warm, my health improved further. I even started to farm.

As Gao was wrapping up his story, I asked some more questions: "Did the guard search for you that night? As far as I know, those who had escaped from Mingshui wouldn't dare to take a train at the Mingshui River Station. It was too close to the camp and the guards could easily capture the escapee. In addition, after you returned to your hometown, did the local Public Security Bureau try to search for you? I have been told that many escaped Rightists would stay away from their hometowns or villages. Authorities at Jiabiangou would notify the hometown police and seek their assistance in capturing the escaped Rightist."

Gao paused for a few seconds. "Those are good questions. The camp did send security guards to search for me that night. I just omitted that part because I didn't mean to tell you about it . . ."

There is something that still haunts me, and causes great pain. Let me share it with you. When I escaped that night from Mingshui, I wasn't alone. I had another person with me. The two of us walked out together. His name was Luo Hongyuan.

Let me start from the beginning. At Jiabiangou, I was a founding member of the carpentry team, but that didn't mean I had the best skills. The most experienced and skillful carpenter on the team was my mentor, Luo. He didn't start out as a carpenter. Luo had graduated from the prestigious Qinghua University in the 1930s and become an architectural engineer. In 1949, he was fired from his job because he had joined the Nationalist Party under Chiang Kai-shek. He became a carpenter and was transferred to Baiyin Nonferrous Metal Company. During the anti-Rightist campaign, his past involvement in the Nationalist Party resurfaced. He was labeled a "historical counterrevolutionary" and ended up in Jiabiangou.

I don't know how he performed as an engineer, but his carpentry skills were first-class. Unlike the other skilled carpenters, most of whom were illiterate, Luo was well educated. He could draw and design. Luo had noticed that the horse-drawn carts at Jiabiangou and in the Hexi Corridor region were equipped with huge wooden wheels, which were taller than the actual body of the cart, clumsy and uncomfortable. Luo designed a cart with smaller wheels. When assembled, the new cart looked good and operated efficiently. When Rightists rode the cart to collect manure in local villages, we attracted a crowd.

Why did I make Luo my mentor? When I first settled in Jiabiangou, I considered my incarceration to be the end of my career. Even if I served out my time, there was no way the government would allow me to practice medicine. I felt dejected. I made up my mind that I would learn to make a living with my hands. Being a blue-collar worker would shield me from political campaigns. I was attracted to carpentry, and so I picked Luo as my teacher. We had a traditional ritual, in which I knelt down and kowtowed to him, making my apprenticeship official.

What happened later in my life proved that I had made the right choice. The carpentry skills that I acquired from Luo enabled me to survive those turbulent years under Mao. After I escaped and went back to my home village, I grew crops and took on carpentry jobs in the winter to earn money for the village and for myself. During the Cultural Revolution, the Red Guards in my village found out about my past and were ready to denounce me publicly. I escaped once again. I wandered all over the region and picked up odd jobs. I made enough money that I was able to move my wife and kids out of the village.

In my previous story, I mentioned that I was quite close to Niu Tiande. But Luo was like a father to me. He taught me every type of carpentry skill and even imparted to me knowledge of construction design. In return for his kindness, I took on the role of caregiver, doing his chores and running errands for him. Being an intellectual, he was proud and maintained his dignity, and refused to go out and steal. As a consequence, he always went hungry. Whenever possible, I would help him get extra food. Since Luo's wife and children lived in the northeast, nobody ever came to visit him; his family probably didn't realize how miserable life was at Jiabiangou.

One time, the "rabbit team" invited me to repair a fence. As you know, the camp was set on two hills. Rightists put fences around the smaller hill and raised rabbits. When I was working on the fence, several rabbits jumped out at me. They must have been surprised to see a human being there. Nobody else was around, so I aimed a wooden yardstick at two rabbits and whacked them on their noses. They plumped onto the ground, dead. I put them in my toolbox and snuck them back to the camp. I concealed them under a pile of lumber, hoping to find an opportunity to boil them for a meal. A chance came the next day. The camp authorities ordered every team to pick some members to collect firewood for the mess hall. The carpentry team had to send two volunteers. Since the job required a long walk to a desert area on the far north side, nobody wanted to go. I raised my hand and volunteered me and Luo. He was reluctant to go out in the cold. He stamped his feet and winked at me, asking me to remove him from the list, but our team leader selected us. As we were struggling through the desert, he complained bitterly and became upset. Once we were away from everyone, I brought out the dead rabbits from the inner pocket of my cotton-padded green winter coat. He smiled and cursed me for not telling him earlier. We found a spot behind a sand dune, collected some firewood, lit a fire, and roasted the rabbit. It was delicious. After the meal, we buried the fur and the innards out of fear of being discovered.

As I mentioned yesterday, our carpentry team was disbanded in the summer of 1960. Luo and several other members were assigned to the agricultural team. We rarely saw each other.

I was in one of the first groups to arrive at Mingshui. I had a small cave all to myself and lived not far from the camp's administrative offices, which were inside a row of makeshift tents. This living arrangement made it easier for the leaders to summon me for any carpentry jobs that might arise.

One afternoon, Luo showed up at my cave looking awful—unshaven, his hair disheveled, and thin as a twig. His clothes were literally in tatters. I was appalled. When we were on the carpentry team together, Luo shaved and kept his clothes clean. He had maintained the dignified appearance of an old-time intellectual.

"What happened to you," I asked.

He didn't answer my questions directly. "I lost my luggage," he murmured.

It turned out that he and twenty other Rightists from the agricultural team had just been put on a freight train from Jiabiangou to Mingshui. After several hours, the train stopped in the middle of the desert. The guards ordered everyone to toss their luggage to the ground and jump off. Then the train moved on. When the camp sent a horse-drawn cart to collect his luggage, they found out that his was missing.

I couldn't bear to see him so dejected, so I tried to comfort him by offering to share my cave. For a couple of days we slept on one bed, sharing a quilt. Later, I scouted around and stole a quilt from another cave, left by a Rightist who had died. I set up bedding for him inside while I slept near the cave entrance to block the wind, so it wouldn't be too cold for him. We lived like that for two weeks, but the cold became intolerable. I picked up cow dung on the grassland and started a small fire near the cave entrance to help ward off the early winter cold.

Not much later, Luo came down with cirrhosis. His stomach bloated like a drum. His waist became so thick and his whole body so swollen that he could barely fit into his clothes. I went to get Dr. Deng at the camp clinic. After an examination, he suggested that Luo be hospitalized right away. The camp's patient ward, housed in a large cave, was located not too far away. I collected Luo's belongings and checked him in there. About thirty dying Rightists slept side by side on the floor. They shifted around and managed to make a small space for him to lie down. When I visited him a week later, his stomach had shrunk, but his body was still swollen. When he sat up, he didn't have enough strength to talk with me.

It was at that time that the edema struck me. As my body weakened, I decided to escape. Before my departure, I visited Luo.

My original intention was to say a quick goodbye and leave. I knew for sure that he wouldn't live long. I wanted to see if he needed me to do anything after his death. After I started talking with him, however, I was gripped by sadness. The thought of him dying in this wild desert, with his body abandoned by the sand dunes, intensified my grief. I couldn't help lying down next to him, and whispering in his ear, "Teacher Luo, I'm going to run away. Do you have anything to say to me?"

His lips didn't move, but I could feel his body trembling. One of his hands reached out from under the quilt, and held mine tightly. Then, slowly, he turned his face toward me. I knew he wanted to tell me something. I moved my ear close to his mouth.

"You're really leaving?"

I nodded. He opened his swollen eyes and pressed my hands. "I will go with you."

I was taken aback by his words. Emaciated and sick as he was, how could he expect to endure the long, arduous journey? At the same time, I was touched by his strong desire to live. I meant to tell him, You can't move anymore. Just stay here and tough it out. In a couple of days, the authorities might release everyone.

But I didn't say this out of the fear that I might hurt his feelings. It was like telling him to wait for his death. Instead, I just remained silent.

"Please take me," he said. "I can walk."

Lines of tears streamed down his nose from his swollen eyes. I knew deep down that he wouldn't be able to leave, but he had made it impossible for me to say no. I stopped myself from crying anymore and whispered in his ear, "Meet me at my cave tomorrow evening, after dark. Dress warmly."

I got up and walked out without turning my head.

The next evening, after eating my bowl of corn gruel, I began to prepare for my adventure. There wasn't really much to do. I put on my long winter coat and tied my pants with a piece of linen rope. I also swallowed two corn and vegetable buns that I had stolen from the mess hall to boost my energy. I lay down in bed, covered myself with a quilt, and lay waiting for darkness to descend. While lying there, I fretted over my plan with Luo. Was it possible that he had changed his mind? Was he too weak? My original plan was to run west, all the way to Yuanshanzi station, to catch a train there. But if Luo came along, I would have to take the easier route and go to the Ming-shui River Station. There were added perils to this plan—guards were everywhere and the chances of getting caught were greater. But I had no other options.

My mind was entangled with all sorts of ideas. Luo tottered in before it was fully dark. He had lied to the nurse, saying that he was dying and that he wanted to discuss his will with me.

I asked him to sit down and rest up. Once it was pitch-dark, I crept out of my cave, making sure that the coast was clear. Then we set off.

There was no moon that night. Officials who happened to come out of the mess hall or the administrative building wouldn't be able to see very far. In addition, the guards hadn't yet started their usual rounds. I told Luo to put his hand on my shoulder for support.

We had covered less than a kilometer before Luo collapsed to the ground. I had one of his arms around my shoulder and one of mine wrapped around his waist. We dragged on, like two wounded soldiers retreating from a battleground.

We wobbled along for another three hundred meters. He fell to his knees, sweating and panting, "Go ahead, Little Gao. I can't go on."

I knew that he had tried with all his might. I told him that I would carry him on my back. Once he was on top of me, I started to reconsider. He wasn't as light as I had expected. Even though his health had deteriorated, every part of his body had retained water. His waist was thick, his legs and arms swollen. He was heavy.

I only managed to stumble on for about one hundred meters before my legs gave out on me. I was gasping for air and sweating profusely. After all, I had shed so much weight during the previous year and I was very weak myself. I put Luo down and said, "Let's take a quick break."

We stood facing each other, panting. I said apologetically, "I'm no longer as strong as I used to be. In the old days, I could carry you all the way to the station without any breaks."

He didn't speak. He simply stared at me. I looked at him but couldn't see his face clearly. The desert was impenetrably dark and eerily quiet. Only a few stars winked feebly down at us. A strong wind roared by, freezing the sweat on my forehead. I reached out my hands to Luo, but he pushed them away and turned his back on me.

"I don't want you to carry me. Why don't you go ahead? I'll follow you slowly."

"Nonsense," I said. "If you walk slowly, you'll never be able to catch the train. Hurry up, let me carry you."

Luo backed away. "Listen to me. You won't be able to take me along. If we continue like this, I'll drag you down. In the end, neither of us would be able to leave."

I was stunned. "Do you mean to say that you don't want to go?"

"I have overestimated my strength. There is no way I can reach the station. Don't waste your time here. If the guards come, you won't be able to escape."

He was probably right. By that time, the officials and walking sticks on patrol had probably discovered that we had escaped. They could be on their way to search for us. But I couldn't leave my mentor behind. I seized one of his arms and dragged him for another nine or ten meters. He collapsed. I was too tired to pull him up anymore. He was too exhausted to speak. I was at a loss. I looked up at the dark sky, and watched the stars.

"If that's the case," I said, "why don't we go back together?"

He was silent for a minute, and then barked, "You stupid idiot. Do you know what would happen to you if we got caught? It's better that one of us gets out of here safely. If they capture me, what can they do? I'm sick as a dog. But you're different. They could tie you up and send you away."

I understood what would happen to me if I got caught. But I couldn't just leave him like that.

"My son, if you really respect me as a father, please listen to me. I would feel better if you managed to escape. I won't freeze to death. I'll just wait for them to drag me home."

"Take care of yourself," I said, and burst out crying.

He waved his hands: Go, go.

I got up and ran a few steps. But then I returned, helped him lie down on the ground, took off my long winter coat, and put it on him. Luo kept waving his hand and saying, "Please go, run quickly." I wiped my tears and walked quickly toward the Mingshui River Station, leaving my mentor alone in the desert.

In April 1961, I was told that the government had released all the survivors from Mingshui and Jiabiangou. I returned to Lanzhou to inquire about work and learn the whereabouts of my mentor. I asked several of my fellow Rightists and they all said that they had heard from the camp authorities that Luo had escaped. I was puzzled. How could he have managed to run away? He was sick and exhausted.

The day before I left Lanzhou, I found out the truth.

I told you earlier on that I had a watch, which had been confiscated by a group leader named Chen Fenglin. He was employed by the Lanzhou Commercial Bureau, so it wasn't difficult to track him down. I located his home and knocked on his door. As soon as he saw me, he started screaming. "A ghost, a ghost!"

He dropped to the floor and was shaking all over. I reached out, trying to help him get up, but he shrank away from my touch. After I reassured him again and again that I was a real human being, he finally regained his composure and told me why he was so scared.

At about eight-thirty on that memorable night, Chen and Hou, another supervisor, noticed that I was missing. They immediately reported me to the camp authorities, and were dispatched to search the train station. Halfway to the station, they spotted my winter coat lying on the road, with bloodstains all over it. They poked the coat open with a stick, held the flashlight closer, and saw my name embroidered on the collar. They searched the surrounding area and found a broken skull and some bones. They assumed that I had been attacked and eaten by wolves. So they walked back to the camp with the coat and didn't pursue things any further.

I asked Chen if he knew anything about Luo. Nobody knew that Luo had been missing until three days later. The leadership just assumed that Luo had pretended to be ill and deceived the people around him. The camp notified Luo's work unit and the police in Luo's hometown, asking them to catch him, but they never heard anything back. Since Luo's family lived in the northeast, it was too far away to send anyone to investigate. The leaders simply dropped the case.

I asked about my watch. Chen said he had simply turned it over to the camp authorities. He didn't know who had it.

Many years have passed and I still haven't forgiven myself. Should I be blamed? I shouldn't have brought Luo along with me in the first place. When he changed his mind halfway through, I should have taken him back. Don't you think?

The Way Station Manager

On March 26, 1958, the staff of the Gansu Provincial Transportation Department was called to a meeting where they witnessed the arrest of forty-eight officials. The meeting was later to be known as the "March 26 Incident."

Xin Xiu, an inspection manager at the Gansu Auto Repair Factory, affiliated with the Transportation Department, had no idea that he would be arrested that day. During the Hundred Flowers campaign, he happened to supervise a group of interns and hardly had time to participate and speak out against the Party. When he arrived at the auditorium on that fatal day, he saw several policemen with machine guns guarding the entrance, and sensed that something big was about to happen.

The Party charged Xin with being a "historical counterrevolutionary," because he had joined the Nationalist Party when he was in college, before the Communist takeover. He was fired from his government job and ordered to receive reeducation at Jiabiangou along with his colleagues.

At Jiabiangou, Xin was given work as a mechanic. He said he didn't suffer too much: repairing trucks and farm equipment relied more on skill than physical labor. Since his job wasn't labor-intensive, he could easily get by with the food allotted per month. The rest of his former colleagues were not as fortunate. Most of them were bookish intellectuals and technocrats who were all assigned to

*the agricultural and construction teams. I spoke to Xin about a close
friend of his, Wang Yufeng.*

Wang Yufeng was the oldest of my former colleagues. When he
started in Jiabiangou, he had just turned sixty. I knew Wang
from way back. In the fall of 1944, at the tail end of the War of
Resistance Against Japan, I graduated from what is now known
as the Southwest Industrial College. I majored in automobile
repair and maintenance. The Northwestern Transportation
Management Bureau recruited technical staff from my hometown, Chongqing. I was offered a job at the bureau's third
brigade, which was stationed in Jiuquan. So I moved there and
became an auto mechanic, taking charge of one hundred-
eighty trucks and cars.

During the war against Japan, the Military Commission of
the Nationalist government established a way station on the
border of the Gansu and Xinjiang provinces. It was surrounded
by desolate low hills that, from a distance, resembled the
rolling waves of the sea. A valley, called Star Valley, ran through
those hills and formed the only passage from Gansu to Xinjiang. The way station was located at the west end of the valley,
on a long stretch of flat grassland. Its courtyard could accommodate more than two hundred trucks. Five houses, each
holding twelve guest rooms, stood at the back. If you count the
manager and attendants, between thirty and forty people
worked there.

The way station played a critical role in the war. All the military supplies from the then Soviet Union—tanks, gasoline,
crates of unassembled airplane parts, and ammunition—were
transported on Soviet trucks to the way station. Chinese staff
would unload the supplies and reload them onto Chinese vehicles that delivered the supplies to the front line. Sometimes
the Soviet drivers simply left their trucks at the way station and

flew back after the mission was over. The way station also served as a motel and as a rest stop for commercial truckers. Even the businessmen riding camels to traverse the Badan Jilin Desert would replenish their supplies at the way station before starting out once again across the sea of desert that stretched hundreds of kilometers in every direction.

Wang Yufeng was the way station manager.

I first met him in the winter of 1944. Two trucks from my brigade got stranded on the Gansu-Xinjiang highway, not far from Star Valley. I hopped on a car and brought two mechanics with me. After we took care of the emergency, we stayed at the way station.

Wang struck me as warm, honest, and dedicated. After my small group checked in, Wang knocked on our doors and asked if we needed anything. He led us to the dining hall and treated us to roast lamb, a local delicacy that you eat with your hands. I initially thought I had received the special treatment because of my affiliation with the Transportation Management Bureau. But during my subsequent stays, I saw that he was equally nice to every guest who walked in the door—merchants, government officials, tourists, and drivers. One time, a veteran driver told me a story over dinner:

"Sheng Shicai, a warlord in Xinjiang, launched a massive hunt for Communists in his region and brutally murdered those he captured. Many Communists fled the region by secretly getting rides on commercial trucks, hoping to sneak through Star Valley and escape to the interior provinces. Sheng dispatched agents to the Star Valley way station. On several occasions, Wang protected the runaway Communists who showed up at the station. One time, Sheng's undercover agents broke into the rooms of two guests and tried to take them away. Wang stopped the agents at the front gate and scolded them, saying, 'I don't care who sent you here. I don't give a damn if these people are Communists! Once they step into this court-yard, they are my guests and clients. You can't kidnap them and take them away. If you don't let these people go, I'll have my guards arrest you.'

"Sheng's agents quietly released the Communists. Wang then called his security guards and kicked the agents out, telling them that they weren't allowed to loiter around the property."

I believe the veteran driver's story. The way station was part of the Transportation Management Bureau, a quasi-military unit under the direct control of the Military Commission, so the local governments in Gansu and Xinjiang held no jurisdiction over it. Star Valley had its own guards. If Wang ordered them to lock up Sheng's agents, the guards would comply.

Wang was born in Shandong Province and followed his father to the far northeast at the age of six to escape a devastating famine that hit his hometown. He attended school in the northeast for several years before he was recruited by the Zhongchang Railroad Company. When the Japanese troops occupied China's northeast, he refused to collaborate with the invaders and retreated to Xian. He participated in the construction of the Gansu-Xinjiang highway and later he was transferred to Star Valley to manage the way station.

Wang's wife died of an illness soon after he became the station manager. Their son was only four years old at the time, and Wang never remarried. A couple of times, I saw his son pulling at his father's shirt behind the counter when Wang was checking in guests.

As the war with the Japanese neared its end, the Soviets were tied up fighting the Germans and their aid to China dwindled. The Americans picked up the slack. With the arrival of trucks carrying U.S. aid, the volume of goods traveling in and out of the region increased. The area surrounding Star Valley was transformed into a noisy town, with new shops and hotels. You can imagine the hustle and bustle at the way station. Wang had seven assistants, but he personally tended to everything— from supervising the loading and unloading of aid supplies, to managing room and board for his guests. The busy life took a toll on him. Wang was only forty-seven, but he already had a bent back and wrinkles on his forehead. During the day, you could never find him at his office or at home. He never had a moment of peace.

On August 26, 1949, the Communist troops took over Lanzhou. Several high-level Nationalist officers in Jiuquan staged a mutiny and surrendered themselves to the Communists, who also seized the Star Valley way station. Since he was well liked and respected, the new government assigned Wang to the Gansu Provincial Transportation Department.

In the early 1950s, the government strongly promoted Sino-Soviet friendship from top to bottom. The press published glowing reports about how peasants in the Soviet Union had willingly participated in the collectivization movement and how happy and prosperous ordinary citizens had become. Having met many Soviet drivers during his days at the way station, Wang questioned the authenticity of these reports. He asked the authorities at the Transportation Department, "Have you ever talked with a Soviet? Do you know what kind of food they eat? When the Soviet drivers dropped off supplies at the way station, they claimed they could only afford to eat stale brown bread, hard as a piece of rock. The poor drivers didn't even have enough money to buy a shirt, and they wore nothing under their overalls. They were also drunkards, and constantly stole truck tires from the warehouse, which they traded for liquor."

In 1957, when the anti-Rightist campaign started, the leadership dredged up Wang's remarks and charged him with being "a bad political element." He was sent to Jiabiangou.

As I mentioned earlier, I was doing fine at the car repair shop in Jiabiangou. When the food ration was reduced, I'd often sneak into a vegetable field to steal beet leaves and boil them to fill my stomach. Sometimes drivers who brought their cars in for repair would drop off steamed buns or small bags of wheat and peas that they had stolen. I would boil the wheat and peas, and hide them in my pocket to snack on when I was hungry.

Wang was not so lucky.

One afternoon in the spring of 1960, I bumped into Wang at the mess hall. He was lining up with members of his agricultural team, waiting for the cook to dish out food from a large pot. His looks startled me: his face was swollen, his eyes squeezed into tiny slits. His skin shone like a piece of oily paper that one could poke through with a finger. He had the long and unkempt hair of a lunatic. His beard had grown untrimmed, like strands of wild grass. I stood outside and waited until he received his food. I called his name. He didn't seem to hear me, and kept walking. I called a few more times before he turned around and shot a blank stare in my direction. Then he asked haltingly, "Are you Xin Xiu?"

"Yes," I said. "How do you not recognize me?"

"I'm losing my eyesight," he said, by way of apology. "I can hardly see things after the sun goes down."

It wasn't that dark outside. The sun had set but the sky was fairly bright. I felt sorry for him.

"What has happened to you?" I asked.

He burst out crying. "Xin, when we get to this point, you realize that life is just so meaningless."

We stood by the side of the road. Wang interspersed his talk with occasional sobs and slurped the murky vegetable soup. Seeing how hungry he was, I dumped my food into his bowl. Tears streamed down his cheeks as he savored the extra food.

"What sin did I commit? I must be paying for something I did wrong in my previous life."

That night I couldn't blot Wang's miserable looks from my mind. I had to find a way to help him. He was such a genuine, kind person—God wouldn't forgive me if I didn't lend a hand.

Yet how could I help him? I toyed with all sorts of ideas. I sought advice from a truck driver named Huang, the brother of Huang Zheng, who was director of the Zhangye District Public Security Bureau. Huang was a true friend. The day after I told him about Wang's situation, he went to the mess-hall kitchen and fetched several bean-paste buns for Wang. Several days later, Huang's truck needed repairs. He dropped off his vehicle at the shop and went to talk with the camp director about Wang. He lied to the director, saying that Wang had driven trucks before and knew how to do mechanical work. As a result of his recommendation, Wang was transferred to my team on a temporary loan.

In reality, Wang couldn't offer me any help. He had never touched a car in his life. But the transfer offered him a much-needed break from the backbreaking fieldwork. When I was repairing trucks, he would sit beside me. I'd put a basin next to him, fill it with kerosene, and drop in a few screws to soak up the oil. Whenever a camp official passed by, Wang would pull the screws out of the basin and pretend to clean them with a brush. When the officer left, he could sit and doze off in the sun.

My car repair skills became quite well known both in and outside Jiabiangou. Drivers working for other labor camps would bring their vehicles to me for repair. The Jiuquan Reeducation and Reform Bureau owned two jeeps and eight trucks.

Drivers there constantly sent them over for mechanical work. Sometimes the camp authorities would allow me to travel to other camps so that I could fix their vehicles on-site. I jumped at the opportunity, in part because I was treated like a special guest. My hosts prepared meals for me that were normally reserved for officers. I ate steamed wheat buns, served with nicely prepared stir-fried vegetables. More important, I could fill my stomach. On these occasions, I would bring Wang along.

Time went by, and the director made Wang's transfer permanent. After two months, Wang's edema disappeared. I took great pride in his restored health. I felt like I had done something worthwhile by rescuing him from the harsh living conditions he was in. Then something else happened.

The day before Labor Day on May 1, 1960, Wang and I put the finishing touches on a truck sent in by a camp outside Jiuquan. We took a quick rest inside the shop while we waited for the driver to pick up his vehicle. A supervisor from the agricultural team rushed in with a stranger.

"Let me introduce you to Comrade Zhang. He's the driver for Chang Zikun, the Anxi County Party secretary. His car just broke down outside our office. Can you take a look?"

According to the driver, the car had been running fine on the way to Jiabiangou, but when he tried to leave, it wouldn't start. He couldn't figure out what the problem was. He told me it was a Ford jeep. It must have been one of those leftover American vehicles from World War II. With those jalopies, anything could happen. I asked Wang to grab my tool bag, and walked out with the driver and the supervisor.

The driver was a young man, very talkative. Within a few minutes, he had told us everything about his trip. He was driving the Party secretary to a meeting in the Zhangye region. On their way home, the Party secretary wanted to stop by Jiabiangou to visit an old acquaintance, the former chief of Jinta County.

The car was parked in front of Deputy Director Liu Zhenyu's office. The driver helped me open up the hood and I examined the engine. The problem wasn't serious—a wire had gotten loose. I reattached the wire and the engine started rumbling.

The Party secretary heard the sound of the engine and came out of the office. He was a dignified man in his fifties. He was wearing a long gray coat with a fur collar and carrying a light brown suitcase, a kind that was popular in the 1940s. Director Liu followed him out. Party Secretary Liang Buyun, who had just been transferred to Jiabiangou, also came out to say goodbye.

Secretary Chang shook hands with Liu and other officials, thanking them for their hospitality. He walked right past us toward his jeep. Knowing that senior government officials wouldn't bother to thank a Rightist like me, I stepped aside and motioned for Wang to do the same. Strangely enough, Secretary Chang suddenly stopped, turned his head, and looked at Wang, sizing him up for a few seconds. Then he stepped into the jeep and the driver shut the door.

They started to pull away, but then we heard a shout, and the jeep abruptly stopped. Secretary Chang jumped out of the car and came up to Wang.

"Are you Wang Yufeng?"

Wang didn't answer.

"Didn't you work at Star Valley way station?"

Wang finally opened his mouth. "I recognized you when you first came out of that office. You're Chang Zikun."

"You remember me? Why didn't you say something? I almost walked past without recognizing you."

Wang simply stood there, staring at the ground. Chang continued with his questions. "How'd you end up here?"

"They accused me of being a bad political element," said Wang.

"Why was that?"

"I served in the Nationalist government and said some bad things about the Soviets to my supervisor."

Now it was Secretary Chang's turn to be silent. He raised his face toward the sky and seemed to be lost in thought. Finally he spoke again.

"Stay here. Wait for me."

He went up to Director Liu and Party Secretary Liang. "Let's go inside," he said. "I want to tell you something."

Wang and I were left alone, waiting for Secretary Chang to come out. I asked Wang how he knew Secretary Chang.

"I knew him at Star Valley. He had escaped from Xinjiang and was planning to go to the Communist branch office in Lanzhou."

"Did you know he was an underground Communist?"

"Of course! Sheng Shicai dispatched his agents to catch him. They chased him all the way to Star Valley. I disguised him as a truck driver and had one of my employees escort him to Lanzhou."

I was excited to hear Wang's story. I thought if Secretary Chang had just a shred of gratitude, he'd figure out a way to help the man who had saved his life. He could at least offer Wang some money or extra grain coupons, or he could put in a good word with Director Liu.

About ten minutes passed before Secretary Chang and Director Liu reemerged from the office. Liu gestured to Wang.

"Go pack your quilt and clothes. Bring them over here."

Wang didn't fully understand Director Liu's words. He simply stood there.

Director Liu spoke again. "Go. Go pack your stuff. You can leave with Secretary Chang today."

Wang was dumbfounded by the good news and stammered, "You mean to say that you are releasing me?"

"Yes," said Director Liu. "I'm releasing you. Go quickly. Get your quilt and clothes. You can leave in Secretary Chang's car."

"Where am I going? Back to Lanzhou?"

Secretary Chang jumped in: "Stop asking questions. We're not going to Lanzhou. You'll come with me to Anxi County first. You can rest up at my place for a few days and then we'll take care of the other stuff. Where is your bunkhouse? Let's go get your luggage together."

Wang's story created quite a stir at Jiabiangou. People envied his luck. Some couldn't contain their curiosity and came to the auto shop to ask me for more details. I could only tell them what I had seen. I had no idea how Secretary Chang had persuaded the camp director to release Wang. A week later, the supervisor of the agricultural team brought another local official to the shop and asked me to fix his car. Since he had happened to be in the office with the camp director the day that Wang was released, I begged him for details.

According to the supervisor, when Secretary Chang invited Director Liu back to the room, he said, "I want to put forward a request to you. I don't know if it's doable or not. I want Wang Yufeng out of here. I'll do everything in my power to warrant his release." Director Liu and the other officials were too shocked to say anything. There was no such precedent at Jiabiangou—a senior official willing to risk his political career to get a Rightist released.

"Why do you seek his release?" said Liu. "You need to give us more details."

"He saved my life once," said Chang. "Without his help, I would have been killed during the War of Resistance Against Japan. I escaped to his way station in Star Valley, and he hid me at his house for a month. He cooked for me and paid a doctor to care for me, as I had gotten deathly ill. After I recovered and was able to move around, he offered me some of his own money, disguised me as a driver's assistant, and put me on a military supply truck. He bribed a Nationalist army officer, who escorted me directly to Lanzhou. I wasn't the only one he helped. Many of our undercover Communists received protection from him when they stopped by his way station. He's made a tremendous contribution to the Communist revolution. How could I leave him here in Jiabiangou without offering help?"

Director Liu rolled a cigarette, and said slowly, "The issue isn't whether we can help him. We just have to go through some bureaucratic procedures. You need to submit a report to the upper level of the government. If your request is approved, we'll be able to put him on parole. Without going though these procedures, we'll be held accountable should anything go wrong."

"What about if I write you a note?" said Chang. "You can submit it to the Provincial Reeducation Committee, saying that I'm the one who bailed out Wang."

Director Liu shook his head. "We can only allow you to take Wang once we've received approval from the provincial government. It would be a violation of the Party policy to act before you petition for approval."

Secretary Chang paused for a moment. "I can submit my request and wait for his parole. But what if he dies during the process? Look at him now. He's in bad shape."

Party Secretary Liang spoke up: "Secretary Chang, it looks like you won't leave here until you can bring Wang with you. Am I right?"

Secretary Chang nodded. "Why don't we avoid using the word 'parole'? I can just say that I'm taking Wang to see a doctor. Once I arrive in Anxi County, I will write up a request to the provincial government. If my request is granted, I'll come back here to fill out the various forms. If I receive a denial notice, I'll send Wang back. What do you think?"

"Okay then, just write us a note," said Liang. "We'll handle a special case with a special solution. I just hope you keep your word and submit your request as soon as possible, so that we can make up the paperwork here."

Not long after Wang's departure from Jiabiangou, I was transferred to a prison factory—the New Life Automobile Engine Factory in Jiuquan, which ran the best auto mechanics shop in the Hexi Corridor region. The factory president somehow heard about me and came to visit me at Jiabiangou. He admired my skills and arranged to have me transferred through the bureau. He appointed me director of the auto mechanics shop. My life improved considerably. I ate at a special kitchen for prison officers and was able to survive the devastating winter of 1960, when thousands of people died of starvation at Jiabiangou.

But the transfer had its drawbacks too. In January 1961, when survivors at Jiabiangou were allowed to return home, I had to stay on at the factory. The factory president called me to his office.

"We need you," he said. "I promise your future here will be much better than that of those Jiabiangou survivors. Do you know why the government closed the camp? It's not because the inmates served out their terms. The leaders wanted to prevent mass death by starvation. Our government's policy toward Rightists remains unchanged. When those Jiabiangou Rightists go home, they'll face similar problems, and none will be able to get their jobs back."

The factory president's remarks proved to be true. Many of those who had gone home suffered terribly. The factory removed the Rightist label from me at the end of 1962. I lived through the Cultural Revolution unscathed. In a morbid way, the thick walls of the prison factory actually shielded me from greater persecution. In 1978, my verdict was officially reversed and I was finally allowed to return to the Gansu Auto Repair Factory.

Let me tell you what happened to Wang Yufeng. One day in 1962, Secretary Chang's driver showed up again at the factory. He recognized me and was surprised to see me there. I told him about my transfer. As I examined his jeep, I asked whether Wang was back in Lanzhou.

"Wang died," said the driver. My heart sank.

"How did he die?"

"The day we took Wang, we drove him directly to a nice county-run hotel in Anxi County. Secretary Chang told the hotel manager that Wang had saved his life, and ordered him to treat his friend nicely.

"The hotel didn't want to mess around with the Party secretary's personal savior! They put him in the best suite and served him three hearty meals a day. But three days later, Wang dropped dead. The doctor said he had stuffed himself with too much beef and eggs. Since he had lived on vegetables for so long, his stomach couldn't handle the rich food, and his intestines burst.

"After learning about Wang's death, Secretary Chang scolded the hotel manager and ran to the hospital. He sat by Wang's body, grabbed Wang's hand, and burst out crying. 'It was I that killed you,' he sobbed."

After I returned to Lanzhou in 1978, I tried to locate Wang's son. An old neighbor told me that not long after Wang was sent to Jiabiangou, his eighteen-year-old son was forced to leave Lanzhou. He went back to live with some distant relatives at Wang's birthplace in Shandong Province. Nobody knows if he is still alive.

The Clinic Director

I heard these stories from "Dr. Zhao," who asked that I withhold his real name. He was a well-known physician in Lanzhou in the 1950s, but was convicted as a Rightist and forced to leave his hospital. At Jiabiangou, Dr. Zhao was allowed to practice medicine at the camp clinic, where he served three and a half years.

In January 1961, after all Jiabiangou Rightists were released, Dr. Zhao was ordered to stay and make up medical histories for those who had died of hunger. Six months later, he returned to Lanzhou. His former hospital refused to give him back his job, so Dr. Zhao went back to his native village and lived the life of a peasant until 1978, when the Party cleared his name.

You want me to talk about Chen Tiantang, the clinic director? I can't say I know everything about him. He and I belonged to different classes. I was an incarcerated Rightist, trying to reform my thinking through hard labor at Jiabiangou. Since I was under the strict control of the camp authorities, I was cautious with my words and behavior and kept my nose to the grindstone. Director Chen, on the other hand, was different. He was a Communist Party member and a Korean War veteran. He was an official at the camp, taking charge of the medical clinic and supervising Rightists doctors like me.

I spent three and a half years in custody, first at Xindiandun and then Jiabiangou. I shared an office with Chen and came to know a thing or two about him and his character. Chen was a native of Zhengding County, Hebei Province. He was in his thirties, married, with two girls and a boy.

Chen was classified as a doctor even though his medical skills were almost nonexistent. He couldn't read the Latin alphabet, yet he was authorized to prescribe medicine. His medical qualifications were considered less important than his political status within the Party. One time, a Rightist became sick and went to see Director Chen. After examining the patient, he wrote these comments on the prescription form: "This patient wears a shirt that used to have two breast pockets. I noticed that the pocket on the left side of this patient's shirt has been torn off. The fact that he chooses to keep the pocket on the right side indicates that he is still clinging stubbornly to his Rightist bourgeois opinions." The prescription baffled Dr. Deng Lizhi at the pharmacy.

Another time, when Chen came back from the patient ward, he told me that he was planning to report to the camp director about "a serious political offense" committed by a Rightist from Wuwei County. "This Rightist likes to sing. Yesterday, while he was performing a well-known revolutionary song, I heard him deliberately changing the lyrics of 'Following Chairman Mao' to 'Chasing away Chairman Mao.' That's a daring counterrevolutionary act, don't you think?" he said.

I was shocked. If the camp director learned about that, the Rightist would be in big trouble. On the other hand, I couldn't believe that the person would be so stupid and bold enough to insult Chairman Mao publicly. I decided to find out. I went quietly to the patient ward and tracked down the Rightist. He told me that he did sing the song. When I asked him to repeat the lyrics, I realized that he spoke with strong Wuwei accent. When he pronounced *gen* (follow), it sounded like *gan* (chase away). I felt relieved and explained to Chen about the misunderstanding. I even imitated the man to demonstrate the accent. My efforts eventually helped put the case to rest.

Chen's wife moved from their hometown in Hebei to join him at Jiabiangou in 1959. His eldest daughter had turned eighteen that year, and he soon married her off to a camp official. In the winter of 1960, his newlywed daughter caught a serious case of tuberculosis, for which she needed at least six months of antibiotic treatment. But Chen had no clue. He found morphine more effective than antibiotics because it stopped her coughing and moaning. I advised him against the use of morphine.

"You can't inject her with morphine all the time. It won't cure her, it will only disguise the infection. Furthermore, the city has allocated us only a few bottles of morphine. We need to limit usage and save the shots for real emergencies."

Chen was upset. "Are you suggesting that I stop giving morphine to my daughter, and save the shots for criminal Rightists?"

I shut my mouth and said nothing more after that. A month later, we ran out of morphine. His daughter's situation worsened. He eventually decided to send his daughter to the county hospital for treatment. In 1961, after the Jiabiangou Rightists were released, I learned that his daughter had died. Later on, Chen and his son-in-law were reassigned to work at Heqing Farm.

Let me tell you a couple of stories that might shed light on Chen's personal character.

At the Xindiandun operation center, there was a Rightist called Ho Bingling. He was raised in Shanghai and moved to Taiwan two years before the Communist takeover. He landed a job as an accountant with a big company there. After mainland China fell to the Communists and the Nationalist government escaped to Taiwan, he lost contact with his parents, wife, and children in Shanghai. He missed home terribly. The pain of separation strengthened his desire to return home. In the mid-1950s, Ho left Taiwan and relocated to Hong Kong, where he was able to reconnect with his family. With the help of a friend, he obtained a government permit and crossed the border to the city of Guangzhou. His friend had promised that he would be allowed to see his family in Shanghai, but upon his arrival in Guangzhou, he found out that a family reunion was no longer on the agenda. The government had assigned him a job with an oil company in the far northwest. He was shipped to Yumen city in Gansu. A year later, when the anti-Rightist campaign started, his past life in Taiwan made him an easy target. He was labeled a Rightist and was sent to Jiabiangou.

Ho had a hard time adjusting. He was plagued with stomach ailments and chronic diarrhea. He was a frequent visitor to the clinic, so I got to know him well. Before the Chinese New Year in 1960, he caught Chen's attention during a regular hygiene inspection.

The camp authorities attached special importance to public hygiene. Rightists were constantly having to clean up their own bunkhouses and public areas. There were regular inspections by a large contingent of people: the camp director, the Party secretary, the reeducation department director, and other supervisors. The clinic director and the doctors were also required to be present. Even though the inspection was supposed to focus on personal and public hygiene, we all knew the real motive lay elsewhere. It was an excuse for security checks. The camp authorities intended to find out whether anyone had hidden weapons or stolen any food. We all had to open up our suitcases, roll up our bedding, and pull off our pillowcases. Officials would confiscate anything that they considered dangerous. They wouldn't spare even a nail. Before any major holiday such as May Day, National Day, or the New Year, there would be organized cleanups followed by an official inspection.

One day, Chen came back from a regular hygiene inspection and asked me, "Have any of you noticed a Rightist named Ho Bingling? He came from Taiwan and stands out from everyone else."

I asked Chen why he thought Ho was different.

"Have you seen his suitcase? There are all sorts of valuables in it: a gold necklace, a thick stack of government bonds, a gold watch, and two Western suits."

"There's nothing strange about that," I said. "He worked in Taiwan for eight or nine years. Those objects probably represent his savings and gifts for his family members, whom he never got to see."

Chen didn't say anything.

When summer approached, Ho Bingling fell sick again. He must have eaten unsanitary food and it triggered his stomach ailment. For several days he suffered a severe form of diarrhea. I prescribed various medicines that were available at the clinic, but none worked. Like so many other members of the camp, he had suffered for two years from hunger and physical exhaustion, and his emaciated body couldn't take another blow. He collapsed. I knew that he wouldn't survive, but I wanted to exhaust all means available. I phoned Chen, saying that Ho was suffering from a severe form of toxic dysentery. I asked if Ho could be tranferred from Xindiandun to Jiabiangou to be hospitalized at the camp clinic right away. Chen granted my request.

I enlisted the help of Yang Wancang, an herbal doctor from Wuwei County. Together, we carried Ho out and placed him on a horse-drawn cart. Knowing that Ho wouldn't be coming back alive, I packed his luggage and suitcase and loaded them onto the cart. If anything happened to him, I figured the doctors at the camp clinic could dispose of his possessions. I just didn't want to leave his suitcase unattended in his bunkhouse. Under the harsh conditions at Jiabiangou, moral standards had deteriorated, and theft was prevalent.

It was about three o'clock in the afternoon when the cart finally left. Dr. Yang accompanied Ho on the short trip.

After about an hour, the phone rang. It was Director Chen.

"Why did you send me a dead person?" he barked.

His question shocked me. "How could it be? Ho Bingling was alive when I carried him to the cart. I even chatted with him and he was fine."

Chen responded with anger in his voice. "Nonsense. He was already dead. Don't you think I can tell the difference between a living person and a dead one?"

I didn't dare try to defend myself, I was so baffled by what he had said. I kept asking myself how it could be. Was it possible that the bumpy ride from Xindiandun to Jiabiangou had aggravated his illness and caused his sudden death?

"All I can say is that he was still able to speak when he left here," I stammered. "He must have . . . died suddenly . . . on the road."

Chen ignored my explanation and continued to berate me.

"You were handling an emergency case. Why didn't you equip Dr. Yang with emergency meds?"

I felt wronged, but I simply had to surrender myself to his harsh criticism. I felt like a mute person who couldn't articulate his misery after swallowing a dose of bitter herbs. All I did was listen and apologize. I offered one round of self-criticism after another: It was my negligence. I should be blamed. I failed to perceive the gravity of his condition.

Chen finally softened his tone. "You need to be careful in the future. I don't want to see another blunder like this happen again."

I promised him over and over that it wouldn't happen again.

After I hung up the phone, I realized that I was in a full sweat. I was a Rightist. My negligence had led to the death of a patient. If the leadership decided to launch an investigation, I would be the chief culprit. That was a liability that I couldn't afford.

I was overwhelmed with anxiety. When Dr. Yang stepped in the door, I immediately asked him about Ho's sudden death. But Dr. Yang gave me a different version of the story.

"Before our cart reached the camp, Director Chen met us near the steel mill," he said. "He had apparently been waiting by the side of the road. He examined the patient perfunctorily and started yelling at me for sending him a dead person for treatment. I pointed to Ho and said that the patient was still breathing and moaning. Chen interrupted me with more scolding and swearing and then ordered me to direct the cart to the steel mill. Ho was groaning and shaking his head. He refused to get off the cart. Director Chen called some workers over, and they then carried him to a large room."

The old steel mill, located at the northwest corner of the camp, was constructed during the Great Leap Forward campaign. In the winter of 1959, when the campaign fizzled, the two buildings in the mill were converted into a morgue.

Dr. Yang and I had a long discussion, but we couldn't figure out the motivation for Chen's actions. In the end, even though there was no disciplinary measure initiated against me, the incident left an indelible shadow on my mind. How could Chen send a patient to the morgue when he was still alive?

In September 1960, two months after Ho's death, Rightists at Jiabiangou began their swift transfer to Mingshui. The authorities decided to abandon the Xindiandun operation center. I was asked to pack up, and that's when I moved into the same office as Chen at Jiabiangou. In the ensuing months, I witnessed a series of events that helped me unravel the mystery step by step.

The first one involved a relative of mine. His name was Lu Changlin. Lu was a celebrated scholar. After new China was founded, he headed the Gansu Provincial Education Department and became the chief curator of a new provincial museum. During the anti-Rightist campaign, the local Party branch asked him to select four Rightists from his staff. He was able to come up with three. The leadership pressured him repeatedly, urging him to choose one more. Eventually, he felt cornered and lost his temper.

"There is no way I can find another Rightist. Do whatever you like. If you can't get another person to fill the quota, you can put me in the spot."

And that's what they did. The leadership accused him of boycotting the anti-Rightist campaign and labeled him a Rightist. He ended up in Jiabiangou. Considering his advanced age and poor health, the authorities didn't send him to Mingshui. He stayed behind, living in a patient ward. One day, Lu heard that I could travel to Jiuquan to purchase medical supplies at a pharmaceutical company there. He took out his bankbook and asked if I could withdraw some money from his account and buy him some oven-baked cakes at a black market.

As you probably know, there was a bank branch, a post office, and a small store at Jiabiangou. Many of those in the first group of Rightists to arrive at the camp had brought their own money. Initially, the camp ordered Rightists to turn over their money to the Finance Department for safekeeping. As more groups swarmed in, the amount of money handed over by Rightists became larger. Yao Wenhua, director of the Finance Department, was a prudent person. Worrying that he could be blamed if problems occurred, he invited a clerk from the local bank to set up an office at Jiabiangou. Rightists could deposit their money directly at the bank branch and keep their own account books. In this way, when they needed cash, they could withdraw money from the bank themselves, without going through the Finance Department.

One day, I went to the bank branch with Lu's account book and filled out a withdrawal form. To my surprise, the bank denied the transaction. A clerk asked for an approval letter from Chen. When I asked why, the clerk said, "Director Chen has instructed us to seek his approval before granting withdrawals to clinic patients at Jiabiangou. The goal is to stop patients from getting the money and escaping. It's also a foolproof way to prevent patients from stealing other people's money."

I found the new requirements ridiculous.

"How can the camp clinic tell the bank how to operate? Has your manager in Jiuquan approved his practice?"

"No," said the clerk. "But at this branch, we have to follow the instructions from your clinic director. I won't give you money until I see an approval letter."

I was thirty that year, young and hot-blooded, but I had experienced the ups and downs of life. I might have been a Rightist, but I wasn't ready to put up with such unfair treatment. I toughened my tone and said, "I'm going to talk with the manager in Jiuquan and inquire about this new rule."

Hearing that I intended to seek answers from his manager, the young clerk gave in without any further argument. He handed me the money.

I left without giving it any more thought. In the evening, Chen questioned me about my visit to the bank.

"Did you withdraw money today?"

"Yes," I said. "A clerk requested an approval letter from you. I had a fight with him. I didn't think it was fair."

Chen repeated the same explanation as that of the clerk, but conceded that he had officially notified the bank that I didn't need his approval for any future transactions.

At the same time, Chen persuaded me not to complain to the manager in Jiuquan.

"That young clerk is well intentioned," he told me. "He's trying to help us."

I wouldn't have thought about this any further if he had not gone out of his way to explain the matter. His words aroused my suspicion. Could there be a secret collaboration between Director Chen and the bank clerk? Anytime a patient died, Director Chen would personally handle the possessions of the deceased, including the patient's bank accounts, bonds, watches, and so on. Could it be possible that Chen was cashing out the money from the patient's bank accounts with the help of the bank clerk, and then splitting the profits with him?

My suspicions weren't supported by any evidence. There was no sign Director Chen had documented any illegal dealings. Even if he had stolen the money, I wouldn't have the guts to report him to the senior leadership. If he found out that I was the whistle-blower, he would fix me in no time. Given his position, punishing me couldn't be simpler. He could easily reassign me to the agricultural team, for instance. Hard field labor would kill me fairly quickly. He could also invent some criminal charges against me and send me to prison.

So I chose to keep my allegations to myself. Another incident, however, confirmed my suspicions and helped solve the mystery.

One morning in early November, while I was sitting in the office with Chen, Party Secretary Liang Buyun suddenly walked in and summoned Chen to his office. Liang sounded like he was in a hurry, and appeared anxious. Chen followed Liang out.

A few minutes later, I heard people's voices outside the office. Someone was calling for a meeting. All camp officials and Rightists who could still move around gathered outside the clinic. It turned out that Liang had received a phone call from the Jiuquan Reform and Reeducation Bureau, informing him that a work team dispatched by the Central Party Committee in Beijing had arrived in Zhangye County. They were planning to visit Jiabiangou that very morning. Liang ordered everyone to clean up and prepare to welcome the work team. At that time, hundreds of Rightists had already died in the camp. The administration worried that they might be reprimanded.

I didn't participate in the emergency meeting that day. I had to treat a patient who had just been rushed in. After the patient left, I was jotting down some notes when I heard a knock on the window. I turned around and saw Chen waving at me, his face pressed against the glass. I moved closer to the window and tried to figure out what he wanted.

"Can you look to see if my drawer is locked?" he asked me.

His desk and mine were pushed together, and we sat across from each other. I leaned over his desk and pulled open his drawer. It wasn't locked. I was shocked to see that the drawer was filled with stacks of government bonds. I paused for a second and then turned back to Chen. I told him he had left it open, and that I would lock it for him.

It was harder to close than it had been to open. I had to stand up and walk over to his side of the desk. Before I closed the drawer I noticed that in addition to the bonds, there were stacks of cash inside it.

At that moment, all the pieces came together. I understood why Chen wanted to take care of the dying patients himself and then handle their personal belongings after they passed away. I knew why he requested an approval letter for patients who intended to withdraw money from the bank. I also figured out the real reason he had forced Ho Bingling to be wheeled into the morgue while he was still alive.

As I was standing there, pondering the meaning of what I had witnessed, Chen was watching me from outside. He realized that I had seen the secrets hidden in his drawer. Afraid that I might relate his dirty secrets to the leadership, he concocted a small scheme. When I came to work the next morning, I noticed a big expensive watch in my drawer. I knew right away that Chen had placed the watch there—that he thought he could shut me up with a bribe.

I didn't touch the watch. I wondered if it had been taken from the wrist of a deceased Rightist. Taking the bribe would be against my conscience. So that watch lay in my drawer quietly for several days before it disappeared. My guess was that Chen had been gauging my reaction. I didn't take the bait. Nor did I intend to report him. Realizing that I wouldn't be a threat to him, he had taken the watch back. In those days, a watch like that could sell for two hundred yuan—three times as much as his monthly salary.

I never shared what I had discovered with anyone. Chen was a Communist Party member and I was a prisoner. If he turned around and accused me of stealing the watch, I wouldn't be able to clear my name. Nobody would believe my story.

In January 1961, all the Rightists were sent home. I stayed behind and continued to work for six months. My job was to rewrite and make up medical histories for the deceased Rightists. The leaders at Jiabiangou didn't believe the Central Party Committee would hold anyone accountable for the tragic deaths occurring at the camp. Yet at the same time, they didn't want so many deaths from unnatural causes to be recorded in the history books. They had to cover it up. I was designated to execute this plan. As a Rightist myself, I had no idea whether the provincial government had ordered us to rewrite the records or whether the camp authorities simply came up with the idea on their own.

I made up case histories for those who had died of hunger. For patients who did have medical records, I added new information. So if anyone bothers to check the medical records of these incarcerated Rightists in the future, they would no doubt find that all of them had died of natural causes: heart failure, cirrhosis, dysentery, stomach cancer, and so on.

These days, people are always complaining about the phony products so prevalent on the market. There are also reports about how people forge their college diplomas and fabricate their résumés. Many are amazed at the incredible ability of these market "geniuses" to pirate name-brand goods and create almost impeccable fake credentials. Compared with what I had to do at Jiabiangou, these deceptive practices are nothing. If someone were to grant professional titles to swindlers, I'd deserve the title of a grand master.

In those six months, the camp authorities provided me with a registration book that listed the names of the Rightists who had died. As I went through the book, I noticed a line item for each individual, which listed the "personal possessions of the deceased." There were plenty of mentions of clothes, quilts, and sheets. Nowhere could I find bank accounts, government bonds, cash, or watches.

How could it be? In the 1950s, many Rightists at Jiabiangou were young government officials and scholars. Since they were single and their families lived far away, they ended up carrying their savings along with them. Many had brought government bonds with them. They couldn't spend them, or cash them at the bank, so they kept the bonds in their suitcases. Do you know why so many people held government bonds? In those days, our country was quite poor. The government issued a large number of bonds to raise money for public projects. For government officials or even ordinary workers, the amount of government bonds a person had purchased would be used to measure his patriotism and his love for the Party. Many people tightened their belts to save money just so that they could buy government bonds.

I thought of Ho Bingling. On the day I carried him to the horse-drawn cart, I put his suitcase with him. Since I worried that his suitcase might be stolen, I removed his gold necklace, his cash, and his government bonds. With his permission, I tucked everything in the pocket of the suit jacket he wore that day. I'm sure other Rightists had money left in their bank accounts, because they couldn't withdraw cash without Chen's approval. Where did all the money go? It ended up in Chen's drawers.

I told you earlier that Chen used to personally tend patients on their deathbeds. One day, I was treating a young man from Tianjing who was dying of cirrhosis. He asked me to invite Chen to the ward to see him. I knew the young man fairly well. He had been an actor and an official at the Dunhuang County Cultural Bureau. After relocating from Tianjing to Dunhuang, he married a local girl. At Jiabiangou, he didn't adapt well to the routine of hard labor, and he fell ill within a year. When I saw him at the clinic that day, his pupils had begun to dilate. He kept asking me to get Chen. I said, half jokingly, "You sound like you're some kind of big shot. What makes you think Chen wants to see you?"

"Go call him," said the young patient. "He will come. He can't afford not to."

So I phoned Chen, and sure enough, he came by on his bicycle. I led Chen to the dark ward. The patient heard his voice and beckoned him to come close. Chen sat on the edge of the bed. The young man reached out to Chen—first holding his hand, then touching his arm and moving up to his face. With all of his remaining strength, he pinched Chen's cheek. This unexpected move shocked Chen. He uttered a loud yell, and jumped back. Half an hour later, the young man died.

Even today I can't figure out why that young man pinched Chen on the face. But I never saw Chen go close to another patient again.

Jia Nong

Of the three thousand Rightists at Jiabiangou, about nineteen were women. They formed a separate section, affiliated with the agricultural team. Qi Shuying was one of the survivors. She told me the story of Jia Nong.

Jia Nong was the name of a boy. His mother's was Li Huaizhu, a Rightist. She gave birth to him in the winter of 1959, while she was undergoing reeducation at Jiabiangou. You may think that Jia Nong is a strange name for a baby. In those days, there was nothing strange about it. You've probably heard the name Jing Sheng, which means "born in Beijing." I once met a girl named Jinjin because she came from Tianjin. In Chinese, Jia Nong is the acronym for the Jiabiangou State Farm, the official name of the camp.

I've been thinking a lot about Jia Nong lately. I'm getting old. I just turned seventy. Most of my days are spent reflecting on the good things that happened to me in life and the hardships I've endured. Memories of Jiabiangou keep coming back. I miss those Rightist women who were like sisters to me. Most of all, I can't seem to get over Jia Nong. So many memorable things happened around Jia Nong.

I was labeled a Rightist in March 1958, when I worked at the Gansu Provincial Public Security Bureau. I was born and raised in Zhangye County. My parents used to own two hectares of prime farmland. They leased the land to farmers and lived on the rental income. I graduated from a local teachers' training school in 1947. My plan was to become an elementary school teacher. My father, however, vehemently opposed my choice of career. Since he never had a son—there was just my sister and me—he wanted me to attend college and marry a rich husband. That way, my parents could depend on me for their retirement. Around that time, my sister married a business-man from the central province of Shanxi. My brother-in-law went bankrupt not long after their marriage. My sister's situation spooked my father. I gave in to his pressure and enrolled in the Chinese Department at Lanzhou University, where I studied for two years. On August 26, 1949, Lanzhou was taken over by Communist troops. Before the troops moved into the city, the university stopped all classes.

On the fourth day after the takeover, I was eager to return to school. I took a trip to campus, hoping to find out the start date for the following semester. The campus was still empty, but I ran into a classmate of mine, Zhang Zongchang. He told me he was going to quit school and join the Communist army. Many of his friends had already done it. He asked me whether I wanted to join the army with him. I agreed on the spot—I had always wanted to be part of the revolution. We walked over to the Military Recruitment Committee, which had set up a booth in front of the Lanzhou Hotel. One officer asked briefly about our family background and encouraged us by saying, "The army badly needs educated people like you."

At the army registration desk, I began to hesitate. If I joined the army, it was likely that I would be sent off to some faraway place. I wouldn't be able to see my parents. Who was going to take care of them? The recruiter was sympathetic and under-standing. He mentioned that the law enforcement agencies were short of staff. The new government in Lanzhou needed a large number of police to keep order. I was quite eager to join the revolution and decided to follow his advice. Seeing that I wanted to be a policewoman, Zhang Zongchang changed his mind and promised to come along with me.

Several days later, we both received letters of acceptance and invitations to attend training for our new jobs. At our training, we met two of my other schoolmates—Na Xiuyun of the Foreign Languages Department and Chen Yuming, a history major. They were married, with children.

We were supposed to complete six months of training at the academy. But there was such a high demand for police enforcement that we were plucked out of the academy after two months and assigned to the newly formed Public Security Bureau. Chen Yuming and Zhang Zongchang became detectives. Na Xiuyun and I ended up at the Propaganda Unit. We wrote publicity materials and coordinated training for newly appointed government officials.

In 1951, Zhang Zongchang and I got married. My husband came from a family of capitalists. In 1954, during the campaign to purge the counterrevolutionaries within government agencies, he was demoted and transferred to a local factory, where he had to supervise prison workers. The next year, when a new branch office was established in Zhangye, my hometown, I was transferred there. That's when the anti-Rightist campaign began.

I used to be pretty careless. During my time at the Provincial Public Security Bureau, my bosses never trusted me with any important duties. I helped out whenever another section was short on staff. It never bothered me. I was never promoted, but I didn't get into trouble, either. However, my personality didn't work well in Zhangye, and I ended up getting categorized as a Rightist.

I felt strange about the label—it didn't really fit me. You've probably heard about Zhang Bojun, the famous Rightist in Beijing? He deserved the label because he tried to challenge Chairman Mao. He claimed that the Chinese president's position should not be held for life. There was another well-known Rightist in Lanzhou, Yang Ziheng. People criticized him for harboring ulterior motives, because he argued that the province of Gansu should be managed by people in Gansu. Zhang and Yang deserved public denunciation, because they competed with the Communist Party for power. But what did I do? I was nowhere near as qualified as they were. I didn't even finish college and I certainly wasn't smart enough to come up with sophisticated counterrevolutionary ideas.

All I did was to criticize the leadership when they encouraged us to speak out. I questioned the distribution of government subsidies, since oftentimes the money ended up in the pockets of those in leadership positions instead of those with low incomes. If we allow this practice to continue, I said, the poor will become poorer and the rich richer. The Communist Party will be as corrupt as the Nationalist Party.

The bureau chief immediately accused me of attacking the Communist Party and the socialist system. He demanded that I write a self-criticism. I complied, but after I submitted the report, the bureau chief called me to his office for a private talk.

Our bureau chief was a notorious scumbag and womanizer. He always liked to talk dirty to women in the office. He pulled over a chair and sat down next to me, and looked at me lustfully. His lecherous behavior made me nervous. I told him to move away from me. He acted deeply offended.

The next day, he organized an all-staff meeting and denounced me before it, threatening to make me a Rightist. I was upset and sought help from the director of the Zhangye District Public Security Bureau, Huang Zheng, who was an old acquaintance of my husband's. Director Huang was sympathetic to my situation and called up my bureau chief to plead for mercy for me.

"Qi Shuying's mouth is faster than her brain," he said. "She really didn't mean what she said. Her remarks are not serious in nature. Since her husband has already been convicted as a Rightist, she has to take care of her two children by herself. Why don't you give her another chance?"

Following Director Huang's phone call, the bureau chief asked his assistant to pass on a message to me, saying that he would change his mind if I agreed to testify against two other female staff members. I couldn't accept the proposal. I just couldn't see myself betraying two other colleagues. I asked whether the bureau chief would put his request in writing. He was outraged.

"Qi Shuying is shrewd," he told his assistant. "She wants to gather written evidence against me."

After that, the bureau chief began to hold a grudge against me and was determined to punish me with a Rightist conviction. Finally, in March 1958, the bureau chief officially labeled me a Rightist. I was expelled from my job and sent to receive reeducation at Jiabiangou.

The day after the announcement was made, I went home, left my two kids with my sister, and broke the bad news to my parents. The following day, I boarded a train for Jiabiangou. Ironically, it was March 8: International Women's Day.

At Jiabiangou, the nineteen female Rightists formed their own group. We became part of the agricultural team. Our group leader was my friend Na Xiuyun. We had joined the Public Security Bureau together in 1949 and nine years later landed in a labor camp at the same time. Her husband, Chen Yuming, was also in Jiabiangou. They had four children. After they were both convicted as Rightists, they gave one kid up for adoption and left the other three with relatives.

The female Rightists lived in a small courtyard house, which was divided by makeshift walls into four smaller bedrooms. Four of us—Na Xiuyun, Li Huaizhu, Dou Weike, and I—shared one room. Mao Yingxing and Zhang Qixian lived in an adjacent one. We all slept on one big *kang*, a long sleeping platform made of bricks and clay. Its interior cavity was connected with the woodstove. In the cold winter days, the heat of the cooking fire could be channeled to heat up the bed, but at Jiabiangou, this was not allowed. Even so, we had it better than the men, who had to sleep on the floor, twelve or thirteen to a room of the same size.

Li and Mao came to Jiabiangou at the end of June. They were both teachers at the Lanzhou Agricultural Academy. Li was a northerner, tall and slender with smooth, pale skin. Mao, a southerner, was just the opposite—short and dark.

Dou had just turned twenty-three and worked at the propaganda section of the Provincial Transportation Department. She had left two children behind to receive reeducation at Jiabiangou. Zhang Qixian, who was thirty-five, was a former legal assistant at the Jiuquan Intermediate People's Court.

Everyone was overwhelmed with sorrow when they arrived at Jiabiangou. Some were even suicidal. It was understandable: we were forced out of our jobs, separated from our families, and had to live in the Gobi Desert without enough to eat. It was like being thrown from heaven to hell. Many of us were in our twenties and early thirties. As idealistic intellectuals, we had joined the Communist revolution around 1949. All of a sudden our lives had been turned upside down, and we found ourselves imprisoned in a labor camp. Many of us were stunned: how had our lives so quickly been ruined and become meaningless? We were also under pressure from our families. Imprisonment led to divorce, and meant children and elderly parents left without care.

Every day after work, we'd try to strike up conversations, hoping to get better acquainted with one another. But as soon as the how-did-you-end-up-here topic came up, someone would burst into tears. Once that happened, it wasn't long before the whole room was filled with sobbing.

In the women's quarters, Zhang Qixian and Li Huaizhu were the two women who cried the most. Zhang had been married to a man who served as the chief judge of the Jiuquan Intermediate Court. One day, she went to deliver a confidential file to the provincial government and ran into an old friend. During their conversation, she mentioned to her friend that she was carrying a court document relating to an important case. Zhang's own husband turned her in and accused her of revealing state secrets to strangers. Zhang was convicted as a Rightist and sent to Jiabiangou. Immediately after her sentencing, her husband filed for divorce and married a young college graduate. It was clear that the husband had been having an affair with that woman for some time and had deliberately framed his wife.

Li Huaizhu had a totally different story. Both she and her husband were targeted as Rightists and ended up at Jiabiangou soon after their marriage. She was twenty-five and had just graduated from school two years earlier. Li couldn't handle the blow. She could never have imagined that the Communist Party, to which she had pledged to devote her whole life, would inflict such cruelty on her. One evening, the Agricultural Academy held a public denunciation meeting against her. Later that night, she suffered a brief bout of insanity. She jumped out of bed and ran around the streets naked. She just didn't want to live anymore.

After her first several weeks at Jiabiangou, she reached a new low. She was four months pregnant, and she swallowed ashes and baking soda in an effort to abort the fetus. "It's enough to have two counterrevolutionaries in the family," she said. "I can't bring another counterrevolutionary into the world, and have the child go through the same amount of torture and humiliation."

Since Na Xiuyun and I were mothers, we cited our own life experiences to persuade her to keep her baby. But Li wasn't convinced.

"You gave birth at home, before your incarceration. I have to raise my child here. How can I? Our experiences here would have a devastating impact on his young mind."

We couldn't convince her. Worried that Li might hurt herself and her baby, the camp authorities granted an exception and brought over Li's husband, Bi Kecheng. He was allowed to stay with Li for a few days and provide some emotional support.

There were several married couples at Jiabiangou, including Na and her husband Chen Yuming, but only a few were so lucky. Under most circumstances, the other couples weren't even allowed to see each other, let alone live together. Liang Jingxiao, our division director, specifically arranged for Li's roommates to move out temporarily so Li and her husband could spend one night alone.

Time was the best healer. As summer turned into fall, we gradually became accustomed to life at Jiabiangou and learned to accept its cruel reality. We even began to work on reforming our political thinking through hard physical labor. And Li stopped crying.

The female Rightists were scattered among different teams. Na, our group leader, worked at a mill shop with six other women. Mao, who studied fruit trees and vegetables in college, was asked to grow vegetables. Dou, Li, and I were sent to the agricultural team.

In the field, there were strict requirements for male Rightists. At harvesttime, each man had to harvest one *mu* (667 square meters) of wheat, plow one *mu* of farmland, or dig ten cubic meters of dirt per day, while helping out with the construction of the irrigation canals. The male Rightists had to stay late at night in order to finish their quotas; otherwise they would be denied dinner. Female Rightists received preferential treatment—we didn't have quotas. We were just asked to follow the guys and work as much as we could.

None of us abused that privilege. We all worked hard. One incident stood out. One time in mid-October, we were digging in a canal to remove the alkali from the soil. Water started to seep into the canal. Our feet were chilled to the bone. Dou made a special effort to show off her fearless revolutionary spirit. In only a vest and red underwear, she dug side by side with all the men. Her bare skin attracted quite a lot of glances from our male coworkers.

Our intense workload put Li in a difficult situation. Her belly grew bigger by the day, and it got to the point that she could hardly bend over, let alone shovel mud. She was expected to give birth in a couple of weeks, but still the camp authorities wouldn't give her a break. She faced a dilemma: If she continued working, she might have a miscarriage. But if she didn't show up, the authorities might accuse her of not taking seriously her process of thought reform. Her compromise was to stand outside the canal and remove excess mud. Na finally begged our team leader to transfer Li to the mill shop, and he gave in.

Of course, milling flour was quite labor-intensive too.

Workers started at six in the morning and finished after dark. They spent the day at a grindstone. First they would empty a heavy sack of wheat into a container, wash the grain, and then move it outside to dry in the sun. After that they would manually sift the husks through large bamboo colanders and grind the wheat. There were seven donkeys pulling seven grindstones all day long. Often, at the end of a workday, Na and the other workers would be too tired to walk back to their bunkhouse. Fortunately the other women took care of Li. All she had to do was watch the donkeys to make sure they pulled the grindstones and didn't stop to eat the wheat or the corn.

Li went into labor on an extremely cold November day in 1958. We had been hit by a blizzard the previous night; the snow had stopped by morning, but a freezing wind started to blow. At breakfast, members of the agricultural team were told to take the day off. There were no weekends at Jiabiangou—we only took breaks during inclement weather. We didn't have any heating in our room, so I wrapped myself up in a quilt and went directly to bed. At about three o'clock that afternoon, I woke up to someone yelling and banging on the door. I jumped off the *kang* and opened the door. Na walked in, with Li leaning on her shoulder. Li looked pale and sickly. She said she had a terrible stomachache. I knew she could go into labor at any minute. Na asked me urgently to heat up the *kang* with firewood.

Two weeks earlier, Liang, our division director, bumped into Li's husband, Bi Kecheng, and advised him to collect firewood on the grassland in his spare time.

"You should make sure you have some firewood ready," he told Bi. "When your wife goes into labor, you have to heat up the *kang* nicely."

Bi was a bookworm from the city, and had no clue how to collect firewood. After three days he had brought back only several small bundles of dried grass, which he piled up in our courtyard. So I told him to borrow two rakes and a flatbed tricycle and I took him to the grassland, where I taught him how to collect material that would burn well. Since the Hexi Corridor region is prone to droughts, there are hardly any trees. But I knew from childhood that tall, dry grass could be used instead. Bi was quick to learn how to find the kind we needed. Every day after work, he would go out on the tricycle and bring back more piles of dry grass.

On that November afternoon, I hurried to the courtyard with a bundle of grass and heated up the *kang*. I dug out a baby quilt and some diapers that Li had made. Worrying that there might not be enough diapers, I tore up some of my old clothes and added them to the pile. Li didn't have a pillow for the baby, so I went to the mill shop, found some peas, and poured them into my handkerchief, which I sewed up to form a pillow.

Bi heard about his wife and rushed to the room to find Li moaning with pain. Bi was scared and kept asking what he should do. Finally Na slapped him.

"Hold her hand and say something sweet to comfort her," she said.

He followed orders well. He sat by her side and held her hand. Soon the *kang* warmed up the room. Around midnight, Li gave birth to a little boy.

When Song Youyi, a political director on the agricultural team, heard the news, he came to visit Li at our bunkhouse. He generously granted Bi several days off so that he could take care of his wife. Song also ordered the cooks in the mess hall to send over a bottle of vegetable oil, fifteen eggs, and some flour.

During her pregnancy, Li hadn't had any access to nutritious food, and she'd been under a great deal of emotional stress. All of this had affected the baby. He was thin and ugly, and weighed only two kilograms. The skin of his face and body was all wrinkled up. He looked more like an emaciated old man or a cat than a newborn baby. His tiny voice was hoarse when he cried, and his legs and arms were weak and soft.

Jia Nong may not have been an attractive baby, but everyone loved him to death. After Bi had to go back to work, the rest of us moved back in. Every night, I volunteered to sleep next to the baby. I would play with him, pinching his little feet and toes. When he cried, I always woke up first and changed his diaper, or swayed him gently in my arms and sang him lullabies.

I wasn't the only one who was crazy about the baby. So was Dou Weike. Dou was quite a beauty, well proportioned, with pale silky skin and a pretty face. But she was arrogant. Even though she was an incarcerated Rightist, she always considered herself a Rightist with style. She wore a short black Lenin-style woolen jacket and walked with her head high. She was extremely active at Jiabiangou. Once every two weeks, she would submit a long progress report about how reeducation had changed her way of thinking. When she found out that two female Rightists had stolen food from the flour mill, she reported them to the authorities. The camp director showered praises on Dou. Everyone hated her and nobody could get along with her.

But Dou doted on the baby. Every day, after work, she would cuddle and kiss the boy before she went to change and wash. She knew that several women were stealing flour and cooking it at night on a kerosene stove for Li and the baby, but she kept quiet about it. One evening, she came back from the field and took a small bag of beans out of her coat pocket. She poured the beans into Li's basin and said, "Boil them tonight. They're rich in protein."

I asked where she had gotten the beans. She told me that she had grabbed them from the mess hall. Her love for the baby helped melt our past anger and brought us closer together. There was another woman who lived at a different bunkhouse and cared deeply about the baby. Her name was Yo Tian, and she was a former English teacher at the Lanzhou Medical College. She grew up in the northeastern region and escaped to Beijing after Japan invaded China in 1938. Following her graduation from Chengdu University in Sichuan Province, her husband went to study in the United States and stayed on as a professor there. Yo Tian remained in China to take part in the resistance movement against the Japanese invasion. She later moved to Lanzhou and took a teaching job at the Lanzhou Medical College. Her husband returned to China in the early 1950s and became a professor at Lanzhou University. Frustrated with the leadership at his university, he quit in 1956 and was planning to ask the government to assign him to a position in Beijing. Then the anti-Rightist campaign began. Yo Tian was labeled a Rightist, though fortunately her husband survived the campaign because he was between jobs at the time. They had three children. The youngest son, thirteen years old, was in junior high. He was an avid stamp collector. One day, he was caught tearing off a stamp from a letter in his school's mailroom. The Lanzhou Medical Academy sent him along with his mother to Jiabiangou. The camp authorities put him in the "bad element" category and assigned him to work with adults on the agricultural team.

Yo Tian was devastated by her Rightist conviction and soon lost her mind. When she arrived at Jiabiangou, she behaved and spoke strangely. During work breaks and after lunch, Yo would always take out a huge book and read it. When guards intervened, she would scream at them, "How could you ban reading here? Physical labor can toughen a revolutionary's body, but reading a book improves a person's thinking."

The other Rightists didn't know her background and they all laughed at her idiotic remarks. Several months after her arrival, she became furious with the destitute situation in the camp. The camp was short of funds and was no longer able to offer the monthly stipend of three yuan (40 cents) that allowed Rightists to buy toothpaste and toilet paper. So she went up to Director Liang and volunteered her services.

"May I have your permission to take a couple of days off?" she asked him. "I'm planning to travel to Beijing and ask the premier in person for funding."

Liang ignored her request, but she wouldn't give up. She went straight to the deputy camp director, Liu Zhenyu, with the same request. Director Liu dismissed her and told other Rightists, "Nothing can fool me. I have seen a lot of feigned insanity around here. Only an idiot would fall for her act."

The news spread around the camp that Yo Tian was acting crazy as a cover. But none of the women at Jiabiangou bought it. Yo's insanity came in bursts. At times she seemed perfectly normal—she was quiet, gentle, and rational. When she was in her insanity mode, however, and she started to talk nonsense, other Rightists would tease her about her proposed Beijing trip.

"What kind of a special relationship do you have with our premier? What makes you think he'll grant you funds?"

When this happened, she would purse her lips and reply in a contemptuous tone, "That's confidential information. I can't divulge it to you!"

One day, while we were outside plowing the field, an airplane flew over. It triggered another bout of insanity.

"Premier Zhou has sent a plane here to get me," she said. Her remarks set off snickers among the other Rightists. Yo became incensed. "I'm not kidding—I'm leaving for Beijing right away." She dropped her shovel on the ground and headed in the direction of the Jiuquan highway. We ran after her and tried to drag her back, but she wouldn't listen to us and kept going. Once she crossed over the edge of the camp and walked past several sand dunes, Liang dispatched two guards to seize her. Leaving the camp property without permission was considered an attempted escape. The guards grabbed her and tied her up with rope. They locked her up inside the isolation cell.

Crazy as she was, Yo Tian acted sensibly around Li's baby. She would stop by our bunkhouse every night to hold him in her arms. At first, however, Li was nervous about Yo Tian's mental condition and worried that Yo might hurt him. Each time she walked in, Li would pretend to breast-feed the baby and refused to let Yo touch him. Yo would have to seize the baby out of Li's arms. In an intimate tone that we had never heard before, Yo would whisper to the baby, and then bend over and kiss him, giggling. One time, as she held the baby close to her bosom, tears welled up in her eyes and she blurted out something in English. I understood some of the words she uttered: "My son, my baby, the apple of my eye."

We all cared for the baby. After supper, all the female Rightests would gather at our bunkhouse and take turns holding the baby. He was Li Huaizhu's boy, but also ours. Li's child brought sunshine to our unheated bunkhouse and to our lonely life at Jiabiangou. He lifted our miserable, lonely spirits.

The baby was thin because he was malnourished. Women working at the flour mill regularly stole wheat flour and cooked it for Li. When she had had enough, she could breast-feed the baby. Song Youyi, the political director in charge of our team, would check up on us occasionally. Seeing that Li had started to gain some weight, he grew suspicious and wanted to find out how she had gotten access to food. We planned carefully to make sure that Song didn't find anything, and only cooked for Li at midnight. During the Chinese New Year, the women were asked to help the kitchen staff prepare holiday food for the three thousand detainees. We stole some lamb from the kitchen, and that night at midnight, we cooked a lamb noodle soup for her.

When the baby turned one month old, we held a small celebration. Mao Yingxing unraveled her sweater and reknitted it into small baby overalls. Yo Tian offered her son's harmonica.

On that day, we discussed what we should name him. Na recommended we call him Jia Nong.

"When he grows up, he will remember he was born in Jiabiangou and think of the meaningful period of time he spent with his mother and his aunties."

Nine months passed. Jia Nong was growing into a healthy child. His bony, wrinkled face began to fill up. When he smiled, he had two nice dimples. His skin started to show a healthy color. His limbs became stronger. He still couldn't walk, but when someone reached out a hand, he would hold a finger tightly and try to leap forward. He knew only one word: Ma. He called every woman Ma. We loved it.

But this grace period was about to end. Following the summer harvest in August 1959, the camp authorities suddenly changed our job responsibilities. The female Rightists were put on the livestock team. Nobody knew why. Was it because we didn't do a good job grinding the crops, or was it because the leadership found it easier to have all the women on one team?

No longer were we able to steal food from the mill shop, and people began to starve.

Fortunately for us, feeding pigs wasn't labor-intensive. We

took charge of more than two hundred pigs, a woman to every pigsty. At that time, China was still in the throes of the Great Leap Forward campaign, in which Chairman Mao attempted to transform China rapidly into an advanced industrialized country. In the rural areas, communes competed with one another to use new methods, hoping to produce bumper crops and raise the largest pigs. To meet the impossible government quotas, many officials engaged in deception. Our camp was swept up in the campaign. Officials procured the highest-quality feed so that they could create five-hundred-kilogram pigs. The pigs ate much better than we did. We fed them boiled potatoes and ground beans, while we got served vegetables, corn gruel, and corn millet buns. We were always hungry. When the hunger became unbearable, we would steal potatoes in the pig feed.

Starvation was not the only disaster that befell us.

As I told you, all nineteen women lived inside a courtyard house. No men were allowed to enter without permission, including husbands. Since we were surrounded by young, sex-starved men, illicit affairs were bound to happen. Na and I had an arrangement with Li where we smuggled her husband into our room for a reunion every week or so. When Bi came, the rest of us would squeeze in with other women in a separate room. He would sneak back into his bunkhouse before dawn.

Before the Chinese New Year in 1959, the camp authorities picked several male and female Rightists to prepare some performances for the celebration party. Dou Weike was assigned to sing a duet with a young Rightist from the agricultural team. The two of them fell in love. For quite some time, we would create opportunities for them to get together in the same way we did for Li. We figured that life was dull and miserable at Jiabiangou. If a young man and woman were courageous enough to have an affair under such difficult circumstances and have a little fun, there was nothing wrong with it. But Dou and her boyfriend were too reckless. Dou quickly became pregnant and their affair was exposed. She was forced to have an abortion at a medical facility for prisoners in Jiuquan. Her boyfriend was transferred to the specially monitored team.

Misfortunes never came singly.

The pigsty was located on a piece of grassland about two hundred meters south of the Jiabiangou administrative offices. Three huge makeshift houses, with a total of eight large rooms, created a horseshoe-shaped courtyard. In the middle of the courtyard there was a well, which was surrounded by stone steps. On the west, there were rows of pigsties. We spent most of our time there, mixing the feeds in the trough, feeding the pigs three times a day, and then cleaning out the manure. The job wasn't that tiring, but Song Youyi hated to see us idle. He ordered us to scrub the trough and wipe it clean with a piece of cloth each time we had fed a pig. Even so, between feedings, we still had time to go back to the bunkhouse for a nap, mend our clothes, or play with Jia Nong.

One afternoon in late November, after finishing the second round of feeding and scrubbing, we gathered in the office for a quick break. It was windy and freezing outside. Our hands were numb after the feeding. There was a stove, and one person brought some firewood from the courtyard and started the fire. The room warmed up.

Li walked in with Jia Nong in her arms and said, "Our bunkhouse is like a frozen cave. It's too cold to sit."

Since our bunkhouse was close by, it was convenient for Li to take care of Jia Nong. She could go back inside anytime she heard him crying or screaming. Before we left for work each morning, we would tie one end of a rope around his waist and the other one to the window near the *kang* to prevent him from falling.

Since the room was warm, Jia Nong fell asleep in Li's arms. We urged her to take the boy back to the bunkhouse.

"Go put a heavy quilt on him," we said. "It's exhausting to have to carry him like that."

Li went back to the bunkhouse, but soon came back, holding her baby. We were surprised, and asked her why she hadn't left the baby at the bunkhouse.

In a somewhat ludicrous, girlish voice, Li said, "Why don't you do it for me?"

Na shot her a reproachful glance.

"Okay, I'll do it for you, my spoiled little princess."

Na took Jia Nong from Li and stepped out. A couple of minutes later, she rushed back with the baby. She had a strange look on her face.

"Li," she screamed, "you're such a liar. How could you be so evil?"

"What happened?" I asked.

Na waved her hand. "It was embarrassing and scandalous."

I probed further, but Na wouldn't say what she was talking about. She pointed at Li.

"Let her tell you. She knows."

A mysterious smile appeared on Li's face.

"Go find out for yourself!" she said. "Our bunkhouse is haunted."

Seeing that I couldn't get anything out of those two, I turned around, left the office, and raced to our bunkhouse. I pushed the door but found that someone had locked it from the inside. This was highly unusual. I bent down and peeped through a small crescent-shaped crack in the door. My goodness! I was shocked by what I saw, and almost screamed. The house was haunted: Dou was lying on the *kang* stark naked. Song Youyi, also naked, was on top of her.

I ran back to the pigsty.

"Dou is shameless," I said. "How could they do this in broad daylight?"

I recounted the scene to the other women, who were all shocked. There was a moment of silence, followed by a heated discussion. Our voices must have sounded like the rapid trills of frogs.

"I always knew Dou was a slut," someone said.

"Song's no angel either," said someone else.

As we were gossiping, Zhang Qixian, who was standing by the door, suddenly put her fingers on her mouth and said, "Look—Song Youyi is coming this way."

We ran to the window. Song hurried past the well and headed out of the courtyard. Two women couldn't control themselves. "Shameless scoundrel!" they said.

It seemed as if Song heard them. He looked in our direction and turned pale.

We had long suspected that there was something unusual going on between Song and Dou. Song constantly showed up to watch our livestock team and plunged right into our bunkhouse. He would only talk with Dou. When Dou fed the pigs, he would follow her. Sometimes he would take Dou away alone, saying that he wanted her to help write a speech. We didn't see it as anything abnormal. Dou was notorious among the Rightists for being a suck-up. She seized every opportunity to show off her reeducation progress to the camp officials. Who could blame her? Everyone at Jiabiangou hoped to have the Rightist label removed, and longed for an early release. As this went on longer, however, there were rumors: Dou and Song were never at the office; they constantly hung out near the sand dunes. What did a man and woman do behind the sand dunes? The answer was obvious, but nobody dared to discuss their affair openly. Song was a political director and had the power to determine our future. Everyone was afraid of him.

But the situation was different on this day. All the female Rightists witnessed their shameless behavior. Everyone began to talk, and soon the news spread all over the camp.

A storm was brewing and danger was imminent.

One night after dinner, about five days later, Na was asked to gather all the female Rightists for a meeting near the administrative building. We lined up and walked over there. All the members of the agricultural team had already sat down on the ground in front of the building. Song came out and delivered a lecture.

"Some Rightists are still clinging to their reactionary ideology and refuse to reform themselves through proletarian thinking. They spread rumors and gossip, slander our Party officials, and instigate trouble, all with the sole intention of creating chaos at Jiabiangou and subverting our Communist government. We cannot tolerate these kinds of activities here. We'll impose tough punishment on these rotten apples."

Then Song raised his voice. "Li Huaizhu and Zhang Qixian, stand up!"

Li was visibly shaking, and Zhang's face had become as pale as a piece of paper. Song looked them in the eye. "Do you know what crimes you committed?"

Both of them answered simultaneously. "We are counter-revolutionary Rightists—"

"I'm talking about the crimes you committed last week," said Song, interrupting them.

Li didn't know how to respond, but Zhang spoke up.

"Comrade Song, I've been doing honest work. I don't know what you could be referring to."

"You're both dishonest and crafty," yelled Song. "Put them in handcuffs."

Song pulled two pairs of handcuffs out of his pocket and tossed them on the ground. A couple of his lackeys from the agricultural team came forward and handcuffed them in the brutal traditional way: one hand was pulled over the shoulder from the front to join the other hand, which was pinned to the back.

The young women had never been subjected to such physical abuse before. We could hear the click of their joints and their screaming when their hands were forced behind their back. When their torturers let go of their hands, Li and Zhang slumped to the ground.

Song bent over them and yelled, "Will you continue to spread rumors and start trouble?"

The women couldn't even breathe, let alone answer his question. They were writhing with pain. Song straightened up and told his lackeys to lock them up. Several men dragged Li and Zhang away to a small room next to Song's office. They couldn't stand up with their hands tied like that, so their bodies curled up in a ball, their heads tilting back and their legs curled, jutting into the air. I could see tears and sweat streaming down their faces.

After the meeting, Na and I stayed behind, stunned. We were the ones who had spread the news and deserved to be handcuffed. Song knew that Na and I used to work in law enforcement and were still well connected. Instead of punishing us, he picked the timid Li and Zhang, employing the strategy known as "killing the chickens to intimidate the monkeys."

As we were about to leave the meeting, a male friend of ours on the agricultural team came up and whispered, "You two should be careful. It might be your turn tomorrow."

Li and Zhang were released the next morning. They couldn't stand or move, but simply lay on the ground, as if paralyzed. Several Rightists from the agricultural team carried them back to our bunkhouse. According to the two women, they had been forced to kneel on the ground with their handcuffs on all night long. Zhang happened to get her period that day. Blood oozed out and soaked her pants.

Our friend's remarks made us nervous. Li and Zhang's experience scared the daylights out of us. We dreaded the thought of attending another meeting the next day and getting the handcuff treatment.

The next afternoon, while we were scrubbing the troughs, a green jeep pulled into Jiabiangou. Half an hour later, my husband's friend, Huang Zheng, the director of the Zhangye District Public Security Bureau, showed up at the pig yard and asked how things were going. Na and I almost burst out crying simultaneously. We told him about Song's affairs and his intimidation tactics.

Upon hearing our story, Huang went back to the then Party secretary of Jiabiangou, who was a friend of his. (This Party secretary was replaced by Liang Buyun in late 1960.) The Party secretary used to be a judge. He was a big fan of Chinese chess. One time, while playing chess during work hours, his clerk handed him an approval letter from the provincial People's Supreme Court regarding the sentencing of several criminals in his area. He was so preoccupied with his chess that he had mistakenly circled a wrong name. A non-death-row inmate was wrongly executed. As a consequence, the judge was demoted and reassigned to be the Party secretary at Jiabiangou.

At the camp office, Huang told the Party secretary, "They shouldn't treat female Rightists like that, and they especially shouldn't use such brutal handcuffing methods. Listen to me— no one is allowed to hold a public denunciation meeting against Na and Qi Shuying. I'm going to come back in a few days and have them transferred. This kind of behavior is unacceptable. Song has done something indecent. He needs to wipe his own ass. Instead, he spanks others. It's unlawful."

Several days later, Na and I were transferred, along with seven other women, into a labor camp near Jiuquan. A Rightist doctor offered us a short-term training course in medicine. Upon completion of the training, Zhang Qixian and several others were recruited by a prison hospital in the region, to serve as medical assistants. Na Xiuyun, Li Huaizhu, Mao Yingxing, and I were considered too old for the job. We were shipped to the Gaotai Farm, which employed a large number of former prisoners.

Li and Mao worked on the vegetable-growing team. Na and I took care of accounting. We enjoyed the same benefits as the staff members, who earned a monthly salary of thirty yuan ($4.40).

We stayed at Gaotai for more than a year. Li soon turned into a skeleton. So did Jia Nong. This was because she had to save food from her monthly ration to support Bi Kecheng, her husband at Mingshui. Li sent food to her husband once a month.

I can never forget what happened on the morning of December 13, 1960. I was about to leave for the office when Li showed up with Jia Nong. She wondered if I could babysit Jia Nong for a day. She needed to take a bus to Mingshui, to drop off some food for her husband. I agreed. I left Jia Nong in my bunkhouse and came back to visit him once every hour or so. Jia Nong had turned two and was well behaved. He had become accustomed to being alone in the bunkhouse when his mother was at work. I'd often give him a piece of an old newspaper, which he'd fold and unfold, and then tear up into small pieces. Normally he was very absorbed by his newspaper folding and he never cried. But on this day, he behaved strangely. He cried nonstop, screaming for his mother, so I ended up spending the rest of the morning with him. I put him to bed after lunch and went back to work. Later on, a neighbor rushed into my office, saying that she heard Jia Nong crying again in my bunkhouse. I stopped working and went back again. No matter how hard I tried to comfort him, it didn't work. By dusk, I figured Li would return at any minute, so I went out with Jia Nong in my arms and strolled along a small path outside the farm. We waited by the side of the road for almost an hour before Li appeared. Under normal circumstances, she would grab the baby from me and kiss him all over. But that day she acted very differently. Although she saw me holding her son, she kept her slow pace, and seemed oblivious to us. When Jia Nong ran up and asked his mommy to pick him up, she seemed indifferent to his excitement. She carried him in her arms and walked on in silence. Thinking that she might have been exhausted from the trip, I didn't say anything. After a while, I asked about her husband. She stopped and turned around to look at me. I noticed that her eyes were red.

"He died," she said. A sad, faint smile flashed across her face.

My heart sank. I didn't continue our conversation for fear that it would lead to more tears. I was surprised that, after we returned to her bunkhouse, she didn't cry at all.

"When I arrived at Mingshui this morning," she said, "his roommate told me he had been dead for over a week. One of his friends there took me to the burial site and we located him." Li was calm and finished her story in a monotone . . .

It was toward the end of that month when the order from the Central Party Committee came, and the living Rightists were released.

Let me tell you briefly what has happened to the people I mentioned. When news came that we were allowed to leave, I didn't wait for the government trucks to get me. I got on the first train and found my husband, who had been locked up at a different labor camp. He was ill, so as soon as we returned to

Lanzhou I checked him into a local hospital. I went to the Provincial Public Security Bureau, and officials told me that since I had been fired, they couldn't take me back. I would have to go seek employment on my own. But I refused to budge and wouldn't leave the office. In the end, they gave in and assigned me a job as a cleaning lady for a hospital attached to the bureau. My monthly salary was thirty yuan. It wasn't until 1978, when the local government officially cleared my name, that I was transferred to the Provincial Bus Manufacturing Plant. I worked there as a deputy manager in the propaganda unit.

Dou Weike returned to the province's Transportation Department. I saw her once in the late 1970s, after the Cultural Revolution. She was in her fifties, but she still had her looks. She wore lipstick and rouge, which was considered quite daring in those days, when plain looks were considered proletarian. But the makeup still couldn't cover up her wrinkles.

Na Xiuyun was luckier than I was. Her verdict was overturned in 1962 and she stayed on at the Provincial Public Security Bureau, where she became a director. People always said to me, Na and you started working at the Public Security Bureau together. Both of you were considered veteran Communist officials. How come you were never promoted?

Well, my former bureau chief, whom I offended in the 1950s, successfully sabotaged every one of my attempts to have my verdict reversed. That's why I had to wait until 1978.

Remember Mao Yingxing, the single woman who made a sweater for Jia Nong? She was executed by the government during the Cultural Revolution. After returning to Lanzhou, she had married another former Rightist. She was thirty-six at the time. The school authorities didn't think she and her husband were fit to be teachers. So they were assigned to work at the Jingning County Agricultural and Herding Center. Her husband tended a pepper tree garden in one commune, and she grew wheat in another one. The two of them were allowed to visit each other only once a year. During the Cultural Revolution, many former Rightists became targets again. Both Mao and her husband were accused of "viciously attacking Chairman Mao's campaign." I was told that before they were executed, the soldiers cut her throat to prevent her from shouting antigovernment slogans at the public execution meeting.

As for Yo Tian, after returning to Lanzhou, she went completely insane. She became homeless and wandered the streets. Her former employer, the Lanzhou Medical College, sent her to a mental asylum, and she stayed there for two years. She's now retired and lives in a nursing home. Remember her young son, who had been locked up at Jiabiangou for tearing a stamp off someone's envelope? He was exonerated in the fall of 1959, but wasn't released until January 1961. He and his mother reunited with his father, who had gotten a job at Ningxia University. During the Cultural Revolution, his father was charged with being an American spy and sentenced to life imprisonment. He died in prison in 1975. When China opened its doors to the outside world in the late 1970s, Yo's younger son attended night school. After graduation, he took an English test and was enrolled at an American university. He now teaches in the United States. He should be in his late sixties now.

Zhang Qixian, the woman who was framed by her husband, the judge, had a tragic life. Upon her release from Jiabiangou, she also returned to Lanzhou, where she eventually married a factory worker who was an ex-convict. He constantly beats her. I met her once and asked her why she was willing to stay with him.

"As a Rightist," she told me, "no one wanted to marry me."

As for Li Huaizhu, she wasn't allowed to work at the Lanzhou Agricultural Academy. In the end, she went to teach at an agricultural school in Pingliang County. She got married again.

If Jia Nong is still alive, he would be fifty this year. He'd probably be married with a child of his own. Before I get too old to move, I'd like to travel to Pingliang County and visit Li Huaizhu. I hope to see Jia Nong. Here we are, so many years later, and I still can't get that adorable little face of his out of my mind.

TRANSLATOR'S ACKNOWLEDGMENTS

Woman from Shanghai, which stands as a unique memorial of a dark chapter in contemporary Chinese history, was made possible by interviews with more than one hundred Jiabiangou survivors, who braved the political risks to share their stories with author Xianhui Yang. This English version is a testimonial to their suffering and endurance.

I have never met Xianhui Yang in person. For four years, we labored over the book through phone conversations and e-mails. His trust in me and his patience with the process made the adaptation and translation a pleasant experience.

My gratitude goes out to the PEN Translation Fund for recognizing the merits of this book at an early stage. I am forever indebted to Esther Ellen at PEN for jump-starting my career as a translator.

I'm fortunate to have as my agent Peter Bernstein and his wife, Dr. Amy Bernstein, who took me in and assisted me in every possible way with patience and encouragement. As always, I'm grateful to my editor, Erroll McDonald, for granting me the creative freedom and to my publicist, Vanessa Schneider, a tireless advocate of my works, and, of course, to Lily Evans for making the process so easy and enjoyable.

I also want to express my gratitude to Philip Gourevitch, editor of *The Paris Review,* who continues to be a mentor and champion of my work and to my young, talented "itinerant" editor, Nathaniel Rich, for his valuable editorial assistance.

Martina Lu, a friend of Xianhui Yang, volunteered to represent Yang in the United States. Thanks to Martina, the contract process went smoothly.

Professor Robert Crowley, a connoisseur of Chinese culture, has diligently read and advised on every single story in this book. In addition, I want to thank the following close family members and friends: Bill Brown; Maria and Warren Tai; Monica Eng; Linda Yu; Tish Valva; Tao Zhang; Megan Eng; Xiaoping Chen; Xiaobo Liu; Jie Yu; Colin McMahon; Patrick Tyler; Andrea Dunaif; Scott and Caroline Simon; as well as my beautiful goddaughter, Lina Simon, and her sister Elise; Mary and Brent Bohlen; Bruce Kinnette; Wilson Toy; Judy and Richard Shereikis; David Alexander; Eiko Terao; Jan and Karen Futa; Mike and Lynne Coyne; and Caren and Dale Thomas.

Most of all, I want to take this opportunity to thank my bosses and coworkers Lisa Sodeika, Diane Bergan, Kate Durham, Josie Fongaro, Cindy Savio, Juanita Gutierrez, and Linda Recupero, all of whom have offered enthusiastic support and encouragement for my avocation.

ABOUT THE AUTHOR

Xianhui Yang is the author of highly acclaimed collections of short stories such as *Farewell to Jiabiangou, Jiabiangou Stories, Chronicles of the Dingxi Orphanage,* and *This Big Stretch of Beach.* Yang's works have won numerous national awards in China, including the National Best Short Story Award (1986) and the Chinese Novelist Academy's Best Short Story Award (2003). Yang, a member of the Chinese Writers Association, lives with his family in Tianjin, China.

ABOUT THE TRANSLATOR

Wen Huang is a Chicago-based writer and freelance journalist whose articles and translations have appeared in *The Wall Street Journal Asia,* the *Chicago Tribune,* the *South China Morning Post, The Christian Science Monitor,* and *The Paris Review.* He translated *The Corpse Walker: Real-Life Stories, China from the Bottom Up* by Chinese writer Liao Yiwu and was the 2007 recipient of a grant from the PEN Translation Fund.

A NOTE ON THE TYPE

The text of this book was set in Filosofia, a typeface designed by
Zuzana Licko in 1996 as a revival of the typefaces of Giambattista
Bodoni (1740–1813). Basing her design on the letterpress practice of altering the cut of the letters to match the size for which
they were to be used, Licko designed Filosofia Regular as a rugged
face with reduced contrast to withstand the reduction to text
sizes, and Filosofia Grand as a more delicate and refined version
for use in larger display sizes.

Licko, born in Bratislava, Czechoslovakia, in 1961, is the co-
founder of Emigre, a digital type foundry and publisher of *Emigre*
magazine, based in Northern California. Founded in 1984, coin-
ciding with the birth of the Macintosh, Emigre was one of the first
independent type foundries to establish itself centered around
personal computer technology.

Composed by Creative Graphics, Allentown, Pensylvania
Printed and bound by R. R. Donnelley, Harrisonburg, Virginia
Book design by Robert C. Olsson